Praise for author Hannah Alexander

"I always look forward to the next Hannah Alexander novel. Her books always have great characters and page-turning suspense."

—Lyn Cote, author of *Autumn's Shadow*

"Alexander is great at drawing the reader into her storyline and keeping them hooked until the resolution of the plot."

—*Christian Retailing*

"Alexander's skill at meshing spiritual truths with fascinating suspense is captivating."

—*RT Book Reviews* on *Safe Haven*

Hannah Alexander is the pseudonym of husband-and-wife writing team Cheryl and Mel Hodde (pronounced "Hoddee"). When they first met, Mel had just begun his new job as an ER doctor in Cheryl's hometown, and Cheryl was working on a novel. Cheryl's matchmaking pastor set them up on an unexpected blind date at a local restaurant. Surprised by the sneak attack, Cheryl blurted the first thing that occurred to her: "You're a doctor? Could you help me paralyze someone?" Mel was shocked. "Only temporarily, of course," she explained when she saw his expression. "And only fictitiously. I'm writing a novel."

They began brainstorming immediately. Eighteen months later they were married, and the novels they set in fictitious Ozark towns began to sell. The first novel in the Hideaway series won the prestigious Christy Award for Best Romance in 2004.

Books by Hannah Alexander

Love Inspired Suspense

Note of Peril
Under Suspicion
Death Benefits
Hidden Motive
Season of Danger

Love Inspired Historical

Hideaway Home
Keeping Faith

Steeple Hill Single Title

Hideaway
Safe Haven
Last Resort
Fair Warning
Grave Risk

Visit the Author Profile page at Harlequin.com for more titles.

HANNAH ALEXANDER

HIDEAWAY

LOVE INSPIRED

INSPIRATIONAL ROMANCE

LOVE INSPIRED®

INSPIRATIONAL ROMANCE

ISBN-13: 978-1-335-50293-3

Hideaway

First published in 2003. This edition published in 2021.

Copyright © 2003 by Hannah Alexander

This edition published by arrangement with Harlequin Books S.A.

For questions and comments about the quality of this book, please contact us at CustomerService@Harlequin.com.

Love Inspired
22 Adelaide St. West, 40th Floor
Toronto, Ontario M5H 4E3, Canada
www.Harlequin.com

Printed in U.S.A.

This book is dedicated to the Great Physician

For my Father's will is that everyone
who looks to the Son and believes in him shall have
eternal life, and I will raise them up at the last day.
— *John* 6:40

Acknowledgments

Long ago we realized that any success in our efforts
to write a readable novel was dependent on the goodwill of
many people. Many thanks to Joan Marlow Golan, our editor,
whose enthusiasm for this work has been a great encouragement.
We also thank our agent, Karen Solem, whose wisdom
and sweet spirit have guided us.

Thanks to Lorene Cook (Cheryl's mom),
who continues to put feet to her prayers for us.

Thanks to Ray and Vera Overall (Mel's mom and dad),
who never cease to encourage.

Thanks to our writing families online, ChiLibris and WritingChambers,
who touch us from across the country and around the world.

Thanks to Jennifer Whitt,
who was willing to allow us to pick her brain for her expertise
with dreadlocks.

Thanks to C.J. McCormick, DVM,
who lent us access to his vast knowledge of
the peculiarities of animals.

Thanks to James Scott Bell, author and friend,
who gave us his legal expertise.

Thanks to Jon Suit, former mayor of Monett,
who was able and willing to tell us far more than we will
ever understand about small-town politics.

Thanks to Barbara Warren of Blue Mountain Editorial Service,
for the nice slash and repair job, and for the input on gardening.

Thanks to Brenda and Doug Minton,
for having a heart for the children most in need—
and for having a garden that refuses to grow beneath the walnut trees.

Thanks to Jackie Bolton,
who understands the psyche of a teenager—
because her own heart is still young.

Thanks to Jack and Marty Frost,
who never let up on us to do our best,
and who quickly forgive us when we fail, time and time and time again.

Thanks to Jim and Louise Brillhart and Ardis Bareis
for allowing us to take your names in vain.

We wish to give credit where it is due,
but any mistakes or discrepancies are purely our own.

We earned them, we intend to keep them.

Chapter One

The scream of an ambulance bounced through the mauve-and-burgundy corridors of the Missouri Regional Hospital on the west side of Columbia. An elderly man moaned. A baby's cry stung the air through the center of the eight-room emergency department.

Dr. Cheyenne Allison slipped into the untidy doctor's call room, closed the door and locked it.

If only she could collapse onto the bed and stay there for a week. Or the whole month of March.

Ordinarily, she could breeze through a twelve hour shift and still have enough energy for a nighttime jog along the Katy Trail. But today, at 2:00 p.m. she already felt as if she'd been on duty for twenty-four hours without a break. In spite of her flu shot, in spite of the antiviral she had begun soon after experiencing the first symptoms, she felt like the framed green-and-purple blob on the wall that some idiot had mistaken for art when this department had been remodeled.

She had a full-blown case of influenza.

Cheyenne sank onto the chair and pressed the left side of her face against the smooth coolness of the desk. If only she could stay here until shift change at seven.

The telephone buzzed above her head. Without opening her eyes, she reached up and punched the speaker button. "Yes."

"Dr. Allison? How you doing, hon?" It was Ardis Dunaway, the most seasoned nurse in the hospital and a good friend.

"You don't want to know," Cheyenne said. "Did you get those orders on bed one?"

"I got 'em. You need to see the baby in five. Fussy, with a fever of 103.7 in triage."

Cheyenne resisted the urge to request a physician replacement. "I'll be there. Is the cefotaxime hanging on Mr. Robb yet?"

"Got it, and the shoulder X-ray on the girl in five."

"Did I hear an ambulance a minute ago?"

"That's right, it sped right on past us to University Hospital."

Good. Why couldn't they do that with the rest of their patients today? Divert them all to the big boys. It amazed Cheyenne that this place stayed so busy, with two trauma centers only moments away. Apparently, the homey atmosphere here drew them in.

"I'm coming, Ardis."

Ninety seconds later, wearing a fresh mask to protect her patients from any stray germs, Cheyenne checked out a fussy infant with a red ear. As she used a bulb insufflator to blow air onto the eardrum, the baby's cries blended with the wail of another siren. Must be a busy day for University and Boone County.

As Cheyenne reassured the mother and comforted the child, the wail outside grew louder.

It stopped. Too close.

When the siren died the baby fell silent, and his mother relaxed noticeably.

Moments later, Ardis stepped to the exam room door. Gone was the motherly grin of the seasoned nurse. "Dr. Allison, we need you in room three."

"Coming." Cheyenne patted the mother's shoulder, jotted a quick order for the nurse and followed Ardis down the hallway. "What's up?"

"Ambulance brought us a chest pain patient. Twenty-eight years old."

"Suspected drug abuse?" For someone so young, that was the norm.

"The attendant says it looks more like a panic attack, and I was told she's been calling for you by name."

"For me? What's *her* name? Did she say why—"

"She won't give the attendants any information," Ardis said. "Nobody told her you were here, she just asked for you. I thought you'd want to see her quickly."

Cheyenne entered the exam room behind the nurse. An ambulance attendant hovered next to the patient with his chart, checking blood pressure as another nurse transferred EKG leads from the ambulance monitor to the hospital's equipment.

The patient's trembling hands covered her face. Silky black hair, as dark and glossy as Cheyenne's, fanned across the pillow.

Cheyenne stepped to the side of the bed and touched the woman's shoulder gently. "Hello, I'm Dr.—"

The hands fell away.

Cheyenne caught her breath. *"Susan?"*

Tears dripped down sharply chiseled, honey-tanned cheeks. Cheyenne's baby sister reached for her.

"Oh, Chey, I'm so scared. My chest hurts. What's happening?"

★ ★ ★

Dane Gideon stepped down from the broad front porch of the ranch house, studying the line of dust clouding the atmosphere above the quarter-mile drive that led from the highway. The early March sunlight dazzled nearby Table Rock Lake with shafts of jeweled colors that built a prism around the small village of Hideaway along the opposite shore.

The sound of tires crunching gravel rippled the peaceful silence as the car pulled into the parking area. Dane saw the dark outline of the passenger. The kid had dreadlocks, skin the color of untouched espresso, eyes narrowed with obvious apprehension—the typical mask of disillusionment in a face too young to bear it.

Clint, the social worker who sometimes seemed to haunt this place, parked beneath the bare oak tree and nodded to Dane with a grim smile. He spoke to the passenger. The teenager shook his head and looked away.

Dane read resentment in every movement.

Clint got out of the car, leaving the door open. "We've got another reluctant one for you," he said, loudly enough for his voice to carry back to the car. "Can't seem to convince him this place'll be like summer camp."

Dane grinned. "Or boot camp."

Clint took Dane's hand in a firm shake. "Thanks for accepting Gavin. Knew you'd be perfect for him. Good kid."

The "good kid" flinched, shot a glare at Clint, crossed his arms over his chest.

"His room's ready," Dane said. "He's bunking with Willy." Clint had escorted Willy here four months ago, under similar conditions.

Richard Cook came striding around the side of the large, two-story house. Apron in place, hair combed back in a wispy gray cap, the older man—who answered only to the surname that also described his job at the ranch—walked across the barely green lawn and nodded to Dane. Willy came rambling up from the barn, obviously curious about his new roommate and—just as obviously—trying not to show it.

Dane grinned at the skinny fourteen-year-old who had taken so well to ranch life. Maybe he would help Gavin settle in.

While the social worker turned to greet Cook and Willy, Dane stepped to the car, slid behind the steering wheel and closed the door.

Gavin breathed with studiously quiet drags, as if the activity caused him pain.

"I'm Dane Gideon."

Only a short break in breathing rhythm indicated the teenager had heard.

Knowing Clint, Dane surmised that the fifteen-year-old had been filled in on all aspects of his new home, from the duties he would have on this thriving ranch, to the size of the house, to the school he would be attending. No doubt he'd also been given thumbnail sketches of the other "inmates" at the ranch.

With a quick glance over his shoulder in the direction of the town, Dane allowed himself a moment of doubt. Was he taking on too much this time?

"You going to tell me your name?" he asked the teenager.

The kid's lips parted, his throat muscles worked, but no sound came out. He cleared his throat and turned to Dane with a garish smile. "Howdy, partner," came the mocking cadence of his surprisingly baritone voice. "You can call me Blaze. It's who I am, it's what I do according to my mama—and mamas never lie, do they?" Bitterness dripped from his words.

"Depends. Did you set the fire?"

The smile sifted from his face like wisps of sand blown from the surface of a rock. "Think I'm stupid? If I say I didn't, you'll call me a liar. If I say I did, I'd *be* lying."

"Then why don't we talk about that later? Right now, let's unload your things and show you around. Your roommate left school early so he could meet you as soon as you arrived. Since this is Friday, you'll have the weekend to settle in and learn your chores before we enroll you in school."

The kid's scowl deepened. "Not going to no school."

"You don't have a choice, and neither do I, Gavin."

"Blaze! My name's Blaze. It's what my—"

"You were acquitted."

"You want to tell me what I'm doing here, then?"

"You wouldn't be at this ranch if you'd been found guilty of a crime."

"But I'm not home with my mama, am I?"

It was Dane's turn to be silent. That was one of the most difficult things he had to deal with here—boys who felt unloved, unwanted.

"You got that straight," Gavin said. "My mama's judge and jury on this case. Long as I'm here, my name's *Blaze*."

Cheyenne pressed several facial tissues into her sister's left hand. "I know it's scary, Susan, but try to relax so we can get a good reading on your heart. You're going to be fine. I picked up on the murmur right away—I think it's your mitral valve problem, but I want to make sure."

Susan nodded, blinking back tears.

When Cheyenne was in eleventh grade and Susan still in elementary school, Cheyenne had discovered her baby sister's mitral valve prolapse with her new Christmas present from her parents—a stethoscope. From that time on, Cheyenne had taken Susan's condition on as a personal responsibility. It was what had motivated her through those first horrendous two years of med school.

She still took that responsibility seriously.

Susan's hand trembled as she mopped her face with the tissues. "It's never hurt like this before, Chey."

"Why don't you tell me what led up to it? Heavy exercise? Did something happen that upset you?"

Susan hesitated, then nodded, glancing at the others in the room. "I guess you could say that," she murmured.

Cheyenne respected her sister's unspoken plea for privacy. She glanced at Ardis, who stood in her usual spot, checking the monitor while the tech from Respiratory handled the EKG machine.

The tech handed the printout to Cheyenne, then disconnected the leads from Susan's chest. "Want me to leave the machine in here, Dr. Allison?"

"Yes, we'll do another test after the heart rate slows down and we get rid of the muscle-tremor artifact." Cheyenne gave her sister a reassuring grin. "It looks good, but we need to find out what's causing this."

"I've never felt like this before, Chey. I'm sorry to be such a big baby, but it scared me."

"You're no baby. Are you sure the pain doesn't radiate to your jaw or your arm? Nothing in your back?"

"My hands feel tingly."

"Both of them?"

Susan flexed her fingers. "Yes."

"That could be from hyperventilation."

"Is this what they call a panic attack?"

"It could be." Panic attack would have been Cheyenne's diagnosis if this were anyone else. But Susan was not one to panic. So what had sent her heart into overdrive?

Susan inhaled deeply and closed her eyes, but they flicked

open again when the outgoing EKG tech greeted the incoming radiology tech, who pushed a portable X-ray machine in front of him.

"Susan, we're going to get a picture of your chest," Cheyenne explained. "Just relax. You know I'll take care of you." She leaned over the bed and held her sister's gaze.

Susan took another deep breath and lay back, the midnight strands of her shaggy-cut hair splaying across the pillow. She looked up at Cheyenne, dark eyes filled with trust.

Cheyenne squeezed her arm. "You want me to have the secretary call Kirk?"

"No!" Susan's head raised from the pillow once more. "Please, I don't want him to know about this."

"It's all right," Cheyenne said. "I won't call." She stepped out of the room long enough for the tech to get the X ray of Susan's heart—just in case. "It's going to be okay," she called reassuringly from the doorway.

What was the problem between Susan and her husband?

Chapter Two

Dane stood beside Clint at the far edge of the yard and watched Willy and Gavin walk toward the barn—Willy's typically talking hands graced the air to emphasize whatever verbal point he was trying to make with Gavin.

What a contrast—the scrawny fourteen-year-old with closely cropped brown hair and glasses was nearly a head shorter and fifty pounds lighter than Gavin. Where Gavin had muscles, Willy had skin. Where Gavin had dreadlocks, Willy had—practically—skin.

"The dreadlocks will take some adjustment," Dane said.

Clint chuckled. "For Blaze or for you?"

"For Hideaway. And I refuse to call him Blaze. It's derogatory."

"You've been living out here in the sticks too long, Dane. You need to get to the city more often."

"No, thanks."

"Still hiding out?"

"I'm not hiding from anything." Dane used his "back off"

voice as he nodded toward Gavin. "He's already got two problems fitting in."

"Do I want to hear this?"

"He's a 'ranch kid,' and he's got dark skin."

"Hold it." Clint made a show of covering his ears. "It isn't politically correct for me to hear this."

"You don't like the term *ranch kid?*"

"You know what—"

"Deal with it. That's the way it is here. When I came to Hideaway, I moved back twenty years in time—in some ways, more like fifty. Many of the natives have been here for two or three generations. They hate change. Many of them are still leery of me because I'm divorced with no children of my own. And it's no coincidence that everyone within a ten-mile radius of Hideaway looks askance at Jason because he has a deeper tan than most of the natives."

"Then move somewhere else. Take the kids with you. You can afford that."

Dane shook his head. "I belong here."

Clint snorted. "I suppose God told you that."

Dane ignored his friend's cynical tone. "We all have our place in life. I've found mine." He watched with growing interest as Willy introduced Gavin Farmer to Gordy, the most cantankerous cow of the herd, through the barn lot fence. Gordy was short for Gordina—the name of a bossy woman he had admired in his church.

"A perfect place," Clint murmured. "Taming wild teenagers to become model citizens? Putting up with Austin Barlow every time he wants to make you a target for one of his special vendettas?"

"I hate to admit this, but I'm enjoying the challenge of those vendettas. Austin isn't invincible." Dane gestured toward Gordy. The cow stood close to the fence, allowing Gavin to scratch her ear. "Would you look at that? I've never seen her do that before."

"The kid has a way with animals. He worked with his father in his veterinarian practice."

"I knew from the report his father was a vet, but it didn't give much information about the mother," Dane said. "Any insights there?"

"All I know is the parents were long estranged, and that she had her own demanding job. Wouldn't even leave it long enough to collect her son when his father was killed in the wreck last year. Social services stepped in, suggested foster care, placed him and he ran away. His mother finally, reluctantly, agreed to take him, but three weeks after he moved in with her, their house burned down."

"None of that's in the report."

"We don't always put everything in those reports, because we don't always have all the information we need."

"So what does the kid's mother do?"

"She's a manager for a fast-food chain down in Arkansas. She does pretty well, seems efficient at her job, but when it came to Gavin, she couldn't cope."

"So she claimed Gavin deliberately set fire to their house?" Dane exclaimed. "Does she have any reason to believe that?"

"Only an episode when he accidentally set the living room on fire when he was a child."

"Nothing since then?"

"Not on record."

Dane gave him a quick look. "That isn't reassuring."

"He's an innocent kid caught in a mess, Dane."

"You're sure? I've got other kids to think about, and the town is always watching—"

"Give him some time and see what you think," Clint said. "Anyway, his mom isn't able to keep him. I feel he needs a mother, though. Frankly, you weren't my first choice for him—you don't even have a woman on the ranch, unless you count Gordy."

"She's a good mama. Her calves always grow well."

"Think you can work one of your miracles, Dane?"

"I don't work miracles."

"You seem to know Somebody who does."

Cheyenne wrote discharge orders for two patients, washed her hands and replaced her mask. When she entered Susan's exam room again, no other medical personnel were there.

Cheyenne closed the door behind her and went to her sister's bed. "How are you feeling?"

Susan nodded. "Better. It doesn't hurt as much. By the way, what's with the mask?"

"Flu." Cheyenne slumped onto the stool beside the bed. "I don't want to risk passing it on to a patient." She tapped the mask with her fingers. "This is just a precaution. I don't feel too bad." *Liar. You feel wretched.* "Your lab reports all look good, but let's get a repeat EKG before I discharge you. Now that your heart rate is slower and you aren't shaking so badly, we'll get a better reading."

Susan nodded.

"Speaking of shaking," Cheyenne said, "what could have set this off? I've never known you to have a panic attack before."

"So you think that *is* what happened?"

A question instead of an answer. "I don't know for sure, but that *could* have been what disturbed your mitral valve. I've already scheduled an outpatient echo for you for next Monday."

"Oh, Sis, do we have to do that? I don't really want Kirk to know about—"

"We have to make sure that valve isn't going to cause any major problems." Cheyenne touched Susan's left hand. "I'm not taking any chances with you. If you're worried about Kirk knowing, I'll have the hospital send me the bill." But why shouldn't Susan's husband know?

"No, don't do that. It's…it isn't that bad."

Cheyenne leaned forward. If it wasn't that bad, why was Susan suddenly avoiding eye contact? "I know you don't like to take medication, but I've ordered something to calm you down."

"A tranquilizer?"

"Yes. You won't have to worry about any more needles, since you already have the IV. It won't fix the problem, but it might help make everything more bearable until we can find the real culprit." But of course the real culprit was Kirk Warden—Cheyenne had known that for some time.

Susan swallowed, then nodded. "Could you give me something…to take with me?"

"I'll write you a script." Cheyenne hesitated. "You'll need a ride home. I'd let you take my car, but you can't drive under the influence of this medication. If you can't call Kirk—"

"I'll get a taxi. Can I work? I have an appointment with a client whose house I'm decorating this afternoon. She's a neighbor who lives just three houses west of us, so I won't have to drive there."

"Sure, you can work…if your client doesn't mind a little drug-induced creativity." Cheyenne got up, battling a wave of nausea. "Since you're getting a taxi, I'll dispense some tablets for you here so you won't have to stop at a pharmacy."

"Thanks." Still no eye contact.

Cheyenne leaned closer. "Honey, what's going on with you?"

Susan dabbed at her face with a tissue. "It's no big deal, Sis, okay?"

"Wrong answer. I'm your doctor right now, not your sister.

You don't have panic attacks for 'no big deal.' What happened with Kirk today?" *Please talk to me, Susan.* The sound of another ambulance siren barely reached them from the highway.

"We had a little disagreement over the telephone," Susan glanced toward the closed door. "Are you sure no one can hear us?"

"Positive."

"I decided to file my taxes separately from his this year. When I told him, he went ballistic. I wouldn't have done it, except I've been comparing notes with his secretary, and we don't jibe. If he's cheating on taxes, I don't want any part of it."

Cheyenne closed her eyes, glad the mask over the lower portion of her face would conceal some of her dismay.

"If he finds out she talked to me, he'll fire her," Susan said.

Anger intensified Cheyenne's nausea. For her sister's sake, she had put up with Kirk's borderline antagonism since he and Susan had become engaged eight years ago. Cheyenne had sat through countless uncomfortably silent dinners, had timed her visits to the house when Kirk would be at work, had run interference when Mom and Dad flew up from Florida to visit. Occasionally, Susan spent the night with Cheyenne, when Kirk was out of town on business—he had his own computer networking firm.

"The stress with Kirk could be a trigger for your chest pain," Cheyenne said.

"I'm not sure what I can do about it."

Cheyenne decided not to mention the obvious solution. "What else is going on with you?"

Susan looked down at her hands, picking at her cuticles. "Kirk isn't…always happy with me."

"Happy in what way?"

"The problem is, he thinks I've become too independent with my business, and he's decided to tighten the reins."

Those weren't reins, they were more like screws. "In what way?" Cheyenne asked gently.

Susan closed her eyes and raised a hand to her face—a shaking hand. "He's taken all the money out of our joint account and placed them in a different bank, using his name alone."

Cheyenne willed away her own outrage. Susan couldn't handle that right now. "Do you think he's planning to divorce you?"

"We don't believe in divorce."

We? Was Kirk cheating on his taxes but still pretending to be some upstanding, good "Christian" man? What a laugh.

"I just don't know what to do next," Susan said. "It's so... so hard to realize that the man I married isn't the man I'm married *to*. You know what I mean?"

Cheyenne nodded, though she didn't really know. Her whole life had been caught up in her career, with only one serious relationship. That had ended in pain when the man she loved couldn't endure her hours—or her success. "You could move in with me, Susan. You'll never have to put up with that kind of treatment while I'm alive."

"I'm the one who got myself into this mess," Susan murmured. "I'll stick it out."

Cheyenne bit her tongue and remained silent. Blast the too holy standards of Susan's religion. Didn't anyone at their church see what a hypocrite Kirk was?

"If you need money to get you by—"

"Chey, I'm doing fine." Susan touched Cheyenne's arm. "Thanks. It seems like half the neighborhood has decided to redecorate, and they're calling me to do it. I've opened a bank account in my name alone. I'll be fine. Maybe Kirk's just going through a bad time right now, and I... I need to be more understanding and...pray for him."

Cheyenne clamped her teeth together. Susan could exercise her Christian principles and turn the other cheek all she wanted, but Cheyenne wasn't—

There was a knock at the door, then Ardis opened it and came inside. "Got you some snooze juice, my dear. Just relax." She injected the syringe into Susan's IV port. "It's a temporary fix, but you'll start to feel better real quick."

Susan nodded. "Thanks. Chey, everything'll be fine."

Cheyenne patted her sister's hand. *I'm not so sure.*

Chapter Three

Dane Gideon stepped through the barn door and switched on the overhead light. The remaining Holstein heifer could be inoculated and released into the pasture.

No problem. He would have it done before the boys came home from school.

Not until he had the calf cornered in a stall did he recognize the little white bell on her otherwise black face. Too late, he heard the deep, rumbling moo of an angry mama cow behind him. Gordy.

He should have waited.

She lowered her head and came at him, her huge nostrils snorting so forcefully her breath swept dust and particles of straw into a tiny cloud at her feet.

Dane jumped up the side of a nearby stall, grabbed the ladder and climbed to the loft. He turned in time to see Starface skittering out of the barn ahead of her indignant mother.

"Should've sold that ornery animal years ago," he muttered, slowly descending the ladder.

Gordy hurried after her baby, ears perked forward, her long, Holstein body all bulk and bones in the reflection of the afternoon sunlight.

Dane reached the barn floor in time to hear a loud whistle, followed by a "Yeehaw!" from outside.

He ran to the door to find Starface running back toward him, with Gordy in hot pursuit. He scrambled backward against a concrete stand, leaped atop it.

Another whistle pierced the gloom of the barn. Metal slapped wood—the slamming of the barn lot gate—then came another whistle.

Gordy waggled her head at Dane, big ears fluttering as she turned to investigate the sound.

"Cook? Is that you?" Dane called.

A familiar, broad-shouldered form came striding inside, dreadlocks bouncing, thumbs hooked over the belt loops of his jeans. "Don't you want to vaccinate Starface before—"

"Gavin, get back!"

Gordy lowered her head and charged as Gavin scrambled sideways. Dane jumped down and ran after the cow.

"Gordy, over here!" He waved his arms over his head. "You old battleaxe, get away!"

Gavin leaped over the fence in one youthful motion.

Gordy swerved and rammed Dane with her shoulder. He hit the ground as she swerved away, kicking out with her foot to land a solid blow to his left thigh.

A loud grunt echoed in his head as he fell against the fence. The gate swung back and a hand grabbed his shirt, then jerked him, half dragging, half lifting, him, out of the lot. As soon as he was clear, Gavin slammed the gate in the cow's face.

Dane slumped against the outside of the fence while Gavin shoved the gate latch home.

"You okay?" Gavin asked, bending over him.

Dane gritted his teeth against the pain in his thigh. "I'll be fine."

"Sorry, I forgot Willy said Gordy had a mean streak." Gavin gestured over his shoulder toward the cow and calf. "I know better."

Dane caught sight of Gavin's blood-streaked sleeve. "You're bleeding."

Gavin held his arm up and inspected a small cut at the base of his wrist. "I'll get that taken care of. Guess that old cow hasn't seen many black guys with locks like mine, huh?"

Dane rubbed his thigh. "I don't think that had anything to do with it."

"Do you want to vaccinate the calf while we've got her in the lot?"

"Thanks, Gavin, but I think we'll let them go this time."

"When're you going to start calling me Blaze?"

"When it becomes your legal name. What are you doing out of school early?"

"Last hour's PE, and I didn't have dress-out clothes, so I told the teacher I'd be good and come straight here if he let me leave early. Why do you have such a fuss with a silly ol' nickname? Everybody else calls me Blaze."

"Good for them. We'll find you some exercise clothes and shoes tonight."

"Guess you know I'll be sixteen in three weeks."

"Yes. What do you want for your birthday?"

"To quit school."

"Sorry, no way. Anything else?"

"It'll be legal then. A guy doesn't have to go after his sixteenth birthday."

"He does if he plans to stay here at the ranch."

Gavin blinked at Dane. "You mean I have to keep going to school just to stay here?"

"That's the deal. Gavin, you're still bleeding." An inch-long cut should have stopped bleeding by now, unless it was deeper than it appeared. The end of Gavin's sleeve was soaked red.

The teenager pressed his fingers over the wound. "Nobody told me about that rule when I agreed to come here."

"You may find there are a lot of things around here nobody told you about."

Gavin gave a disgusted grunt.

"Come on," Dane said. "Let's get you to the house and clean your—"

"Okay, fine, then there's something else I want for my birthday."

"I hope it's Gordyburgers," Dane muttered, still aching from the kick.

"Call me by my chosen name."

Dane put a hand on Gavin's shoulder and nudged him toward the house. "I don't understand the logic of calling yourself Blaze when you aren't an arsonist."

"Something my daddy taught me."

"I thought he was a veterinarian."

Gavin gave Dane an impatient look.

"Sorry. What did your father teach you?"

"To take the sting out of the name. Beat 'em to the punch."

"Did kids at school call you names?"

"That's for me to know. Why're you limping?"

"Gordy kicked me."

"Better get some ice on it."

"I plan to."

"Come on, you can say it. 'I plan to, Blaze.'"

"For three more weeks, your name is Gav or Gavin, take your pick."

★ ★ ★

"Missouri Regional, this is 841, we are currently inbound for your facility...."

Cheyenne glanced at her watch, groaned, straightened at her desk, still fighting the nausea. "Go away," she muttered. Twenty more minutes, and Brillhart would be here. Why hadn't she asked Ardis to call him sooner?

"...Caucasian female, late twenties, class one trauma from an MVA. Patient's car was struck in the driver's side, had to be extricated. Patient is fully immobilized, responsive only to pain. We are attempting to establish IV at this time. BP sixty over forty by—"

"Coming *here?*" Ardis exclaimed. "Did you hear that? They're bringing us a class one."

Cheyenne reached for the ambulance radio and keyed the microphone. "Eight-forty-one this is medical control. Divert to University Hospital. We are not a designated trauma facility."

"Missouri Regional this is 841, we copy but cannot comply. University and Boone are both on full trauma diversion at this time. ETA of five minutes."

Cheyenne pressed the button again. "Eight-forty-one, this is medical control. We roger your last transmission. Please advise of any change in patient's condition. This is medical control at Missouri Regional out." She disconnected.

"Oh, my. What do we do now?" the secretary asked.

"Advise RT and X Ray we've got a hot one coming in fast." Cheyenne turned in her chair. "Quickly, Deanna."

"G-got it, Dr. Allison." The secretary swallowed and jerked up the telephone.

Cheyenne nodded to Ardis. "Have Lab get four units of O-negative blood STAT. I want it in this department when the patient arrives. Then attempt to notify the surgeon on call for backup. Let him know what we have."

Ardis went to work.

Cheyenne found the intubation kit in the trauma room and selected the appropriate size ET tubes. What a time to have the flu.

The radio came alive again. "Missouri Regional, this is 841. Be advised our patient is now in full arrest. I repeat, our patient is in full arrest. Following ACLS protocol. ETA less than two minutes."

Cheyenne made eye contact with Ardis. They would do all they could, but the odds were against this patient surviving.

"Everyone get your protective gear on," Cheyenne said.

"I hear the sirens now," the secretary called.

"Make sure RT and X Ray are on their way down," Cheyenne said. "Ardis, check on that blood." The trauma room was ready. "Aprons, masks, gloves, everyone."

Stepping to the window that overlooked the ambulance bay, Cheyenne caught sight of the red-orange-red-orange flash of lights as the van safety-sped into the lot. Tension thickened the air in the Emergency Department.

"We can do this," she said. "Get ready."

The RT tech came racing down the far end of the corridor pushing her supply cart.

Ardis hung up the telephone and swung toward Cheyenne. "They're getting the blood ready, Dr. Allison."

"Good. Come with me." Cheyenne looked for the ER tech. "Rick, you too." She led the way out to the bay, where the driver was yanking open the back doors of the ambulance.

The attendants pulled the intubated patient from the vehicle. Cheyenne's first sight of the patient was the flash of red blood marring a half-naked body—the attendants had stripped her to check for all injuries.

"Rick, take over compressions," Cheyenne ordered the tech. "What's the rhythm?" she asked the attendant, standing back as they wheeled the stretcher toward the door.

"PEA," the paramedic said.

Pulseless electrical activity. No surprise, judging by the apparent blood loss. The patient was unrecognizable.

"How much fluid have you given?" Cheyenne asked, following them through the door.

"We've only been able to give about a hundred cc's," the paramedic replied. "I could only get a twenty-two gauge IV started."

Not big enough. "We need at least a twenty gauge." She turned to Ardis. "I need you to establish a large-bore IV, have her ready for the blood when it arrives."

"I'll get right on it."

They helped transfer the patient to the ER trauma bed while the respiratory tech took over bagging the patient, helping her breathe. Cheyenne moved to the patient's left side to check for placement of the ET tube, leaving her right side accessible to Ardis.

No breath sounds over the abdomen. Good. That meant the patient had been intubated properly. Pressing the bell of the stethoscope over the patient's bloody chest, she raised a hand for Rick to delay the next compression.

No heartbeat.

She nodded for him to continue.

As she removed the stethoscope from the patient's rib cage, she saw a dark blotch on the skin. A large birthmark just below the left breast.

She looked at the face again, reached for the blood-matted hair.

Black. It was the length of...

She looked at the paramedic. "You said she was the driver?"

"Only person in the car. We pulled her from beneath the steering wheel."

Cheyenne couldn't catch her breath. "And the car? Did you notice what kind...?"

"Dark blue Sable sedan."

The edges of Cheyenne's vision went black and she felt herself slipping backward. *It can't be—I told her not to drive, she said she wouldn't....*

"Dr. Allison!" Ardis yelled.

"Oh, Susan. Oh, please God, no." Cheyenne fought to regain her composure. "Where's that blood!" she snapped.

"Right here," Ardis said. "Hold on, Dr. Allison, I can't get the large bore IV."

"Have you heard from the surgeon?"

It couldn't be Susan. She was only going to a neighbor's house.

But her sister's silhouette—the undamaged part—was obvious now.

"Our on-call surgeon is also on trauma call for University," Deanna said. "We're trying to reach someone else, but—"

"Ardis, get me a central line kit," Cheyenne ordered. "She needs blood now. And get X Ray in here for a trauma series. Now!"

"Dr. Allison?" came a voice from the hallway. It was her replacement. Jim Brillhart. His tall, lean form filled the doorway. "How can I help?"

She looked up at him, felt the floor rock beneath her.

He rushed forward and caught her arm. "Are you okay?"

"I'm getting ready to do a central line on this patient. I'll take the jugular so I won't interfere with CPR."

"You want me to do it?"

"I'll be fine." She refocused on her procedure, felt the sweat coat her neck and chest and trickle down the sides of her face as she tried to keep her hands steady

A tech reported on the CBC and Cheyenne prepared for a transfusion as the respiratory tech came into the crowded room with a report on Susan's blood gas that deepened Cheyenne's frown.

"That could be venous," she said. *They missed the artery and got a vein.* "Take it again."

"Dr. Allison, I really don't think it's—"

"One more time."

The X-ray tech brought in the trauma X-ray series and mounted them on the view box.

It showed multiple left rib fractures with a massive collection of blood in the left chest cavity. Multiple pelvic fractures with a ground glass appearance on the X ray.

No, Susan. No!

"Get me a chest-tube setup. And wrap a sheet around her pelvis and tighten it as much as you can."

Rick looked up from his compressions, though he continued in perfect rhythm. "You want me to stop doing compressions when you put in the chest tube?"

"Yes, but no longer than absolutely necessary. Get somebody fresh to spell you."

"Let me do the chest tube," Jim said, "then I'll take over for Rick."

"Check for fine V fib," Cheyenne said as he placed the tube. *Susan, baby, work with me. Don't you dare die on me!*

The monitor remained an agonal rhythm, but it now appeared more asystole.

Flatline.

No! She would not let that happen!

"Where's that surgeon? I need him *now.*"

"I'm sorry, Dr. Allison, but he's already been called to University Hospital for disaster code," Deanna said.

"Then it's up to us," Cheyenne said. "Get me a thoracotomy tray."

Jim looked at her in surprise. "Cheyenne, are you sure about this?"

"Push the epinephrine, Ardis," Cheyenne said, ignoring him. The thought of opening Susan's chest and massaging her heart was unthinkable. But it was her sister's only chance.

"Ardis! Epi. Now."

"Dr. Allison," Jim said.

"I've got to try it," she said softly. "This is my sister."

He gave a shocked, "Oh, dear God no," then, "Rick, take over back here." Jim came around the bed to Cheyenne, placed a hand on each shoulder and tried to draw her away from the bed.

She resisted. "I'm still the doctor in charge, Jim. You can't take me off this case."

"I'm your director, Cheyenne, and your friend. Listen to me for a moment."

She looked up at him. "Did you hear me? It's my *sister!*"

"I know, but what if it weren't? What would you do?"

She turned again to Susan's side.

"She's a blunt trauma victim, right?"

"That's right, Dr. Brillhart," said the paramedic.

"Pulseless for more than twenty minutes?"

"Twenty-five," Rick said.

"Cheyenne," Jim said gently. "You need to let her go."

"I can't do that. Ardis, push the epinephrine again."

"You've done all you can," Jim said.

No! I'm still in charge! "I haven't called this code yet."

"Cheyenne." Jim leaned closer. He placed a hand over hers.

She jerked away. "Ardis, why are you waiting? Push the epi! Any word on the second blood gas?"

"Dr. Allison," Jim said, this time with authority. "You have to call it. She's gone. She wouldn't want to come back, even if she could. There's too much damage."

Cheyenne felt the dizziness strike once more with blinding swiftness. She couldn't bear it.

"I can't call it," she whispered.

"I'll do it, then," Jim said.

"No!"

Silence descended except for the sounds of the monitor, Rick's labored breathing and the efforts that kept this hopelessly damaged body functioning.

Let her go? She's already gone.

Cheyenne looked at her watch, then reached for Susan's hand, covered in blood.

Everyone waited.

I'm so sorry, my baby sister.

"Time of…" Cheyenne swallowed, took a breath of air, which was strong with the scent of blood. "Time of…death, 18:14."

Rick stopped compressions. The respiratory tech stopped bagging. Ardis set her equipment down and rushed around the bed to Cheyenne's side.

As Cheyenne felt herself falling, felt hands catching her, she willed herself to descend into death with her sister.

Chapter Four

Dane found Cook in the pantry, sorting through institutional cans of tomato soup.

"Barbecue tonight?" he asked the bony old ranch hand.

"If I can find the molasses," Cook said over his shoulder.

"If we're out, I'll make a run to town." The boys loved that recipe. "Cook, did Blaze get into the medicine chest?"

The older man turned and frowned at him. "Why would he do that?"

"He had an injury out in the barn lot. Gordy got after us."

"That blamed ol' cow's going to get somebody kilt someday. Since when did you start calling him Blaze?"

Oops. "Since three seconds ago. I'd better go see about him."

Dane took the stairs and saw a spot of blood on the railing. He went to the closed door of the bedroom Gavin and Willy shared. When he pushed it open he saw Gavin in the center of the room, holding the end of a syringe against the bare flesh of his stomach.

"What are you doing?"

"I'm a bleeder." The boy wiped a smudge of blood from his arm.

"What's in the syringe?"

"A coagulant to stop the flow." He rewrapped the syringe and set it on the top of his dresser.

"Nobody told me," Dane said.

"Not a lot of people know."

"How could you keep something like that a secret?"

"You don't believe me?" Again, that expression of irritable impatience, thick brows lowered over eyes narrowed with disappointment.

"I didn't say that."

Gavin sat on the chest in front of the window that overlooked the barn. "About two years ago my old doctor died, and nobody took his place. The guy was in his eighties, only had a few patients. My prescription for this stuff's always refillable, so I didn't go to a new doc for a while. When I did, he never said anything about sending him my old records. I guess they kind of got lost."

"That's dangerous, Blaze. You need to take responsibility for your own health care now. What would happen if you ran out—"

"What'd you call me?"

Oh, no. He'd done it again.

"You called me Blaze."

"Happy birthday. Why didn't your mother tell the social worker about your condition?"

"She doesn't know."

"I can't believe she wouldn't—"

"There you go again." Blaze shook his head and gestured toward the bed. "You want to sit down and let me tell you a few facts of life?"

"I want to know where Clint can get a copy of your medical records."

Blaze unwrapped a paper towel from around his wrist. "See? The stuff's already working. No big deal."

"It's a big deal when we don't know—"

"Thing is, I didn't figure they'd let me come to the ranch if they knew I was a bleeder. You know, working with the animals can be a little tricky sometimes. But I've got this—" his voice wavered "—this need to be around...." He swallowed and studied the wound on his wrist.

"It's okay," Dane said. "I think I understand. You probably worked with your father a lot in his practice."

"All the time."

"You lived in Rolla?"

"Edge of town. Saw my mother maybe three times after the divorce was final, and maybe six times before that. Until Dad died."

"I'm sorry."

"About what? That my own mother doesn't want me? Not your fault. You ever put any ice on that thigh?"

"I will."

"Sure. You gonna kick me out?"

"You got any other secrets you need to tell me?"

"I'm not an arsonist."

"That's no secret."

"I don't think I'll make it at school."

Dane eased himself onto the bed at last, groaning at the increased soreness of his leg. "Why not?"

"Don't read too well."

"You need glasses?"

"I've got good vision, I just can't catch on to reading."

"Maybe I can help you."

"How're you going to do that?"

"Has anybody ever suggested you might have a learning disability?"

"All my life."

"Your father could have helped you—"

"Don't you say anything about my father," Blaze snapped. "He got dumped by the same woman who dumped me. He did the best he could, but he was busy."

"Maybe you need to learn a different way to process information."

"I process just fine—I just can't read the letters."

"Backward? Maybe if we played with that a little."

"Maybe you should just use me here on the ranch to take care of the animals. Maybe that's all I need to do. I could just be a ranch hand here on the place."

"I didn't bring you here to work. I brought you here to take care of you. That means you get an education."

Blaze hooked his thumbs into his belt loops. "I'd like to see you try."

"You'd better believe I will."

Hothouse flowers saturated the atmosphere, nauseating Cheyenne as she slid into the pew beside her mother. Organ music threaded through the gloom of the church, trickling over her like black oil, punctuated by her mother's quiet sobs. She felt oppressed by the crowd in this auditorium, though she knew the outpouring of kindness by so many should give her comfort.

But nothing could give her comfort. Some evil entity had gut-kicked her, and it amazed her that she was still breathing.

Kirk sat across the auditorium, wiping his face with a white handkerchief. In a haze of pain this past weekend, Cheyenne had tried twice to contact him. No response. Her parents had called his number three times yesterday. No answer. No matter what had transpired before now, he must be hurting horribly.

Cheyenne's fingernails sank into the flesh of her hand. Could he be hurting worse than she was? She had lived with the nightmare of seeing her beloved baby sister—her only sibling—wheeled into the ER mangled and bloody. She had plunged her hands into the blood, had fought desperately for Susan's life. She had lost.

If not for the overwhelming support of extended family— aunts, uncles, cousins—Cheyenne wouldn't be able to handle this day, or her parents' grief. Or her own.

Mom hadn't stopped crying since she and Dad arrived yesterday. Dad looked closer to seventy than fifty-six.

A young minister sat on the stage behind the podium, fidgeting with his tie.

Someone touched Cheyenne on the shoulder. She looked up to see Ardis Dunaway standing in the aisle, her dark eyes peering through bifocals with deep compassion.

"How're you holding up, hon?"

Cheyenne nodded. She still wanted to die. "I don't know how to thank you for all you've done to help these past few days."

"Don't you even worry about that."

Not only had this dear friend taken care of her when she collapsed the day of Susan's death, but Ardis and Jim had been the ones to call Kirk in and tell him about Susan—a task Cheyenne would traditionally have undertaken.

Ardis leaned closer. "Have you spoken to Kirk at all?"

"He won't communicate."

"And so we still don't know why she was driving under the influence—"

"Please." Cheyenne felt the stab of fresh pain. "Does it matter, anyway? She's dead, and no amount of fact finding will bring her back. The wreck wasn't her fault, according to the police report. That's all I need to—"

"I'm sorry, honey, of course you're right." Ardis squeezed her shoulder, then indicated the crowded church. "Look, I know you don't believe in all this, but I hope it comforts you to know that Susan was very well loved."

"My sister found...comfort here, apparently," Cheyenne said.

"She's receiving more comfort now than she ever received here on earth."

Cheyenne nodded, too overwhelmed to argue. She respected Ardis's faith even though she didn't share it.

Ardis squeezed Cheyenne's shoulder and returned to her seat several rows back.

The organ music drifted to silence. The deep baritone voice of a soloist echoed through the auditorium—waxing poetic about gardens and dew and talking with the Son of God.

Cheyenne focused her attention on the closed casket and the picture of her laughing sister, whose life hadn't been lived long enough for her to ever be complete.

At the cemetery, the funeral director escorted Cheyenne beneath the canopy to the seat next to her brother-in-law.

He edged away from her, his firm features set.

She endured the minister's attempt at consolation as he eulogized her sister.

He meant well, but he didn't know Susan the way she did.

She took her mother's hand and held tight, forcing away the memories of Friday. Almost every night, she dreamed of the blood. She dreamed of Susan's battered body. She relived that horrible time over and over in her head.

The pastor finished his eulogy and said a prayer, then reached for Kirk's hand. "She was a precious soul," he said softly. "We'll miss her so much, but I know it'll be nothing compared to what you're going through."

Kirk's tears looked real, the pain on his face unrehearsed. It reflected Cheyenne's own loss.

For one unguarded moment, she felt the kinship. As the pastor stepped away, Cheyenne touched Kirk's arm. "We're both going to miss her," she whispered.

He jerked away, turning on her with the swiftness of a striking snake. "How are you going to live with yourself, knowing you killed your own sister?"

The viciousness of his words, his voice, sent a sting of shock through her. "How can you say that? I did everything I could to—"

"Save it for the jury." He turned his broad back to her and stood.

Cheyenne stood at the foot of the casket, barely heeding the voices that surrounded her as she watched Kirk shaking the hand of the funeral director. He waved and nodded to others, like a gracious party host.

He looked aside and caught her watching him. His expression hardened.

She stepped backward and stumbled.

"Cheyenne? Are you okay?" Uncle Chester caught her by the elbow.

She felt a wash of dizziness. "I'm not sure."

Mom rushed to her side. "Chey? What's wrong? Are you sick again?"

"No, I... I'll be okay." How could he blame her? She'd done all she could do. She would gladly die herself, if only it would bring Susan back.

But nothing would bring Susan back—and Cheyenne didn't know how she'd be able to bear it.

Chapter Five

Susan's face floated into Cheyenne's vision, interrupting a perfect in-house nap. The dark brown eyes were lit with humor, the classically high cheekbones glowed with health.

"I want to see you again, Chey." Her soft voice floated through the darkness. "Make sure to come—"

With a cry, Cheyenne plunged from the dream, startled awake by its vividness.

She gasped, tugging the comforter around her shoulders. "Susan!"

The telephone beside the twin-size bed beeped at her.

"Leave me alone." She turned away from the sound, covering her ears, desperate to catch another glimpse of the dream, to hear that sweet voice again.

Another beep, and the speaker came alive. "Dr. Allison? Hello?" A male voice. Tom, the R.N. on duty.

She turned and snatched up the receiver. "Yes?"

"Dr. Allison, I'm sorry to wake you. Are you okay?"

No. She cleared her throat. "What's up?"

"We've got a patient with chest pain."

"I'll be there." She disconnected and looked at the bedside clock. Six-thirty on Saturday, April 2. Exactly a month since...

How many dreams did that make now, thirty or so?

How much longer could she function this way? She felt the sting of tears as she reached for her stethoscope. "Oh... Susan."

She quick-stepped to the ER and found Tom waiting for her at the central desk.

"Vitals?" she asked.

"Arlene's in the room doing the patient assessment."

Cheyenne selected a T-sheet and placed it on a clipboard on her way to the cardiac room. She stopped in the doorway and caught the faint scent of body odor.

The patient had black hair...olive skin...dark eyes...

Cheyenne's clipboard clattered to the floor.

Arlene looked up from the monitor. "Doctor, are you okay?"

Stop this! It isn't Susan.

"Doctor?"

"Yes. Sorry." Cheyenne picked up the clipboard and looked at the patient again. Not Susan. Of course it wasn't Susan. *Get a grip!*

"H–Hello, I'm Dr. Allison."

The patient watched her closely, and Cheyenne realized Arlene was still staring at her from the other side of the room.

"Arlene, is something wrong?" she asked.

The nurse shook her head slowly.

Cheyenne questioned the patient, did an exam and ordered a drug screen, all the time aware that the nurse continued to watch her a little too closely. It rankled.

While she waited for the test results to come back, Cheyenne sat down at her workstation and struggled with the memories. As she often did, she planned to drive to the cemetery with a bouquet of flowers from the grocery store.

And then she would sleep through the day. After that, she had vacation for two weeks, which she desperately needed.

She checked her mail slot in the E.R. call room. There were the typical copies of old lab reports and hospital memos, a request for her to stop by her director's office before she left on vacation.

No problem, she could do that. Jim had a shift today. Besides, it wasn't as if she had plans to do anything but sleep. With the physician shortage in the past few weeks, she'd worked several extra shifts in March, half of them nights. It kept her occupied, but it also kept her tired, especially combined with the insomnia caused by her frequent nightmares.

Jim walked past her desk. "You ready to talk to me in a few minutes?"

"Let me finish up a patient and I'll be there." He was obviously serious about something. Might as well see what it was.

Dane heard the familiar crunch of gravel announce the arrival of a macho engine. Opening the barn door, he saw the big red pickup floating in a cloud of dust, and the mayor of Hideaway behind the steering wheel.

This was not the best possible morning for Austin's kind of company, but then, Dane couldn't think of a time when he would welcome this man. Too much ugly history came between them.

With a final glance at Willy and Blaze hovering over the cows in the milking room, Dane strolled from the barn and ambled up the incline toward the house, catching a whiff of dust in his nostrils. They could use a good rain. In fact, he wouldn't mind if the sky chose this time for a cloudburst.

Austin Barlow lit from his truck like some cowboy hero

alighting from his trusty steed. Minus the hat, for once. At forty-two, Austin had a full head of auburn hair with barely a streak of white, while at thirty-eight, Dane knew his silver-blond hair was already more silver than blond. His beard had even more snow in it. His father had been the same way.

"Morning, Austin." Dane reached out a hand, bracing himself for the man's exaggerated grip. He didn't wince when his knuckles squeezed against each other. "Breakfast will be ready in about thirty minutes. It's our Saturday special—"

"No time for that today, Gideon, we've got other things to worry about." The man loomed a little too close and tall, a sure bet he had conflict on his mind.

Dane suppressed a groan. At six feet even, he was barely an inch shorter than the mayor, but he'd never learned to intimidate quite so well. "Time for a cup of coffee?"

"I need to know where your boys were last night."

Not this again. "All snug in the house as soon as the milking was done."

"You know that for sure? You have padlocks on all your outside windows?"

Don't react. "I have squeaky floorboards, and I'm a light sleeper. Why don't you tell me what's going on, Austin?"

The mayor kicked at a rock with the pointed toe of his boot and gestured across the lake toward the town of Hideaway. "Someone set a boat afire on the new dock last night."

Dane sniffed the air. He'd caught the scent earlier, but several neighbors heated with wood stoves and fireplaces, so he'd thought nothing of it. "Was anybody hurt?"

Austin shook his head. "Edith Potts called the county sheriff this morning—she found her cat lying on the front porch, shot through the side."

That was even more disturbing. In spite of Austin's suspicions, the fire could have been an accident. The cat could not.

"Know anybody who'd do those things?" Austin's gaze combed the outskirts of the ranch.

"Not a soul."

"What about that new boy you got last month? Black kid with that stupid mop-head hairdo. What do you know about—"

"I know where Gavin was last night, Austin. Don't try to drag my kids into—"

"Didn't I hear somebody calling him Blaze? I hear he's not doing too well in school."

"He's just settling in." *Temper, Dane. Control the temper or suffer the consequences.* "I've told you before, my kids aren't delinquents." They were just unwanted teenagers who'd fallen between the cracks in the social system.

"Yeah? How long were you in the hospital when your kid Bruce Wickman ran over you with the tractor?"

"That was seven years ago," Dane said curtly. "He was here by mistake." Bruce was still a touchy subject between them. One of several.

"How do you know your little Blaze isn't a mistake?"

From the corner of his sight, Dane saw "little Blaze" walking up the hill with Willy—all five feet ten inches of brawn. Time to get rid of this joker before tempers flared or feelings got hurt.

"Austin," Dane said, forcing an edge to his tone, keeping his voice low, "I appreciate your coming out to check on us, but your fears are unfounded. Why don't you wait until the sheriff checks out the source of the fire before you start pointing fingers in our direction again?"

"Don't blow me off like—"

"It seems I remember you were the most outspoken against the new boat dock. If the sheriff knew that, he might be more likely to check *you* out."

"You know I wouldn't—"

"And didn't you and Edith Potts have some heated words a few weeks back about her property line?" Most of the time Austin Barlow was easy to handle. He hated bad press.

"Hi, Mr. Barlow," Willy called.

Austin turned and looked the boys over, nodded, then turned back to Dane.

"Thanks for coming by, Mayor." Dane opened the truck door and stepped back. "Sorry you can't stay for breakfast."

Dr. Jim Brillhart was seated behind his minuscule desk in the director's office by the time Cheyenne arrived.

She slumped into the empty chair across from his desk. "So, what's up, Jim?"

He hesitated for a full second before unfolding his long legs from their cramped position. He stepped around the desk. "Can I get you a cup of coffee? Ardis brought some dough-nuts. I know you like the chocolate-iced ones."

Cheyenne studied his expression. "No, thanks. I'm not really hungry right now." Something was making Jim edgy. "Is everything okay?"

He closed the door and returned to his chair, folding himself beneath the desk once more. "I noticed you're scheduled for two weeks of vacation. Going anywhere special?"

Please don't tell me you need me to work. "I hadn't made any plans. Why?"

"I was just checking your records, and you have an anniversary date coming up next month."

That had to be it. He wanted her to work. "Yes, and I haven't had a vacation for a year."

"Exactly." He tapped the tip of a pen on the desk, watching the movement of his hand.

"Is there some trouble covering the shifts?" It wasn't as if she had something special planned.

He stopped tapping. "I don't need you to work." He straightened and scooted forward, still looking at the pen. "In fact, if you haven't used up the four weeks before your anniversary date, you'll lose what you don't take, according to company policy."

"I was afraid of that, but I just couldn't find the time...."

"I have a proposition for you. I would like you to take all four weeks, starting now. In addition, I'd like you to take additional leave time."

"Additional?" She tried to read his expression. "Why?"

He met her gaze, held it, sighed. "You need it."

"I'm doing fine. I don't—"

"I heard about your episode this morning. It's obvious to me and to the staff that you're still struggling with your sister's death." His words tumbled over one another. It was well-known to the staff that their director hated confrontation.

"I dropped a clipboard, for Pete's sake. Big deal."

"Arlene said you were shaking visibly."

Cheyenne made an ostentatious show of looking at her watch. "It's been barely forty-five minutes since that happened. Arlene sure didn't waste any time."

"And the fact that this annoys you tells me you're still being affected by grief over Susan's death, because I know you, Chey. You don't get rattled that easily." His chair squeaked as he leaned forward to place his elbows on his desk. "Face the facts. You had a devastating experience, and you haven't been given the time to deal with it. I'm giving it to you now." He held up an April schedule. "I've already removed your name."

Cheyenne stiffened. "Over a silly little incident this morning? You can't be serious."

"That kind of thing has happened more than once in the past month."

"Three times. Yes, Jim, I know that. I've had some trouble sleeping, but don't you think that's normal after a loss like mine?"

"Sure. It's perfectly understandable after what you went through, and you need time to deal with the loss. You're one of our best doctors, Chey, and your emotional health is important to everyone here, including your future patients. You know how quickly ER docs burn out."

"Save the lecture, I've heard it all before." This was crazy. How could he do this to her? "Are you telling me I can be replaced that quickly? We're already working a doc short."

"Another Missouri ER is closing near Saint Louis. The physicians there will be out of a job in two weeks."

"Why is it closing?"

"The hospital couldn't afford the increase in their insurance rates. Three of their docs are looking for temporary work, and I plan to grab them up and use them as much as possible. That'll give all of us a break. The rest of us will hold out until they come on board."

"Jim, I don't need that much time off."

He gestured to a stack of files on the far right corner of his desk. "Your quality control reviews have not been impressive lately."

That hurt. She hadn't seen the reports for this past month. "I've worked fifty percent more shifts than last month, Jim. All of us are a little tired."

"I saw your patient this morning," he said. His voice was soft, sorrowful.

"Which one?"

"The one with the chest pain. Crosby. The one who looked like Susan."

"But I did everything appropriately. I did a cardiac workup and EKG and she was fine."

"Chey, did you even consider a pulmonary embolus?"

"No, why would I? She was young—"

"She had multiple risk factors. She was a smoker, she took birth control pills."

"Yes, but—"

"She was wearing an air stirrup splint." He dropped the pen onto the desk and leaned back, as if he wanted to cross his legs but didn't have room beneath the dinky desk. "She'd been practically immobilized for three days with a badly sprained ankle. I did a D-dimer test on her."

Cheyenne's thoughts froze. "The result?"

"Positive."

She gave herself time to recover from the blow. "The woman was having a pulmonary embolus?"

He nodded.

"I'm sorry, Jim. I—I told you I'm not sleeping well." The woman could have died! If Jim hadn't seen that ankle brace…

"You're not focusing, Cheyenne. That isn't like you. Your tragedy is way too fresh. For your own good and the patient's, I have to consider you an impaired physician and take the necessary steps to help you."

"Impaired! Jim, I'm not an alcoholic, and I don't have a drug—"

"The problem is, the last place a physician's struggle ever shows up is at work. You must be going through some nasty stuff at home."

She nodded, her mind still reeling with shock.

"It took you three weeks to recover from your flu. You worked sick during that time. I want you to take some sick leave."

"But I'm not—"

"End of discussion. I'm sorry. Why don't you go see your parents? Florida should be nice this time of year."

Cheyenne slumped in her chair. "They wouldn't know what to do with me." She heard the plaintive sound of her own voice. "Okay, I'll take off. The whole four weeks."

"Eight, with an option for more the minute you request it, but give us enough notice to line our people up. And remember, we'll have third year residents available in July."

"July?" He was trying to get rid of her. "No, Jim. You can't do—"

He held up a hand. "You don't understand what I'm doing yet. Trust, me, Chey, I've been there. It took me twelve months to recover from burnout eight years ago. It nearly ruined my marriage and destroyed my family. I don't want that to happen to you."

She blinked. This was news. He had three beautiful children, and the youngest was eight.

"But I don't have a family," she said softly. Most of her friends worked right here in this department. What was she going to do with herself for two months? What about her nightmares, with no work to distract her from their impact?

She forced herself to stand and walk to the door, hoping she didn't look as stunned as she felt.

"Chey?"

She turned around, hoping he'd changed his mind.

"You might want to try some grief counseling. I'm speaking to you as a friend, not your boss. We all know how losing Susan—"

"Save it, Jim, you don't have a clue." She knew she sounded ungracious, but something in her had snapped, Jim couldn't imagine her life as a single ER physician, whose schedule was never the same, who could seldom arrange for her own time off to coincide with that of her friends—even less could he understand her grief.

What was she going to do now? How could this day possibly get any worse?

She picked up the next envelope on the mail stack at her work space. She opened it, forgot to breathe.

This was a request for the release of Susan Warden's medical records to Hodgkin and Long, a legal firm. The request was signed by Kirk Warden.

Cheyenne covered her face with her hands.

Her former brother-in-law had meant his threat at Susan's funeral. He believed she was instrumental in the death of her own sister.

Was she?

Chapter Six

The smoky aroma of sausage and onions permeated the ranch kitchen and mingled with the chatter of the boys around the extensive breakfast table. Cook knew how to make Saturdays special with a big spread of food.

Dane ate quietly, watching and listening. If Willy and Blaze had any idea what Austin's visit was about, they didn't let on as they joked and laughed with the rest.

No way could any of them have sneaked off the property in the wee morning hours. Dane would have known.

Wouldn't he?

He had good kids. Austin Barlow enjoyed reminding him of that solitary incident when a problem child had slipped through the screening process for the ranch, but nothing like it had happened since.

Seventeen-year-old Jinx leaned toward Dane, his red hair sticking out in fifteen directions. "So what'd he want?"

Dane sipped his coffee. "What did who want?"

"Couldn't've been good," Willy said from the other end of

the table. "The mayor never drives all the way out here just to visit. Notice he didn't just take his boat across, like the others do. He drove all the way around."

Dane speared another sausage link as the platter passed by. "Our local vandal is up to more of his activities."

Jinx put down his fork. Willy rested his elbows on the table. One by one the boys fell silent.

"How would Austin know it's a *him?*" Cook demanded. "Could be a her."

"Anyway," Dane said, "a boat burned at the new dock. The fire apparently started sometime last night or early this morning."

Surprise registered on all faces. Tyler and James glanced across the table at Blaze.

"You have a local vandal?" Blaze asked. "Like this is a normal thing?"

"It's happened before. Dane got his tires slashed last year, and now it seems to be escalating," Cook said. "We're right uptown with the big boys. Anybody get hurt, Dane?"

"Austin said no."

Cook grabbed the empty pancake platter and carried it to the stove for a refill. "Not sure I believe anything that blowhard would say," he muttered, breaking a house rule against name-calling. Long strands of gray hair fell loose over his right ear, baring his shiny scalp. "You're the one who pushed so hard to get that dock approved, Dane. So why'd he come running to you soon as something happened?"

"Don't know."

"He expect you to know something about the vandalism? Or may he just wanted to gloat a little. He never wanted that dock. Whose boat is it? Belong to anybody we know?"

"He didn't say."

"He thinks one of us did it," Willy said.

"He does, doesn't he?" Jinx blinked sleepily, his bright-red hair reflecting itself in the freckles that covered his face like an uneven tan. He'd been up late last night playing chess with Cook after chores and homework.

Jinx, the "big brother" of the family, would be graduating from high school with honors in a few weeks. He took it personally when someone criticized his foster brothers.

"Austin ought to know better," Cook said.

"He wants to blame us," Jinx said.

Willy tugged one of Blaze's dreadlocks. "Bet he thinks it's you, Dr. Doolittle."

Blaze leaned away and shoveled potatoes onto his fork. "Blaze is my name, blazing's my game."

"This isn't something to joke about," Dane warned. "And there's more. Mrs. Potts found her cat shot dead on her front porch this morning."

The kids stopped eating. Blaze displayed an unappealing glimpse of his breakfast.

"Close your mouth, please, Blaze," Dane said.

Blaze swallowed. "Somebody killed her cat?"

"That's what the mayor said."

A storm gathered in Blaze's eyes.

"Bet it was Danny Short," Willy said. "He'd do it. Danny's such a jerk."

"Watch the names," Dane warned.

"He's always picking on the littler kids at school," Jinx said. "And just about everybody's littler than he is. He calls Blaze a—"

"He don't call me anything I haven't been called before," Blaze said. "Let him talk."

"If Dr. Doolittle didn't wear pigtails, Danny wouldn't pick on him," Willy said.

"They're not pigtails, and he'd do it anyway," Blaze said. "All he sees is my color."

"Austin has no real reason to blame any of us," Dane said. "We'll just have to stay squeaky-clean."

"I don't know how we can get any squeakier," Jinx grumbled.

Blaze pushed his plate back. "I need to go check on Starface. She was limping this morning."

Dane nodded and watched him leave.

As soon as the mudroom door closed, Willy said, "Blaze wouldn't do anything like that, Dane."

"I know."

"Guess somebody started the fire, though. And somebody killed that lady's cat."

Dane nodded. He hoped they caught the culprit quickly, because until the town had someone else to blame, his kids would take the brunt of it.

"I'd like to see Barlow try to prove anything," Cook muttered.

Dane picked up his cup of coffee and took a sip. "Maybe we should do a little sleuthing ourselves."

By the time Cheyenne finished reading the final page of Susan's medical record her whole body trembled and she felt sick to her stomach. Leaning away from the call-room desk, she rubbed her eyes and stretched her arms over her head.

"Hey, there, pal," came a comforting voice from the corridor. Ardis hovered in the open doorway, looking fresh and well rested in her green scrubs. Her curly salt-and-pepper hair looked damp.

"Hey." Cheyenne gestured for her to come in. "Raining?"

"Haven't you heard the thunder? What's up?" Ardis entered

the untidy room and perched on the side of the unmade bed. "You should've been gone hours ago."

Cheyenne held up the legal request for medical records.

Ardis tilted her head backward so she could read the print through her bifocals. Her lips moved silently, then her eyebrows lowered. "You're kidding."

Cheyenne shook her head.

"Your brother-in-law hired an attorney? He's going to sue?"

"Maybe they're going after the people who hit Susan," Cheyenne said. "I don't know."

"When they read the report, they won't come after you, that's for sure. You did everything right. You did far more than most—"

"What I did was prescribe a controlled substance for her. She wasn't supposed to be driving."

"I'm the one who administered the drug, and I heard you tell her not to drive. You told her more than once, and so did I."

Cheyenne returned the request form to the desk. "But she was under the influence of a tranquilizer when we told her."

"She also received her discharge sheet, which she signed. It clearly stated that she was not to drive under the influence."

"Again," Cheyenne said, "she signed that sheet after you administered the IV dose. And I didn't document as completely as I ordinarily would have, because she was my sister. I had… other things on my mind."

"I don't know what she was doing behind that wheel, but she—"

"Ardis, you're a Christian. Would you tell me how someone who claims to be a good servant of God could defraud the government *and* a spouse?"

A soft whisper of air escaped Ardis's lips as they parted. "What on earth are you talking about?"

Okay, that *had* sounded pretty stupid. "I'm sorry." Cheyenne closed the folder that held the medical records. "Forget I said anything."

"You're talking about your brother-in-law?"

It was tempting to spill what she knew—that Susan's initial visit the day of her death had been because of Kirk.

"Fraud, huh?" Ardis murmured.

"It's…probably not something we should even be discussing."

"Okay, you're right. If the unthinkable does happen, and Kirk decides to slap a suit on you, then I could be forced to tell what I know on the witness stand. So don't tell me anything."

"Fine."

"But let me tell you something." Ardis leaned forward and touched Cheyenne's hand. "Don't let Kirk's behavior affect your impression of Christ."

"I don't have any impression of—"

"People attend church for different reasons. Some are earnestly seeking God, even if they haven't found Him yet. Others are making business contacts, improving social skills, looking for entertainment or warm fuzzies. Church attendance doesn't necessarily make nicer people with high moral standards."

"Good sermon, Ardis."

"I haven't even warmed up."

Cheyenne forced a smile.

"I'm sorry."

"I've been relieved of duty."

There was an uncomfortable silence. Cheyenne turned in her chair and studied Ardis's face. Obviously, this wasn't news.

"Medical leave isn't the same thing," Ardis said.

Cheyenne straightened. "You *knew* about this?"

"Kind of hard to miss the schedule change for two months. Dr. Brillhart explained it to me."

Cheyenne felt as if she'd been slapped. "Jim told you? Who else did he tell, the whole ER staff?"

"Calm down, I think he just told me."

"You *think?* How do you—"

"Would you relax for a minute?" Ardis reached into the pocket of her scrubs. "Jim had a reason to tell me. In the first place, he knew we were friends, but he also knew I had just the thing you need right now." She pulled out a key on a plastic ring shaped like a daisy.

"What's that?"

"I've told you about our place on Table Rock Lake, haven't I?"

"Barely."

"It's a farm near the Missouri-Arkansas border. It's on sixty-five acres, about a mile drive from this tiny town called Hideaway. Closer by boat. Isn't that the perfect place to spend some downtime?"

"On a farm? Tell me you're kidding."

"Nope." Ardis swung the key back and forth. "Just take it and listen to me, Chey. The place is in the middle of nowhere. It belonged to my husband's aunt before she died. We were down there last year, but we haven't had a chance to get back. It needs a woman's touch, but I know you helped Susan some when she was starting her business."

"I know how to paint under supervision. That's it." But Cheyenne took the key.

"There's some basic furniture," Ardis continued, "and I could call and have the electricity turned on if you want. I'm not promising it would be connected over the weekend, but definitely by Monday. It's on well water, and the pump works. The heat is electric. There's no telephone, no television."

"You're saying I should leave Columbia."

"That's what I'm saying." Ardis sat back, eyes hiding behind lenses that reflected the overhead light. "You've buried yourself here too long, even before the accident. What with the nightmares, you need a complete change of scene. Hideaway would be quite a change."

Cheyenne couldn't believe she was actually considering it.

"You're in a rut here," Ardis continued. "And the rut keeps getting deeper, especially now. Down at our place, there's a dock on the water just right for fishing. You could get involved in some of the community activities, or you could hole up and read, listen to audio books, take a trip or two into Branson. The drive's about forty minutes over winding roads. You could be in Springfield in about an hour and a half, maybe less if they've got the new road completed."

Cheyenne studied the faded green-and-yellow plastic key chain, turned it over in her hand. "This place is close to town?"

"If you want to call Hideaway a town. There's a general store open all year long, and I heard they've got a nice new boat dock, which should bring in some tourist trade. There's a mechanic and a café, a school and a beautiful little bed-and-breakfast down by the water." Ardis paused, fingers linked around her knees. "What do you think?"

The thought appealed. Very much. Cheyenne had to admit that the name "Hideaway" drew her. Right now, she wanted nothing more than to hide away.

Dane found Blaze sitting on the front porch steps, tossing pebbles over the wooden railing.

Blaze looked up at him. "Somebody's wicked around here."

Dane sat beside him. "That kind of thing has happened before."

"They killed an animal before?"

"No. They've broken into the general store, damaged a few vegetables, knocked some boxes off the shelves."

"When did that happen?"

"Couple years ago."

"Anything else?"

"A tire slashed on our pickup, a hole in the canoe, maybe a year ago."

"You make somebody mad?"

"Maybe a few people," Dane said.

"Just because you had this ranch with all us delinquents?"

"You aren't delinquents."

"The mayor thinks so."

"How did you guess?"

"Not hard, once you learn to read the signs. You know, like trying to get your ranch hands in trouble."

"Speaking of reading, has yours progressed lately?" Dane asked.

Blaze tossed another pebble, shaking his head. "We're learning about the minerals and stuff in science right now. I can look at a rock across the room and tell the teacher all about its composition, but that don't work. He wants me to write it down."

Dane selected one of the pebbles Blaze had accumulated for tossing, held it up to the sunlight. "This one's calcite."

Blaze picked up two others. "This here's dolomite, and this one's chert."

Dane nodded.

"You show me a globe of the world, and I'll tell you pretty much every country."

"Then why are you flunking geography?"

Blaze tossed another pebble and didn't reply.

"I know a retired teacher over in Cape Fair who worked with children with learning disabilities."

Silence again.

"I'd like you to meet with him," Dane said.

"You don't think my dad tried all that, over and over again?"

Dane leaned back against the railing, frustrated.

Blaze shook his head. "It's like my brain puts up this invisible armor every time I try."

"Then we need to find a way past that armor."

"So the mayor thinks I blazed the boat and killed the cat?"

"Don't change the subject."

"You changed it first. We were talking about the fire, remember? About how the mayor thinks I did it. I think he called me the black kid with the stupid mop-head hairdo."

Dane winced. There was nothing wrong with Blaze's hearing. "I think you made a poor choice for a nickname."

"You know what's weird? Ramsay Barlow and I are buddies at school. I guess his daddy don't like it."

"You let me handle his daddy."

Cheyenne wrote a final check, signed it, then slid it into the envelope addressed to the local rescue mission. It was her pet project—and the reason she still lived on the third floor of an apartment building without an elevator, still drove a four-year-old Lumina sedan.

All her bills were paid up for the next three months. The mission would be supplied with food. She had ample money in her debit card account.

Everything would be okay.

Then why did she feel so frightened?

She picked up the telephone and hit speed dial. She got a recording.

"Hello, Mom and Dad? It's Chey. I just wanted to let you know I won't be at my apartment for a few weeks." Could she do this? Just take off? "I'll call you later with a contact number, in case you need me for anything. I love you."

As she hung up, she saw that her hand was shaking.

Maybe she did need this time off.

The nightmares had haunted her sleep for so long, she had trouble closing her eyes at night. She seldom even slept here anymore, preferring the cramped quarters of the call room, with the overhead speakers blaring every so often, just to remind her she wasn't alone.

Strange that this apartment triggered the dreams more often than the actual place where Susan had died. But Susan's signature was stamped all over this place—her special, decorative touches, her color schemes with those just right shades, the deep violet-blue of tanzanite, alexandrite, rose quartz. Susan's favorite colors. And Susan had stenciled the wisteria around Cheyenne's living room doorway.

Cheyenne pulled a suitcase from the closet in the spare bedroom. Ardis was right. It was time to escape the memories before they took over completely.

Chapter Seven

On Sunday night Dane Gideon wandered through the upstairs hallway of his sprawling house. He overheard Tyler and Jinx arguing about synonyms versus antonyms through the closed door of the bedroom they shared at the end of the hallway. Tyler had a test tomorrow, and Jinx was helping him study.

Dane knocked softly. "Keep it down in there, guys. Willy and Jason have to get up early to milk."

He heard a boyish chuckle, then silence. Good, the atmosphere around here was calming a little. The boys had been upset all weekend about the vandalism Friday night, and especially about the fact that some of the townsfolk showed signs of blaming Blaze for the whole thing.

Dane saw light coming from beneath the door of the room Willy and Blaze shared. He knocked. No answer. He opened and peered inside. Willy lay sacked out on the top bunk with all his clothes on. Blaze's bed was as pristine as when he'd made it this morning.

Dane switched off the light and closed the door, then went downstairs to check the kitchen.

Empty.

He peered out the window toward the barn. No lights glowed, but that didn't mean much. Blaze could be sitting there in the dark, talking to a cow or a chicken. The kid had an interesting emotional link with the animals. It was as if humans had let him down, and now he preferred the company of other species.

Dane sometimes felt the same way. Not that he ever resorted to talking to the cows except when it pertained to their milk production. He would never sit in the barn and spill his guts to Gordy.

Blaze was different. The chaos that often seemed to reign in this house—with so many male teenagers clamoring for attention—obviously stressed the kid at times. Up until his father's death, Gavin Farmer had lived quietly, assisting his dad in the veterinary practice, avoiding extracurricular activities at school. Dane knew he craved solitude.

Switching on the outside floods, Dane picked up a flashlight from the end of the cabinet. If Blaze was in the barn, fine, but he tended to wander from the property. Once, Dane had found him on the island in the middle of the lake, fishing from the cliffs with Red Meyer, an eighty-five-year-old neighbor across the lake who was like a grandfather to the boys. Another time he'd been out on the highway, trying to rescue a dog that had been hit by a car.

Two weeks ago Cook had found Blaze inside the vacant house across the lake. The kid had sworn to Cook that he'd heard crying sounds inside. He had no explanation about what he was doing there in the first place, however. At this ranch, three strikes and the ranch hand was out the door. Blaze had been warned once already.

Kicking Blaze off the ranch was not something Dane wanted to do.

Cheyenne swerved to miss a jagged chunk of rock and hit yet another pothole the size of the Grand Canyon, the latest in a series on this road of Ozark gravel. Her head pounded from the tightness that had crept through all the muscles of her body on her drive from Columbia.

It was a four-hour trip, but she felt as if she had driven halfway across the world, from the bustle of Missouri's premier university town to the backwaters of the borderland between Missouri and Arkansas—this part of the Ozarks was a whole 'nother country.

"I'm crazy," she whispered.

Maybe so, but if she stayed in Columbia, she could lose her mind for sure.

Dense forest closed around the road on both sides, blocking out the moonlight. The darkness mocked her. She took a deep breath and tightened her grip on the steering wheel.

In the weeks since Susan's death, Cheyenne had tried desperately to sidestep emotion. She'd been aware of a deadly canyon somewhere inside her mind, where she stumbled at vulnerable times. Then she felt devoured by the pain.

She knew better than to go there tonight.

Right now she was wishing she'd known better than to come *here* tonight, especially since there'd be no electricity until tomorrow. But this afternoon, pacing through the beautiful prison walls of memory in her apartment, she could take no more. Better a sleepless night in an old house in the wilderness than another sleepless night surrounded by images of the depth of her loss. And in the morning, perhaps the beauty of the countryside in April would keep her mind away from the dark canyon.

But morning was still hours away. Tree frogs shouted "cree-cree-cree" from the thickets alongside the road, so loud they nearly drowned out the sound of the car's engine. Now the forest huddled in clumps, the tallest trees converging over the top of the road.

The eeriness of the night intensified Cheyenne's sense of isolation.

A gate loomed ahead, shiny aluminum panels fastened with a rusty chain and padlock. Ardis had described it perfectly.

Cheyenne turned onto the grassy track and stopped at the gate. She pulled the key chain from the bottom of her purse and opened the door.

The interior light flashed on. Something rustled in the brush barely three feet from her. She slammed the door and locked it.

A raccoon shuffled across the road in the beam of headlights.

Cheyenne slumped against the steering wheel. "It's okay," she whispered to herself. "This is still just Missouri. No wolves, no grizzlies, no anacondas." The biggest danger to humans in this area of the world was other humans. And she hadn't seen another human being in the past thirty minutes.

Everything would be okay.

"Blaze?" Dane called from the doorway of the milking room. The barn was empty. Dane saw Starface out in the lot, heard the rustle of another animal somewhere in the darkness. Probably Gordy.

They had purchased two sows last week, both heavy with piglets, due to come any day. The flashlight revealed the door to their abode securely fastened.

Stepping to the fence, Dane leaned his elbows against the top rail. "Are you out here, Blaze?"

No answer. He turned off the light for a moment.

A break in the trees revealed a reflection of moonlight against the surface of the lake. There was a soft, rhythmic splash, followed by a silent ripple in the glow of the moon.

Without turning on the flashlight, Dane strolled down to the private dock. The small canoe was gone. He sighed and stepped onto the wooden planks. Time to intervene before something happened that he and Blaze would both regret.

A coyote cried in the distance. Cheyenne shivered.

The wooden gate swung back on its metal hinges with a screech of complaint. She wouldn't close it again tonight. Why bother? There wasn't any livestock on this acreage. Judging by the thick growth of trees, there wouldn't be much room for cattle.

She got back into the car. Now to find the house and settle in for a night without electricity. She pressed on the accelerator. The car surged forward, hesitating, jerking, as if it echoed her own thoughts. The road grew rougher, rockier, forcing her to slow to a crawl.

The shadow of an animal darted across the far reaches of the headlight beams. It stopped to gaze toward the car for just a moment, its eyes glowing red, then disappeared into the deep foliage. A dog? Another raccoon?

Or maybe the darkness of her dreams was coming to life at last. She wouldn't be surprised.

She completed a curve in the road, and her headlights reflected against the pale sides of a building—her home for the next couple of months. She stopped and stared at the house in the headlight beams. The paint was dingy gray, dried and peeling. It looked as if no one had lived here in ten years.

Dead weeds covered the yard and wooden porch. So this was what Ardis had meant when she said the house needed "a woman's touch." All the sensible women Cheyenne knew would hire a dozer to level the place.

She pulled up to the edge of the yard, where the fence had collapsed, and turned off the engine as she scanned the place with distaste. Sixty-five acres with a solid, two bedroom house. Now that she thought about it, Ardis hadn't said anything about a bathroom or a kitchen, or even a living room. What else had she failed to mention?

Cheyenne pulled a flashlight out of the glove compartment. This place surely couldn't be so depressing in the light of day.

The frogs, which had momentarily stopped their singing at Cheyenne's arrival, took up their chorus again as she crept across the yard and up the chipped concrete steps of the front porch. The door unlocked easily. She pushed it open. The rusty hinges caught and held. She pushed harder, and it gave way with a loud creak.

A scuttling sound came from somewhere inside. That would be mice, or perhaps rats? Maybe squirrels.

Nothing to be afraid of. She aimed her flashlight beam through the room and saw a floral sofa in blue and white. Stepping across the threshold, she caught the faint scent of a dirty kitty litter box. Yuck.

Cheyenne shuddered as she edged into the center of the fifteen-by-fifteen room and saw cobwebs hanging in multiple layers from the ceiling, barely discernible in the dimness. Cheyenne had always prided herself in her bravery in the face of barking dogs, invading mice, and even her own hostile brother-in-law. She could handle a few spiderwebs.

She walked through the door at the far right corner of the living room to the kitchen, complete with a sink, stove and refrigerator. Modern faucets gleamed. At least this section of the house was in better repair than Ardis had remembered.

Cheyenne inspected the cabinets on her way to the west side of the kitchen, then entered an open doorway beside the refrigerator to find a small bedroom. The beam of her light picked out the wrinkled folds of a burlap bag in the far southwestern corner. She pushed open the door to her right, saw the sink, clawfoot tub, commode. She nodded with satisfaction. It wasn't until she saw the curtains over the sink billow inward with the breeze that she realized the window was open.

The floorboards creaked loudly underfoot as she stepped to the window. The pane slid down easily, but there was no latch. "Great," she muttered. No telling how long it had been that way.

As she turned away, she thought she caught a flash of light from the corner of her vision. She frowned and returned to the window. In the backyard, barely outlined by the quarter moon, was a small shed. Past that about a hundred and fifty feet was the barn Ardis had told her about. No light.

Maybe what she'd seen had been distant headlights from a nearby, unseen road.

A small chest of drawers had been placed against the door that Cheyenne presumed led to the other, larger bedroom, but she didn't feel like heaving the chest out of the way tonight. She retraced her steps to the living room and was about to push open the closed door adjacent to the entryway when she heard a muffled thump from the back of the house.

She froze in place.

She heard another creak of floorboards—from the bathroom. She stopped and stared at the threshold ahead of her, then swallowed. Her hands trembled, making the flashlight beam flicker against the far wall as she fought for control over her imagination.

No mouse had made that sound. She hadn't imagined it.

She aimed the light at the kitchen doorway.

"Willy, that you?" came a deep male voice, accompanied by the sound of footsteps, the scritch of shoes on old linoleum. "I told you to get to bed. If Dane knows you came over here, he's gonna kill me for sure." A large man stepped through the doorway. "Get that flashlight off before someone sees it."

Cheyenne caught her breath and stumbled backward.

His clothes were dark, and his skin so black he would have merged into shadow except for a huge smile, with teeth all over the place. He squinted in the light. Dreadlocks sproinged from his head in every direction.

"Quit teasing me, Willy. How'd you get in here? I don't want to get you in…trouble…too." He took a step forward. The teeth disappeared. "Willy?"

Cheyenne shuffled backward, collided with the half-open door, dropped her light with a clatter of plastic on wood.

Chapter Eight

"Well, that was stupid. You okay?" The deep voice cracked through sudden darkness as footsteps drew closer.

Cheyenne stopped breathing. Had she stumbled into illegal drug activity? The smell of a dirty litter box…meth lab?

"Stay back! I've got a gun." She reached into the right pocket of her jacket and pulled out the tiny pistol. He didn't have to know what it contained.

The footsteps stopped. "A gun! Who are you?" The voice came again, deep, but hoarse with the defining echo of adolescence.

Her heart thumped a dance against her ribs as she fought panic. "I don't think that's the question right now, since you're the one trespassing." Her voice sounded shaky in her own ears.

She crouched, feeling along the wooden floorboards with her hands. Could she pull the trigger on a teenager? "What are you doing in this house?" She should have run when she'd had the chance. Why had she hesitated? Stupid, stupid!

No reply. No movement. Only loud breathing that sounded

more terror-stricken than her own. He could be a meth addict who was tweaking—desperate for another fix, and willing to go through anyone to find it. She'd had a few of those as patients in the ER.

Her fingers came into contact with the flashlight. She grabbed it and straightened, switched on the light and aimed the beam upward so it would diffuse throughout the room—less threatening, she hoped, if he truly was tweaking. She saw his silhouette and held the pistol high, so he would be sure to see it.

Straight dark brows rose over wide-open eyes. The young man whose shoulders nearly filled the doorway wore a black sweatshirt and dark-blue jeans that looked new. His work boots that were stained with mud.

This was crazy. He could be a killer. Why had she come out here at night?

If she didn't continue the bluff, he could reach her in three strides. If she tried to run, she risked being shot in the back if he had a gun. She needed to gently ease out the front door, get to the car and test the capacity of the car's acceleration.

"That a...real gun?" he asked, voice hoarse with obvious tension.

"You want a demonstration?" She tried to instill a threatening tone to her voice. It sounded phony to her.

He held his hands out to his sides, shaking his head. "No, I don't need anything like that. How'd you know I was here?"

"I'll ask the questions! Tell me who you are and what you're doing in this house." She was pushing it, she knew, but so far she had him fooled. How she would manage to get him out, she didn't know.

He glanced out the front window, as if searching for her car—or maybe looking for his buddies? Who was Willy?

Somehow, the kid didn't seem like a tweaker. In fact, he

didn't seem dangerous at all, and he had obvious respect for the teensy weapon in her hand. Good. It needed to stay that way. "Answer me!"

His attention refocused on the pistol. "I'm Gavin Farmer, and I live across the lake at the boys' ranch. I'm not doing anything bad over here, honest. I'm sorry, I thought nobody lived here." His gaze swept past her, out the window again. "You're alone?"

"I'm never alone." She fingered the small pistol of pepper mace. "And I plan to live here for a while. As I said, you're trespassing." It had been a long time since she'd knocked a man to his knees, but she still knew the moves, even for a big, tough kid. Still, something about him didn't seem tough.

"They said this place wouldn't ever sell, that it was tied up in some dead woman's estate," the kid said. "Austin Barlow send you here?"

"No."

"The sheriff, then. He send you?"

"Do I look like a deputy?" she asked.

"I don't know many deputies." There was some familiar emotion in his voice, in his movement. It wasn't anger so much as resentment. Despair, even.

"I'm not under arrest, then?" he asked.

She studied the shadows of his face for a moment. "Why would you think you were under arrest?"

"Well, for one thing, you're still holding that gun."

"I think I'll hold it a little longer, if you don't mind. Are you cooking meth in this house?"

His eyes widened. "Meth! You mean drugs? No way!"

Her instincts said he was telling the truth, though she didn't know how far she could trust her instincts these days. She lowered the mace slightly, and heard him release a quiet sigh.

"Ardis Dunaway sent me here," she said.

"Don't know him."

"Obviously not," Cheyenne said dryly. "You climbed through the bathroom window?"

He nodded. "It wasn't latched."

"Just because a door isn't locked doesn't mean you have a right to trespass on someone else's property. Who's Austin Barlow?"

He lowered his hands to his sides. "The mayor of Hideaway, population a thousand plus some change."

"Who's Willy?"

"Another ranch boy like me."

Okay, things were beginning to make a little more sense. Not a lot, but some.

"So what are you doing here?" Cheyenne asked. "And why would the mayor call the sheriff on you?"

"Because he doesn't like my hair and he doesn't like my nickname, and he likes to blame the ranch boys for everything that goes wrong around here."

"In that case, don't you think it's time you got back to the ranch?" she asked.

"You going to tell Dane about this?"

"I don't even know Dane." She waited for him to make for the door, but he just stood there in the middle of the living room. Something about this kid intrigued her—and he was definitely stalling for some reason. Were the police actually looking for him? "You never told me what you were doing in my house."

"Thought you said it was Ardis Dunaway's house."

He had a good memory for names. "It is, and I'm going to sleep here tonight, so if you don't mind—"

"No electricity."

"Good. I like to camp out."

"You won't like the ghosts."

"Right." *Ghosts?*

"And you'll have to use the old outhouse, because without electricity there's no water."

"That'll be my problem, won't it? Go home."

Still he hesitated.

Her internal tension meter kicked back up a notch. Why wouldn't he leave?

He glanced at the pistol she still held in her hand. "That a twenty-five caliber?"

"No."

He nodded and gazed around the room.

"Is there something else you need to tell me?" she asked.

"This place has cockroaches."

Lovely. "Do you plan to do something about that?"

"No, but ol' Bertie Meyer says all you have to do is throw a few hedge apples under the house and the bugs'll leave."

"Who's Bertie Meyer?"

"Your nearest neighbor. She and Red are eighty-something and going strong."

"What's a hedge apple?"

He frowned at her. "You sure you want to stay here? You got a lot to learn about farm life."

"I didn't say I was a farmer."

"You're moving in here? All alone? You just came out here to live all by yourself?"

She glared at him. Her hand automatically tightened around the pistol. What was his game?

"All I'm saying is, don't you need some help carrying your things in?"

"No."

Without turning her back to him, she reached for the front door and shoved it open wide. She hadn't completed the task when she heard the slap of shoe leather on concrete behind her on the porch. The long spring on the screen door twanged as it opened.

"Blaze, I guess you know you're dead."

Cheyenne pivoted with her flashlight and her pistol as a hulking, short-haired Santa Claus in denim filled the door-way like a mafioso hit man.

He looked at the gun, then looked past Cheyenne toward the kid and lunged forward.

"No!" the kid shouted. "No, don't shoot! He's—"

Her scream and the contents of her pistol blasted at the same time as she scrambled away from him. The man fell back-ward onto the porch with a cry of agony. Cheyenne caught the rebound effect of the spray in her face. It burned like fire, blinding her.

"Dane! No!" The kid shoved past Cheyenne. "You shot him? I can't believe you shot him!"

Chapter Nine

"I didn't shoot him, I sprayed him."

"This is Dane!" Blaze's voice barely reached through the curtain of fire that scorched Dane's face and eyes. "This is the director of the ranch, how could you do that?"

"I'm sorry, we can—"

"He wasn't hurting anybody, he was just coming to find me and take me home. Dane, it's okay, we're going to get you help. Just hold on!"

Dane groaned a response, writhing in agony on the concrete.

"Help me get him to water," the woman said. "Quickly! It's pepper mace. If we can get to water, we can dilute the pain. Where's the nearest—"

"Get away, I'll take care of him myself! You just get back." Gentle hands urged Dane to his feet. "Come on, let's get you to the lake, it's just down the hill. I can't believe that crazy woman did this to you."

"I'm sorry," the woman said again. "I didn't know—"

"I said get back, just leave him alone! Haven't you done enough? It's okay, Dane, we're going to take care of it right now," came the tender voice Blaze used with injured or frightened animals. "Just walk with me. No, not you, lady. You just stay right here and keep that gun in its holster."

"I need the water too, if you don't mind," the woman snapped. "I caught the spray in my face. It isn't as if I do this kind of thing every day. I didn't know it attacked everything in a five-foot—ouch!"

"Watch that hole," Blaze said.

"Thanks."

The cloud of pain stalked Dane as he allowed himself to be guided across the yard. His groans persisted as if as if he had no control over his voice. When they finally reached the lake, Blaze told him to kneel, then splashed the frigid water into his face.

The relief was sweeter than anything Dane had ever felt in his life. He bent forward and plunged his whole head beneath the lake's surface, held his breath until his lungs threatened to burst, then emerged only long enough to inhale, then plunge again.

Several moments later, after the burn began to subside, he realized Blaze had gone silent. The only sound he heard was splashing.

"Blaze?"

The splashing stopped. "He left," came the mellow feminine voice of his attacker. "Are you okay?"

"Much better. You?"

"I'm fine, but you took the brunt of it." She didn't sound like a mad mace sprayer. She sounded like a reasonable human being.

He dashed the water from his hair and beard with his hands

and glanced up at her shadow in the darkness. "Wow. I can't believe the difference a lakeful of water can make."

"It's pretty dramatic." She switched on her flashlight, illuminating her drenched face, hair, red flannel jacket. "Come on, let's get to the house before we freeze. Your ranch hand already excused himself."

"You mean he went back to the ranch?"

"No, up to the house, I think. I wasn't paying much attention at the time."

"I can't believe he just took off like that. It isn't like him." Dane pulled out his own flashlight and joined her.

"You must have been underwater when he said he was leaving. He's pretty upset with me."

"He has a lot to learn about women."

"Oh, really." There was an edgy pause as they walked side by side up the steep slope of the yard, shoes crackling the overgrown grass. "I take it you've been maced before."

Ah, yes, that mellow voice sharpened nicely. In spite of his recent shock, he felt his lips twitch with a smile that was probably unwise at the moment. "What I meant was that he needs to understand that any woman in her right mind would have done the same thing, accosted by two strange men out in the middle of nowhere."

There was another pause as she glanced sideways at him, as if to determine his sincerity. "Good save."

"Thank you." The smile would not behave. He knew it was a reaction to the relief he'd just experienced, but he'd learned long ago to look for the humor in any situation. He could enjoy a slapstick comedy routine on occasion—and this was definitely that. "I apologize for frightening you, and when I hunt Blaze down, I'll beat an apology out of him, too."

Too late, he realized how that must sound. He felt her disquieted gaze. "Figure of speech," he said. "I don't beat my boys."

"You called him Blaze?"

"It's his nickname, and believe me, it isn't a slur. He chose the name himself." He glanced at her. She had an expressive face that revealed her continued concern. Dark eyes that seemed warm, intelligent. She was only three or four inches shorter than his six-foot frame, with straight black hair, now heavy with lake water, that fell in layers across her neck and forehead.

She took the porch steps with athletic grace, then turned to him. "I can't tell you how sorry I am about this."

He stepped into the beam of her flashlight. "I know it's a little late for the amenities, but I'm Dane Gideon. I run the boys' ranch across the lake."

"So I gathered from Gavin. I'm Cheyenne Allison. A friend of mine inherited this place, and I'm on... I'll be staying here for a while. Does Gavin have a habit of wandering away from the ranch in the middle of the night?"

"On occasion. He's accustomed to more solitude than he gets with us. I'd like to keep him at the ranch more consistently, but I've decided to use my own discretion about discipline with this kid, instead of going strictly by the rules. Until now, Blaze hasn't let me down." He opened the screen door and held it for her.

She hesitated, thoughtful eyes focusing intently on him.

Right. She was less confident about the situation than she appeared. "Actually, I don't need to go inside," he said. "I just need to collect Blaze and take him home. I'm not sure what it is about this place that draws him, except that it's peaceful here. Its previous inhabitants were very kind people, and they took good care of the house." Why was he chattering all of a sudden? Perhaps it was the superastute gaze of those dark eyes.

"Come on in," she said at last, stepping over the threshold. "Gavin doesn't seem to be in any hurry to go back to the ranch. Do you know anything about Austin Barlow calling the sheriff about him?"

As she passed, Dane caught a faint scent of vanilla. "I don't think Austin would do that. He has no reason to."

Blaze wasn't in the living room.

"Maybe he bolted again," she said.

"He wouldn't," Dane replied. What was Blaze up to? He glanced around the room. "Obviously you don't have electricity yet. Did you just get here?"

She nodded, looking around the barely furnished room—complete with cobwebs—with an expression of dismay.

"You know, there's a cozy bed-and-breakfast about a mile from here, on the lakeshore," Dane said. "I'd be glad to call Shatzi and see if there's a room available for the remainder of the night." He would negotiate a good price for her—it was the least he could do after terrorizing her tonight. "There's usually a vacancy this time of year. That way you could have a nice hot breakfast before you come back out here to finish unloading your car and put everything in order." He was talking too much again.

She gave him an enigmatic smile. "Thanks, but I'll be fine. The owner will have the power turned on first thing in the morning—she just didn't expect me to arrive so early." She raised her voice. "Gavin, are you in here?"

They heard a thump and a mutter of unintelligible words through the door at the western end of the room.

Dane opened the door and stepped through. "Blaze? We need to go home now, son." He aimed the beam of his light around the plain, paneled bedroom, which contained a twin-size bed and small dresser in the southwest corner. There was a brown mess of stains in the center of the bare mattress. Something stank.

A grunt drew his light to the closet, where a denim-covered derriere presented itself to them. "Blaze."

"Yeah."

"Okay, you want to let me in on the little mystery?" Dane asked. He felt the victim of tonight's onslaught step up behind him. He turned to her. "I'm sorry about all this, really. Crazy as it seems, Blaze usually has a reason for behaving the way he…does. Blaze, we see your photogenic side, now would you show us your face and try hard to explain why you're hiding in a closet in a stranger's house?"

"Not hiding," Blaze muttered. "Seeking. Come here, little darling."

Dane could almost feel Cheyenne Allison's alarm. She must think he ran a ranch filled with lunatics.

"Aha!" Blaze said. "There you are, you little fighter. Come here, let me take you to some milk. I bet you're starved half to death. Where's the rest of your family?"

Dane cleared his throat. "Blaze."

"Ah, gotcha!" Blaze backed out of the closet, cuddling four mewling balls of golden kitten fluff beneath his chin. "Finally found them. You know the cat that was executed Saturday? I'm pretty sure these are her babies."

Cheyenne caught her breath. "Somebody executed a cat?"

"We have a repeat offender who likes to vandalize the community every so often," Dane explained. "Blaze, how did you—"

"I was hoping I could do this without getting in trouble." Blaze nuzzled one of the kittens, then wrinkled his nose. "Phew, you stink. Didn't Mama teach you how to use the kitty litter?"

"Blaze."

"Okay, okay, but you're not going to write me up over this, are you?"

"I'm not sure I—"

"I heard them crying the first time I came over here a couple weeks ago." Blaze untangled one kitten from two of his dreadlocks and squatted to place them all on the floor. "I couldn't tell what the sound was, and before I could find out, Cook caught me and made me go home, then ratted me out to you."

"But of course you had to come back and investigate," Dane said.

"Not for a few days, and that was when I saw Mrs. Potts's cat coming in through the window. I only did it then because—"

"I know, you were afraid there was some animal trapped in here." Dane strolled over to the bed and studied the stains. "Apparently, she gave birth to them in the bed." He glanced at Cheyenne. "Sorry. It's a mess."

"I'll sleep on the sofa tonight."

"The babies have been without food at least since Friday night sometime," Blaze said. "We need to get them fed. Can we keep them in the house tonight?"

"Nope. Barn."

"Oh, come on, Dane, they don't need to be alone tonight."

"They won't be alone. You know the rule about animals in the house."

"But we kept the racing pigs in there last week."

"That's different. Cook isn't allergic to pigs."

Still grumbling, Blaze went to the other room. "Fine, I'll just get the bag and close the bathroom window."

Cheyenne picked up one of the kittens that had wandered from its siblings. The kid was right, these kittens needed to be fed soon.

She looked up and studied Dane Gideon's face more carefully in the dim glow from their flashlights. The hair wasn't Santa Claus white, it was more silver-blond, and carefully trimmed. Dane's silhouette was craggy, with intense green eyes, slightly prominent nose and firm chin outlined by the short silver-blond beard.

Gavin's words finally sank in, and Cheyenne frowned when he reentered the room with the bag. "Racing pigs?"

Dane and Gavin looked at her as if she should know exactly what they were talking about.

"You race pigs?" Had she just stumbled onto the SciFi cable channel?

"Sure, Dane told me they do it at the September festival every year," Gavin said. "We brought ours into the house when the old sow got cantankerous and started hurting them."

"And you kept them in the house?"

"Lady, don't you know nothing about farm life?"

"Apparently not."

"Blaze," Dane warned. "You're in enough trouble already. Count your blessings that I've decided not to write you up about tonight. Now let's leave Cheyenne in peace."

Cheyenne found herself intrigued by this man. Though he had a tough appearance, there was a gentleness in his voice, in the way he handled Gavin-Blaze.

She handed off the kitten to the teenager. "Do you mind if I ask why the nickname? Why Blaze?"

"It's my reputation." He eased the kitten into the cloth bag. All four of the felines protested their new environment. "Hush up, we'll get you dinner soon."

"Reputation?" Cheyenne asked.

"I accidentally set fire to a house. It's why I'm here."

"Accidentally?"

"I was building a fire in my mom's fireplace, and it got away from me. Burned half the house." He peered into the bag to check on his foster kittens. "I got in big trouble for that, and then there was a fire the next week at school. They tried to blame me for that, too."

"It didn't work," Dane explained to Cheyenne. "They weren't able to pin the blame on him for that one, because he had an alibi."

"It worked, all right," Gavin said. "My mother got me out of the way, didn't she?"

"It worked for us at the ranch." Dane placed an arm over Blaze's shoulders. "We've practically got a veterinarian living under our roof—whenever he decides to stay home."

Gavin grinned at him. "How else are you going to get your exercise if you don't go chasing all over the county after me?"

Cheyenne could sense the kid's affection for Dane, and once again she felt ashamed for panicking and spraying him.

"Let's get these babies to the ranch and get out of Cheyenne's hair," Dane said, nudging Blaze toward the door.

The teenager stopped in front of Cheyenne. "Sorry about tonight."

"Thanks, Gavin. Apology accepted."

"I'm Blaze."

"Why would you want to be?" she said. "It sounds like you're admitting you're guilty of the arson."

Cradling the burlap bag in his arms, he shrugged. "By the time the townsfolk get ahold of you tomorrow, you'll believe them instead of me, anyway."

"I don't intend for any townsfolk to get ahold of me," she protested.

Dane and Gavin said good-night and let themselves out the front door.

"They'll be good milk cats, soon as they're big enough."

Gavin's voice drifted through the still night air, fading as they walked toward the dock.

When all sound died from outside except for the singing tree frogs, Cheyenne pulled the hook of the screen door into the corresponding eye in the threshold. "Racing pigs in the house…hedge apples under the house… I've fallen into a psych ward, lockup division." She sank onto the sofa and wrapped herself up with the comforter, then gazed out the large front window into the brilliant moonlight that kissed the earth with silver. "But maybe a psych ward is where I belong for coming here in the first place. Ardis, what have you gotten me into?"

Chapter Ten

"Suppose they ain't up yet?"

"'Course they will be. Sun's been up an hour."

The murmuring voices penetrated Cheyenne's sleep and dragged her eyes open. For a moment she thought she was back at the hospital, snoozing in the call room after a wild shift.

But if she was in the call room, that marshmallow they called a bed had been replaced by a...sofa

With a groan, she rolled over on her side and threw off the comforter. Its weight wasn't nearly as heavy as the oppression that dragged her down when she remembered. She always remembered when she first woke up. *Susan...*

A sudden movement in the far corner of the room startled her, then a mouse scuttled out of sight.

She picked up the comforter and folded it, recalling how Susan had always panicked, screaming and jumping onto the nearest piece of furniture, whenever she heard a telltale squeak or saw a small furry body racing across the room. She'd always called on big sister to come and chase it away. That had been when they were growing up, when Dad was off on a business trip and Mom was working late at the office.

Cheyenne's throat constricted. Would it always cripple her like this when she allowed herself to think? Would she always have to battle this horrible, gnawing guilt when she thought of Susan?

The voices reached her from outside again.

"Don't let her eat the flowers!"

"What now?" Cheyenne tossed the comforter over the sofa, combing her fingers through tangled hair. This was supposed to be Ozark wilderness, where she could hide out and not see anybody for weeks at a time. So far, if she counted the mice skittering around the living room half the night and the howl of coyotes that had awakened her sometime in the darkness, she'd had very little solitude.

She drew the lacy curtain from the window and looked out.

Three wizened faces peered at her over the ledge of the three-foot-tall concrete wall around the porch. One was an older woman, at least in her eighties, with pure white hair framing her face. An even older man hovered next to her. He was bald with white tufts sticking out around his pink head, and age spots covering his face. Most startling was the third face—that of a mottled brown goat.

As Cheyenne's lips parted in surprise the man's smile widened in a toothless grin. He nodded sagely as she backed away from the window.

Cheyenne took a sustaining breath and pulled the door open. Three heads bobbed as the visitors filed to the steps.

The man smiled again, and the woman turned to look at him. She stopped, placed her hands on her hips and shook her head. "Oh, honey, you went off and forgot your teeth again. What's she gonna think?"

The man leaned forward. "What's that?"

"Your teeth! You forgot your teeth!"

"Oh." The man dashed his hand over his mouth, caught sight of Cheyenne watching him and gave her an embarrassed smile.

The woman sighed and turned toward Cheyenne. "Mornin'." Her strong, hearty voice held the warmth and spice of hot apple cider. "Heard you'd moved in here. I'm Bertie Meyer, this here's my husband, Red and the one with the teeth is Mildred." She pointed to the goat.

Cheyenne blinked at Mildred. The animal blinked back.

"Don't worry, she don't butt no more," Bertie assured her. "Used to, but I broke her of it. Told her I'd trade her off for one of the ranch racing pigs."

Cheyenne groaned inwardly. Racing pigs and pet goats. If she had any sense, she'd load all her things back and get out of here. She could go stay with her aunt Sarah in Sikeston. Nobody would visit her there. Or she could just buy a tent, drive to the nearest park and camp out for the next few years. Come to think of it, New York City probably wasn't as populated as Hideaway.

She realized that her visitors were watching her expectantly. "My name's Cheyenne Allison." She stepped onto the porch as she glanced at the goat. *Mildred?*

Red took an unsteady step up one of the concrete steps, tottered on the edge until Cheyenne was sure he would fall backward, then gained his balance and found his smile once more. "We're Red and Bertie Meyer. What's your name?"

"She told you, silly goose!" Bertie shouted at her husband. "Name's Cheyenne!"

"Hmph. You mean she's too shy to tell us her name?" he shouted back.

Bertie shook her head at Cheyenne. "Don't mind him, he's deaf as a flowerpot. We just came over to see if you needed any help settling in. This is a good ol' house, in spite of what some thinks. Knew this place'd sell someday. You and your husband planning to farm it?"

"Not at this point." Why bother to explain the whole situation?

"Knew the Jarvises. They lived here until a couple of years ago, did a little farming."

While Bertie talked, Mildred stepped daintily up onto the porch and sniffed Cheyenne's leg. She darted a glance down at the goat, who gazed up at her with an air of innocence, then took the leg of her jeans in her mouth and tugged. No one else seemed to notice.

"Tell her about the Jarvises," Red instructed his wife.

Bertie grimaced and shook her head conspiratorially at Cheyenne. "Okay, Red, I will!" She lowered her voice. "It helps to humor him. He gets mad if he thinks you're ignoring him. Lizzie Barlow called me this morning to warn me they saw lights out here last night, and that there was probably vandals messing up the place."

Cheyenne tugged the hem of her jeans out of Mildred's mouth. "Lizzie?"

"Austin Barlow's mother. He's the mayor of Hideaway. Lizzie hears everything that goes on around here." Bertie snorted. "You have to watch her. Sometimes she gets ahead of herself. Not that she likes to pass judgment on people, but...well...anyways, don't tell her anything you don't want the whole town to know. Would you listen to me? Now I'm doing it. Anyways, around here, everybody knows everybody else's business. You'll be needing a cat."

Mildred took another tug at Cheyenne's jeans, and Cheyenne jerked back. "A cat?"

"For mice, unless you want to share a bed with 'em."

Cheyenne nudged the goat out from between her legs.

"Our cat's a good mouser, and you're in luck. We've got some almost grown kittens that'll do you fine. I'll bring one over."

"No, thanks, I don't need a cat."

Bertie blinked up at her.

"I mean… I'm not moved in yet." Cheyenne hesitated, looking at the three expectant faces. "I'm only here temporarily. I won't be staying."

Bertie's shoulders drooped slightly. "Don't you worry, those cats'll be with us awhile. No hurry on that." She turned to Red. "Guess we'd better be going. We got the goats to milk yet this morning, and I need to work in the garden this afternoon." She patted Mildred's behind and nudged her off the porch, then herded Red along behind the goat.

Red nodded smilingly at Cheyenne again. "Nice to meet you, young lady. You come and see us real soon." He turned to his wife as he stepped to the ground. "I bet she could use one of those kittens for the mice around here."

Bertie chuckled. "I bet she could, too." She turned to Cheyenne and said, "If you need us for anything, we're the next house on the road south from your gate."

As they strolled back toward the gate, Cheyenne called out, "Why don't I drive you there?"

"Thanks, but Mildred wouldn't appreciate us cuttin' her walk short," Bertie called over her shoulder as they continued down to the rocky driveway.

Cheyenne chided herself for her lack of hospitality. They were just two harmless senior citizens…and a goat who liked to chew on pant legs.

She went down the steps and strolled around the yard, surveying the place that would be her home for the next few weeks…months?

Seven cedar trees congregated at the center of a grassy knoll twenty-some yards south of the house. New leaves sprinkled bright green across the tops of the otherwise naked gray-and-brown oaks in a forest that formed a natural barrier between this property and the rest of the world, except for the shoreline. Jonquils bloomed in splashes of yellow where the woods met fields.

The house sat on the crest of a hill that overlooked Table Rock Lake, and across the lake she saw a big red barn. The boys' ranch, no doubt.

Judging by the position and lack of warmth of the sun, it was probably about six or seven o'clock in the morning, but Cheyenne had no way of knowing. She had purposely left all clocks and watches back in her apartment. Someday, perhaps, she would rejoin the human race, but now she wanted to forget.

Behind the house she found a small barn within a fenced corral, with two other outbuildings, apparently in good condition. One outbuilding was the well house, built of whitewashed blocks. The other looked like a chicken shed.

Chickens...mousing cats...milk goats. She'd never lived on a farm, though she'd often thought it might be interesting.

So far, she could definitely call this experience interesting.

Before she stayed here another day, she would need some supplies. Maybe Hideaway, small as it was, would carry what she needed. She'd finish unloading the car, then take a short drive to town.

Dane loved the smell of freshly cooked bacon, even if it was poison to arteries. He especially got a craving for it on Monday mornings, when he had a whole week of work to face. This morning, Cook had also made biscuits, fried eggs and potatoes with onions, and whipped up a batch of cream gravy that could tempt a man to sin.

Snatching a strip of bacon from the platter on the warming tray, Dane nodded good-morning to Cook. "Where's your kitchen help this morning?"

"I sent him to town." Cook grabbed an oven mitt and opened the oven door. "Our hens are getting a little carried away lately, and they were low on eggs at the store."

Dane paused with the bacon halfway to his mouth. He checked the schedule on the side of the refrigerator. Gavin Farmer.

"How long ago did he leave?"

Cook stirred the potatoes and onions, then peered at Dane over the rims of his reading glasses. "About thirty minutes ago. Something wrong?"

"I hope not. It doesn't take that long to go over and back." The dock was barely a block from the store. After the hullabaloo this weekend...but searching for problems never did anybody any good. Dane crunched the bacon.

"You know how Blaze likes to hang around and shoot the breeze with ol' Cecil when there's time," Cook said. "He got the milking done early and already had the potatoes shredded when I got down here. He was just underfoot, driving me nuts. I figured—"

"It's okay," Dane said. "He'll be back anytime, I'm sure." He strolled to the back door and peered out the window.

"You worry about that kid too much," Cook said, stepping up behind him.

"And you don't?"

"He's a piece of work, all right. Charmer. He got Bertie Meyer to bake him a batch of her chocolate black-walnut cookies last week, then he traded half of them to Willy to do his chores one morning so he could sleep in."

"Well, if he doesn't get back soon, he's going to be eating the rest of them for breakfast. We're not waiting around if he's late."

★ ★ ★

Brightly colored houses graced the narrow, roughly paved road into Hideaway. The peridot green of budding springtime gave the morning a crisp, fresh feel, the multitude of pink-and-white dogwood trees providing a splash of elegance to a progression of postage-stamp-size yards. Larger, more elegant brick and stone homes graced the cliff line across the lake. Other houses were set deeply into the hillsides above the road.

As Cheyenne entered Hideaway proper, she realized that the whole community was built on a peninsula, surrounded on three sides by Table Rock Lake, with docks situated along the shore the way parking lots were situated within the vicinity of retail shops back home in Columbia. The downtown area of Hideaway, which at first appeared to be a one-block-long succession of brick-front shops, was actually an inverted town square, with shops along a four-square block that faced a street encompassing them. It seemed the inhabitants of Hideaway traveled via boat as often as they did by automobile in this town that focused itself along the shore.

Cheyenne drove around the large square, three sides of which overlooked the lake that was glittering in the sun. A substantial community boat dock extended well out into the lake, providing slips for perhaps twenty-five vessels, and docking space for at least twenty more. A total of six boats occupied slips. A canoe was parked onshore. This place must really rock in the summertime.

The view across the lake made her catch her breath. The morning sunlight was reflected from the cliffs in splashes of red and orange, bordered by green and inset by yellow jonquils. She knew from casual research that Table Rock Lake squiggled across this part of the state from Branson to the Missouri-Arkansas border. Somehow, the squiggles on the page didn't do justice to the reality.

Before she realized it, she had driven through town and found herself approaching the bed-and-breakfast Dane had mentioned to her last night. She turned the car around in front of a bright-yellow gazebo and was headed back toward the brick-face street square when she caught a glimpse of movement from the near end of the community dock.

Two young men stood facing each other on the grassy shore, arms stiff, bodies radiating the tension of apparent conflict. One of them had dark skin and dreadlocks. As Cheyenne drew closer, she recognized Gavin Farmer. His forehead gleamed with bright-red blood.

She stomped on the brake and pulled to the edge of the pavement, then shoved the gearshift into park as the two young men tangled—or rather, the blond-haired kid shoved Gavin toward the dock. Gavin didn't retaliate.

Cheyenne got out of the car and ran down the grassy slope. "What's going on down here? Stop it!"

The blonde glared over his shoulder at her. "This is none of your business, get back!"

Gavin stepped away from him. "Look, I don't want to fight you, I just want to get to my boat and—"

"You just want to find your next victim, but it ain't gonna happen." The kid rounded on him again, shoving him toward the water, an angry red suffusing his face. "How many people you gonna hurt around here before they haul you off and lock you up?" His foot shot forward and hit Gavin in the side of the knee. "It's stoppin', right here, right now."

"Look," Cheyenne said, reaching for the bully's arm, "this isn't going to settle any—"

The kid drew his arm back. Hard. The force of his movement shoved his elbow into Cheyenne's eye socket and the pain of a thousand needles shot through her head. The sky spun to black as she felt herself hitting the ground on her back, the breath forced from her lungs.

Shouting male voices surrounded her. "You're a real loser, Short. You know that, don't you? You think you can beat up on a helpless woman just because she gets in your way?"

"I didn't do it on pur—"

"Get away from her!" There was a scuffle of feet. "You're just a bully, you're not so big and brave—"

"I don't set a stranger's boat on fire, or shoot cats."

"Somebody does, and it seems someone who would smack a woman in the face wouldn't mind stooping to shooting some poor animal. Cheyenne? You okay?" A hand touched her arm.

She opened her eyes to find two angry young faces peering down at her. Racing tentacles of pain exploded through her head. The tow-headed kid leaned closer.

"Leave her alone!" Gavin shoved him aside. "Get away, just go on."

"I didn't mean to—"

"Get out!"

As Cheyenne scrambled to sit up, Gavin dropped to his knees beside her. "You okay? He really whacked you."

"You don't look so great yourself," she muttered, trying to focus on the blood that still dripped down the side of his face from a cut past his hairline. "Is there a doctor's office someplace around here? You might need some sutures."

"No doctors here. I've got to get back to the ranch."

"The police, then. We need to call the police."

"Are you kidding? Nobody'll take my word over Danny Short's, even if he is a bully. I don't need a doctor if I can just get back to the ranch."

There was a splash behind them, and they looked around in time to see Danny paddling the canoe away from the shore.

"Is that your boat?" Cheyenne asked.

"Nope, it's Dane's," Gavin muttered. "No telling where Short will paddle that thing, then he'll leave it. He's always doing things like that at school." He took her arm. "Can you make it to the car?"

"I can make it, but what about you?" She reached up and pushed a dreadlock aside to locate the source of the blood and saw a gash in his scalp about an inch and a half long. "He must have cut you with something."

Gavin pulled away. "I fell against the dock railing when he hit me the first time."

"Get in my car. I'll drive you home." She led the way back to the car. She opened the trunk, pulled a handful of paper towels from the back seat and folded them into thirds as Gavin slid into the passenger seat. She pressed them against the gash.

He winced. "Ow!"

"Sorry. Here, keep pressure—"

"Yeah, yeah, I know the drill. I'll do it. You sure you can drive? You've got swelling around your eye."

"I'll see if I can find some ice." Now that he'd mentioned it, the pain returned to her face with agonizing precision. As she slid in behind the steering wheel, Cheyenne wondered if her eye would swell shut. It felt like it might.

Don't be a wuss. "Which way to the ranch?"

"You can't drive there from here, it'd take too long. There's no connecting bridge for miles."

"I'll call the ranch."

"No, drive to Red and Bertie's place, just down from you. Red can take me across on his boat. Bertie's got some vet equipment she keeps for the goats."

Cheyenne cringed. "Goats? Don't you have any doctors for humans out here?"

"Nope. Why'd a doctor want to come and live in Hideaway?"

She gently pressed her fingers against her swelling eye socket, then put the car into gear.

She should have stayed in Columbia. It was safer.

Chapter Eleven

By the time they passed Cheyenne's drive, Gavin had his eyes closed, head back, fingers pressing the towels against his scalp. The towels were turning red. The wound Cheyenne had seen must be deeper than she thought.

When she turned into the Meyers' drive a couple of minutes later, Bertie emerged from a concrete building barely twenty feet away, wearing a stained overcoat and black rubber boots, a red bandanna on her head. White hair peeped out the front and sides of the scarf.

She smiled and waved. "Change your mind about the cat?" she asked when Cheyenne got out of the car.

"No, that isn't—"

"Lord a'mighty, what happened to your eye?"

"I had an accident. You know Gavin Farmer from the ranch?" She gestured toward her passenger.

The old woman's dark eyes narrowed as she peered past the glare of sunlight on the windshield. "Blaze! What happened?" She sprang around the front of the car with the en-

ergy of one of her healthy young goats and yanked the door
open. "You all right?"

"Don't get all het up," Blaze muttered. "I've just got to get
to the ranch. Think Red'll give me a lift on his boat?"

"Not before I see where all that blood's coming from,"
Bertie snapped. "What on earth—"

"It's just blood, Bertie." He made no move to get out.
"Cook sent me over to Hideaway to take some eggs to the
store, and Danny Short went after me before I could get out
of town. Some people think I'm the one who did those things
Friday night."

"Cook should've gone hisself!" Bertie tugged on Blaze's
arm. "Come on, let's get you cleaned up."

He slid from the seat and stood up, grabbing the door as
he swayed forward. Cheyenne reached for him, but he pulled
away. "I've got to get to the ranch."

"What's wrong with you?" Bertie asked. "Why are you
wobbly? You lose that much blood?"

"Nope, I just hit my head on the dock a little too hard, is
all."

"Think you might need a doc."

"I know what's wrong, and—"

"Let's just hope Red don't catch wind of this, or he'll tot-
ter to town and bang some heads, yessir he will," Bertie said.
"Come inside."

Cheyenne studied the blood that matted Blaze's hair. There
shouldn't be that much blood—his cuts weren't that deep.
"Blaze, have you been taking a lot of aspirin for some reason?"

"Nope."

"Any other medications that might—"

"I don't do drugs."

Don't interfere.

But she couldn't let him bleed out. She walked beside him to the concrete porch.

He stumbled.

She caught him by the arm.

He didn't pull away. "No use me going inside, Bertie. I'll get blood all over everything. Just give me a lift across the lake."

"Sit down," Cheyenne said.

"All I need's—"

"I said, *sit down*."

He sat.

Cheyenne returned to the car, pressed the trunk release, pulled her overstuffed medical kit—the size of a small suitcase—from the depths of the trunk and carried it to the porch.

"What're you doing with that?" Bertie asked.

"I'm going to see if I can help this stubborn kid who doesn't want to tell anyone he's a hemophiliac."

Blaze groaned and buried his face in his hands.

"We need to stop the bleeding, but I don't have clotting factor in my kit," she said dryly. "I trust *you* have some somewhere."

"It's at the ranch, that's why I need to get there," Blaze said. "You're a doctor?"

"Not much of one, or I'd have picked up on this sooner. I also would have done a neurological check." She pulled some gauze pads from the kit. She had packed this thing Saturday, prepared to spend at least two months in the wilderness. Alone.

What a joke those plans were turning out to be.

"What kind of doc?" Blaze asked.

She removed the bloody paper towels from his head and replaced them with gauze. "Bertie, would you please hold this in place? It needs pressure."

Bertie held the gauze, while Cheyenne reached into the

bottom of her kit for a tiny tube of acrylic glue. She didn't have suture equipment, but she'd read about a procedure in one of her medical journals that just might help.

"Hold it directly over the cut," she instructed Bertie. She withdrew some scissors from her kit and snipped the ends of two snaky braids, one on either side of the wound.

Blaze pulled away. "What're you doing?"

"The best I can do to slow your blood loss." She untangled the hair, then twisted it over the top of the wound until it drew both edges of the cut together.

"You got any idea what you're doing up there?" Blaze complained.

"I've never done this before."

"What?" He pulled away. "Ow!"

"Hold still, I'm doing a rough suture repair using what I have, which is your hair."

"You're ruining my do?"

"Just don't look in the mirror for a while."

"You using a needle?"

"I said hold still. I'm not using a needle. Bertie, hold this tight."

The older lady did as she was told, obviously unaffected by the sight or nearness of blood. Cheyenne coated the hair with glue, then capped the vial, taking care not to glue her own fingers, or Bertie's, together. She pulled the strands tightly together as she continued to twist.

"Now just keep it there a moment, Bertie, give it time to dry. If Red can't take Blaze to the ranch, I'll—"

"Why don't I go call Dane real quick," Bertie said.

"No!" Blaze cried.

"Hold still," Cheyenne snapped.

"Don't you go telling Dane," Blaze said. "He's put up with enough from me for now."

"He'd have all our hides if we kept this a secret from him," Bertie said.

"You won't be able to keep it a secret, Blaze." Cheyenne pulled out a roll of cling gauze. "Not when you walk into the house with your head bandaged. Dane Gideon doesn't seem like he'd—"

"You're not bandaging my head," Blaze protected.

"Yes I am, because this makeshift suture job may not prevent further blood loss, and you've already lost too much." She indicated his shirt, soaked red, his hair and the paper towels they had discarded.

"Lady, who *are* you?" Blaze asked.

"I'm a doctor, okay?" She unwound the gauze and started wrapping it around her patient's head. "An emergency physician, so please listen to me."

"You work in an ER?" Bertie asked. "Like that television show?"

"Yes, but right now I'm on leave, and I would appreciate your keeping quiet about it." Her experience in this area of the country had been that when some people discovered she was a doctor, they took for granted she was rich. Then unscrupulous service people would try to charge her double the going rate for their services.

Besides, if people discovered she was a doctor on leave, they'd want to know why, and she'd rather not talk about Susan with strangers. Not to mention that as soon as people knew she was an M.D., they'd start coming to her with medical questions and problems, and she didn't feel like dealing with those.

She did a quick neurological exam on her patient and was satisfied he'd received no lasting damage. "Please, Blaze, just do as I ask and be careful today. You've lost blood, you need to take it easy."

"Blaze? You called me Blaze."

"Well, I—"

"Blaze is good, Doc."

"Call me Cheyenne, please. I told you I don't—"

"Won't help for Dane to know about this," Blaze said. "He'll just think he's gotta do something about it, and it'll make everyone madder at me. So you keep quiet about it, and so will I."

"Dane wouldn't make it worse on you," Bertie said. "He knows how to handle things. Always has. Besides, he'll take one look at you—"

"Not if he don't see me in the light for a while. I'll wear my knit cap over all this gauze. But I've got to get back to the ranch," Blaze said. "I need my medication."

"Won't work to hide this from him," Bertie said.

"I'll stay out of his way for a day or two. I just want to forget the whole thing. Please, Bert."

Bertie straightened. "Good-looking young fellas always could get around me, you know. If Red don't show up soon, I'll take you over to the ranch in his boat."

Bertie had just gone inside when Red's bald head poked around the side of the house. A smile creased his whole face when he caught sight of Cheyenne, then Blaze.

He nodded at Cheyenne. "Hello, young lady. Did you bring this little scalawag over to go fishin' with me this morning? Crappie are bitin' good, they say." He sank down on the steps next to Blaze, squinted at his young friend more closely, then exclaimed, "What'd you do, get run over by another mad cow? Bloodied your face up good."

"That's right, Red," Blaze said loudly enough for the old man to hear. "You know me, always falling."

"Bertie gettin' you cleaned up?"

"Yup."

"Don't s'pose you'd want to go fishin' for a while afterward." He nudged Blaze playfully with his elbow, eyes twinkling as he turned to Cheyenne. "This here's my fishing buddy. Only kid I ever knew who could sit still for hours in a boat, waitin' for the fish to bite." He turned back to his young friend. "So how about it, want to go?"

Blaze shrugged. "Yeah, we're on spring break. I'll go if you'll take me to the ranch first. I gotta deliver some beans an' tell Cook where I am. You got any beans?"

"What's that?"

"Beans! Dried beans! Got any?"

"Sure, sure. Got two bags, but they're not cooked."

Blaze chuckled.

"You'll need fluids," Cheyenne reminded him. "To replace the blood loss."

"Got some orange juice," Bertie said, poking her head out the door again. "I'll get you a glass."

She came back out with a pan of water, a cloth and a clean shirt of Red's.

"I got me a fishin' partner, Bert," Red announced as he slapped his knees and stood up. "I'll go get our gear ready. Blaze, you come on out to the dock when you finish."

"I will, Red!"

Bertie helped Blaze change shirts, then did some quick cleaning on his face.

"You need your clotting factor," Cheyenne said. "You can clean up later. Are you sure you feel up to fishing today? I think you should rest."

"Fishing'll fix anything. As long as Red doesn't tip the boat over again, it'll be plenty restful out on the lake. I just…got the wind kicked out of me."

"And half the stuffin'," Bertie said. "If the Short kid gets away with this, what's to stop him from doing it again?" She wiped the last of the blood from Blaze's face and dropped the stained cloth into the pan of dirty water. "That's done. You're still bleeding some, I guess you know."

Blaze stood up. "You got those beans?"

Bertie went in to fetch the beans. Blaze looked at Cheyenne. "Most strangers wouldn't've bothered with me."

"How long does a newcomer stay a stranger around here?" she asked.

"More'n a day. They say about ten years. Could be longer. Dane's been here that long, and some still say he's a newcomer."

Bertie brought out the beans, handed Blaze a package of sandwiches and fixed him with a stern gaze. "You make Red take the motorboat."

"I will, Bert. Guess we'd better look for the canoe while we're out there. Danny probably set it free to roam wild." He nodded to Cheyenne. "Thanks. Guess this makes up for last night."

Cheyenne chuckled. "You know where I am if you start having any trouble with the cut."

He collected his beans and sandwiches and headed around the house.

"How are the kittens?" Cheyenne called after him.

He raised an "okay" sign with his hand as he disappeared around a lavender bush.

"I don't s'pose you know you got a shiner yourself," Bertie said. "Better put some ice on it."

"I'll do that." As soon as she found some ice.

"Come on in the house a minute," Bertie said, as if reading Cheyenne's mind. "Sooner you take care of it, the better it'll be. 'Course, being a doctor, you already know that."

Cheyenne followed the older woman into the house, and found herself stepping forty years back in time. A worn sofa in brown tweed faced two avocado-green recliners, well used, by the look of them. Bertie led the way into the kitchen, where an old oak table and chairs took up the center of the room. White metal cabinets gleamed in bright sunlight that poured into the kitchen from a long row of windows to Cheyenne's left.

Sitting Cheyenne down at the table, Bertie dug out a clean rag and wrapped it around several cubes of ice.

"Put this on your eye," she said, holding out the rag.

Cheyenne took it, then winced as the wet coldness stung her skin.

Bertie reached for a cast-iron kettle with steam drifting from the top, then took two mugs from the metal cabinet beside the stove. "How'd you come across Blaze? Just see him getting beat up and leap to his rescue?"

"Something like that." Cheyenne pulled the ice pack away from her eye.

"Leave it right there. It'll still probably turn color, but maybe not so bad." Bertie poured pink-brown liquid from the kettle into the mugs, then set one in front of Cheyenne. "Sassafras."

Cheyenne frowned at the cup. The latest medical reports said sassafras tea was toxic.

"Try it. It'll thin your blood for summer. Here's some honey for sweetener." Bertie pushed a jar across the table.

Cheyenne added the honey and took a sip of the tea. It tasted a little like warm root beer. Not bad.

"The ranch boys are always having trouble with the town boys," Bertie said. "It's no surprise Blaze is catching it now."

"Why is that? Because he's black?"

"That could have something to do with it, but I think the biggest problem is that Blaze and school don't mix.."

"Why not?"

"He don't read so well. He just turned sixteen and he still

can't read a line out of a newspaper." She shook her head. "He's not dumb, not by no stretch. Dane wants to help him learn, but much as Blaze likes Dane, he won't try even for him. Says he's had too much trouble with it. If it weren't for Dane's rule that all the boys have to stay in high school in order to stay at the ranch, Blaze would've quit already."

"Then he'll be able to thank Dane for that rule someday. Good for Dane."

"Yep, Dane's a winner." Bertie stared into the swirl of tea in front of her. "A God-fearing man."

Cheyenne stopped stirring her tea and scowled. She hated those words.

Bertie raised an eyebrow. "You got something against God-fearing men?"

Cheyenne hesitated. She didn't know Bertie well enough to expound on her religious views—or lack thereof. "I'm not sure I know what a 'God-fearing man' is."

Bertie grunted, nodding with sad understanding as she slid her chair away from the table. "I hear you there. Don't seem to be many of them left around these days, specially the younger ones. But mark my words, Dane Gideon knows the Lord and lives a life that tries to honor Him."

Cheyenne said nothing. She didn't want to argue with this kind, elderly lady.

"Got something to show you," Bertie said as she got up. She went to the back door and opened it. "Just sit tight a minute, I'll be right back."

Cheyenne took another sip of her tea. It tasted good, and if it was toxic, why did Red and Bertie look so healthy?

She thought about Bertie's description of Dane Gideon. What *was* a good, God-fearing man?

Cheyenne's parents had been strictly holiday church attenders when she and Susan were growing up. But they had sent Cheyenne and Susan to Sunday school—it made a good baby-sitter on Sunday mornings while the couple went out to brunch at one of their favorite restaurants. But even though Cheyenne quickly memorized the books of the Bible and all the Bible stories, she couldn't help looking at the lives of some of the people who called themselves Christians and becoming skeptical when she observed how little they practiced what they preached. Down deep, she rejected Christianity on that basis.

There were churchgoers who made her wonder if she'd made a hasty decision—Jim Brillhart for one, and Ardis Dunaway, who had loaned her this house at no cost. And then there was Susan, who had "found Christ" during college, just before she met Kirk.

On the other end of the scales was Kirk, her brother-in-law, who certainly didn't "love her in the Lord." There was also the nurse on the second floor at the hospital whose car had a Jesus Reigns bumper sticker, yet she was having an affair with her supervisor.

These people claimed to walk with God? Something was wrong with that picture, and Cheyenne couldn't reconcile the irregularity. Something had always been wrong with it.

Bertie came bursting back into the house, allowing the screen door to slam behind her. She held two half-grown cats in her arms—one was dark gray and the other black and white.

"You sure you don't want a kitten or two?" Bertie plopped them onto the kitchen linoleum. "They take good care of themselves and they're already decent mousers. Be good company for you, all alone over there."

The gray kitten shook himself, glanced around the kitchen, then strolled over to Cheyenne and sniffed her feet. He then curled around her right foot and lay down, purring loudly enough that Cheyenne could hear it over the motor of Bertie's ancient refrigerator.

"Looks like you've been adopted."

Cheyenne reached down and rubbed the kitten behind the ears. The vibration of the animal's purr tingled through her fingertips. "My apartment complex has a no-pets policy. I couldn't take him home with me when I leave here."

"Then consider him a foster cat," Bertie said. "Name's Blue. We'll take him back if you ever decide to leave."

"*If?* Bertie, I plan to leave, of course."

"How long you here for?"

"A couple of months." Maybe. If she decided to stay.

"You'll be needing some cleaning supplies to get that place in order. Why don't you let me gather some up for you?"

Cheyenne smiled. Seemed like she'd been adopted not just by the kitten.

The aroma of breakfast lingered in the ranch kitchen and drifted out onto the front porch, where Dane stood watching across the lake. He heard the familiar grumble of Red Meyer's ancient fishing boat as it putted across the lake toward the ranch dock. As the boat came into view through the trees, Dane had no trouble recognizing his wandering teenager, in spite of that silly brown knit cap Blaze had pulled down over his outrageous hair.

What was he up to now?

Dane continued to watch as Red and Blaze pulled up to the dock and tied up. Blaze stepped off the boat with a package under his arm, but Red didn't pull away. Hmm. Interesting.

Blaze walked slowly up the hill, past the barn lot to the house. The package turned out to be a couple of bags of beans. The shirt he wore wasn't his. Neither was the cap.

"Sorry I'm late," Blaze said, avoiding eye contact as he

reached Dane. "I lost the canoe, and Red is going to help me find it."

"In exchange for a couple of hours of fishing, no doubt."

Blaze gave him a brief grin, nodded and continued toward the house.

Dane fell into step behind him. Blaze was moving slower than his usual dancing, cocky gait. "How did you lose the canoe?"

"Prank."

"Did this prankster take your shirt, too?"

Blaze took the porch steps slowly. "Got it dirty."

"With what?"

Blaze pulled open the screen door and stepped inside the house. "Cook here? I got his beans for him."

"He went to town looking for you." Dane saw the small crust of dried blood just below Blaze's jaw line. "Are you going to tell me what else happened?"

For once the house was quiet. Willy and Jinx were down in the barn cleaning stalls. The other boys had gone on a float trip with a group from their church in Blue Eye.

Blaze carried the beans into the kitchen, then returned to the foot of the stairs, where Dane waited for him with arms crossed over his chest.

"I can handle it myself, okay? I can't go running to you with every little spat I have at school."

"You weren't at school this morning—you went to take some eggs to town, last I heard. What happened, Blaze?"

The kid hesitated, glancing up the stairs. Gavin Farmer had very dark-brown, expressive eyes, which often betrayed the emotions he tried so hard to conceal. Right now they expressed anxiety.

"Go on up and take your shot," Dane said, following him up the stairs.

"I got in a fight," Blaze said admitted. "No big deal. You know how Short's always hammering us about something. Now he's decided I did that stuff Friday night."

"He doesn't have a say. The sheriff checked out the cat, the Coast Guard checked the boat, and no one pointed a finger at you. Just because some people want to make us look like criminals doesn't make it so."

When they entered the quiet room Blaze and Willy shared, Dane waited while Blaze assembled his medication, gave himself the injection and sat down on the bottom bunk for a moment.

"Now will you show me what Short did?" Dane asked.

Blaze sighed and pulled off the knit cap to reveal the bandaging. Someone had rounded the circumference of his head several times with surgical gauze. "Cut my head when I fell at the dock, and it bled too much."

"We need to have a doctor take a look at it."

"It's already been seen to," Blaze said.

"I mean a real doctor. I know Bertie's good with herbs, but I don't want to take any chance—"

"Come on, Dane, I've been hurt worse than this before and didn't have to see a doctor. Give it a few days."

"You might need sutures."

"Got 'em. Sort of."

Dane sat down beside him. "How do you 'sort of' get sutures, and since when is Bertie doing that?"

"Didn't say Bertie did it."

Dane sighed. Why was Blaze being so cagey all of a sudden. "Who, then?"

Blaze hesitated. "The mad macer."

"You're kidding. Cheyenne Allison?"

"She's the one who broke up the fight—got a black eye for her troubles. Then she drove me to Red and Bertie's and pulled a honker of a first aid kit out of the trunk of her car. Did some kind of weird, twisty thing with my hair and closed up the gash in my head with glue. You see any blood up there?"

"A little seepage, but not much."

"So why would I need to see a doctor? I know how to see to myself."

"We'll keep an eye on things for a day or so, but I'll make an appointment for you, just in case. And I have to call the sheriff, Blaze. I have no choice."

Blaze winced. "See there? That's why I didn't want to tell you about this. It'll just cause more trouble. Red's waiting for me down at the dock, Dane. Can't I go fishing with him for a couple of hours? He'll be disappointed if I don't."

Dane rubbed his face, suddenly weary. And it was only Monday morning. He needed additional help here on the ranch, especially if he planned to take on more boys, and that was a definite possibility. There were a lot of discarded kids in this world. Far too many. He wished he could take them all.

"Go ahead, son, but be back by noon, okay? If you haven't found the canoe by then, you and I can go out looking for it later. I need to contact Cheyenne and thank her."

Blaze shook his head. "Maybe you should wait awhile for that. After last night and this morning, I get the feeling she just wants to be left alone."

Chapter Twelve

Cheyenne walked along a cool hospital corridor. Silence took on substance, as close and watchful as a cemetery at night. She couldn't hear the sound of her own footsteps. There were none of the typical smells of antibacterial cleaners or iodine, or even the more human smells of waste. She saw only the broad white hallway.

At the end of the corridor she turned a corner, then tripped over an unseen object. She crashed to the floor and landed without pain beside another prone body.

She found herself staring into the lifeless eyes of her sister.

She screamed, but no sound came from her throat. She closed her eyes and forced the sound. At last it broke through, spiraling around her in a soft moan.

"No... No!"

Plunging from the dream, she shoved the comforter away from her as if it were a shroud. She heard the loud protest of a flying kitten as she rolled from the sofa and hit the hard-wood floor.

Blue's growling cry continued. The dream slithered back

into the darkness. For a few seconds Cheyenne allowed herself the exquisite rush of relief that always came after awakening from a nightmare.

The kitten emerged from the folds of the lavender comforter.

He leaped to her side, meowing loudly as he plunged his head beneath her arm. She nuzzled her face in his fur. It was as if Bertie had instinctively known how well this little living being could provide contact with reality after the nightmares.

"I'm sorry, Blue."

His purr-motor kicked into high gear.

Again, she felt soothing relief. As the sky turned from indigo to denim blue outside, she embraced the strangeness of this room, this house. Gone were the reminders of Susan that had hovered around her in Columbia. Later, she would cherish those reminders. First, however, she needed to recover from the violent reality of her sister's death.

If recovery was possible.

She'd been here in Hideaway a week now. The only neighbors she had spoken with were Red and Bertie Meyer, and Dane, Blaze and that blond kid who had attacked Blaze. A person could get used to the solitude…after a while…probably.

The house was clean, the pantry and refrigerator well stocked with food after a drive into Kimberling City—Cheyenne had been reluctant to revisit the place where she'd witnessed Blaze being assaulted.

She carried Blue out to the front porch and inhaled the mingling of rain-washed earth and the familiar scent of the lake. This afternoon she planned to try the general store again. She'd used her car phone to call Ardis, and overriding her friend's protests had insisted on trying her hand at painting some of the rooms where the walls were faded and the paint cracked. After all, she needed something to keep her occupied for seven more weeks, and there were only so many novels she could read without getting eyestrain. Maybe the general store would have paint.

With Blue trotting alongside, Cheyenne strolled down a steep, grassy path that led from the side of the house through scattered elm trees, ending at the weathered wooden boat dock on the shore of the lake. According to Ardis, this land bordered the east side of the sheltered cove, from which the tops of trees poked from the water's surface—trees long buried beneath this man-made lake.

In the center of the lake, several hundred yards east of the cove, was an island, light green with budding trees, and red rocky cliffs along one edge. Islands had always intrigued Cheyenne. As a child she had dreamed of living on a deserted island in the Pacific Ocean where no one could find her. She could forget the whole world then.

That wouldn't be practical now, but this retreat might do the trick. It had occurred to Cheyenne this past week that she didn't have to stay in Columbia. She had no family there now.

There was something about Hideaway that felt right to her, in spite of her inauspicious beginnings in the place. It almost felt as if she'd lived here before, if only in a dream. A silly thing to be thinking after only a week, but it forced her to pose an interesting question to herself.

What was she going to do with the rest of her life?

Dane was carrying a sack of calf starter from the general store to the back of Mrs. Reeves's pickup truck down the street when he saw a vaguely familiar forest-green Chevy Lumina sedan pull up to the curb. Familiar because he'd glimpsed it in the distance across the lake every time he looked that direction.

Though he had only seen Cheyenne Allison in the dim

glow of a flashlight, he had no trouble recognizing that shaggy cut of shoulder-length black hair, the athletic build.

He placed the sack beside a bale of hay and dusted off his hands. "See you next week, Mrs. Reeves," he called, stepping out of the way so the retired schoolteacher could pull her truck out.

When Cheyenne left her car, he waved to her and strolled down the boardwalk in front of the store. As he drew closer, he realized she was older than she'd seemed the other night—perhaps in her midthirties. She also had a black eye, though the chartreuse and muted blue that outlined the socket suggested it was partially healed.

She nodded to him in greeting. No smile, but she didn't appear unfriendly. She just seemed to have something on her mind.

"Hello. I'm glad to see we haven't chased you away yet," he said.

"That's right, I plan to stay to the bitter end. Besides, I've got free rent for two months. It'll take a bulldozer to drag me away from paradise in springtime."

He nudged an old sleeping hound dog away from the entrance of the general store with the toe of his boot, then held one of the old-fashioned glass double doors open for her. "Thank you for helping Blaze last week." He examined her left eye more carefully. "Looks like he wasn't the only one who took a hit."

She tipped her head away from him as she entered the antique-style store and paused to look around. "So he told you about it, after all?" she said as she reached for a shopping cart.

"With a little encouragement," Dane replied dryly.

"How's he healing?"

"Very well. I took him to the clinic in Kimberling City to have him checked over, and the doctor said it looked like you'd done everything right. That was quite a trick with the hair twisted over the wound."

She gave a noncommittal shrug as she pushed her cart down the first aisle to their right. "This is some store. Looks like it has everything a person could ever need."

He continued to walk beside her. "The proprietor likes to think so." He decided not to try to take the cart for her. She seemed kind of independent—or at least a little wary of him. How could he blame her, after he and Blaze frightened her half to death her first night here?

She selected some nails, a hammer and a screwdriver and placed them in her cart.

"Interesting how you stopped the bleeding like that," Dane persisted, unable to contain his curiosity. "I never would have considered using Super Glue and hair."

She reached for a paintbrush. "I read about it somewhere."

"Blaze seemed to be under the impression you might be familiar with the medical profession."

She selected some lightbulbs and turned down the next aisle. "This is a big place for such a small town. Do they get much business here?"

Hmm. So she wasn't going to answer the question he hadn't asked. "You'd be surprised how much," he said. "Kimberling City is the next closest place with any selection, and a lot of people don't want to drive that far. It's at least a twenty-minute drive from here."

She glanced at him. "At least?"

"For us at the ranch it's twenty, because we're on the south side of the lake. But for those who live on this side it's farther, because they either have to take the long way around the lake and hit Highway 76, or they take the bridge and circle back on Highway 86."

She nodded and put a spray bottle of window cleaner and some towels in her cart.

Okay, he was boring her to tears. "Before long you'll notice a lot more people in town. The bed-and-breakfast stays booked from May through October, and we're hoping with the new boat dock we'll draw a lot more tourism. We have a library, three seasonal restaurants, a nature trail and bike rentals. I don't suppose, being medical, you'd know of any doctors who'd be interested in building a new practice in paradise." He watched her closely.

She turned her cart down another aisle. "If I hear of one, I'll be sure to send him your way." She selected some canned corn, sardines and a box of crackers and put them in the cart.

Dane hesitated. She suddenly seemed uninterested in conversation. That might be an indication for him to leave. Disappointed, he straightened some packages of canned ham and turned to wander back the way he had come.

"They wouldn't happen to carry house paint here, would they?" she asked.

He turned back with embarrassing eagerness. "Several shades. I'll be glad to show you." He fell into step beside her again as he directed her two aisles down. "You don't get out much, do you? Bertie told me she's only seen you drive through your gate once since the day of the fight."

"I had a lot of things I wanted to do around the house and was in the mood to get supplies today."

"Anything the boys and I can help you with?" he asked. "For instance, the painting? I also noticed when we were there the other night that the shutters need nailing."

"Thanks for the offer, but I enjoy painting and such."

"You won't enjoy it if you take on the whole job yourself. Besides, we owe you for trespassing on your place."

"I'll survive. How are the kittens doing?"

"Coming along fine." Dane reached for a gallon of paint. "They're thriving on some milky concoction Blaze mixes for them."

"He seems to love animals."

"His father was a vet, and it was very much a full-time project for the two of them."

"His father isn't around now?"

"He died last year."

"And his mother?"

Dane shook his head. "Estranged." He held the paint can up for her to see. "This is the bestselling color here, creamy off-white with just the barest suggestion of burgundy."

She looked at the can, then at him. "You know a lot about this stuff. Do you work here?"

"You might say that."

As they discussed the paint selections, Dane watched her more closely, trying to pick up on the things she *didn't* say. He'd worked with enough hurting teenagers to develop an instinct about people in emotional trouble. Something about Cheyenne reminded him of Blaze when he'd first arrived.

Of course, Cheyenne was a woman, and Dane's history with women was laughable.

No, not laughable. It was tragic.

She walked with him to the front counter, where a wizened old man in horn-rimmed glasses sat nodding behind a cash register.

"Wake up, Cecil. Time to earn your keep," Dane teased gently.

The man started awake, teetered on his seat, then straightened. "Oh, sorry 'bout that. Been a slow day." He glanced at Cheyenne's cart full of food and supplies, then peered at her. "You sure you want all that stuff? There's a better selection down in Kimberling City. 'Course, you'd have to drive all the way there and back."

"Cecil, would you stop trying to talk us out of a sale and just ring her up?" Dane winked broadly at her. "If there's a worm in a basketful of apples, Cecil will tell you about it, try to talk you out of buying the apple, then dig the worm out and show it to you."

She smiled.

At last!

Cecil rang up the items, checking each price carefully. After Cheyenne paid, Dane helped her carry everything out to the car—glad he had stayed to talk with her and tell her more about the community.

He had just finished loading the last of her purchases in the trunk when a red pickup truck pulled in beside them. Dane glanced at the driver, saw the cowboy hat and tried hard to keep a straight face. Trust Austin Barlow's radar to tell him when an eligible female came within range. He lingered in town every evening during the summer months, when the tourists were thick. Some habits were apparently hard to break.

Austin sat behind the steering wheel watching them for a couple of seconds, obviously intrigued by Dane's companion. He tipped his stupid cowboy hat and nodded to Cheyenne.

"Afternoon, Gideon," he said as he got out of the truck.

Dane nodded. "Hello, Austin. Cheyenne Allison, meet the mayor of our town, Austin Barlow. Cheyenne's the Meyers' new neighbor." *And you look like a hungry hound dog, Austin. Keep your tongue in your mouth.*

The front door of the store opened, and Cecil stuck out his head. "Dane? You need to check this cash register. It's talking to me again."

Dane excused himself and left. Cheyenne Allison had

proved when she arrived last week that she was capable of taking care of herself.

As he entered the store, Dane resisted the urge to imagine Austin facing down the barrel of Cheyenne's mace shooter.

Cheyenne eyed Austin Barlow's dark-brown felt cowboy hat and red-checked Western shirt. She supposed the mayor of a lakeside village that catered to summer tourists had to maintain a certain image…but Will Rogers? The last time she'd seen a man in a cowboy hat, she'd been at a rodeo. Of course, what did she know—she'd practically lived in the hospital for much of her adult life.

She opened her door and got into the car. "Nice to meet you, Mayor."

"Please call me Austin, everyone in town does. And it's *very* nice to meet you." He had a handsome voice to match his strong, perfectly even features. "So you've moved to the old Jarvis place. Funny, I didn't remember anything coming through."

"Coming through?"

"I'm a real estate broker. I handle a lot of the farm sales around here. Last time I called the Dunaways, they told me the place wasn't for sale."

"It isn't, I'm just staying there for a few weeks." Not that it was any of his business.

"Staying out there all alone?"

"Nope."

He looked disappointed. "Well, that's good, because—"

"Bertie gave me a kitten last week. He's good company."

He nodded and pulled a card from the front pocket of his stylized shirt. "If anything comes up there's my number." He smiled. The gently weathered lines of his face made him even more attractive, with that firm chin, those blue eyes. "You don't have to wait until you decide to buy. I make a good tour guide, lived here all my life. Seen practically every Branson show, and it would be my pleasure to take you to one." His eyes narrowed, and he stepped to her window. "Say, where'd you get that shiner?"

She raised her hand to her left eye. "I had a brief encounter with a local bully," she replied as she started her motor.

"Local! Any idea who? Where'd it happen?"

"Down by the dock." She gestured behind her. "Kid was beating up on Gavin Farmer last week. I went down to break it up, and my face interfered with Danny Short's elbow."

"Short." Austin shook his head. "You're right, ma'am, he's a bully. I'll have a little talk with his father and make sure nothing like that—"

"No, please, not on my account. And I'm sure I'll be fine on the farm. Dane Gideon has offered to let his boys help me out with some repairs."

The mayor's smile lost some of its brightness. "I wish you wouldn't do that, ma'am. May I call you Cheyenne?"

She nodded.

"The less you have to do with those people, the safer you'll be."

"Excuse me?"

He leaned closer. "I know that sounds a little abrupt, especially coming from a stranger. Dane's a good-hearted man, there's no denying that. He's good at running a farm, and he seems to have a Midas touch when it comes to making money—that's why this general store's doing so well."

"This store is his?"

"Sure, didn't he tell you?"

She shook her head.

He nodded. "Sounds like Gideon. But he doesn't know diddly-squat about how to raise a teenager. How could he?

He's got none of his own. He's too lax with discipline, if you ask me."

She hadn't, but she decided not to pass judgment too quickly. After all, what did she know about anyone here? "Thanks, Mayor, I'll keep that in mind."

"Remember, it's Austin."

She reached for the gearshift.

"You getting a telephone put in out there at the farm?" he asked.

"Not if I can help it." She gestured to the purse-size carrier on the seat beside her. "Just this car phone."

"Well, if you run into any kind of trouble—ranch boys or otherwise—use that car phone there and call me."

"Thanks, I'll—"

"I mean it, now. Woman out on the farm alone like that needs some contact with the outside world, and old Red means well, but he and Bertie wouldn't be much help in a pinch. You be sure and call me if you need anything, hear?"

"Thank you, I'll keep that in mind." She waved and backed onto the street.

"And don't forget about my Branson offer," he called to her as she drove away.

The man was persistent, she had to say that for him.

She gave her image a glance in the mirror, grinned, then shook her head. The guy must be desperate.

Still, it was kind of fun.

Her grin faded as she drove out of town. Why was the mayor of Hideaway so concerned about Dane Gideon's boys? Was she truly in danger?

Chapter Thirteen

The hospital tile felt cold against Cheyenne's side. She opened her eyes to see her sister's bloody face only inches from her own.

A hand came up and touched Cheyenne's hair. Susan's eyes opened.

Cheyenne screamed and jerked awake to find Blue nuzzling her forehead. The curtains drifted across her face with a cold breeze through the open bedroom window.

She caught her breath, wiping the perspiration from her face. For a few seconds, the horror lingered, shooting her six weeks backward in time. Again.

Blue nudged Cheyenne's chin, his purr vibrating against her neck. Muted morning light gave the room a rosy glow, and the horror retreated for another day. Most likely, she would awaken tomorrow the same way. The only difference between this place and her apartment in Columbia was the absence of city sounds outside her window—no horns honking or garbage trucks chugging by.

She gazed around the room. Normal. Everything was nor-

mal. Her racing heart slowed its rhythm. It was Sunday morning. She'd been here nearly two weeks now, and she almost
felt as if this place was hers, especially after she'd cleaned and
painted and hammered on something nearly every day.

She was pulling on her jeans and sweatshirt when she heard
the sound of male voices coming from the direction of the
lake. Running her fingers through her tangled hair, Cheyenne
peered out the west window of her bedroom and saw Blaze
and another boy coming uphill from the dock.

Vaguely, she recalled the mayor's warning last Monday
about the ranch boys, but she dismissed it as she watched
Blaze joking and laughing with his companion. Somehow, he
didn't strike her as a dangerous person, especially considering
what he'd been doing here the night she arrived and frightened him nearly to death.

She stepped onto the porch when the boys came through
the front gate.

"You have a lawn mower on this place?" Blaze called as he
and his friend waded through the ankle-deep grass toward her.
"If not, I could bring one over from the ranch. If you don't
get this stuff cut down before long, the snakes and ticks'll get
pretty chummy with you."

"Thanks, I think there's a mower out in the barn." Her
attention automatically focused on the scalp wound she had
treated two weeks ago. Although his braids didn't quite match,
Blaze looked good otherwise.

He held up two large, thick paper bags. "Got a present for
you."

"Please don't tell me there are kittens in those bags."

"Nope, Bertie told me you had Blue." His dark-brown
eyes glowed with mischief as he set the bundles gently on the
porch. He jerked his head toward his companion. "Cheyenne,
this is Ramsay Barlow. Guess you've met his dad." He turned

to Ramsay. "This is the newcomer everybody's been gossiping about in town."

"How are they gossiping?" Cheyenne asked. The teenager looked vaguely familiar. He was about an inch taller than Blaze, with short auburn hair and blue eyes.

He held his hand out. "Don't mind Blaze, he's always trying to start trouble." He had a firm grip, a familiar voice. "It's just that everybody knows a single lady moved into the area."

"You're Austin Barlow's son?" she asked.

"That's me." He had a dimple on the left side of his chin when he smiled, like his dad.

"How do you like that?" Blaze readjusted the lip of one of the bags. "Me running around with the mayor's son. If my mama could see me now." There was a faint edge in his voice. "Just don't go telling Austin, okay?" Blaze said. "He's not too crazy about us over at the ranch. I don't want to get Ramsay in trouble." Again, that edge.

"Ramsay, I met your father last week," Cheyenne said. "He seems like a nice man."

Ramsay nodded and looked away.

"So I don't understand his problem with the ranch."

Ramsay shifted uncomfortably.

Okay, there was definitely some undercurrent of tension between Austin Barlow and the ranch boys.

Cheyenne leaned toward Blaze and looked more closely at the wound she had "sutured" the day of the fight. The hair had been trimmed from above the scar. "How's it healing?" she asked.

"Not the best, but it'll be fine. Got your farm started." He gestured to the bags.

"My farm?"

"You wanted a hen and chicks, didn't you? Bertie said last

week you'd like to see what it was like to live on a real farm, and she told you to start small, with a hen and some chicks."

"She told you that?" Cheyenne recalled a casual reference to the possibility one day when Bertie and Red came over to visit, but she hadn't been serious.

Blue sniffed at the bags.

"This is them," Blaze said. "You've got an old chicken coop out back. I checked it out when I was looking for the kittens."

"You mean the night I maced Dane?"

There was a surprised cackle of laughter from Ramsay. "What? You sprayed Dane?"

"It wasn't funny when it happened," Blaze said. He picked up the bags. "You want them in the chicken coop, don't you?"

"Uh… Blaze, you do realize I don't plan to—"

"I'm going to hang out down at the dock," Ramsay interrupted.

"See you in a few, and don't wander too far. Your church starts in an hour." Blaze carried the bags around the side of the house toward the outbuildings in back. "Just remember not to let the hen out of the pen unless you want to corral her," he told Cheyenne.

Cheyenne rushed to catch up with him. "But I don't have anything to feed them. I wasn't expecting—"

"No problem, I brought enough feed to last you a week."

She gave up the argument. "Why don't I hear anything? Shouldn't they be clucking or something?"

He turned and quirked a thick eyebrow at her. "You really don't know much about farming, do you?"

"Well, excuse me for being a city girl."

"All you've got to do is put chickens in a dark place, and they'll usually be quiet."

"Okay, fine. What's the gossip you were talking about? I've hardly even spoken to anyone since I arrived."

"That's what they're gossiping about. Somebody told Willy you're running a meth operation."

"Why would anyone say—"

"Don't blame me, I'm just repeating what I hear. That's the biggest problem around these parts. You've got to get out and mingle with the natives more often, let them know you're harmless."

"I did that once. It got me a black eye."

Blaze reached the chicken coop and opened the rough wooden door. "Yeah, I hear you there. Still, you can't just give up and hide out." He stepped into the darkness ahead of her and pulled a flashlight out of his back pocket. "There's nothing to taking care of chickens."

"Yes, but—"

"Don't need more than a little scoop or so of feed once a day—you'll be able to tell if she's eating it all or not. Keep fresh water in the coop. She'll take care of the rest, and I'll be over to keep an eye on things, make sure you aren't killing her." He set his bags inside. "Before you know it, unless Blue eats 'em, you'll have a whole coop full of banties. You'll be selling your eggs to the general store." He grinned, and she realized it was not a grin of mischief but of excitement.

She didn't have the heart to remind Blaze she wouldn't be around that long. She stepped through the door after him and watched as he inspected the coop, found a likely spot for the nest and gently opened the first sack to expose a cluster of five small brown eggs.

She stared at them. "That's it? I thought you had chicks."

"They'll hatch soon enough." He placed them in the nest site, then opened the other sack and pulled out a small, suddenly squawking black hen.

The hen clucked with alarm, circled the coop several times

and finally settled on the newly placed nest, fluttering her wings over the cluster.

Blaze gestured for Cheyenne to climb out of the coop, then followed and closed the door securely. "You've got your beginnings of a farm." He stepped to the side of the coop, where chicken wire formed a roomy enclosure. "See that door? After the hen has a few minutes to settle down, release the hinge and open the door so she can come outside and scratch in the dirt."

"Thanks," Cheyenne said. "Now all I need is a cow, pig, goats, maybe a horse...."

"Can't have my racing pigs."

"Oh, come on, Blaze, be a sport," she said dryly. "That's all I need to make my life complete. What will I—"

"Shh, listen!" Blaze went to the door and peered out. "Hear that? A goat. Red and Bertie must be paying you a visit." He looked at his watch. "They'd better hurry if they plan to make church this morning. Probably coming to invite you."

If so, they were wasting a trip. What had suddenly happened to her peaceful solitude?

As they left the coop, Cheyenne heard Mildred's characteristic alto bleat and saw her two elderly owners strolling up to the porch, one on either side of the mottled brown milking goat. Bertie carried an oblong cake pan. Red carried a brown paper bag.

Cheyenne glanced at it cautiously. Another paper bag. What kind of animal did this one have in it?

"Don't you have a lawn mower?" Bertie called when she saw Cheyenne and Blaze. "If you don't start cutting the grass, you'll have ticks and snakes knocking at your door."

"Told you," Blaze murmured.

"Fine, I'll pay you the going rate to come over and mow."

"Can't do it."

"What?"

"Dane wouldn't let me take your money after I nearly scared you out of your skin that night. Then there's the fee you never charged us for this." He gestured to his healing scalp. "I'll be over after school tomorrow." He greeted Red and Bertie and Mildred, then left to join Ramsay down at the dock.

Cheyenne invited her new visitors into the house. She'd already learned Mildred was housebroken. If her friends in the Columbia ER could see her now… Still, she'd always enjoyed older people. She'd had a good relationship with her grandparents when they were alive.

"I don't suppose you'd be interested in setting up a clinic while you're here," Bertie said. "You'd have people knocking your door down. Shoot, you could probably support half your practice with Cook alone." She shoved the pan at Cheyenne, who took it.

"Who's Cook?" Cheyenne asked.

"He's the older fella who lives over at the ranch. He's a chondromaniac with hemorroids."

Cheyenne paused for a moment to allow time for that statement to make sense. It didn't work. "He's a what?"

"Chondromanaic. You know, one of those folks who always thinks they're sick."

Ah, a hypochondriac. "Sorry, Bertie, I didn't know. But I can't open my own practice. My professional liability insurance is through the hospital where I'm employed. It only covers me in that facility, and it's against the law in most states to practice without insurance."

"Hmph. Can't you get your own?"

"I couldn't afford the premiums."

"Couldn't afford it? I thought doctors made all kinds of money."

Cheyenne sighed. Why bother to explain? She lifted the lid from the pan. "What's this?"

"Black-walnut cake," Bertie said as she, Red and Mildred crowded into the living room. "Figured you hadn't ever tasted one, down from the big city like that."

Cheyenne thanked them and led the way through the house to set the cake on the kitchen counter among all the cleaning paraphernalia.

Red handed her the package he'd been carrying. "Goat cheese," he announced, his blue eyes shining with pride. "Make it myself. Boys at the ranch love it, and Dane purty much buys all I can manage to make." He leaned forward and winked. "But I saved this out for you." He patted the lump of cheese lovingly. "Been making it for years. Had no complaints."

"And you won't get any from me, I love cheese." Cheyenne opened the package and took a knife out of her utensil drawer. "Would you like a piece?"

Red cocked his head forward. "Cheese!" he shouted. "It's cheese!"

"Red, she knows that!" Bertie shouted back. "Why don't you wear your hearing aid?"

"Hmph. I cain't hear with that stupid thing. It just stops up my ears," he grumbled. "When the wind blows, those things make it sound like a storm's about to hit."

Bertie reached out and touched Red's arm, watching his face with focused concern. "You feeling okay?"

"Fine," Red muttered. "I feel fine."

Cheyenne reached in the cupboard for some plates. "Can you stay and share it with me?"

"Sure would like that," Bertie said. "Have a seat, Red." Again, that focused concern.

Cheyenne cut the cake into generous pieces and added some goat cheese to each plate. It smelled delicious.

"You like goat's milk?" Bertie asked as they settled at the

table. "It's good for you, and if old Mildred here doesn't stop trying to get my cake, you can have goat burgers, too."

"I've never tried goat milk," Cheyenne said. "But I don't think I could eat Mildred." She watched the goat inch up beside Red and sniff at his plate.

Red nudged Mildred away, brushed cake crumbs from his overall bib and looked at Cheyenne, blue eyes wide. "How d'you like that cheese? Good stuff?"

Cheyenne sampled it. "Delicious." The texture was smooth but not too soft, and the flavor was mild, almost sweet.

Red's face flushed with pleasure. "Knew you would." He took another bite of the cake. "This cake of Bertie's ain't bad, either. Her black-walnut cake's won ribbons at the fair." He jerked his plate away from Mildred's eager nose and spilled crumbs across his leg, which the goat snatched up.

Under Bertie's watchful eye, Cheyenne cut a small corner from the square of cake and put it in her mouth. She tried not to gag as the strong aroma and taste of dirt filled her nostrils and coated her tongue.

Ugh! People *liked* this stuff?

Bertie leaned slightly forward, just as eager for approval as Red had been.

Cheyenne couldn't spit it out. She would not make a face. She forced a smile through the tears forming in her eyes, smashed the moist cake with her tongue and chewed. She tried not to breathe until she swallowed.

"Well? What do you think?" Bertie asked.

Somehow, Cheyenne managed to smile. "So this is black-walnut cake, is it?" She swallowed again. "It's very different from English walnut."

Bertie beamed. "It sure is. Lots of people say it's a delicacy. It's richer than pecan, and makes English walnuts taste like baby food, no flavor. If you like this, you ought to try my black-walnut pies."

Cheyenne silently vowed never to be in that predicament.

"So you two walk everywhere you go?" she asked, hoping to distract Bertie's attention. "You don't have a car?"

"Nope. We use the boat to get to town, and when we need to go to a bigger place for something, Dane takes us."

"What's that she's asking about?" Red asked his wife.

"About why we don't have a car!"

Red frowned. "A car? What would we need a car for? Them things ain't nothing but trouble."

"Oh, what d'you know?" Bertie jeered. "You only drove once, and gave up because you couldn't get the hang of shifting."

Red turned a playful glare on his wife. "Well, you didn't do no better! You drove into the goat's pen and crippled our best doe!"

While they continued to glare at each other, Cheyenne crumbled some of her cake and slipped the crumbs to Mildred.

"If you hadn't been in the back seat, screaming to high heaven about us all dying, we'd've been okay!" Bertie retorted.

Mildred nudged Cheyenne's elbow for another bite, and the swift movement caused Cheyenne to drop her fork, which attracted Bertie's attention.

"Goat, you're a nuisance. Red, take her on outside, would you? We've got to be going in a few minutes."

"Ain't you gonna invite her to church?" Red asked. "I thought that was why—"

"Sounds like that's what you just did," Bertie said.

"Thanks, but not this morning." Cheyenne hoped they wouldn't push it.

As Red stood up, he reached toward his chest and stumbled

backward, nearly tripping over the goat. He righted himself and left the kitchen, limping slightly.

Cheyenne looked at Bertie. "What's wrong with Red?"

Bertie avoided her gaze and reached for her husband's plate. "He gets a little gimpy once in a while." She carried the plates to the counter and set them in the sink, suddenly quiet.

"That wasn't just gimpy—he reached for his heart. Bertie, how long has it been since he's seen a doctor?"

Bertie ran water over the plates and covered the cake pan. "A while."

"How long?"

"Long enough we don't even have a doctor. Maybe twenty, twenty-five years."

Bertie's earlier comment made sense now. "Why don't you let me listen to his heart with my stethoscope? I don't have to have insurance to do that."

Bertie hesitated. "I didn't mean to come over here and take advantage of you. I just thought if you could take a look at Red's left leg, we could pay you for—"

"What's wrong with his leg?"

"He fell last week and bruised it up pretty bad."

"Did it break the skin?"

"Yes, and now it's all hot and red and pitted, like an orange peel. He's got a lot of swelling farther up...you know..."

"In the groin area?"

Bertie nodded. "I've been trying my own home remedies, and nothing works."

"Why don't you let me drive him into Kimberling City? There's an urgent-care facility—"

"He won't go. Says he's made it this long without a doctor, he'll make it fine now."

"Is he having fever or chills?"

"He felt warm to me this morning. That's one reason I

wanted to come over—that, and invite you to church—but I didn't know about all that insurance stuff."

"Forget about that insurance stuff. See if you can get him back in here. And see if Mildred wouldn't mind waiting on the porch."

Dane watched Blaze and Ramsay pull up at the dock, thick as thieves. He automatically glanced toward Hideaway, which was only about a quarter of a mile from the place where Cheyenne Allison was staying—by boat. By car it was about a mile.

For some reason, he'd glanced that way quite a few times the past few days. He'd considered boating over there, but didn't have a clue what he'd say once he arrived.

He envied Blaze, who seemed capable of plunging into any situation headfirst and keeping up a running monologue of words—Blaze's own special defense mechanism. When he wouldn't let them get a word in edgewise, people were prevented from asking questions or interacting with him.

Apparently, Cheyenne had accepted the hen and eggs, because Blaze and Ramsay got out of the boat without the sacks.

Soon afterward, Ramsay got into his own boat and sped across the lake toward town. He'd be wise to make sure his father didn't know he was muddying the waters here at the ranch. Austin Barlow had his good points, but leniency wasn't one of them.

Dane glanced again toward the farm across the lake as Blaze came up the slight incline from the dock, past the barn. "Did she take them?" he asked when Blaze drew near.

"She took them. I think I bullied her into it, though. I don't think she was ready for her own little farm."

"You did assure her, didn't you, that you'd be over to help her with them?"

"Of course I did. I couldn't let that hen and her chicks suffer just because we're trying to be nice to the neighbors. I'm going over to mow for Cheyenne tomorrow."

"Good."

"Red and Bertie are over there now."

"I saw them walk up."

Blaze gave him one of those knowing grins. "Oh, you did, did you? Watching the place pretty close lately, aren't you?"

Cocky kid. "Breakfast is ready, and you're running late."

Red's leg was, indeed, warm to the touch, and he had a temperature of 101.5. He wouldn't let Cheyenne get close to the area where his lymph nodes were affected, but she took Bertie's word for it.

"Ain't worth shooting, am I Shy Ann?" he said as she placed her stethoscope against his chest.

She nodded as she listened. He had a rapid heart rate, low blood pressure, swollen nodes and other symptoms of serious cellulitis. Unfortunately, these were also symptoms of deep vein thrombosis—a blood clot deep in the leg.

She removed her stethoscope and sat back. "Red, you need to see another doctor so they can run some tests." She nearly shouted the words so he would hear her.

"What's the problem?"

"I can't be sure, but your symptoms imply you have a serious infection caused by the injury you suffered a few days ago. Your body has been invaded by some kind of bacteria, and if that's the case, you need a strong antibiotic to go after the germs. With tests, another doctor might be able to find out what—"

"Don't want any of them new-type tests," he said. "If you

can't do anything for me, I'll be fine. I'll just get back on home and tough it out."

Rats. She'd been afraid he'd say that. Cheyenne glanced at Bertie, who shrugged at her helplessly.

"Okay, look, is there a pharmacy in town?" Cheyenne asked.

"Nope," Bertie said. "Dane tried to get a pharmacist to set up shop at the back of that little soda fountain beside his store, but without a doctor here, he can't get one to come."

This was ridiculous. There was no earthly reason Red couldn't let Cheyenne take him to Kimberling City, swallow a little pride, see a doctor at the urgent-care center and get this thing taken care of.

But then, how many patients had Cheyenne seen in the past year with this kind of problem? Columbia had a high population of retirees, many of whom did not have the best of incomes. They went to a doctor—sometimes even came to the ER—got their prescriptions, paid for the medication if they could. If they couldn't pay, they did without.

If Cheyenne's diagnosis was correct, Red would need the big guns to stop it. That meant a hundred dollar prescription, and she wasn't even authorized to write a script outside the ER.

And yet, what was she supposed to do? Risk Red's life over a few rules?

Rules that could give someone a reason to yank her medical license.

She put her stethoscope away. "Okay, you two, Red doesn't need to be walking, he needs to lie still with his leg up as much as possible. I'm going to drive you back home."

Bertie frowned at her. "Mildred, too?"

"Of course. I'm taking a trip to town, so I'll pick up the medication Red needs while I'm there."

"You're going shopping on a Sunday?" Bertie exclaimed.

"That's right. Now, let's get you back home."

Thankfully, Bertie didn't offer her any kind of animal in payment.

Chapter Fourteen

The bells echoed across the water from the community church in Hideaway, where Dane had attempted, years ago, to attend with his boys. Now they belonged to a smaller congregation down in Blue Eye, right on the Missouri-Arkansas border. It was a little farther to drive, but Dane felt the degree of acceptance his boys received from Doug and Brenda, the minister and his wife, far outweighed the deficit in transit time.

Not only were his brood welcomed with enthusiasm, but they were encouraged to take part in the small ministry— not quarantined to the right front pew every Sunday, watched carefully for any sign of mischief by Austin Barlow and his mother.

Jinx sat in the driver's seat of the van while the boys and Cook climbed inside. Dane was just about to lock the front door of the house when the telephone rang.

Ordinarily, he would let the answering machine get it, but he'd been waiting for a telephone call from Clint about a new prospect to replace Jinx in a few weeks. Jinx had been accepted at College of the Ozarks, and he had a summer job lined up, working in the restaurant on campus.

Dane picked up the receiver before the machine could respond. It was Cheyenne Allison.

"I need some directions," she said after the greeting. "Do you know of a pharmacy anywhere in the vicinity where I could fill a prescription for an antibiotic?"

"This morning? It's Sunday."

"It's an emergency."

"Are you sick? Is something—"

"No, it's Red Meyer. He has a bad infection, and I need to...anyway, I was hoping you'd know where I might be able to find a pharmacist open on Sunday morning."

"I see." Why would a vacationer know more than the rest of the town about Red Meyer? Red hadn't said anything this past week about any infection. "You don't have a boat, do you?"

"No, I was going to drive to—"

"You stay put and I'll be right over. I have a friend near Kimberling City I can call. He'll fill the script, and he's close to a dock. It'll be quicker for us to get there by boat. What's the script for?"

"Antibiotic, but—"

"Give me the dosage and I'll call it in. We can give him the prescription when we get there. Meet me down at your dock."

By the time Cheyenne stepped out the front door, she heard the boat racing across the lake toward her cove. Dane sat behind the wheel of a Mystique power cruiser, dressed a few notches up from casual.

"Thanks for coming," she said as he pulled up to the dock. "Really, if I'd had directions, I could have driven."

"You said it was an emergency."

"It is."

"Then get in." He tossed her a life jacket. "Buckle up. I didn't realize you knew Red and Bertie so well." He backed away from the dock. "Ordinarily they don't like to share their problems with anyone."

She fumbled with the jacket and finally figured out how to put it on. She hadn't been in a boat in years. "I just happened to be nearby at the right time."

"But where's the prescription coming from? They don't have a car, and Red hasn't been to a doctor—"

"I got it for them. Don't worry."

Their speed gradually increased as they aimed north along the smooth lake. Cheyenne huddled behind the windshield, aware of Dane's curious attention as he glanced at her from time to time.

"I'm still impressed by that little trick you used to stop Blaze's bleeding," he said at last.

She nodded.

"And now here you are rushing to get some medication for Red Meyer. With the prescription in hand, I presume."

"That's right." *Good grief, just tell him. It isn't like this is some big secret.*

"I guess Blaze warned you this morning that half of Hideaway is talking about the mysterious stranger who moved in two weeks ago."

"He warned me. I'm not manufacturing meth, in case you're worried."

He chuckled. "I'm not, but I am curious."

"About a crazy woman who charges at you with a mace gun?"

"No, I understood that perfectly. I guess what I meant to say was, I'm interested in how you're doing, and the boys and I have wondered if there's anything we can help you with besides mowing the lawn and—"

"And sending me a stewing hen and those delicious eggs?" From the corner of her eye she saw him glance at her.

"You don't like to talk about yourself, do you?" he asked.

She held her hand over the side of the boat and felt the cold spray on her skin. "I'm on a long vacation—leave of absence, forced on me by my director." Had she suddenly developed verbal diarrhea? Being compelled to take leave was humiliating enough, but to recite the whole mess to the first inquisitive stranger—

"Vacation from where?" he asked.

"My job."

A short silence. "You don't have to tell me what that is, of course."

"Thank you. I appreciate that." She knew she was making too big a deal about this, but her privacy had long ago become a matter of principle. Why did everybody have to know everybody's personal business?

"But if you don't, someone else will."

She rolled her eyes. "I've made a habit of not telling people what I do for a living because they tend to prejudge." And especially now, she'd just as soon forget everything.

"Oh." Heavy silence. "That's fine. There's no shame in making an honest living."

"I'm not ashamed of what I do." This was ridiculous. "I'm a physician. I work in an emergency department in Columbia."

He gave a low whistle. "A doctor. Why are you hesitant about telling people your profession?"

"I guess because I'm a private person."

"Shy?"

She smiled in spite of herself. "It's difficult to remain shy when you're forced to examine two or three naked strangers every shift."

"I guess it would be. I have a friend who is a surgeon in

Springfield. He never tells anyone what he does for a living because he was once sued for pitching a ball during a softball game at a company barbecue."

Ick. Lawsuits. Another uncomfortable subject. "How could he be sued for that?"

"A woman wandered out onto the field while the ball was still in play. She was struck by the ball and injured."

"And since he was presumed to have deep pockets, he was sued." It figured.

"My friend told me he mentally places people into one of three categories when he meets them," Dane said. "Some people automatically take for granted he's a rich doctor who thinks he's God, and they resent him. He never bothers to tell them about his five adopted children, or the money he gives for college scholarships every year. He's sponsoring one of my boys."

"Other people go overboard in the opposite direction," Cheyenne said. "Being worshiped is just as uncomfortable."

"But there's that third category, where future friends are waiting. Speaking of the future, if you happen to know any physicians who are interested in a very solo practice, there's a great opportunity in Hideaway. We're also looking for a pharmacist and a nurse. For a tiny town, we have a lot of retirees who could use a pharmacy nearby, and for that we need a doctor."

"That sounds like a good plan. Is Austin Barlow the one doing that?"

"No, I'm afraid I've become an irritant to Austin on that issue right now."

"You mean he doesn't want a doctor in town?" she asked, studying him.

His perceptive green eyes returned the inspection as he

shook his head, his silvery-blond hair tufting out in the wind. "I think he's just resentful because it was my idea."

"How long has he been mayor?" she asked.

"A full term. He's running for reelection this year."

"Is anyone running against him?"

"Just me."

She approved. Not that it mattered. She wouldn't be here that long. Now she understood why she'd sensed the tension between the two men the other day, and why Austin had been quick to warn her about the dangers of the ranch. Her opinion of the man dropped a notch.

Dane didn't take the time to chat when they encountered Jonathan Bruner at the dock, but promised him a steak dinner in the near future.

He was becoming more and more impressed by Dr. Cheyenne Allison as he got to know her better, although he reminded himself that she was only a temporary resident. Still, it struck him as a little too coincidental that she just happened to show up in the community in time to treat her first two patients....

Oops. *Stop it, Dane. God will answer those prayers in His time, not yours.*

"So tell me why Austin Barlow is so antagonistic toward you," she requested as they sped beneath the bridge toward home.

"You mean other than the fact I'm running against him for mayor? He blames me, indirectly, for the death of his wife."

For several seconds, the only sound he heard was the powerful purr of the Mystique's motor.

"How?" she asked.

He negotiated a narrow spot between two bass boats. "Seven years ago, one of my boys, Bruce, had more problems than I realized—he slipped through the screening system for the ranch, and I didn't pick up on the problem for several weeks. Back at that time, Austin's wife, Linea, came out to cook for us on weekends as a ministry of the church, and Bruce developed a crush on her. She confided in me about it, and I advised her to stop coming for a while. Our problem boy found out about it and flew into a rage. He ran over me with a tractor out in the field when we were hauling hay."

"I'd say he was dangerous."

"I ended up in the hospital. The same day, Ramsay found his mother dead from a head injury."

There was a gasp. "Bruce?"

"Nobody could ever prove how it happened, but Austin blamed Bruce and, consequently, me, for her death."

"So he's bitter."

"Very."

"Do you think Bruce killed Linea?"

"No."

"If Bruce was capable of running you over with a tractor, why don't you think he would have hurt Linea?"

"Because with me, he was in one of his rages. It was a blind attack, and he hadn't yet learned how to handle anger. Bruce's rages didn't last long, and it wouldn't have been sustained long enough for him to cross the lake, attack Linea at home, then return home to be available for the sheriff to take him into custody. It couldn't have happened."

"Then what did?"

"I've prayed for years to know the answer to that question. My boys have suffered from community suspicion ever since."

"What happened to Bruce?"

"He was removed from the ranch."

"Did he go to jail? Juvenile detention?"

"Last I heard, he'd joined the Coast Guard."

"You're kidding."

"I didn't press charges, and he was cleared of any other involvement. Linea's death was determined to be an accident. I tried to get Bruce into counseling, but he turned eighteen soon after the incident."

"If he was cleared, why did Austin continue to blame him?"

"Austin doesn't have a high opinion of the law enforcement around here. I think for a long time he felt the need to blame someone, and it just became a habit for him."

"And so now Blaze is being scapegoated over something that happened seven years ago. That doesn't seem fair, does it?"

They rounded a bend, and the first tiny island near home came into view. "A lot about life seems unfair. I'm trying to learn patience to wait for the final outcome."

Cheyenne discovered a whole new vantage point of Hideaway as Dane pulled up to the Meyers' dock and helped her ashore. Sheltered as she was in the cove, she hadn't seen the number of boats that belonged to the locals. Hideaway was definitely a water-based community.

Since she hadn't realized Dane would bring her directly here via boat, she'd left her first-aid kit at home, and she sent him to retrieve it.

Bertie was waiting at the back door when Cheyenne walked up the neatly mowed lawn to the house. A few strands of gray hair fell into board-straight rebellion across her worry-lined forehead, as if she hadn't been able to find time to comb them, and couldn't have cared less.

"I thought you said you was driving into town this morning." Bertie held the door open and ushered Cheyenne into the house.

"I didn't say I was driving."

"Have you had anything besides that black-walnut cake for breakfast?"

Cheyenne was trying hard to forget about the cake. "That was plenty for me, Bertie. Is Red taking it easy?"

"Sure is. He tried to go out and milk this morning, and I told him if he tried to go back out that door, I was going to lock him up in the smokehouse."

"Good." Cheyenne opened the package containing the Augmentin antibiotic. "This is potent stuff, and I think it'll work, but you need to make sure he takes it as regularly as possible—twice a day, starting right now. As soon as Dane returns with my medical kit, I'll check that leg again and make sure nothing has changed."

"Changed? You ain't even been gone an hour, what could've changed? Besides, I've made him yank his pants off and climb in bed, and I took his shoes and put them in the barn."

When Dane returned, Cheyenne checked Red, gave Bertie further instructions on the medication and promised to check back the next day. Dane was right, this town needed a doctor—preferably one who made house calls.

After Dane made sure Red was going to be okay, he went to the barn to do the milking for Bertie, while Bertie and Cheyenne left Red in bed on the honor system and walked together out the back door.

"I guess you know you're an answer to prayer for us," Bertie said.

Cheyenne didn't reply. Talk like that always made her uncomfortable.

"Not just *our* prayers, either," Bertie continued as they strolled into the beautiful spring morning. "Look what you did for Blaze, what with him bleeding all over hisself and everybody else. Any other time, he might've bled half out before—"

"Blaze would have been fine. He had medication to treat himself."

"And no telling what would've happened to Red if you hadn't been around this morning. Did you ever think of living out in a small town like this? Away from all the traffic and madness of the city?"

"Yes, I've thought about it, but it would be difficult to do."

"Why's that? You got family up there in Columbia?"

Cheyenne closed her eyes against a flash of pain, devastating in its suddenness.

"Oh, honey, don't tell me you're going through a divorce. I'm sorry I said anything. My best friend, Edith Potts, always tells me I ask too many questions, but it ain't because I like to spread gossip or—"

"It's okay, Bertie. I'm not going through a divorce, I've never been married. My sister was killed in an automobile accident recently, and I've had to take some time off from work to recover."

Bertie led the way to the front porch, and the two women sat on the porch swing.

"It's hard to lose a loved one." Bertie said. She was silent for a moment. "Red and I lost a son, back years ago."

"How many years?" Cheyenne asked gently.

"Forty. He was only seven. A mule kicked him in the head one morning when we were getting ready to plow. We tried to get him to a doctor, but he died before we reached town."

"Oh, Bertie, I'm so sorry."

She nodded. "Took a long time for that to heal, especially when we couldn't have any more little ones. We couldn't just wish it all away and ignore the pain. Life don't work like that." She eyed Cheyenne. "Can't run away from it, neither, but I guess you already found that out. You gotta carry on."

Cheyenne was carrying on. Wasn't she? "Did you ever have dreams about him? Your son, I mean."

"Red did. They weren't bad dreams, but they really got to him. Still, I wished I could've dreamed about him. You know, it might not make much sense to some folks around here, but that ranch of Dane's did something for us, even after all those years of living without kids. Seemed to us those boys needed some love, and it also seemed Dane was asking us to help give it."

"When did he take over the boys' ranch?"

Bertie snorted. "What d'you mean, take it over? He started it. That Dane's a smart man, I'll tell you. He's the one started the general store, borrowing money from his folks up in Springfield to fix the old place up. Made a killing in the summertime, when vacationers overran the place. Austin Barlow sold the old farm to Dane for a good price. Dane had enough money to pay his folks back for the store just after one summer, then started catering to the locals for winter trade. Got a lot of it, too, because it's such a far drive to any other town. And he kept his prices reasonable. He had a pretty young wife at the time, too, and he was willing to spend some money on her."

"Dane was married?"

"That's right. Everybody could tell he adored Etta, but when they got here, they'd been married five years, with no kids. They started taking in foster boys, but things didn't work out. I could tell she was down in the mouth about something. When she left, Dane blamed himself."

"Didn't he go after her?"

"Sure he did. But she didn't come back with him. He even offered to leave Hideaway and move back to the city. She made it clear it was him she didn't want. Broke his heart."

Poor Dane. And poor Austin. Was there anyone in Hideaway who hadn't suffered some kind of tragedy?

"Don't feel sorry for Dane, though. He fell in love with the place and the kids as soon as they got here. He's done a great job. Only one boy went bad, but Dane's heard about it ever since." Bertie glanced toward the sun. "Guess I need to be fixing some lunch. You hungry?"

"No, I need to be leaving, Bertie, unless you want me to help with the...uh...milking." *Please, no.*

Bertie got up quickly. "Dane can handle that fine. Now, Cheyenne, I know you say you can't take money for all this, but that antibiotic had to cost you something. I need to pay you back."

"No, you don't. You've already done so much for me."

"Well, I tell you what, there's one thing more I can do for you." Bertie went into the house, allowing the screen door to slap shut behind her. A few seconds later, she came back out carrying a pie covered in tinfoil. "Here you go, Dr. Allison. It's all yours. My very own, prizewinning black-walnut pie."

Cheyenne hoped her face displayed a delight she was most definitely not feeling.

Chapter Fifteen

Cheyenne awoke the next Friday morning to the sound of distant thunder and the feel of a rough tongue on her toes, which were sticking out from under her comforter.

"Stop it, Blue. Let me sleep." She turned over, trying to keep her eyes closed, but morning light filtered in through the window, and thunder reached her ears once more. She'd have to feed the hen now if she wanted to beat the rain.

She tossed the covers back, climbed sleepily out of bed and fumbled for her jeans.

An eerie moan halted her. She pivoted to look at Blue, who was staring at the window with narrowed eyes. She followed the kitten's line of vision and saw a face staring at her from the front porch.

A goat.

She rushed to pull on her jeans and tugged down the hem of her nightshirt. The appearance of a goat usually heralded the arrival of Red or Bertie, but this time no one appeared. The goat wasn't Mildred, it was a buck.

Cheyenne pattered barefoot through the living room and jerked the door open. There stood the goat, looking up as if he expected her to invite him in.

"Off the porch," she said as she stepped out. She shivered when her feet touched the cold concrete.

The screen door slapped shut behind her.

"Go on, go back home," she said, shooing at the buck with her hands.

The sound of bleating reached her ears from past the north end of the porch. She had just turned to investigate when the blurred shape of her first visitor rushed toward her, butting her in the side so hard she stumbled against the wooden column to the left of the steps.

She gaped at the brown-and-tan goat and took note of the sharp horns, his nervously twitching tail. "Get out!"

The buck lowered his head again. Before he could make another lunge at her, she jumped to the top of the three-foot-high concrete porch ledge.

The goat's horns snapped against the concrete, barely six inches beneath her feet.

A soft bleat drew her attention to the yard. Five female goats stood munching contentedly on the blooming forsythia.

"Stop that!" Cheyenne cried. She bent forward, trying to wave them away.

Too late, she heard the clatter of hooves and received a sharp, painful nudge in her posterior. She went flying over the edge, face first into the mud at the feet of the trespassers. Five curious goat faces peered at her, then lost interest and returned to the forsythia.

The buck on the porch leaped onto the ledge for which he had battled, bleating in triumph.

Five more of the little varmints munched on the honeysuckle in the corner of the yard.

"Get out of here, you little monsters!" Waving her arms wildly in the air, Cheyenne shrieked, running from one group to the next, slapping them sharply in the sides. "You're ruining the whole yard!"

Running amid the now panicking, bleating animals, she stumbled into a hidden hole in the grass and twisted her left ankle. The pain shot up her leg.

The buck advanced toward her, head lowered. She leaped to her feet and hobbled toward the porch, wincing as a band of white heat surrounded her ankle.

Blue jumped to the center of the screen of the door, digging into the screen with his claws from inside the house.

"Move, Blue! Get out of the way!" She grabbed the handle and pulled, but the door wouldn't open.

With a sinking heart, she realized the hook latch had fastened when the door slammed behind her. The buck clattered up the steps and butted her viciously in the thigh before she could move. She staggered against the house as pain radiated through her side.

"Get away from me!" She hobbled to the end of the porch and climbed to the ledge.

The goat followed her. Before he could butt her again, she reached for the latticework that supported the honeysuckle. As she climbed away from the porch ledge and the malevolent goat, Cheyenne hoped the flimsy framework wouldn't collapse with her weight. She reached for the guttering and held it as she felt for a footing with her toes.

The wooden lattice shuddered beneath her. Grasping the corner of the roof, she swung a leg to the rain gutter. The hem of her jeans caught on the corner of the guttering and ripped as she kicked up and over. She clawed her way onto the roof, with the rough shingles scraping her exposed skin. Shaking from reaction, she collapsed on the roof edge.

The thunder echoed around her again.

"This is crazy," she muttered. "I'm insane for staying in this godforsaken place."

Blue's plaintive cry reached her from the porch. She leaned over to peer at the ground and found that hateful buck standing in the yard, munching on the lilac bush in the corner.

"Godforsaken," she repeated, rolling to her back and glaring up at the stormy sky. "That's me, isn't it? It isn't enough that You take my sister...my best friend in the world." *Oh, Susan, where are you now?* "You force me away from my job, my friends, my life. Am I so vile to You that—"

Stop it! Who was she talking to? Her poor sister had been duped by all that God talk. Kirk had used the Bible to manipulate and threaten his wife for years. "Love, honor and obey," he'd said when Susan tried to contradict him about anything during a conversation. What a cruel joke. He had done anything but honor her.

And where had all that so-called "blessed peace" been the day Susan had her panic attack and was rushed to the ER? If Christians were so filled with love and joy and peace, would they have attacks like that?

Cheyenne clenched her fists and glared once more into the sky. "What did You do, take her life because she had a panic attack? She loved You! She thought she was serving her God, and she stayed with that disgusting creep of a husband because she believed that was what You wanted her to do."

Covering her face with her hands, Cheyenne rolled to her side. "Why couldn't You take me instead?" Susan had been the gentlest person Cheyenne had ever known. "I'm the one who should have died."

Blue wailed again, his claws scratching at the screen.

"Stop it, Blue! I'm here. I'm okay."

Or was she? Would a sane person be lying here on the roof

of a house, with a storm brewing, while she argued with a God she claimed not to believe in yet some part of her obviously did? Two months ago she would have immediately found a way out of this situation, and then laughed about it later.

Of course, two months ago she wouldn't have been in this place, so totally out of her element. What had made her think she should come here to heal?

The goats had fallen silent. A cold gust of wind whipped past her so hard Cheyenne grasped the edge of the roof, shivering as the air cut through the thickly knit fibers of her nightshirt.

Lightning streaked across the face of dark clouds that roiled above her. She couldn't prevent a fleeting thought—God was about to get her.

Blue stopped scratching at the screen, but his voice rose in an eerie howl.

Cheyenne peered over the edge of the roof again.

No goats. The yard was empty.

She crawled up to the peak of the roof and looked over the other side. Still, there was no sign of the goats. How had they been able to disappear so suddenly?

A mournful bleat came from directly below her. On the porch.

"Well, sure," she muttered. "Why am I not surprised?" And of course this would happen when it was about to storm, so there would be no one on the lake to see her.

She grasped the side of the eaves and leaned outward to peer onto the porch. Within view were five goats huddled in comfortable shelter, wiggling their ears and twitching their short tails, as if this were all a big joke. The buck leaped back onto the concrete ledge and glared at her.

Cheyenne sighed and sat back. The first big drops of rain splashed into her face. She was locked out of her house, but if she could climb back down the way she had come up—and avoid Old Billy Goat Gruff—she could at least find shelter with the chickens out of the rain. If she could walk that far.

But when she tried to swing her legs over the side of the roof and gain traction on the trellis, it swung away from the house. If she climbed onto it, she realized, as soon as she released the roof, she would fall with the makeshift ladder all the way to the ground.

Soaking in the rain, she scrambled, crablike, around the edges of the roof for some other way to climb down. There was nothing. Drenched, she shivered in the deluge of driving rain.

Blowing sheets of water lashed the roof. Blue had either given up crying or she couldn't hear him over the roar of the storm. Cheyenne's ankle throbbed, but that wasn't her biggest concern. Would she have to make a choice between hypothermia or injury from a jump?

When she was a ten-year-old tomboy, climbing up the trees had always been easier than climbing down, and once her father had even had to climb up on a ladder to get her down from the huge old oak tree in their backyard.

But now Dad was in Florida, and she was on her own. She certainly couldn't depend on prayer, as Susan had always done.

Unable to stop shivering, Cheyenne scrambled back to the front porch and caught sight of a flash of yellow on the driveway at the top of the hill. She glanced up quickly to see a lone figure coming toward the house along the muddy track. On foot. He wore a rain poncho with a hood, but she was pretty sure she recognized Dane's characteristic silver-blond hair and beard.

"Hey!" she shouted. "H-hello! I'm up here!" She waved and tried to stand, but her ankle complained.

He broke into a run. When he reached the yard, she shouted, "Watch that b-buck! He's dangerous."

"I know all about that buck," Dane called up to her. "I'll handle him. What are you doing up there? How did you *get* up there?"

"The t-trellis." She couldn't stop her teeth from chattering. "B-but I can't climb back down b-because it swings away from the house when I try. It isn't anchored at the top."

"Come on over and I'll hold it for you."

"What about the buck?"

"Roscoe's a typical coward. He doesn't abuse men, just women."

He held the lattice for her as she climbed down, then removed his poncho and wrapped it around her.

"You're freezing," he said, squeezing her arms with his warm hands. "Come on, let's get into the house."

"The doors are locked."

"The porch, then."

"Not the front porch! The back." She started around the side of the house.

"Hey, wait a minute, you're limping." He reached for her, and before she could protest, he swung her up into his arms. His warm, strong arms.

Oh, boy.

He carried her to the back porch and set her down gently.

"How long were you up there?" he asked, releasing her.

"A few m-minutes." She could have hugged him. Did he know what a welcome sight he was? "The screen door slammed shut and the hook lock bounced into the eye." She suddenly felt like an imbecile. How incompetent she must look to him.

And since when did she care?

"Do you still have that tricky bathroom window?" he asked.

"Yes, but—"

"How did you hurt yourself?"

"I stepped in a hole chasing the goats."

"The goats are safely on the porch for now, and I'll take care of them later. You stay here while I climb inside." He reached for the hoe leaning against the side of the house. "If Roscoe gives you any trouble, smack him across the horns with this handle. I doubt he'll bother you in the rain, though. He doesn't usually behave badly unless there's a doe in season, anyway."

She accepted the hoe and watched Dane retrace his steps to the bathroom window. As if mesmerized, she couldn't drag her gaze from him. He looked good…really good.

Stop it! Relief and cold were making her silly.

Dane had the window up and was climbing through it within a minute. Seconds later he was helping her inside. He pulled a kitchen chair away from the table and eased her down as he took the poncho from around her shoulders.

"Stay right here while I put this thing in the tub to drip-dry. I'll bring some towels and turn up the heat. Where do you keep your extra blankets?"

"In the b-bathroom closet. Get an extra one for yourself, you're as wet as I am."

"But I'm not chilled." He disappeared into the back bedroom, and she heard the closet door open in the bathroom.

Blue came running into the kitchen, meowing loudly. He attacked Cheyenne's left foot with his tongue, then retreated, shaking his paws when he encountered the water that had dripped onto the floor.

Dane returned with a stack of towels and a thick blanket. "Where's your thermostat control? We need some more heat in here. No, don't get up, you should stay off that foot."

As she complied, he wrapped the blanket around her, wet clothes and all. Once again, she was accosted by the impact of his touch, in spite of the aching foot, in spite of her chattering teeth. How long had it been since she'd enjoyed a man's nearness?

A very kind man, with a gentle touch. She looked up and found him watching her. Simultaneously, they both looked away.

After Dane turned up the heat, he returned and took a towel from the stack, unfolded it and handed it to her. "You still don't have a telephone, do you?"

"C-car phone."

"If you don't mind, I'd like to use it to call Red and Bertie and let them know their babies are okay. Red isn't feeling well, and Bertie's—"

"What's wrong with Red?" Cheyenne had checked on him yesterday, and his cellulitis was healing well.

"Bertie said he was acting a little disoriented and had a temperature this morning. She stuck his work boots in the barn again, and called us for help with the milking. When I arrived, we found only three candidates. Cook is searching along the road. As soon as you're dry, I'll drive you to the urgent care clinic in Kimberling City so you can have that ankle X-rayed."

"N-no, it'll be fine." The attention was nice, but embarrassing. "You need to dry off yourself."

"I'm worried about *you* at the moment," he said as he rubbed at her dripping hair with a towel. He pulled a chair out for himself and sat down, reaching for her left foot. Gently, he examined her ankle. "It's swollen, but not badly."

"It's not b-broken," she assured him. "I was more frightened than hurt. But I'll have some doozy bruises in the morning. That guy's mean."

"I'm sorry about that. Red's talked about getting rid of him—I guess now he'll do it." Dane tucked her more tightly into her blanket. "Do you have an elastic bandage in that first-aid kit of yours?"

"Yes, but I'll take care of—"

"Why don't I wrap your foot. Then you can change out of those wet clothes while I call the Meyers."

He wrapped her ankle expertly, then helped her to her bedroom and closed the door. By the time she'd changed, the temperature in the house had risen several degrees, and her shivering had stopped. When Dane returned to the house, Cheyenne was sitting with her foot propped up on a chair.

He filled her teakettle with water and placed it on the stove, then pulled out a chair and sat down beside her, taking her hands in his. "Better now?"

"Much, thanks. I was getting pretty frantic up there on the roof. You were like an—"

What was she going to say? An answer to a prayer she hadn't prayed? "A rescuing angel," she said.

"Bertie was upset when she found out what happened. She's sending Cook over to get the goats."

"So the animals are still on the porch?"

"All huddled together, watching the rain like it was good television. Where's your tea?"

She motioned toward a cabinet, and he pulled down a cannister of chamomile.

Cheyenne was feeling better by the second. "Imagine how ridiculous I must have looked trying to chase those stubborn little animals out of my yard."

Dane's smile was sudden and devastating, and again, she couldn't look away for a moment. Why hadn't she noticed before how attractive he was?

He held her gaze briefly, then reached into another cupboard for mugs. "You take sugar in your tea?"

"Honey."

As he worked, she watched his strong profile. He had never struck her as handsome, but now that she'd become acquainted with him, she couldn't imagine how she missed the strength in that gaze, the kindness in those eyes.

He turned and saw her watching him.

She looked down at her hands, folded tightly together in her lap.

This was silly. She was thirty-five, he was—what, thirty-eight? Stupid to behave like shy teenagers.

The whole episode on the roof had heightened her sensitivity, but she had no intention of allowing herself to be carried away by the attraction.

The teakettle whistled and Dane reached for it. "How much honey?" Why hadn't he noticed before what a beautiful woman she was? Of course, he'd been attracted the second time he met her, but—

"One dollop, lightly stirred."

He found the honey and carried it to the table. He'd let her do the dollop, since he didn't know what that was.

She grinned. "You're a kind man, I don't care what they say about you."

"For what you've been through since you arrived here, you're taking this well," he said.

"You rescued me from the mean old goat and gave me chickens."

"Chickens? The chicks have hatched?"

She nodded. "Yesterday. All but one." She spooned in the honey, and he watched closely.

Aha. A dollop was half a teaspoon. He would remember that.

"I can't help wondering why you do it," she said. Her voice was as smooth and soothing as the honey she stirred into the tea.

"Do what?"

"Spend your life out here in the middle of nowhere, helping people, running for a thankless political position that doesn't even pay enough to cover your monthly electric bill."

"I'm not sure I'm always much help." But it felt good to hear her say that.

"You should have heard Red and Bertie every day this week when I went over to check on Red. It was always 'Dane says this' or 'Dane did that.'" She shook her head. "They think you're special, and they should know, they've been your neighbors for so many years."

This lady could make a guy feel like a million. "So tell me why you do what you do."

"You mean why did I kill myself in med school and residency, just to set myself up for a lawsuit in a high-risk specialty?"

He was sorry he'd asked. All the good humor had just been distilled from those lovely, dark eyes. "You sound as if you've been asking yourself that very question."

She nodded, still stirring her tea. The sound of the metal against ceramic echoed through the house. "Constantly." She glanced at him, then looked quickly away.

"That's why the two-month vacation?"

"Vacation and leave. I did tell you, didn't I, that my director forced this on me?"

"You didn't tell me why, but if you'd like to talk about it, I've been told I'm a good listener—and not the kind who repeats everything he hears."

"You mean like Lizzie Barlow?" she asked.

He just smiled. Apparently, Bertie had been talking to Cheyenne, as well.

"My younger sister was killed in an automobile accident the first of March."

The sudden announcement startled him. "I'm so sorry."

She pulled the spoon out of the tea, tapped it on the side of the mug, then stared at it, as if trying to focus on anything but what she was saying. "Susan was brought into our department." She swallowed and took a breath, hard and deep. "I was the one who pronounced her dead."

He felt the shock of her words all the way through his body. He couldn't begin to imagine the horror of it. "Oh, Cheyenne."

"What will haunt me to my grave is that I might have contributed to her death. I had given her a sedative in the ER earlier that day for a panic attack. I gave her specific instructions not to drive with the drug in her system, but she drove anyway."

"Then how could you possibly suspect your actions contributed to her death?"

Her eyes filled with tears. "How can I ever know for sure?"

Before he could reply, there was a knock at the front door. Dane answered it to find Bertie standing there, wearing a bright-yellow shower cap and red-plaid coat. She held a brown paper bag in her arms.

He stepped back and let her inside.

"Cook's herding the goats back to the house," she said as she walked past him. "How's Cheyenne? You say she hurt her ankle? What about that Roscoe, what'd he do to her? I can't believe this happened! I told Red to sell that animal last year, but would he listen?"

She walked on into the kitchen. Dane followed, but only to excuse himself to get the van. Bertie would need a ride back home—he didn't intend for her to walk back in this weather. He hoped to have other opportunities to get to know Cheyenne better.

★ ★ ★

Bertie invaded Cheyenne's kitchen with apologies and herbs, scattering droplets of water as she yanked off her coat and shower cap.

Shower cap?

"Now, tell me where that old rascal got you." She pointed toward Cheyenne's wrapped foot. "Twist your ankle? Ice for that, and I brought some comfrey root and onions. Best thing there is for bruises. Did he break the skin anywhere?"

Cheyenne nodded.

"We'll see if we can't do something about that." Bertie opened and closed the cupboard doors beside the sink. "Cheyenne, I need a pot to boil this comfrey root. And a knife."

"Knife?" Cheyenne exclaimed. "For what?"

"To cut the onion. We'll get the juice out of it easier that way."

"Onion?" She was cooking? "What are you going to do with it?"

Bertie found the pot she was looking for and covered the bottom of it with water. "The onion we'll use for your bruises, the comfrey we'll use for everything, but it takes a while to boil the comfrey, so I'll use the onion until the tea's done."

"Tea? Dane just made me some tea."

Bertie reached into the paper bag, drew out a big handful of roots and dumped them into the pot. "Comfrey tea to use for a poultice on you. How do you turn this stove on? Oh, here it is." She set the pot on the burner and returned to the bag. "I brought a rag, but no knife. Got one?"

Cheyenne pointed to the drawer that held her cutlery, and watched as Bertie cut the onion into pieces and wrapped it in a plain white dish towel. Then she beat the bundle on the cabinet until the whole thing was soft and mushy, and the kitchen smelled like an onion-processing plant.

"Now, where's it hurt the worst?" she asked, turning to Cheyenne with the poultice.

Cheyenne watched her with suspicion. "You're going to put that thing on me?"

"Won't do you no good to eat it! Now come on, don't be shy, it's just you and me here now. Dane won't be back for a while. Drop those drawers and let's get to work on you. I guarantee you'll be up and around a whole lot faster. You've done so much to help us, now I'm gonna doctor you for a change."

"Okay," Cheyenne said, glancing around at the windows. "But first, lock the doors and close the curtains."

Bertie snorted, but she did as Cheyenne requested. "Honey, you're living in the country now. There's no neighbors to see you or passersby to peek." Chuckling, she helped Cheyenne with her jeans and searched for the worst bruise, which turned out to be on her right thigh.

"Red and I don't go to doctors much. Don't trust 'em—present company excluded. And I've yet to see a good doctor's remedy that'll beat mine for bruises, cuts and sprains. You listen to me and you'll be up and around in half the time you expected. Might even put some of my wisdom to use in your new practice when you come and join us for good."

Cheyenne nibbled on her lower lip to keep a grin from spreading across her face. "You don't like doctors, huh?"

"We like you, that's for sure."

As the poultice soaked and the comfrey boiled, Bertie settled herself comfortably beside Cheyenne. "Dane's brought his boys over to me for all kinds of ills. He knows the value of good herbs." She shook her head. "But Austin now, he says I'm playing doctor. Maybe I am. Many's the boy I've treated for coughs and diarrhea with my blackberry root and mullein leaves. They never even had to go to the drugstore."

"You mean you make your own cough syrup and antidi-arrheal?"

"You betcha. And lots of new mothers come to me when their babies can't sleep. I just make a syrup out of plain old catnip you find around any barn. Honey, you'd be surprised how many things you can make from weeds. Mama used to make coffee substitute from chicory root."

Cheyenne was surprised when her thigh stopped throbbing as she sat listening to Bertie's soothing voice. Hard to tell if it was the poultice of onions or Bertie's healing touch. For a moment, Cheyenne allowed herself to relax and her mind to drift. What if she did move here? She would desperately miss her job, and her friends. But she was making friends here. And Columbia wasn't the only place with emergency departments.

She focused once more on what Bertie was saying…

"…and I almost bought a couple of kids last year, except the people I was going to buy 'em from changed their minds at the last minute and decided to keep 'em."

Cheyenne gasped aloud. "Bertie! You almost bought someone's kids!"

Bertie got up to check on the boiling brew, chuckling as she went. "Honey, I don't know about Columbia, but down here in Hideaway it's not against the law to buy and sell young goats. After today, though, I'm selling that old buck. There's no use in him beating up on the neighbors like this. Why, if he was to do this to Lizzie Barlow, she'd sue us for the farm."

"Austin's mother?"

"She sure would. She hates our goats, thinks they stink. Why, it's all her imagination, because we keep 'em real clean, keep the lot cleaned out and sell the manure for fertilizer." Bertie took another towel out of her paper bag and laid it on the counter beside the boiling pot. She turned the burner off under the pot and poured some of the brew over the cloth, folded the cloth, poured some more. Next, she strained the roots and put them on the very top of the folded towel. "Now, take off that bandage from your ankle and we'll put this on for a while. Then we'll pack it in ice. You'll be as good as new in no time."

Cheyenne hesitated. "Shouldn't it cool down first?"

"It will be cold soon, trust me. Now, where's your ice cubes?"

Cheyenne groaned. This place did indeed need a doctor.

She was considering the possibility when she heard the approach of a car out on the drive, sloshing through the mud. Against her own advice, she hobbled to the window and peered out to see a car with an insignia on the door. Bertie stepped up behind her and looked out.

"Cheyenne," Bertie said softly, "ain't that the sheriff?"

A large man wearing a tan uniform got out of the car with an envelope in his hand.

Cheyenne swallowed. "Oh, no." She hobbled to her bedroom and pulled her pants back on.

The sheriff stepped up onto the porch and knocked at the screen door. In spite of Bertie's protests, Cheyenne walked to the door and met him there.

He handed her official notice that she was being named in a lawsuit for the death of her sister, Susan Warden. The plaintiff, of course, was Kirk Warden.

Chapter Sixteen

Exactly a week after being served by the sheriff, Cheyenne parked in the front lot at the Missouri Regional Hospital and entered the building through the front entrance. She couldn't remember the last time she'd felt like a visitor in her own place of employment.

Or would she even be employed here after all this was over?

Instead of taking the elevator to the administrative offices on the sixth floor, she took the first hallway to the right and followed it toward the Emergency Department.

The echo of her approach seemed to reverberate all around her. She hesitated, her steps faltering. This hallway was excruciatingly familiar, like the one in the dreams that haunted her. She almost expected to turn at any moment and see her sister's mangled body lying on the floor.

The first person she saw as she entered the ER proper was Ardis Dunaway, who turned from the central desk.

"Dr. Allison!" She rushed forward and caught Cheyenne in a hug, then stood back, grinning. "You look wonderful—

you must be catching up on your sleep. I told you that place would be good for you."

"Sleep? What's that? And speaking of restful, it isn't."

"You're kidding, that little town? I'm surprised you aren't bored silly. Why didn't you call me and let me know you were coming up? We could have had lunch."

Cheyenne lowered her voice. "This isn't a social visit. I plan to head back home as soon as my meeting is over."

Ardis lost the smile. "Meeting? Please tell me you aren't quitting. Doing without you for two months is bad enough, but—"

"Bad? What do you mean? Jim's getting the shifts covered isn't he? I thought he had—"

"Oh, don't even worry about that. I just miss you is all."

"My meeting is with Larry Strong."

Ardis frowned. "Risk Management? Why would you—" She caught herself. "Oh, no, that brother-in-law of yours…"

"Ex-brother-in-law." Cheyenne cringed at the bitterness in her voice. "Sorry. I'm sure you'll be brought in as a witness."

"Good, let me at him. I'd love to prove him wrong."

"Ardis," called a man in a white coat from exam room one. He crooked his finger at her.

"Oops, I'd better go." Ardis patted Cheyenne's arm. "The patients have us hopping today. You going to be okay? Things may slow down here after a while, and we could get together and download."

"I don't know how long the meeting will last, but I'm hoping to be back home before dark."

Ardis studied her face for a moment. "Home?"

"I want to sleep at Hideaway tonight, and the nocturnal animals are so busy after sundown, I don't want to be on the road."

A nod of understanding. "So it's home to you now. You

need a place to heal, Cheyenne, but don't make any impulsive moves, okay?"

"I promise. Now stop mothering me and get to work."

Ardis gave her another hug and rushed to her patient.

Cheyenne watched her go with a feeling of loss. But why? She and Ardis were friends, but Ardis had her grown family, with two grandchildren. It wasn't as if they spent a lot of time together outside of work.

But then, Cheyenne didn't have much of a social life, just a few single friends from college she occasionally got together with for a dinner or movie as her schedule permitted. Until now, that hadn't bothered her much, because she could always take an extra shift or two.

Today she felt cut off from the rest of the world.

When Cheyenne walked into the reception area for Risk Management on the sixth floor, the secretary immediately reached for a green file folder and held it out. "Hi, Dr. Allison. Mr. Strong wants you to read through this while you're waiting. It's all the medical information about the case."

Cheyenne stared at the folder. She tried to swallow, but her throat had suddenly gone dry.

"Dr. Allison?" the secretary said softly. "Are you okay?"

Cheyenne glanced at her. "Thanks, Lisa. I'm fine." She presented the copies of her medical licenses.

After carrying the file back to the conference room Lisa indicated, Cheyenne sat down to study.

Dane was standing at the cash register, giving Cecil a break, when he saw Austin Barlow's red pickup pull to the curb. From the look of Austin's face and the set of his hat, it wasn't hard to guess what was on his mind.

The door opened with a clatter of the new cowbell Cecil had attached to the top, in case he had customers when he was stocking shelves. Not that the bells worked any better than shouting. Customers had to go hunt him down half the time.

The sound of Austin's cowboy boots echoed on the old wooden floor. "Cook said I'd find you here."

"What can I do for you, Austin?"

"I hear you're running for mayor."

"That's right."

"You don't think I'm doing the job?"

Dane leaned against the counter and folded his arms across his chest. "I think you've done a fine job. People like you, and they trust you."

Austin's blue eyes narrowed slightly. He took a step forward. "You wouldn't be mocking me, would you?"

"Nope. I'm not out for a mudslinging fight, I'm just adding my name to the mix." Personally, he hoped he lost. The only reason he was doing this was to put a little more pressure on Austin to improve a few things in Hideaway. Maybe during the next term, if Austin thought he might have competition, he would push for a little more progress instead of nursing a chip on his shoulder over the past.

"Austin, I've asked you several times to consider opening a clinic in town, and you won't even suggest it to the board. I've also asked you about a pharmacy. I've got a corner right here in the back of the store that would serve us well."

"No doctor or pharmacist would come here for what they could make."

"I doubt you've tried to find out." He thought of Cheyenne again. In fact, his mind had been on her quite a bit this past week, especially today, with the meeting in Columbia. "I know this is a small town, but it serves a larger community, especially in the summertime. We're perfectly situated on the water for increased traffic to the dock, and our village is convenient for shopping, church attendance, picnics in the park. If we had a medical clinic here, word would spread."

"Why would we want increased traffic?" Austin asked. "It's a nuisance. Those people pollute our water."

"We share the same lake with every other town in the area. Besides, you never complain about the traffic during the fall festival. Sometimes I think you want to be mayor so you can direct that thing every year." *And honor your dead wife out of a sense of guilt.*

Austin scowled. "I do a lot more than that around here, and you know it."

"Yes, I do." His biggest job was getting underfoot when the sheriff was trying to identify the vandals who had attacked their town several times in the past. "Speaking of that festival," Dane said, "I have four boys entering the pig races this year."

"I'll write them down."

"Wouldn't you like to know their names? Last year you conveniently forgot to include Jinx and Jason, and then you tried to stop them from entering at the last minute."

"I said I'd write them down."

"That's fine, but just in case, I'll check with you on it in a couple of weeks. I know it doesn't seem very important to you, but my boys talk about it all year. They need this sense of community."

"Really?" Austin's voice dripped with sarcasm. "This *community* needs a sense of *safety,* which is something we'll never have with a vandal on the loose. That's one reason you won't win a mayoral election, not as long as those kids are allowed to run wild all over the county."

"Why don't you lighten up on the boys at the ranch!" Dane heard his own raised voice echo through the store. He took a deep breath, allowed himself time to calm down. "I'm sorry, Austin. I don't want to start another argument with you over something that happened seven years ago. I know the loss of Linea devastated you and Ramsay, but you can't make those boys suffer for it."

"You have no idea what it did to Ramsay and me."

"Yes I do, Austin. Divorce is no church social."

Austin looked away. He cleared his throat. "You didn't have a son who was so devastated he couldn't speak for a year."

"I had two boys at the ranch at the time." When their foster mother left, Dane had nearly lost custody of them. The boys had blamed themselves, afraid they'd run her off.

Austin cleared his throat again, still not looking at Dane. "Why don't you mail me a list of your entries."

"Thank you. My boys will appreciate it."

Austin reached for a copy of Dane's weekly list of sale items, folded it and stuck it in his pocket, even though he seldom shopped here. "I don't suppose you'd be interested in a nice, friendly little public debate in September?"

"Name the date."

"How about the festival? Saturday after the pig races. That way people will already be accustomed to the smell of a little shoveled manure."

"I don't plan to shovel manure, Austin, and I don't plan to sling any mud. If it gets dirty, I'm out of there."

Meeting his gaze at last, Austin nodded. Almost as an afterthought, he held his hand out. Dane took it. They shook like gentlemen for the first time in seven years.

Dane only wished it was more than a temporary truce.

Cheyenne was trembling by the time she read through Susan's medical records for the day she died. Lisa had placed a box of facial tissues on the table, and Cheyenne pulled three of them out to wipe her face. She had relived everything as she read. When she blinked, she saw the blood. If she closed her eyes for more than a few seconds, she saw an image of her sister's lifeless eyes staring at her...accusing her?

No, Susan would never do that. Kirk was the accuser.

Cheyenne was blowing her nose when the door opened and two men entered the small conference room. She recognized Larry Strong, the director of Risk Management. She responded appropriately when he introduced one of the hospital's attorneys, Ed Burdock.

The men sat across from her, as if positioning themselves to see every nuance in her expression, hear every change of tone in her voice. She felt her stomach muscles tighten.

"Dr. Allison," Larry Strong began, "Ed and I wanted to discuss the facts of the case with you today. Have you read the complete report?"

"Yes."

"Do you agree with what you've read?"

"Yes." Her voice quivered. "I'm sorry, you'll have to forgive me, but this is a traumatic situation for me, as I'm sure you can understand. She was my sister."

"Yes, I'm sorry to have to put you through this, Dr. Allison," the attorney said. He was an older man, about her father's age, stocky and bald with a white fringe of hair around the sides.

"I know you've heard a lot of horror stories about malpractice lawsuits," Larry said. Strong was about ten years younger than the attorney, more slender and athletic. Both appeared compassionate. "The good news is that seventy percent of the time the plaintiff loses. Unfortunately, in the case of a loss of life, that percentage drops enormously."

Cheyenne felt herself go cold. She knew the risks, but deep down she realized she had never expected something like this to happen to her. Somehow, she'd expected them to tell her this was nothing more than a frivolous lawsuit, and if they made the right motions to convince the judge of that, the whole thing would be dropped. Nothing else made sense to her.

"In order to properly defend you and this hospital," Ed said, "we're going to have to go over and over the details of that day. I'll warn you now, we expect this one to go forward rapidly. Seldom do plaintiff attorneys take action this quickly on a case, so somebody is pushing things, and it's my guess they'll keep pushing to strike while emotions are high about the patient's death."

"Does that mean they expect to win?" Cheyenne asked.

Ed paused as he indicated the medical record. "Any time there's a death, no matter who is at fault, a jury is much more likely to decide for the plaintiff. The typical mentality is 'someone's got to pay' for the loss suffered by the grieving family member."

"But I'm a grieving family member! Susan was my sister, and the impact of her death hit me so hard I've been forced to take a leave."

"Yes, I agree that will put an interesting spin on the situation."

Cheyenne felt her skin tingle with anger. *Stay calm. He's doing his job.* "Interesting? Excuse me, but we're talking about the death of my sister."

The attorney leaned forward totally in control of the conversation with her now, as Larry Strong sat taking notes. "I understand that, Dr. Allison, believe me, I do. But in order to handle this nasty situation successfully, we can't allow our emotions to control us. We have to look at some very cold, hard facts, weigh them against each other and decide what to do about them, keeping in mind that the other side will be playing on the emotions of many people in order to damage you and your testimony in any way they can legally do so. You must keep a cool head."

"I can do that."

"You aren't doing it today. I realize you've had little time to prepare for this emotionally, but you're a doctor. You've learned how to distance yourself from your emotions when you're treating your patients. You need to do the same thing with this case."

This *case* was all about her sister's death. How was she supposed to distance herself from that? And yet she knew she had to.

"We'll try to emphasize your relationship with the deceased, of course, every chance we get," Ed said, "but the plaintiff in this case is Kirk Warden, and his attorneys will attempt to draw the jury's sympathy toward the bereaved widower. If they are able to use your leave of absence against you in court— perhaps to imply you might have been incompetent on the day you treated your sister, as well—"

"But that isn't fair. I'm not incompetent, I'm—"

"Please, Dr. Allison, I understand that. They will, too, but they will turn it against you in every way they can. Unfortunately Warden's attorneys have some finely honed abilities."

"Kirk plays golf with several attorneys on Friday mornings," Cheyenne said. "He's been a plaintiff once before in a malpractice case. He's highly litigious."

"I gathered that," Ed said. "You know, of course, not to discuss the situation with anyone besides your attorneys and Larry. In particular, don't discuss it with the husband of the deceased, or his attorneys."

"Please, would you refer to my sister as Susan?"

"Yes, of course. I'm sorry, Dr.—"

"And please call me Cheyenne. Look, Ed, I've read the records. I may be blinded by my emotions right now, but they can't possibly believe I made any mistakes during the resuscitation efforts. As my director pointed out to me, I resorted to extreme measures to save her, and I left nothing out."

"I think you're right," Ed said. "Our focus for now, until both sides have had more time for discovery, will be the medication you gave Mrs. Warden during her first visit to the Emergency Department, earlier in the day."

Cheyenne had expected that. "You're concerned that she wasn't advised properly about the risks of operating a motor vehicle under the effects of the drug."

"I believe that will be Mr. Warden's chief focus. As you can see, his attorneys have already engaged the services of an expert witness."

"I documented my advisory on the medical record. I also warned her repeatedly, as did the nurse, Ardis Dunaway."

"I believe the plaintiff will try to prove you didn't warn her often enough, or take the necessary measures to keep her from driving," Ed said.

"But that isn't true."

"It doesn't matter if it's true or not. What matters is whether or not the plaintiff's attorneys and their paid medical expert can convince the jury to doubt you, and your integrity, in any way. That's their job. For instance, the records show Mr. Warden wasn't called the first time Mrs. Warden was brought in."

"I offered to call him, but Susan asked me not to. Ordinarily I would have called a family member to come and pick her up, but as her sister, I called a taxi to take her home. As a doctor I emphasized her need to not drive under the influence of the drug. Susan said she had an appointment with a client that afternoon, but the client was a neighbor, so Susan could walk there."

There was a knock at the door, and Lisa opened it and

stuck her head inside. "Excuse me, Larry, the lunch you ordered is here."

"Good, thanks. Let them bring it on in." He looked at Ed and Cheyenne. "This promises to be a lengthy session. We'll need something to keep us going. Cheyenne, your director told me you love Kansas City barbecue, so I've taken the liberty of ordering some ribs. Comfort food. I think we could all use it today."

If only food could be a comfort. Cheyenne felt sick. She had been told that being sued for malpractice was a brutal experience, but she'd never realized how devastating it could be. The petition she received from the sheriff had been worded in a way that implied she was totally incompetent, and it struck at the very core of her life.

She looked up as a setting was placed before her, complete with a bib to deflect sauce. Her sister was dead, and she was being held responsible.

As she reached for her plate, she decided to ask for more time off. Right now, this whole city felt like hostile territory.

Chapter Seventeen

It was about an hour before sunset when Cheyenne crested the hill on the quarter-mile driveway to home. She saw a welcome scene as the car coasted down the rocky track. Red and Bertie worked in her garden, while Dane trimmed the hedge around her yard.

Had they somehow sensed her desperate need for friendly faces? From what she'd learned today, everything she had done for Susan the day of her death was open to question, and she could count on being grilled about every word, every action. Kirk and his attorneys were cashing in on Susan's death—apparently that was more important than justice.

Dane gave her a welcoming grin that engaged his whole face as he walked across the yard toward her car. "Red and Bertie are planting more vegetables," he told her when she got out of the vehicle. "I guess you know they'll be forever sorry about the goat attack."

Cheyenne closed the car door, too weary from the drive and the meeting to reply. Her interrogatories lay on the passenger seat of her car. She was tempted to bury them out in the barn lot, or maybe burn them on the front lawn. She was expected to share all vital information about herself with an enemy who could then take that information and figure out a way to use it against her in court—or sell it on the street corner to anyone interested in stealing her professional identity.

Dane walked with her to the front porch, where she slumped on the top step. "Are you okay?"

"I'll be fine." She'd endured the rigors of medical school, internship, residency, just so her career could be ruined by one vindictive person. "Lawsuits are just another fact of a doctor's life. So is death."

He sat down beside her. "Rough day?"

She nodded. "I feel as if I've been stabbed in the back. Instead of taking out the knife and suturing the wound, people are telling me it needs to stay there until a group of people who know nothing about me, and nothing about my job, decide whether to plunge the knife even deeper. Of course, before that happens, someone may just decide to break off the handle and leave the blade in place."

"They're talking about settling out of court?"

She nodded. "It's like admitting I did something I didn't do."

"I'm sorry," he said quietly.

For a moment she was tempted to rest her head on his shoulder and release the tears that had been building all afternoon. Before Susan died, Cheyenne hadn't cried easily. Now it seemed practically anything could move her to tears.

"The hospital's attorneys seem to feel my sister's widower actually has a case against me." She had explained the whole thing to Dane after the sheriff had served her last Friday. "It looks like I'm going to have a big legal battle on my hands unless I can find some way to make my ex-brother-in-law back off, and here I am spouting when I've been told not to talk about the case."

She got up to go inside. Dane followed. From the living room she caught a glimpse of her bedroom, with a bedspread and curtains in pink and cream. Something about the colors soothed her. The kitchen, however, was the room that matched the soft mint-green stains on the tennis shoes and T-shirt she had discarded two days ago. The house still smelled of paint and turpentine. She decided she loved that strong smell. She needed the distraction of the work she was doing on the house right now.

She led the way into the kitchen, reached into the freezer section of the refrigerator and took out the cake Bertie had given her two weeks ago. "Have a seat and rescue me, will you? I need some major help getting this down."

"Say, is that black-walnut cake?"

"Bertie's specialty. I can't eat it all by myself." *Or any of it.*

Dane reached into the cabinet and took out two glasses. He poured some goat milk from the refrigerator.

A few moments later, after the cake had some time to thaw, Cheyenne drew comfort from the domestic act of cutting the cake, setting out dishes and silverware, feeling her cat's sudden presence at her feet. "There's pie, too, if you want some." *Please.*

"You don't have to beg too hard. Bertie's black-walnut desserts are my favorite." He accepted the overly generous piece of cake.

She was apparently the only person in the county who couldn't stand the smell or taste of black walnuts.

She joined him at the table, picking up her glass. She'd learned she loved goat's milk, goat cheese, gooseberry pie and practically every other food offering from the Meyer farm, unless it contained black walnuts. The elderly couple were generous with their gifts to her, and generous with their time. She had never realized how much she would appreciate that.

"So, how can you make the plaintiff back off?" Dane asked.

"I don't think I can." She didn't want to talk about it anymore. "Tell me, do Red and Bertie make a habit of adopting complete strangers?"

He gave her a brief glance, and his expression showed that he understood. "No, they don't have anything to do with the vacationers." He chuckled. "Red fumes constantly in the summertime because the visitors take over his choice fishing places. The island is one of his favorite spots. He likes to row over there and sit on the rocks of the cliffs, soaking in the sunshine to keep his bones from stiffening up. He's been taking Blaze with him lately."

"Red and Blaze," Cheyenne murmured. "What a combination."

"Red gets a kick out of their nicknames. The two of them have been friends ever since Blaze came here."

"Bertie told me about losing their little boy," Cheyenne said. "Maybe Blaze is easing a little of their loss after all these years."

"Could be. He definitely needs a mother, and Bertie's good at mothering the whole town."

"Is Blaze's own mother that bad?"

Dane grimaced and glanced down at the half-eaten cake. "I think in her own way she loves him." He cleared his throat and looked up at Cheyenne. "She's a difficult person to get along with, and she and Blaze have a dysfunctional relationship. She and Blaze's father were divorced when Blaze was a child. Blaze lived with his father, and only saw his mother sporadically."

"Her decision or Blaze's?"

"I believe it was mutual. After his father died, I think she tried, but Blaze has a learning disability, and she didn't seem to be able to deal with it."

"A learning disability?"

"He's dyslexic."

"So? Big deal. I'm dyslexic and it didn't stop me, just slowed me down a little."

He put his fork down. "*You're* dyslexic?"

"That's right. I had a lot of trouble learning to read when I was a kid, but my parents didn't pawn me onto the foster system because they couldn't deal with it. Is there any hope for Blaze and his mother to reconcile?"

"There's always hope. I have to be careful that I don't allow my own prejudices to affect the way I handle the situation."

"How's that?"

"For instance, I feel Blaze receives more attention from us at the ranch, and from Red and Bertie, than he could ever hope to receive from his mother. I also believe he fills a need in Red and Bertie's lives."

Blue nudged Cheyenne's leg for attention, and she pulled him up into her lap, taking comfort from the warmth and softness of his furry little body, the racket of his purr. "Bertie told me their son died forty years ago. It was a long wait to fill the need."

"Did Bertie mention the possibility that if there had been medical help closer to Hideaway, their son might not have died?" Dane asked.

"Medical care isn't miracle care," she said. "Odds are, that long ago, if he didn't make it to the hospital alive, he wouldn't have lived even if there'd been a doctor right here in town."

"What about now?" Dane finished his cake and nudged his plate aside. "As an experienced emergency physician with the right equipment, would you have been able to—"

"Don't even ask, because there's no answer. Besides, I have a job, and it's in Columbia."

"People change jobs all the time."

"Not if they're happy where they are."

"And are you?" he asked.

"This isn't a good time to ask that question."

A soft breeze puffed the new, muted magenta lace curtains away from the kitchen windows. With the breeze came the scent of sweet clover and honeysuckle. Cheyenne breathed deeply. The trees were all green and beautiful, in their full spring array. Walnut, hickory, birch, sassafras, all grew close around the house.

She had to admit she was enjoying this place, in spite of the goats and the bullies and the sick people who could, conceivably, cost her her medical license if she was caught treating them.

"Cheyenne!" came Bertie's excited shout through the open window. "You'd better get out here quick. Red's fixing to ruin a perfectly good tree."

"Don't you know those things are dangerous?" Red's voice drifted past his wife's from somewhere around the side of the house.

Cheyenne looked at Dane as they got up from the table. "Now paradise has dangerous trees?"

He shrugged, apparently mystified. "Let's go see what he's up to. Just remember he's a superstitious old cuss, but please don't laugh at him. It hurts his feelings."

She followed him out the back door. "I gather you know this from personal experience."

"That's right."

They reached the west side of the house to find Red leaning on his hoe, his wrinkled face etched with worry. "You'll be cursed if you let this rotten old tree live." He touched a small cedar tree with the hoe blade. "Ought to let me cut it down for you."

"Oh, Red," Bertie yelled. "Cheyenne doesn't want to hear our old hill wives' tales. She's a sophisticated city girl."

"The curse'll get pretty girls as fast as ugly girls!" he shouted back at his wife, shaking his finger at her. "I seen it happen. You let a cedar tree grow high enough in your front yard to shadow a grave, and someone in the house'll die. Mark my words!"

"Then we don't have anything to worry about," Cheyenne said. "I'm not going to be here long enough for that to happen."

The sudden silence concerned her.

"What'd she say?" Red shouted to his wife.

"Said she's leaving, and it's all your fault for cutting down her trees."

"Bertie!" Cheyenne said. She turned to Dane helplessly.

"Red, this isn't Cheyenne's place," Dane said. "She can't give you permission to cut down a tree."

"I pulled out the weeds in that garden, didn't I? It's the same thing," Red grumbled. "Even worse! Most weeds don't put curses on people."

Curses? Where on earth had he gotten such a crazy idea? "Dane," Cheyenne said softly, "you're the agriculture guy. What would it hurt to let him cut down a sapling?"

"It isn't as if cedars are indigenous to this area. If it makes him feel better, I don't think it's going to hurt the future of Hideaway's ecological health. Just remember, don't laugh at him."

She sighed. "Fine, Red, cut it down."

"What's that?"

"I said cut it down!"

Red's scowl immediately transformed to a pleased grin. He picked up his hoe, nodded to his wife and raised the hoe high in the air.

★ ★ ★

Dane followed Cheyenne back to the house, admiring the glimmer of blue-black highlights in her hair as the sunlight touched it. He found himself more and more intrigued by this woman—and attracted, not only by her appearance, but her actions, her character.

"Cheyenne, are you still leaving at the end of May?"

She strolled ahead of him in silence.

"Cheyenne?"

"I'm thinking."

That could be a good thing.

"Initially, I'd planned to take two months," she said. "But I spoke with my director today, and he told me my shifts for June can easily be covered. After that they'll have access to cheap labor."

"Cheap?"

"Residents. They're always looking for opportunities to moonlight, because they get paid very little during residency training."

Good, then she wasn't leaving right away, after all. Which meant she might still be persuaded that Hideaway could be a decent place to make a living. To make a home.

"Since you're going to be here awhile, would you be interested in spending some one-on-one time with Blaze? He's been talking about getting his driver's license recently, but he can't get a license if he can't read. He needs tutoring."

"Does he agree?"

Dane chuckled. "Yes, but you can imagine how reluctantly. The problem is, there isn't a summer school around close."

"What about his regular teachers?"

"I've already spoken with the staff there." He sighed. "No one wants to tackle it. How did you overcome your own problems with dyslexia?"

"My parents brought a special tutor to our house who worked with me every day for several months. After that she helped me with my regular schoolwork when I needed it."

"Do you remember some of the techniques the teacher used?"

"I remember it all. That was an exciting time in my life."

"Do you mind sharing the knowledge? You get along well with Blaze—"

"I'd be glad to tell *you* what I know, but I'm not a teacher. Tell me more about your boys. How does the ranch run?"

Okay, so she wasn't thrilled about the idea. Time to back off for a minute or two. "They take care of all the work on the ranch, the cattle, hogs, chickens, the hay hauling and gardening, the feeding in the winter."

"Sounds like they keep busy."

"They learn a lot. Those who don't work outside get to help out around the house, with the cooking and down at the general store. We also have a shop where we build furniture, and they've put up several small outbuildings."

"Do you ever have trouble with them?"

"Of course, especially with the new arrivals. Most of the boys I get are either products of broken homes, or their parents were unable to keep them for some reason. Some came directly from an orphanage. At the ranch we try to find a skill or chore they're especially good at, and encourage them at it."

"How do you keep up with it all?"

He hesitated for a moment. "I don't. And I'm glad I'm not responsible for the results," he said quietly. "I pray with them, I work with them on the ranch and I watch them heal. It doesn't happen all at once, and sometimes they take a step forward and two steps back, but I see them change. I see a lot of my prayers for them answered."

"You sound like a person at peace with who you are," she said. "I envy you."

"I'm the one who gains the most benefit working with the boys." He shook his head. "You're good at changing the subject, aren't you? I was hoping you might be willing to work with Blaze during some of your spare time, in exchange for his helping you around here."

"I told you, I'm not a teacher."

"You're a doctor, right? They say the good docs have to be able to teach their patients."

"Who says I'm good?"

"I do. Anyone willing to take an elbow in the eye to help Blaze get away from a bully, and go so far out of her way for one sick elderly man and shell out over a hundred dollars for medicine, is a good doctor."

She reached across the fence rails and plucked another blade of tall grass and rolled it between her fingers until it disintegrated.

"Blaze needs help, Cheyenne," Dane said. "He's smart. He can learn."

"I don't doubt that." She stepped away from him.

"Won't you just think about it?" Dane asked.

"Sure, right. I'll think about it."

He sighed and turned to stare across the lot toward the forest beyond.

"What made you start taking in the boys when you bought your ranch?" she asked. "Was a boys' ranch in your plans when you first came here?"

He shook his head slowly. "I wouldn't call it a plan, exactly. More like a dream. I loved farm life, and in college I majored in agriculture and studied adolescent psych and education, without a real focus on what I wanted to do with such a hodgepodge of training. Several years after graduating, I moved here with my wife and purchased the general store, and everything just fell into place as I went. Well, most things."

"Just like magic," she commented.

"No," he said. "Not magic. The times I tried to take things into my own hands, I made a mess of it. My marriage, for instance. And I blew it big time with one of my kids a few years ago. I don't suppose Bertie mentioned that I spent some time on a boys' ranch when I was a teenager."

She stopped and looked up at him. "You?"

"Up near Saint Louis."

"What happened?"

"I put a man in the hospital." Why was he baring his soul to her this way?

The silence stretched uncomfortably. Dane felt the warmth of embarrassment flush his face.

"How?" she asked.

"I lost my temper and hit him. He was badgering a friend of mine, wouldn't leave him alone, and I socked him in the face. I hit him wrong, broke his nose, there were complications, and he ended up in the hospital."

"Temper problem, huh?"

He cleared his throat and glanced over his shoulder toward the garden. "Looks like Red and Bertie are finished. Want to go join them?"

She turned to look at them. Then she turned back to Dane. "I wouldn't have known you had a temper."

"I've learned to control it. Usually."

"At that other boys' ranch?"

"It was the best thing that could have happened to me." He led the way toward the garden.

"Was the ranch what changed you?"

"Something happened at the ranch that changed me."

"What was that?" she asked.

"There was a counselor there whom all the boys called 'the Jesus freak.' He was a retired science teacher, which surprised me, because I thought anyone who studied science couldn't still believe all that nonsense about God. But this man did." Dane stepped carefully across the garden to inspect the work Red had done. "That man was the best counselor there, because he taught me, and actually convinced me, that I was loved, and that I could be forgiven because Jesus Christ had already paid for my sins when He died on the cross. I could tell that his faith was solid, something to build a life around."

Cheyenne stopped walking. He could feel her growing resistance.

Dane sighed and turned back to her. No smile there, that was for sure. He bent down and absently crumbled a clod of dirt in his fingers. "God's people have a bad reputation, and I can see why."

"You'd better believe it."

He heard the trace of resentment in her voice. "Some people use the name of Christ the same way they use tickets to a movie theater—to gain acceptance where they wouldn't ordinarily be accepted." He stood back up and looked at her. "It's called taking God's name in vain, and they won't always get away with it."

"But in the meantime they'll continue to hurt others."

"It takes time and patience to be able to sort out the good from the bad."

"That might explain some of the things that have happened to me lately—for instance, the lawsuit from a man who claims to be a Christian," Cheyenne said. She glanced toward Red and Bertie, who had their heads together at the other end of the garden. "I'd love to be able to blame my ex-brother-in-law for my sister's death, but I can't. It was what most people would call an act of God. And the deal with the goats the other morning? Another act of God, according to most. There have been times lately when I've actually wondered if He's out to get me."

"He could be."

She blinked up at him. Was that apprehension he saw in her eyes?

"He is a God who pursues, but it isn't to harm you," Dane said. "If you believe He's making Himself known to you, then also believe it's because He wants a relationship with you." *Lord, please don't let me frighten her away.*

"Oh, sure," she said, turning away. "Who wouldn't want a relationship with a God like that." Irony laced her voice as she stepped carefully past the new sprouts. "Disaster after disaster, constant emotional attack from all sides. I lose my sister, I'm forced from my job and I'm being sued. Thanks, but I'll pass."

"Why don't you let me try to put it into perspective?" Dane said, following her. "When you're treating a patient, you're often forced to perform painful procedures, right?"

"I try to be as humane as possible." She kept walking.

"But you can't always be as gentle as you would like."

"No."

"So you can see the necessity of sometimes causing pain to ultimately cause the greater good for the patient."

She stopped at the edge of the garden and turned to him. "How can this kind of pain bring about my greater good?"

"You'll never be able to imagine it until you take that step of faith."

"You mean that step my sister took that forever placed her in subjection to a bully who calls himself a Christian? As I said, I'll pass."

"It doesn't have to be—"

"Dane, forget the song and dance, okay? I've seen the ugly

side of this Christianity you swear is so wonderful. All I see is corruption and injustice."

"That's *all* you see?"

She hesitated. "Okay, I'm sorry," she said softly, looking into his eyes. "That isn't all I see. There are exceptions. A few."

"For now, that's all I ask," he said.

Chapter Eighteen

The next Friday morning, a week after Cheyenne's meeting in Columbia, she pushed up her bedroom window, took a deep breath of sweet country air scented with honeysuckle, and realized she was falling in love with Hideaway. She was helpless against her feelings. Only time would tell if it was a temporary infatuation or the real thing, but she already dreaded the thought of having to return to Columbia when her leave was over.

She'd never before realized it was possible to love a place. Birds serenaded her from every direction, and the sound of their songs seemed to echo from the early morning fog that hovered over the lake. Soon the sun would roll that blanket away, leaving only puffy remnants of moisture across the deep blue sky.

Two days had passed without intrusion except for the occasional motorboat down on the lake, or a jet flying overhead. She still felt an uneasy sense of waiting, as if, any day, she would hear back from Columbia, and the real world would come crashing in on her once again.

As she stepped out onto the front porch, barefoot, wearing a pair of jeans and a T-shirt, she heard the sound of a motor down on the road, past the rise that gave this place its privacy. A few moments later, to her total surprise, Austin Barlow's shiny red truck topped that rise and bounced over the other side, pulling a horse trailer.

What on earth was Austin Barlow doing here with that thing? Especially this early in the morning.

She went inside to put on some tennis shoes, then walked out to meet the truck as it reached the gate. Ramsay sat in the passenger seat.

Father and son both called a cheery greeting as they climbed out of the truck and walked up to meet her.

"Hello, there," Austin said as he extended a hand and took Cheyenne's in a firm shake. Ramsay followed suit, a younger image of his father.

"We've got us a little problem here, and I was wondering if you could help us for a few weeks," Austin said, gesturing for her to follow him. "I found a poor, half-starved, abandoned horse on one of the properties I'm representing in my real estate business."

She wasn't crazy about the little-boy-up-to-something look in his eyes. "How can I help you, and what do you mean by a few weeks?"

"Depends on how long you're planning to stay around. Come on back and look at the critter, Cheyenne."

She hesitated. He couldn't be implying what she thought he was.

Austin went to the back of the trailer, turned and looked at her. "Come on, he won't bite, unless you're a bucket of grain or a piece of grass." He removed his cowboy hat, dusted it off on the side of his well-worn jeans and placed it back on his head.

Reluctantly, Cheyenne joined the mayor and his son.

"He's apparently used to traveling in trailers," Ramsay said, "because he didn't put up any kind of a fuss when we loaded him in here."

"Could be because he's ravenous," Austin said. "We bought some grain, and this big boy ate a full bucket of the stuff, then tried to eat the bucket. It's a sin, I tell you, what people do to animals."

Cheyenne peered into his truck, where she saw two hunting rifles on a rack in the back window.

"Hunting's one thing," he said, following the direction of her gaze. "Kill them quickly and eat the meat. But don't starve them to death."

She glanced through the bars of the trailer and saw a caricature of a horse. A stick figure with enormous eyes. "You're asking me to keep a horse?"

He turned and gestured toward the field in front of the house. "You've got at least thirty acres of good grass growing out here, and no animals to keep it down. Ramsay and I figure you could feed this boy all summer with just a little extra effort."

"But I'm not going to be here all summer."

"We'd provide the grain, of course, if you wouldn't mind feeding some to him every day, give him some fresh water, maybe a kind word or two. That's all he'd need."

"But I won't be here—"

"At least try it for a few days." Ramsay took a rope from the bed of the truck. He pulled open the back gate and slid the iron bars up. "Come here, fella. You're okay now." He climbed into the trailer with the horse.

The dull thud of unshod hooves gave Cheyenne the impression that this was, indeed, a horse stepping out of the trailer. However, that impression was dispelled as the piteous animal stepped to the ground. The droop-eared, hollow-hipped chestnut ignored everyone in favor of the grass he saw a few feet away. He tugged on the rope, nearly jerking Ramsay from his feet in a rush to the food.

Cheyenne blinked at Austin, then at the horse cropping his food with urgent efficiency. No need to buy a new lawn mower.

But what was she thinking? She had no business keeping a horse. "Austin, don't you have a place you can keep him?"

"Not unless you count my backyard."

"We live in town, Cheyenne," Ramsay elaborated.

She glanced at Austin's hat and cowboy boots. "Sorry. What could I have been thinking? Shouldn't you have a vet look at him?"

"I just took him by. Carol checked him out, gave us some supplements and she'll take a look at him in a week and see how he's doing. You're set to go, Cheyenne, if you'll do it."

She strolled over to the pitiful-looking animal and ran a hand over his side. Why hadn't anyone ever warned her Austin Barlow was crazy? There was no way she could keep a horse.

"What's his name?" She knew nothing about horses.

"We haven't named him," Ramsay said. "We just called him fella."

Not exactly the most imaginative people, these Barlows. "You say you'll keep an eye on him?" So maybe Austin wasn't the only crazy person in this pasture. What could she be thinking?

"Of course we will." Austin took the lead rope from his son. "Come on, fella."

It took some effort to convince the horse that he would indeed see food again, but he finally relented to Austin's heroic tug on the rope, perked his ears up slightly and lifted his head.

In that moment, Cheyenne silently gave him his name. Courage. It took courage to leave a sure thing and strike out for better pastures. Courage, or foolishness, and she wanted to be optimistic.

Austin fell into step beside Cheyenne. "Looks like you've done this place some good." His deep-blue gaze scanned the fresh coat of buttery yellow paint on the shutters of the house. "Who'd you hire for the work?"

"I did it myself."

Courage entered the corral eagerly, and his eyes lost some of their dullness when he saw the abundance of grass that had sprouted all along the fence. Austin had difficulty holding on to the rope, and finally he unfastened it from the halter and handed it to Cheyenne.

"He's all yours," Austin said. "I sure appreciate this, and I don't think you'll be sorry. When I was growing up on the farm, I always loved to look out at the horses in our neighbor's pasture. Ramsay or I'll be over every so often to check on him, but you can do the basics yourself, if you want. Remember, plenty of water, plenty of loving care, and he'll be fine. You've got my telephone number, so you can call me on that car phone any time you need me."

She turned and leaned against the rough, gray-brown wooden fence that encircled the corral, watching Courage crop the grass.

As Ramsay wandered over to check the hen and chicks in the wired enclosure beside the coop, Austin joined Cheyenne at the fence. "You do like to keep to yourself, don't you?"

She smiled. "It's what I came here for."

"Usually when someone's been at Hideaway for just a few days, everyone in town knows all about them. You've been here more than a month, and no one knows any more about you than they did at first. You never did take me up on that offer to see a Branson show."

"I've heard there's a lot of traffic there. I haven't been in the mood for traffic lately."

"No need for that, then. We have our own restaurants right here in Hideaway."

She smiled but didn't reply, and he apparently took the hint.

"What brought you out here all alone, anyway, Cheyenne?"

Here we go again. "I wanted a change of pace, some peace and quiet." She hesitated. "Some solitude."

"Change of pace, huh? We've got that, all right. We're about as different here as people can get." He rested his foot on the lowest rail of the fence. "You don't find places like Hideaway very often, with the convenience of a nice general store downtown, a boat dock on the main street and practically all the solitude you want."

"I've noticed people are very caring about their neighbors," she said. "At least I've found it to be true with Red and Bertie Meyer, and Dane Gideon."

Austin's boot shifted on the fence. "You don't go to church anywhere do you?"

"No."

"Come to ours, why don't you? We have a lot of things going on for a small congregation. The church cosponsors the festival and pig races every fall. We raise a lot of money that way, which goes to help several worthy causes."

"Oh? Is the boys' ranch one of them?"

Austin paused. His expression didn't change, but Cheyenne picked up on some sudden discomfort. "Not now," he said softly. "It was at one time, but we had a…a tragedy. We had to part company to keep it from happening again."

"I'm sorry, Austin. I was told about your wife."

"You were? By Dane, I imagine."

"Yes."

"I doubt you got the whole story."

"The whole story?" she said gently.

"The kid who killed my wife put Dane in the hospital."

"He told me."

"And then when it turned out Dane was the only person who could get this kid off the streets, he wouldn't do it. Dane Gideon allowed my wife's killer to go free." His words fell like hard little pebbles into the silence, each word filled with bitterness.

Ramsay glanced up nervously at his dad.

Austin cleared his throat.

"I'm sorry," Cheyenne said. "I shouldn't have brought up the subject."

Austin was silent for a moment, watching the horse crop grass. "Anyway, I didn't come out here to dig up old ghosts or blast Dane. Some folks have mentioned I'm living too much in the past. It's a hard habit to stop."

"So tell me about the festival."

He looked relieved. "We've got local quilting, wood carving, all kinds of crafts on display and for sale. Red and Bertie Meyer bring goat cheese and pies and little statues she makes out of freshwater clamshells and pebbles. My wife and I helped start the festival about fifteen years ago, soon after Ramsay was born. Linea was always really involved in it, usually won the prize for the best painting."

"I'm sure no one can take her place in the community." Cheyenne turned and strolled toward the house. "I've heard Bertie remark on what a fine job you've done with your son."

Austin caught up and walked beside her. "He's a good boy, always has been. He's been through a lot. The church kept us going, even though I was only a casual attender when Linea was alive. The ladies of the church helped out a lot with Ramsay that first year."

"That must have been a horrible time."

"It sticks with a guy, you know? There's always an empty spot, Ramsay not having a mother. Boys need a woman's touch in their lives to keep them civil."

Cheyenne looked up at him. "Ramsay seems very civil to me."

"You can thank the ladies in our church for that."

"So the church ladies don't go out to the ranch anymore?"

"Not after what happened to Linea. We couldn't take the chance."

"But there haven't been any other problems with discipline at the ranch since then?"

He was quiet for a moment. "I can see what you're getting at, Cheyenne."

"What's that?"

"I'm holding a grudge. I'm being spiteful. Other people have told me that, but it wasn't their wife that was killed."

She stepped onto the front porch. "I'm just suggesting that maybe, after seven years, the ranch has proven to be a safe place again. The boys might benefit if they felt more a part of the community." Not that it was any of her business.

"Dane quit taking his boys to our church years ago."

"You mean after your wife's death? Do you blame him?"

There was an awkward hesitation. He tipped his hat back on his head and frowned at her. "You've been talking to Dane a lot about this, haven't you?"

"The subject has come up. I've become acquainted with Blaze."

"I guess it sounds like I'm a bigot, but there's still the issue of vandalism to deal with."

"I thought no one had caught the culprit."

"That's because our sheriff hasn't been looking in the right place, if you ask—"

"Dad." Ramsay came around the side of the house. "I've got to be at school in ten minutes. We'd better get going."

Austin checked his watch. "You're right, we've got to get." He rushed toward the steps, as if relieved to be extricated from a discussion he was sorry he'd started.

"Cheyenne, your water trough has a leak in it," Ramsay said over his shoulder on his way to the truck. "There's a bucket in the barn you could use for watering the horse. The grain's just inside the barn door, and the supplements are beside it, with directions."

The engine roared to life, and they waved as they pulled out.

"You're sure you have everything packed?" Dane's hands squeezed the steering wheel as he and Jinx bumped over the rocky dirt road that led them from the ranch to the highway. "The notebooks Cook gave you, the presents from the boys?"

"I have everything, Dane." Jinx chuckled, and Dane could hear the tension, the way the chuckle was forced a little too fast and hard.

"I love you, kid, you know that." Dane pressed the brake at the stop sign and brought the van to a standstill, checking the rearview mirror to make sure no one would pull up behind him. "Blaze and Willy and Jason bugged me all night last night to let them ride along so they could say goodbye."

"Why didn't you let them?"

Dane glanced sideways at his red-haired eldest, and fought against the overwhelming rush of emotions. "You think they won't try to take advantage of the opportunity to see a grown man cry?"

Jinx forced another chuckle. With his coloring, he had always flushed easily, and now Dane could see the color rise up his neck. When it reached his face, his eyes filled, as if there were some connection between the blood flow to his face and the water flow to his tear ducts. "I'm going to miss you. I'll miss everybody, but you're the one who's always been there. I wish you were my dad."

"Your dad had his own problems. Sometimes that blinds people to reality."

Jinx brushed the tears from his cheeks as his face turned even redder. "It's like you're the dad of my heart, and I had to run away from home to find you."

Dane swallowed. "That won't change. You've got a home here anytime. It isn't as if you'll be so far from us." He pulled out onto the highway to prevent another awkward goodbye scene—there had already been two back at the ranch with various boys.

"You know you don't have to go right now," Dane said. "You could stay at home until school starts."

"I want to earn the extra money."

"You could work at the general store."

"And put old Cecil out of a job? How could I live with myself? Besides, I have a feeling you'll want to bring in another kid before long."

Dane nodded. It was a possibility. Clint had told him last week how much difficulty they were having with an influx of kids in their teens who needed a home.

"Just don't let the new kid share a room with Monte," Jinx said.

"Why not?"

"Because he snores."

"Maybe we should stick Monte in the closet."

"If you do that, Blaze'll wake him up when he sneaks out the window at night."

"What do you mean, Blaze sneaks out the window?" Dane

had an instant vision of Blaze lighting to the ground and finding Austin Barlow and the sheriff waiting to catch him.

Jinx was silent for a moment. Dane glanced at him, saw
him nibbling his lower lip.

"Jinx?"

The kid slumped within the confines of his seat belt. "I saw
him do it a couple of times. I followed him once, all the way
to the barn to check on the kittens you wouldn't allow him
to keep in the house."

"But there were other times, when you didn't follow him?"

"I don't think Blaze is up to anything, if that's what you
mean."

"Just because you didn't catch him doing anything wrong
the night you followed him?"

"No. I think he does it because he's used to having more
freedom. You know, he had a lot of responsibility with his
dad's vet practice. I think the rules at the ranch rub him the
wrong way sometimes."

"You don't think he already has plenty of freedom?" Dane
asked.

"I didn't say that's what *I* thought. I just remember him
muttering about all the rules he had to learn when he came
here. I know he's just sixteen, but a lot of times he acts like
an adult."

"If he's sneaking out at night, he isn't acting like an adult,"
Dane said.

"Dane, is it really that big a deal?"

Dane didn't want it to be, but could he afford to overlook
this? Blaze wasn't his only responsibility. Even with Jinx leaving, there were seven other boys who depended on Dane to
do the right thing, make the right decisions. If he didn't, he
could lose these kids. He couldn't let that happen.

★ ★ ★

Friday afternoon Cheyenne walked the half mile to the Meyers' to give Red a quick checkup. Although his leg had healed well, he continued to have some heart palpitations that concerned her. But she could not persuade him to go to the clinic in Kimberling City.

After still another argument about the evils of modern medicine, she gave up and went to the garden with Bertie to learn how to weed. Three days ago she had tried to weed her own garden, and had yanked out a row of carrots before she realized what she was doing.

Bertie knelt beside Cheyenne and showed her which of the tender green sprouts would someday grace her kitchen table and which would make her sneeze.

"Bertie, you've known Austin Barlow for a lot of years."

"Most of his life."

"I don't suppose you've noticed a certain… I don't know… chip on his shoulder?"

Bertie snorted. "Is there a person alive in the county who ain't noticed?" She tossed a handful of weeds toward the end of the row of carrots. "He's an active mayor, I'll say that for him. Got to admire that in a man who isn't getting paid for what he does."

"So the position is just a power thing with him?"

Bertie stretched and glanced around the garden. "It is, but he don't see it that way. He thinks he's doing his Christian duty interfering in everybody's lives."

Cheyenne picked up some rocks and tossed them out of the garden. "It seems to me people do a lot of things to hurt others, and call it their 'Christian duty.'"

"I know it seems that way sometimes, but don't let all the meanness blind you to the truth. For instance, you're a doctor. You see a whole lot more sick people than most. Still, you don't think, just because you only see them when they're sick, it means everybody in the world is sick. It's just that when a person's sick, his symptoms draw attention. There's a lot of healthy Christian people in the world who don't draw attention to themselves, who just quietly do what they know God wants them to do."

"So you're saying Austin is a sick Christian?"

"Austin's got a lot of fighting to do if he wants to overcome the poison he was born into."

"Poison?" Cheyenne dashed a sheen of perspiration from her forehead. Gardening wasn't as easy as it looked.

"See that patch of earth over there underneath that black-walnut tree?" Bertie said. "Know why we didn't plant anything there?"

"I thought you just wanted to avoid the shade."

"That ain't it. That tree puts off some sort of chemical in the ground that poisons the plants that try to grow around it. You plant anything over there, it'll die. Austin's daddy was that kind of man. He was poison to his family. Austin grew up going to church and calling himself a Christian just because his folks said he was. His daddy was mean and his mama sharp-tongued, and so Austin grew up thinking that was the way all Christians were supposed to behave—all tight-lipped and disapproving and hating anybody who wasn't just like them. What poor little Austin learned about true Christianity could fit on the head of one of those nails Red used to fix your trellis beside the porch."

"But he's a grown man now. He should know better."

Bertie shook her head. "A man don't just automatically learn a lesson he needs to learn, if nobody's willing to show him the truth. I try to do that by loving him and that boy of his, in spite of the things he does sometimes. He's trying, Cheyenne."

Bertie moved on down the row. "I remember one time,

when Austin was only about twelve, I saw him out working in the field by our back pasture. He'd taken his shirt off, and there were several nasty red welts laid across his back, like someone would've done with a razor strap. Now, I know a child's got to be disciplined, but some folks go too far." She shook her head angrily, remembering. "Another time, Red found him hiding out in our tractor shed with half his face black-and-blue, his eye swollen almost completely shut."

Cheyenne gasped. "What did you do?"

"We brought him in the house and asked if he wanted us to help him tell the police about his dad. We told him there wasn't no reason for him to be treated like that."

"Did he agree?"

"Nope. He said that was his daddy, and he just couldn't do anything like that. He must've told his daddy about it, too, because they was real unfriendly to us after that. Even Austin was."

"But why?"

"Family pride, I guess. It don't matter, because I think we might've done a little good, after all. Anyways, we never saw no more bruises on Austin after that, up to and including the day his daddy died, and we've never seen anything on Ramsay that might suggest he's being abused."

"Austin brought me a horse this morning."

"So that was Austin's truck I saw pulling that horse trailer up toward your house. Don't that beat all! Why'd he do that?"

Cheyenne explained about Courage.

"Sounds to me like you need to have a talk with Blaze. He'll know what to do for the horse if anybody does."

"Austin said he would help keep an eye on him."

"Oh, he would, would he?" Bertie glanced over her shoulder at Cheyenne. "I'm surprised Austin Barlow could tell a horse from a mule. You know what it looks like to me? Looks like Austin's more interested in using that horse for an excuse to come out and see you."

Cheyenne chuckled. "You're right. I'll get Blaze to check on Courage."

Bertie paused from her weeding and looked over at Cheyenne. Approval registered in the deep lines of her face. "Blaze'll love nursing a horse back to health. That kid knows something about everything. Pity he can't read." She bent over again.

"Dane mentioned that."

"He can calculate weights and doses in his head, but sit him down with the *Springfield News Leader,* and you've got a grumpy teenager on your hands."

"Dyslexia."

"What?"

"Dyslexia. It's a perception problem. I have it." Cheyenne tossed another handful of weeds to the end of the row.

"So how do you cure Blaze's problem?"

"You don't. You teach him to function in spite of it."

"Who'd do that?" Bertie asked.

"He'd need a tutor, someone who knows how to work with him."

"You mean somebody who knows what's going on in his mind?"

"That's right."

"Somebody like you, then."

Cheyenne sighed. "Yes, I guess so. Somebody like me."

Chapter Nineteen

On Saturday morning the air had lost its chill by the time Dane and Blaze escaped the ranch to haul the heavy trough across the lake on the bass boat. It was the first week of May, and the sun's rays were warm on Dane's bare arms. It was turning out to be a beautiful spring and he felt like bursting into song. He couldn't help wondering how much of that attitude came from the anticipation of seeing Cheyenne Allison again.

He studied the back of Blaze's head, still thinking about Jinx's revelation yesterday. His instincts told him to trust Blaze. So did his heart. But experience had taught him not to always depend on his feelings.

They were halfway across the lake when Blaze pointed toward Cheyenne's place. "See him? She's already got him out."

Up on the small rise to the house, Cheyenne was leading an emaciated chestnut horse to the pasture just above the boat dock. The animal's nose plunged to the ground as soon as they reached the first clump of grass. Obviously, Cheyenne had little control over him.

"I hope she knows not to leave him out there too long," Blaze said.

"I'm sure you'll tell her."

"I wonder why Austin gave the horse to her. Does she know anything about them?"

"She said she didn't, but she acts pretty comfortable with him. She said Ramsay was with Austin when they brought the horse." Dane hesitated. "I haven't seen Ramsay around much lately. Did you two have a falling-out?"

Blaze looked around at him. "I think his dad found out we were hanging together and got onto him."

"Did Ramsay tell you that?"

Blaze shook his head and turned back to look at the horse.

"Blaze."

"Yeah?"

"What do you do at night when you sneak out the hallway window upstairs?"

Blaze's expression when he turned back around was almost comical. And very guilty. "You saw me do it?"

"No. You're lucky you haven't broken the limbs on that tree—or some of your own limbs."

"I'm not doing anything wrong, Dane. Honest."

"Then why sneak out?"

"I like to check on the animals at night, and then I like to sit out on the dock, and if I say something about it you'll either tell me I can't go or somebody will need to come with me."

"You know the rules."

"But I didn't do—"

"Three strikes and you're out."

"Fine," Blaze muttered. "That's just fine."

"I don't like it, but you know I can't make exceptions."

Blaze cast a resentful glare over his shoulder. "I'm not sure but what you're just looking for a reason—"

"Stop it. You know better." That stung.

They approached the dock, and Blaze jumped out of the boat and tied the rope around the post. Without speaking or looking at Dane, he reached for one end of the trough while Dane lifted the other. Together, in uncomfortable silence, they carried the water trough up the hill.

Cheyenne saw them and left the horse munching contentedly as she strolled toward them. She wore denim cutoffs, a tank top and tennis shoes without socks. Her glossy black hair was tousled around her face, and she wore no makeup. She looked great. Dane tried to imagine her wearing a set of scrubs and a doctor's lab coat. Somehow, the image didn't fit.

"Thanks for bringing that, guys," she said, coming toward them. "I've already had to refill the bucket for Courage at least eight times. He keeps kicking it over."

"I thought we'd let Blaze have a look at him," Dane said.

Blaze gave an impolite snort. "Better not trust me alone with him," he muttered.

Cheyenne gave him a curious look as she rushed ahead of them to open the corral gate. "What's eating you?"

Blaze jerked his head toward Dane. "Ask him, he's got the rule book."

They carried the trough to the corral, removed the leaky trough and set theirs beneath the hydrant at the corner of the barn.

Blaze turned on the faucet, then pivoted and saluted Dane in a poor imitation of a soldier. "Guess I'd better ask permission to go check on that horse, sir."

"Permission granted."

Blaze saluted again, then leaped the fence like an agile cat and whistled to the scrawny animal. Dane watched him leave, and sighed.

"What was that all about?" Cheyenne asked.

"He's pouting over the rules." Dane watched Blaze walk around the side of the house and out of sight. "We have a lot of them, and one has to do with curfew. He apparently had a lot of freedom and responsibility from an early age, and he's chaffing."

"I'd say. I've never been great about following the rules myself, but I can understand why you need them."

"Thanks. I'm glad someone does. Sometimes I wonder if I'm being too strict."

She touched his arm. "Do you have a habit of worrying too much?"

"How could you tell?"

"I've seen that look in the mirror a few times. I'll tell you what I tell myself—stop it. It'll age you fast. While Blaze is making friends with Courage, how about a piece of gooseberry pie?"

"Bertie's?"

"Mine."

"Lead the way."

"I'm warning you," she said as he held the corral gate open for her, then closed it and followed her to the house, "it's the first pie I ever made, and I'm not known for my culinary abilities."

"What a shame. You mean you wasted all that spare time during medical school and you never learned how to bake?"

"I could do a cake mix, and I learned how to pick up the phone and order a great pizza."

In the kitchen, Cheyenne took a pie out of the refrigerator and cut a wedge of flaky crust filled with green, tart-sweet gooseberry filling. "Bertie helped me with it. She said it was almost as good as hers."

"Bertie never lies." Dane took the pie and pulled a chair out for her.

"She might exaggerate a little." Cheyenne sat down and leaned back. "I want to watch your face when you take your first bite."

Dane obliged, and was pleasantly surprised. "Your first pie, huh? You know, if you decided to change professions, maybe you'd be interested in opening a bakery in the little shop next to the general store." For that matter, she could open that shop anyway, and treat patients instead of selling pies. It would be a whole lot healthier for everyone, and a whole lot more rewarding for her, if she'd be willing to do it.

"I'm glad you like it." Cheyenne leaned her elbows against the table. "I remember one time, when I was about fourteen, when my cooking efforts ruined a whole weekend. I'd been invited to a bunking party by some girls at school, and I was so thrilled about it that I rushed straight home Friday afternoon and decided to bake some cookies for the party." She shook her head. "I didn't get invited to a lot of parties, so this was special. I got the recipe out for my favorite oatmeal-raisin cookies and tried to make them myself."

"What happened?"

"It took me so long that I just barely had time to get ready to go, and I didn't have time to taste the cookies. But the girls at the party tasted them, and those cookies were awful. I'd misread the instructions, cooked them too long, and they were so hard we could barely bite into them. And they were too salty. The girls all got a good laugh out of it."

"What did you do?" Dane asked quietly.

She got up and covered the pie, set it in the refrigerator and sat back down. "I walked home, and took my cookies with me. I never told my parents about it, but that was when I finally decided to learn to read as well as anyone else."

"You've improved since then, obviously."

"That tutor I told you about made a world of difference

to me. She helped me see letters in a way that made sense. I'm not a teacher, but I still remember the things that helped me." She glanced out the window toward the corral. "I have a feeling Blaze might want to spend some time over here for the next few weeks. What could it hurt to try a few simple exercises with him?"

"Exercises?" Dane could have hugged her. "You want to help him learn to read?"

"I'll try. What worked for me might work for him. Recalling that one baking incident when I was a kid helped clarify Blaze's situation for me. Isn't it strange what we remember about our childhoods?"

"Not strange. I think it tells us a lot about ourselves, why we react to particular circumstances in particular ways." He finished the last bite of pie and carried his plate and fork to the sink, then sat down again. "For instance, I was raised in the city and I hated it, so every chance I had to be in the country, I went. I've loved farm life ever since. How about you?"

"I'm not sure you would call this place a farm," she said.

"Did I mention that I had considered trying to buy this place before I bought the ranch?"

"What changed your mind?"

"I wanted more acreage to grow hay and graze cattle."

She rested her arms on the table. "I love it here. I've never seen so many wildflowers in one field. I've identified them, too. Daisies, yellow clover, spring cress, fire pink."

She loved it here. He resisted the urge to leap on that statement and run with it. Still… "If you don't mind my saying so, you seem a lot more relaxed and at peace than you did when you first arrived."

Her dark eyebrows drew together quizzically. "That's not exactly a stretch. It just means I haven't maced you recently."

"And I appreciate that. So tell me more about how you inherited Courage."

"I didn't. Austin found him starving on a property he's selling and thought this would be a good place to fatten him up."

"So he's Austin's horse?" It sounded to Dane like he wasn't the only one who was hoping Cheyenne might stay around a little longer. "And he's paying you for the use of your pasture and your time?"

"I don't think so. We didn't discuss it."

The cheapskate. "In that case, I don't suppose you'd mind if we brought a load of cattle over to graze." He couldn't help himself.

She had a smile that engaged her whole face and made her look barely older than Blaze. Dane had been captivated by it the first time he'd seen it. He only wished he could see it more often.

There was a loud knock on the screen door behind them. "There you are," Blaze said as he opened it and came inside. "Cheyenne, you got a currycomb or a brush around here anywhere?"

Dane couldn't help noticing that Blaze was apparently still pouting.

"Not unless there's one in the barn I haven't found," Cheyenne said. "Would you like a piece of gooseberry pie and some milk?"

"Bertie's pie?"

Cheyenne's lips twitched in mock exasperation. "No. Mine."

"Blaze, meet your new tutor," Dane said.

Cheyenne gasped audibly. "You don't believe in thinking things over, do you?"

"No thinking to it. I don't turn down offers as good as yours."

"What do you mean, she's my tutor?" Blaze asked.

"Have some pie and we'll talk about it," she said.

"You say you baked it?" Blaze asked.

"Yes, and it won't poison you."

He pulled a chair out and sat down, giving Dane a side-long glance.

Cheyenne served the pie. "You want to learn to read, don't you, Blaze?"

"I thought you were a doctor."

"I'm on leave, remember? This will be a definite change of pace for me."

"Well, I've dealt with a few teachers in my time." Blaze tilted his chair backward and folded his arms across his chest. "So what've you got they haven't got?"

"Dyslexia. Please don't abuse the furniture, you big brute."

Blaze grinned suddenly and straightened his chair. "You're kidding. You've got this, too?"

"I would appreciate it if you would help me around the farm when you come, like taking care of Courage, keeping the weeds down, painting the barn. I'll pay you, of course."

Blaze picked up his fork. "Tell you what, if one dyslexic can teach another dyslexic to read, you won't have to pay me a thing."

"It's a deal."

Blaze took a long swallow of milk and glanced hesitantly at Dane again, as if maybe he regretted his little digs earlier. He set his glass back on the table. "Just do one thing for me, okay? Don't tell anybody about this."

"Why not?" Dane asked.

"Because if it won't work, I don't want to be embarrassed in front of my friends."

Cheyenne shrugged. "Fine with me. That'll take the pressure off both of us."

"Hey, you two," Dane protested. "I want you to put some effort into this."

"I'll do my best," Cheyenne assured him, "but I won't beg Blaze to listen, and I certainly can't bully him into it."

Dane raised his eyebrows at Blaze. "Well?"

"You know I can't make any promises."

"But you'll try?"

"Sure I'll try, but I've tried before, and after all these years you'd think something would sink in. It hasn't."

"Why don't you come back this afternoon?" Cheyenne suggested. "If it seems to be working out, then we can plan a schedule."

Blaze's expression softened as he glanced at Dane again. "Would that be okay with you?"

"I think it would be great."

Cheyenne watched the bass boat leave the dock, then turned around in time to see Austin's pickup truck—minus the trailer—coming downhill along her driveway. Just like yesterday, Ramsay was in the passenger seat. As Austin pulled to a stop beside her on the drive, father and son gave her a half wave and a nod in mirror-image motion.

"Guess what we've got for you, Cheyenne," Austin said through the open window.

"Water trough," Ramsay told her before she had a chance to guess. "Dad felt sorry for you having to keep that bucket filled, so—"

"Thanks, but I don't need a trough," Cheyenne said.

They both fell silent for at least three full seconds.

"Oh, no, don't tell me you already went out and bought one," Austin said. "If you did, I know you can get your money back."

"Where's Fella?" Ramsay asked.

"I've renamed him Courage, and he's out in the corral," she said. "Why don't you go visit him? Thanks for the trough, but I didn't pay for the one that's out there, some neighbors brought it by."

As Ramsay went to see the horse, Austin put his truck into park and switched off the ignition. He reached for his ever present cowboy hat and got out. "Couldn't have been Red and Bertie who brought it. I can't see them hauling a heavy—"

"Dane and Blaze just brought it over a few minutes ago," she said. She pretended not to notice Austin's sudden grimace, which looked very much to her like offended pride. "Too bad you didn't come a little sooner, you'd have met them as they left."

"Yep. Too bad." Heavy sarcasm.

"Then you and Dane could have had a boxing match on my front yard, and maybe gotten this seven-year feud out of your systems."

He scowled at her. "I said I'd be out to help take care of fella."

"His name's Courage now," she reminded him. "Did you know Gavin Farmer's father was a veterinarian? I wanted to give the boy an opportunity to work with Courage, and since I'm new here and don't know any better, I thought it would be a good idea." She could dish out the sarcasm, too.

"What's the kid doing here in Hideaway instead of back home with his father?"

"His father died last year," she said quietly. "You and your son aren't the only ones with pain in your past, Austin."

He cleared his throat and strolled to the lilac bush at the corner of the yard. For a moment he stared out across the lake, arms crossed over his chest. When he turned and walked back the scowl was gone.

"I'm sorry. I guess, to an outsider, it must look like I'm trying to carry on a seven-year feud with the ranch. I'd like to think I'm being a little more noble than that."

"Of course you would."

"I didn't just come to bring you that trough. I came to ask you a question and tell you about a rumor making the rounds in town."

"I thought you said yesterday you hadn't heard much about me in Hideaway."

"I heard this last night down at the Lakeside Restaurant."

"What's the question?"

Austin hesitated. "Don't you care about the rumor?"

"Not particularly."

Austin hesitated. "Are you a doctor?"

"Is that the rumor or the question?"

He jerked his hat off, rubbed his head, shoved the hat back. She suppressed a grin.

"A simple question," he said. "That's all. I was just curious about your occupation."

"Well, it isn't that simple, really. If I were a teacher or a doughnut maker or a computer operator, no one would expect me to be on duty twenty-four hours a day, seven days a week. But when you throw a doctor into the mix, everything changes. That's when complete strangers come up to you in the grocery store and take off their shoes to show you their ingrown toenails."

"So you are a doctor."

She shook her head. He wasn't getting the point. "Okay, what's the rumor?"

"I heard you're treating Red Meyer and the ranch boys."

"You heard wrong."

"I got the information from a good source."

"Doesn't sound so good to me." Glueing Blaze's scalp wound to help stop the bleeding wouldn't have been considered a comprehensive treatment plan, and writing a script for Red's cellulitis was an act of desperation because the old coot was so stubborn.

None of those things meant she was "treating" Red or the kids. Besides, if she *were* treating them, this would be a case of doctor-patient confidentiality.

Ramsay returned to the truck. "He looks happy here, Cheyenne. Dad, did you ask her?"

"Never mind." Austin climbed back into the truck. "I meant what I said about keeping an eye on the horse, Cheyenne. I'm not the kind of man to ask someone else to do his work for him. I'll be back around."

Cheyenne had a copy of the local weekly news in her hand when Blaze arrived that afternoon. "Show me what you can do, then we'll get to work on what you can't do."

"Dane tried this."

"I'm going to get tired of hearing you say that before we're finished. I'm not trying to teach you right now, I'm trying to learn from *you* how to teach you, so humor me."

Blaze sat down on the porch steps. "Crazy Columbian."

"Right. Now, read."

He spread the paper out before him. "Says here, 'Tonya Whittaker and Jerry Fulp were united in holy matrimony on—'"

"No good."

Blaze grimaced. "Why not? I'm telling you what it says."

"You're telling me what the picture says. I shouldn't have picked a local paper." Reading pictures had been one of Cheyenne's favorite ways to keep people from knowing she couldn't read the print.

"I bet you've fooled a lot of people that way," she told Blaze.

"Almost fooled Dane, but he caught on soon enough. Not as soon as you, though."

"Maybe I'm better than you thought. Now read this article here." She pointed at a paragraph without pictures.

"Tonya and Jerry are too young to get married. They're both still in high school."

"I'm sorry about that. Read."

"I heard tell Tonya was in the family way."

"It happens. Read."

Blaze tapped his fingers against the paper. "Don't you care that two kids may be ruining their lives?"

"Right now I'm concerned about your life, which may be shorter than you think. Read, Blaze."

Blaze grinned broadly as he sat back down. "See why my teachers hated me?"

"Of course. Read."

His smile died. "I can't read. Don't you hear what I'm telling you? I can't."

"Do you know your ABC's?"

"Sure, I know the song by heart. Want me to sing it?"

"I want you to write it." She pulled out a pencil and note pad she had stacked with the newspaper. "Make an *a* for me."

His lips tightened. "I hate this."

She waited.

He fumbled with his pencil a moment, then wrote a backward *a*. "See what I mean? I can't write. The letters won't work for me." He threw down the pencil and notepad and stood up to pace across the yard. "You should be proud. You got more out of me than most does."

"More than most *do,* and stop trying to play stupid with me."

"Do you ever get over dyslexia?" he asked.

"Maybe not completely. I still have problems with left and right coordination."

"You still have trouble? Old as you are?"

"Watch it."

"Sorry."

"Usually I stay in control. When I'm stressed and in a hurry, letters come out funny, and my director complains all the time about my bad handwriting."

Blaze shook his head. "I can't see myself being able to read enough to go to college. I can't even see graduating high school, but I've got to get my driver's license. Why are you wanting to do this for me? I'm not the only dyslexic in the world, you know."

"But you're the only one in my world right now."

He was silent for a moment. "When do we get started on the real stuff?"

"Come with me to the barn."

She had found a few carpentry tools last week, stacked in a box in the corner of the barn. This afternoon, while she waited for Blaze to arrive, she had spread the tools out on a makeshift table she had built of plywood atop two sawhorses.

As she opened the barn's great central doors and pulled them back to allow the sunlight in, she saw the look of mystification on Blaze's face.

"We're going to build the alphabet," she said.

Blaze went immediately to the saw, hammer and nails on a rickety table. He strode over to a small stack of various sizes of wood and picked up a two-by-four. "How did you know I like to build things?"

"Red mentioned it a couple of times. We're going to go through the alphabet, one letter at a time, upper and lower case."

Blaze put down the two-by-four and picked up the saw.

"We'll start with the letter *A*. I'll go get a pencil." She started toward the house.

"Cheyenne."

"Yes?" She turned back.

Blaze watched her for a moment, looked away, cleared his throat. "Do you ever… I mean…what do you think about God?"

"God?" Why was that subject always coming up lately?

"Yeah. Do you believe in God?"

She ambled back toward him. Since she'd railed at God that day on her roof, she'd realized that she did believe he existed, but she wasn't sure she wanted to explore the subject. She still doubted the benevolence of this Deity, and her feelings toward Him were not exactly benevolent, either.

"Do you?" she asked.

"I believe because Dad did. This past year it's been hard for me to even think about stuff like that, though, because I get so…mad."

"At God?"

"Yeah. Not just God, though. It seems I get mad at everybody lately."

"I know that feeling, too."

"Dane told me the other day he was praying that I would learn to read."

"Do you think his prayer will be answered?"

"Maybe. If it is, that means you're part of God's answer."

Some lines she'd learned in Sunday School years ago suddenly came into Cheyenne's mind; "God moves in a mysterious way, His wonders to perform."

Chapter Twenty

After completing the interrogatories and returning them to Columbia, Cheyenne heard no more word about the lawsuit. She wasn't naive enough to think the case was forgotten, but she liked to believe she had recovered from the shock of it. The nightmares were less frequent. If she could just remain in this place, in this little space of time, life would be good. She had plenty to keep her occupied here.

While the buds of May bloomed into the lush green of June, Blaze proved to be a faithful student. As every day passed, Cheyenne felt the joy of watching him learn, and experienced, vicariously, the excitement of seeing a whole world of possibilities develop. When school ended for the summer, Blaze increased his time at Cheyenne's.

On the second Tuesday in June, he arrived later than usual, after a long weekend break. When he stepped on to the porch, the first thing Cheyenne noticed was that his black hair had been cut to within an inch of his scalp.

She pushed open the screen door and stepped out. "Blaze! You cut your dreadlocks off?"

There was no answering grin, no greeting. He didn't even look at her, but turned and slumped onto the top step of the porch. "Cheyenne, I thought you said I was doing good." There was accusation in his tone.

"You are. You're doing great. What does that have to do with your hair?" She sat down beside him and put a hand on his arm. He'd loved those dreadlocks.

He drew away. "I thought I was doing everything right," he said. "I even had Dane get a copy of my birth certificate, and I was studying the manual and I got all the hair cut off so I wouldn't scare the people at the Motor Vehicle—"

"You went to get your driver's license?" *Oh, no, Blaze. Too soon. Far too soon.* "Why didn't you tell me what you were planning?"

"Same reason we don't tell people what I'm doing here."

"But why keep it from *me?*"

"Because you would have told me not to go yet."

"You'd better believe it."

His thick brows drew together. He looked down at his hands clasped between his knees. "Guess you would've been right. I would've passed the driving test fine, but I flunked the written before I could show them what I could do."

"Dane took you?"

"He told me not to do it, but he took me when I asked."

"Why didn't he tell me about it?"

"I told him not to."

"You froze up?"

"Okay, yeah, I froze up," he muttered. "So rub it in. How much longer are you going to stick around Hideaway?"

"I'm scheduled to go back to work in July." The thought

of returning to Columbia depressed her, but she couldn't just hide out here forever. "I have the rest of this month."

Blaze groaned and closed his eyes. "That only gives us a couple more weeks."

"You have the rest of your life. You don't need me in order to learn."

"Want to bet? Why didn't I learn to read until you came along?"

"Blaze, it isn't as if I'm a lucky rabbit's foot. You've broken through some kind of barrier, and you can do it yourself now. Let's make the most of the time we have left. Did you bring your manual?"

He shook his head. "There's another reason I think I flunked."

"What's that?"

"My mother drove up to see me Sunday night, interrupted my study time."

"She did? Were you happy to see her?"

He gave a soft snort. "Sure. You know, she has this special little tone in her voice when she asks me what my grades are in school."

"She drove all the way to the ranch to ask you about your grades?"

"She wanted to apologize."

"For what?"

"For sending me away."

Cheyenne studied his impassive expression. "Something tells me you didn't forgive her."

"I told her I was happy here, and it was the best thing that could have happened to me. I want to stay here where I belong. Dane needs me on the ranch."

"Yes, but your own mother—"

"Don't even say it. Oh, hey, I brought you something." He

reached into the back pocket of his jeans. "Cecil called from the general store this morning, said a guy named Larry Strong wants you to call him." He pulled a note from his pocket and handed it to her. "Dane wrote it all down."

She looked at the note in his hand, recognized Dane's bold cursive. She didn't want to read what it said.

"Go ahead, it won't bite. All it says is for you to call this Larry dude."

Apparently, the legal process was still in motion. Her idyllic interlude was coming to a close more swiftly than she had expected. That queasy feeling stole through her with familiar swiftness.

"Dane said he'll be over later with that paint you wanted for the kitchen cabinets." Blaze stood and strolled across the yard. "Want to tell me something? How come you're trying to fix up this house when you aren't going to live here? And why are you seeing Dane and Austin both, when you don't act like you're going to get close to either one of them—not that I think you should be friends with Austin, anyway."

"I'm painting the house for my own personal satisfaction, and because it belongs to a good friend who has allowed me to stay here for free." It also helped her feel close to Susan. Cheyenne knew she didn't have the creative flair her sister did, but after working with her on days off, she had picked up a basic feel for her own color preferences and combinations.

"And Dane?" Blaze asked.

"What about Dane?"

"And Austin?"

"He comes out here to check on Courage. Period."

"Might be period to you, but it probably isn't to him."

"Let's get to work. I'll call Columbia while you're practicing." She stood up and headed for the barn.

"Hold it," Blaze said, catching up with her. "You didn't say anything about Dane."

"There's nothing to say. We're friends who come from two completely different worlds." She had enjoyed Dane's company, and she was pretty sure he enjoyed hers. They had developed such a comfortable relationship in the past few weeks that there were times he could complete her sentences, and she his.

"I guess your friends in Columbia miss you," Blaze said, stepping ahead of her to open the barn door.

Her friends in Columbia? Ardis had a husband and three grown kids. Jim and Louise kept busy with soccer practice and church activities and work. It was the same with her friends from outside the hospital. They might miss her, but she knew there was no empty spot in their lives because she was gone.

"I guess they do," she said. "Let's get to work."

On Wednesday morning at ten o'clock, barely twenty-four hours after calling Larry Strong, Cheyenne found herself once more in Columbia.

As soon as she walked into the conference room with Larry, she saw bald-headed Ed Burdock sitting at the end of the long, mahogany table, with papers spread around him in neat stacks.

He stood as she entered, shook her hand, and smiled while conveying a sense of gravity. She felt immediately on edge.

"We're continuing with the discovery process," Larry told her as she sat in the chair he held out for her. "Mr. Warden's attorneys are pushing for a deposition date."

"First," Ed said, "has anyone claiming to be a representative of the hospital, or of my law firm, contacted you in any way?"

"No."

"Good. If anyone does so in the future, I want you to call Larry or me before you talk to them. You have the card with my number on it?"

"Yes."

"Good. Second, do you wish to obtain legal defense of your own choosing, at your own expense?"

Cheyenne couldn't conceal her surprise. "Why would I want to do that?"

The two men exchanged a quick glance.

"What's going on?" Cheyenne asked.

"You need to keep in mind that I've been retained by the hospital to represent you," Ed said. "If the hospital decides the most expedient avenue of action is a settlement, then we will attempt to settle. If you disagree, you might want your own attorney on board at that time, but I must warn you that you would then assume the risk."

"Meaning I won't be covered," she said.

"Yes, I'm sorry."

"So if they do convince the jury on a multimillion-dollar decision, I pay it myself."

"Remember a majority of cases are settled before trial, due to the exorbitant cost."

"I understand that, but I'm not guilty of malpractice. I don't want to settle."

"We'll continue to prepare," Ed assured her. "But you do need to keep in mind that it's a knee-jerk reaction for a jury to decide for the plaintiff if there's been loss of life."

"But won't they see—"

"Mr. Warden's attorneys will make sure there are no physicians, and no family members of physicians, on the jury. They'll play hard on the jury's sympathy. There are hundreds of ways to make you look bad—what you say will only account for about twenty percent of the final decision."

"So you're saying the truth doesn't mean diddly-squat?" She detested this whole process.

"It always depends on the insight of the jury, of course," Ed said, "but this is a gamble for both sides."

"I'm sorry, Cheyenne," Larry added, "but the first priority of the hospital will be to keep costs down as much as possible so we can stay open and keep treating patients. With the health-care crisis we have on our hands, that's getting harder and harder to do."

Cheyenne closed her eyes and sat back for a moment. "But with this case there's an extenuating circumstance," she said quietly. "Susan was my sister. If the jury is going to decide with their emotions, then my relationship with the patient should carry some weight."

"We've already made sure the plaintiff's attorneys are aware of that," Ed said.

"So let's get started on preparation." Larry opened a notebook. "We believe Mr. Warden and his attorneys will focus on the fact that you failed to warn Susan about the danger of driving under the influence of the drug, so we'll focus on that today. However, you need to reacquaint yourself with every aspect of the case, every word spoken, every procedure undertaken."

Cheyenne placed her arms on the table and leaned forward. "I've had nightmares about that day ever since it happened. I've gone over and over every little thing in my mind."

"Do it again," Ed said.

This was going to be a long meeting.

Cheyenne was still smarting when she drove away from the hospital. Larry and Ed had both assured her this happened to the best physicians in the city, and if she continued working in the ER, sooner or later she could probably count on another lawsuit or two during her career.

Depressing.

She took Providence south to Nifong in the extreme southwest section of Columbia. For the first time since Susan's death, Cheyenne approached the exclusive subdivision where Susan and Kirk had moved three years ago. She turned onto Red Cedar Circle and cruised past the huge, three-car garage, two story brick house where Susan once lived.

Cheyenne had spent a lot of hours in that house when she'd helped Susan choose flooring and wallpaper, select fixtures. Susan had taught her a few new methods of texture painting, which she had found, to her relief, could be easily painted over when she became a little too enthusiastic with the brush.

Susan's spirited personality was reflected within the walls of that house, and Cheyenne longed to stroll through it again, remembering.

When Susan had completed her work in the house, she'd used it as a showroom to display her talents. She had received so many new clients from the neighborhood and her church community that she had remained busy without advertising until the day of her death.

Cheyenne parked half a block from the house, and walked to the front door. She steeled herself and rang the doorbell. It was after Susan and Kirk moved here that Cheyenne noticed a growing tension in their relationship, and an increased hostility from Kirk.

It was also here that she and Susan began compiling a family album with pictures of their childhood.

When the door opened, Cheyenne braced herself. Kirk's tall form and broad shoulders shadowed the entryway. The squared features of his handsome face froze in momentary surprise, and then his gray eyes hardened.

"Hello, Kirk."

"What are you doing here?" His voice held all the venom she remembered from the funeral.

"I came to pick up the family album Susan and I were working on before she died." Cheyenne didn't ask to be invited in.

"You don't have any right to be here." He stepped back and started to close the door.

With a rush of frustration, she took a step forward and shoved it back. "I didn't come here to violate any legal rules, I came here to collect property that belongs to my family. All I want is the album. It has a red cover—"

"There isn't any album here."

"But I left it here the last time Susan and I worked on it. She was going to buy some extra pages and have some old photos—"

"Honey, who is it?" came a feminine voice from somewhere in the house.

Cheyenne caught her breath and blinked up at Kirk.

"My attorneys are going to hear about this," he said as he shoved the door shut.

Cheyenne stood on the bricked front porch, lips parted in astonishment, staring at the wood grain of the front door for a long moment. It wasn't until a car breezed past on the street that she turned and walked away.

The jerk was suing her for pain and suffering and loss of income, and he already had another woman? How long had she been in the picture? It sure didn't take the poor, grieving widower long to overcome his disappointment.

She got into the car and slammed the door, imagining Kirk's head in the way, and then ashamed of herself for the feeling of satisfaction it gave her. As she turned the key in the ignition, she recalled where Susan had said she would be working that afternoon. Three houses to the west.

Two minutes later Cheyenne found herself ringing another

doorbell at another elegant home down the block. A frumpy looking man in a business suit answered, smiling pleasantly.

"Yes, can I help you?"

"Hello, my name is Cheyenne Allison. I'm Susan Warden's sister. I believe she was doing some interior design here."

As she spoke, the man's smile gradually faded.

"The day she died, she mentioned to me that she would be working here," Cheyenne continued. "Is it possible…could I speak to the person who would have been here that day?"

He was shaking his head before she finished. "I'm sorry, my wife isn't home right now." Nothing more. No explanation about why he had suddenly shut down when he discovered who she was. A friend of Kirk's, perhaps?

"Please, if I could just leave a number where your wife could contact me? I just want some idea about what was said during my sister's visit here that day, maybe some idea about why she was driving, what time it might have been when she left here." She jotted the number of the general store in Hideaway, handed him the slip of paper. "She can leave a message and I'll call her back."

He took the slip of paper hastily, then stepped back inside and closed the door.

Stung by his reaction, totally discouraged, Cheyenne returned to her car for the long drive home.

Chapter Twenty-One

A loud thump from upstairs awakened Dane with a jolt. His first thought was that Blaze was sneaking out the upstairs window again. He was pushing the blankets back when he saw an eerie glow outside, and heard another thump.

"Fire!" Someone screamed from upstairs. "There's a fire!"

Dane frantically pulled on his work jeans and shoes and ran from his room across the living room to the front bay window, where he saw flames lick the sky above the barn. Blaze came racing down the stairs, wearing only sweatpants and tennis shoes. He ran past Dane to the back door without stopping.

"Animals!" he called over his shoulder. "We've got to get the animals out of—"

"No, Blaze, get back here!"

Cook tumbled out of his bedroom, pulling on his jeans and shoving on his shoes, nearly colliding with Dane in the back hallway.

"Cook, call the volunteer fire department, and keep the boys in here if you can."

"Where're you going?"

"I've got to get Blaze before he does something stupid."

As he raced out the back door, he caught the stench of smoke and heard a scream piercing the air. The sound shot through his whole body.

"Blaze!" *Oh, God, no, please don't let it be,* he prayed as he ran downhill toward the fiery inferno. The scream grew louder, splitting the sky with agony as it plunged through the darkness.

Blue's familiar feline growl dragged at Cheyenne's consciousness until the darkness of sleep retreated. She opened her eyes to a faint, eerie glow that seemed to fill the room.

Dreaming. She was dreaming. She closed her eyes and tried to recapture the peace of a dreamless sleep.

Blue's sharp claws, barely unsheathed, scraped against her left arm and brought her sitting up in bed.

"What is it, Blue?" she whispered, frowning at the strange, yellow-orange glow of light against the wall. She glanced toward the window as the warm memory of sleep vanished. "What's going on?"

The cat leaped to the floor and ran crying into the back room. Cheyenne leaned across the bed and peered out the window. She saw the flames across the lake and caught a whiff of smoke at the same moment.

"A fire...the ranch!"

She threw the blankets back and leaped from bed, grabbed her clothes and pulled them on. Was it the house? An outbuilding?

She found her car keys and ran to the car to call for help, then grabbed her first aid kit from the trunk of the car and hauled it down to the dock. She leaped into the rowboat and untied the rope. Her movements were awkward, and she backed into a tree stump hidden beneath the water's surface before she could get her bearings. She shoved away from the stump with a paddle, then pushed out into the center of the cove as she grew accustomed to the rhythm of paddling.

Thank goodness Red and Bertie had loaned her this boat.

When she reached the mouth of the cove, she could see the flames more clearly. The smoke nearly choked her. She pulled the neck of her T-shirt up around her nose and mouth and continued to paddle, staring with horror at the flames.

It was then that she heard the scream.

"Blaze!"

The barn door stood open, engulfed by smoke and flames. The panicked cry of a calf reached Dane from the corral to his left, and then he heard the sweet sound of Blaze's voice.

"Get out! Go!" The gate swung open and Starface came trotting toward Dane, calling for her mother.

"Blaze, get out here now!" Dane shouted.

Blaze retreated back into the barn, toward the flames. There was a crash, and a loud, bright whoosh of fire. Dane ran into the corral. "Blaze, get out of there. Blaze!"

The kid came bursting through the side door with a Holstein calf in his arms. "Get back, Dane! It's okay, this is all the calves we put in last night, but I can't find the white sow."

The scream. "I think I heard her go into the woods."

Blaze set the calf down well away from the fire and smacked her behind to drive her away. "Gordy made her own doorway out the other side of the barn. Come on, let's get out of here before it does something crazy. Where're the guys?"

"In the house."

"We need to be fighting this fire!"

"You need to get some clothes on for protection. If you cut yourself—"

"Aw, Dane—"

"Just do it!" He ran to the water hydrant at the side of the house. "Get into the house and put on a long-sleeved cotton shirt on before you come back outside. Send the other boys out here to me."

Blaze slammed back into the house while Dane connected the garden hose to the hydrant. He would put the boys to work soaking the house and outbuildings to prevent the fire from spreading.

A siren reached him from across the water. It would take the Hideaway Volunteer Fire Department awhile to drive here.

There came a crack of wood and a loud *whoosh,* then smoke and sparks flew toward heaven. Past the barn, Dane saw sparks flicker in the tops of two big oak trees.

"Oh, Lord, please, don't let this thing spread!"

The other side of the lake looked miles away as Cheyenne pushed forward by the light of the moon—and the flames.

The scream continued—not a human sound, but a guttural keening of pain. An animal. The lake was smooth and clear, without a ripple. It gave back an indistinct reflection of flames from the top of the hill at the ranch.

Sirens echoed through the night, at first bouncing across the water in a shriek, then softening as the firemen drove out of town on the circuitous route to the nearest bridge.

As Cheyenne left the moon's glow and entered the shadow of the trees on the ranch side of the lake, ripples from somewhere ahead reached the tip of the rowboat. She looked up in time to see the silhouette of a canoe gliding along the edge of the shoreline. The lone passenger was silent.

She didn't call out as she allowed her boat to drift past the ranch dock.

The animal scream continued to pierce the night, a heavy sound of agony, louder as Cheyenne drew closer to it.

The rowboat grounded in mud and rocks beneath over-hanging trees, and Cheyenne leaped forward awkwardly. Her shoes squished in mud as she stumbled out and flung the paddle into the bottom of the boat, then pulled the boat farther up to keep it from drifting away. She needed to leave room for others who would be coming to help.

She grabbed her heavy first-aid kit and hugged it protectively in her arms as she pressed through overgrown brush, fighting the thorns. If only she'd remembered to bring a flashlight.

The crackle of flames reached her as she stumbled blindly up the hill, and she followed the sound. Along with the acrid burn of smoke in her nostrils.

The brush cleared, and Cheyenne breathlessly stepped out onto an open path that led to the crest of the hill, where the huge barn seemed to dance in the dark with the flames. She rushed along the path toward the house.

Dane came running from the house, followed by five of his boys. "Stay away from the barn!" he told them. "Willy, you grab another garden hose from the garage and hook it to the hydrant at the pump house. Jason, you help him. The barn's lost, guys. We've just got to keep the fire from spreading."

Cheyenne ran up to him. "Is anyone hurt?"

"One animal, can you hear her? The boys are okay, and I intend to keep it that way."

"What can I do to help?"

"Find Blaze. He was here a moment ago, then he disappeared. I couldn't find him in the house. Willy, don't go back into the barn, it could collapse."

"I have to get my calf! I put him in the back stall last night with his mom, and—"

"Blaze said he got all the animals out already, son. Get Tyler and James to help you. We've got the fire department on the way, but until then we've got to make sure nothing else ignites."

Cheyenne entered the house through the back door and found herself in a mudroom filled with boots and coats and a huge, industrial-size deep freeze. "Blaze, are you in here?" she called as she ran through the kitchen—which extended the width of the back of the house. She stepped through a broad entryway into the living room, where she set her kit, the size of a carry-on suitcase, on the coffee table and took the stairs that separated the dining area and living room at the far eastern wall.

"Blaze! Are you here?" she called as she reached the top of the stairs.

There was a clunk, then a scrape of wood against wood above her head. In the attic?

"Blaze!"

More shuffling, the squeak of footsteps on loose floor-boards, then the small door opened to her right and Blaze stepped out, holding a rifle and a box of bullets.

"Blaze, what—"

"Dane's old hunting rifle from the attic." He rushed past her. "I've got to do some hunting."

What on earth was he talking about? *Hunting?* She followed him down the stairs and out the back door, but as he rushed across the lawn into the night, two figures stumbled around the far side of the barn. Dane braced blond-haired Jason, both of them coughing, streaked with soot. Cheyenne ran to them.

"What happened? I thought you weren't going back in the barn."

"Jason was after his calf, just born yesterday," Dane said hoarsely. "I told you to stay away from the barn, but you didn't listen. You could've gotten us both killed."

Hideaway

"Got him and his mama out." Jason coughed again. "Blaze didn't know he was in there."

"Both of you get into the house," Cheyenne said. "I'll check you over. You may need medical treatment, and all I have is my first-aid kit, which won't do much if you've scorched your—"

"Dane!" Cook ran up to them, holding a garden hose spurting water. "Anybody else in that barn?"

"No." Dane caught his breath and nudged Jason toward Cheyenne. "You go with her, and I don't want you stepping foot outside the house again tonight."

"But, Dane—"

"Go. Now! No more warnings."

Jason coughed again. "But Blaze went out, I saw him."

"Blaze is in trouble, too. Get to the house. Cheyenne, check him out, and if he needs to go to an ER, would you arrange it? Cook, you go with them and don't let him out of your sight!"

"I need to check you, too," Cheyenne said. Should she tell him about Blaze?

"Later." Dane turned to shout at the other boys. "Wet down everything, starting with the house. Get the others to help you. The barn's lost, but we may still save the rest." He swung around and grabbed up the shovel he had thrown down earlier.

"Dane, wait," she said. When he turned back to her, she hesitated.

"What is it, Cheyenne?"

She trusted Blaze, and Dane had enough to worry about. "Never mind."

"Hey, Dane!" called a man coming uphill from the boat dock. "Show me how I can help."

Five more people came up behind him, and the sound of sirens reached them, growing louder as the fire trucks drew close. Two pickup trucks pulled into the drive and parked out of the way. Austin Barlow jumped out of his vehicle and reached in the back for a shovel and a water hose, which he looped over his shoulder.

Cheyenne followed Jason and Cook into the house.

"Where'd that Blaze get to?" Cook asked. "Wouldn't put it past that kid to get himself hurt, and him with that bleeding problem."

"I'll go look for him as soon as we get Jason checked out," Cheyenne said as she reached for her kit on the coffee table.

"Won't do any good," Cook said. "If you don't know this place, you could get lost, and that wouldn't be safe out there tonight."

"Okay. Have a seat on the sofa, Jason."

"Say, look at that medical kit you've got there," Cook said as Cheyenne opened the case and reached for her stethoscope, a tongue depressor, and a light. "You a nurse or something?"

She winked at Jason, whose golden-brown eyes had begun to widen with a touch of white-coat phobia she occasionally saw in the ER. "Something. Don't worry, Jason, I'm just going to make sure you didn't get too much of that smoke into your lungs."

"Doctor, then?" Cook asked, leaning closer.

"Cook, would you bring me a wet towel? I'd like to clean off some of this soot and see what's underneath." *And keep you out from underfoot as long as possible.*

"Sure thing." Cook rushed to the kitchen.

The sirens grew louder, lights flashing through the windows until the sound abruptly ended. Doors slammed, men shouted and Jason's attention was distracted away from Cheyenne. She checked his throat and listened to his lungs.

"You're lucky, Jason. You could have done a lot of damage running into the barn like that."

"You mean I'm okay?"

"You'll be fine." She touched his arm. "I need to treat that burn, and I wish I could give you a breathing treatment, but otherwise I think you'll heal." She reached into the kit for some cleaning pads and burn ointment.

"Wasn't much burning out in the back stall." Jason coughed. "Just smoke. I checked to see if the sow and her babies were in their pen, but they weren't. Guess Blaze got them, too."

"Say, Cheyenne," Cook said as he handed her a large bowl with a wet towel in it, "no kidding, are you a doctor?"

She stifled a sigh. "I'm on leave from my job in the ER at Missouri Regional in Columbia. Are you going to look for Blaze?"

"Nope, I need to keep an eye on this live wire," he said, tapping Jason's shoulder. "Tell you what, supervising these kids is like trying to walk on a layer of marbles. They're always going six different directions at one time."

Cheyenne finished bandaging Jason's arm and replaced her supplies, closed the kit and started to lift it down from the table.

"Here, I'll get that," Cook said. "You don't need to be hauling the heavy stuff when there's a man can get it for you."

"You know, Cook, on second thought, why don't we just leave the kit right here on the table?" Cheyenne glanced out the window again, to see another car pull into the drive. The firemen were focusing their attention on the barn and the trees surrounding it. The flames in the treetops had been extinguished.

Cheyenne counted about twenty people milling around at the edge of the yard, shovels useless by their sides. For several moments they stood there, and then a sudden crash sent them rushing backward, while the roof of the barn collapsed, shooting sparks upward. One of the women screamed, a couple of men shouted.

Someone behind Cheyenne sniffed loudly, and she turned to see Jason wiping his eyes. Cook stood beside him with an arm around his shoulder as they both stared outside at the conflagration.

"I can't believe it," Cook murmured.

"What's going to happen now?" Jason asked, wiping at his face again.

"What do you mean? We'll build back," Cook said. "Meanwhile, I have a feeling we'll get some hungry, thirsty firefighters trooping through here in a bit."

Cheyenne followed Cook into the kitchen, knowing it was nervous energy that rushed him through the kitchen, opening cupboard doors and laying food and packets of drink mix on the counter.Willy came stomping through the back door. "Cheyenne! You in here?"

She turned to meet him as he entered the kitchen. "What's wrong?"

"Dane wants to know if you found Blaze. The mayor's out there trying to start another fight."

She followed Willy outside, where Austin and Dane stood in the shadows, voices lowered, words clipped, angry.

"This is getting to be a habit lately," Austin said. "Don't tell me you can't see it, too."

"If you came over here just to point fingers at my boys, you can drive right back to town," Dane snapped.

"There's something bad wrong around here. You've got a kid with a history of arson, and you just keep closing your eyes to it—and your mind. What'll it be next, Dane, the house? With you and some of those kids inside?"

"You're jumping to conclusions again," Dane said. "Gavin Farmer was keeping his racing pigs in that barn. He wouldn't have done it to any animal, but no kid is going to torch a barn and destroy his own project."

Austin yanked his hat off, stalked away, then swung back. "You're going to mess around and get somebody else killed, and you won't—"

"Stop it."

Austin leaned closer. "You don't have the common sense it takes—"

Dane grabbed Austin by the shirt collar. "I said stop it, Austin!"

Surprise froze them into silence. Cheyenne could almost feel the tension as she descended the porch steps toward them.

Dane released Austin and stepped away. "I'm sorry," he said softly.

Austin cleared his throat and glanced toward Cheyenne, then toward the small crowd of onlookers whose focus had switched from the work of the firemen to the show on the lawn.

"I guess it's me who should be sorry." Austin dusted his hat against the leg of his jeans. "Guess I don't know how to pick my moments, do—"

The loud report of a rifle echoed through the air.

"What was that?" Austin asked, shoving his hat back on his head.

A tall human shadow came walking slowly toward them from the direction of the lake. As he drew closer to the light, Cheyenne could see it was Blaze, carrying the rifle.

"Blaze?" Dane called.

"It's me." He wiped quickly at his face. "Did you hear the screaming?"

"I heard. Rosie?"

Blaze stopped, and a sob escaped his throat. "There was no saving her. She was in the stall where the fire was the worst, right in the middle of it. I couldn't let her suffer like that."

"I know you couldn't, son. What about her babies?"

"I put them in the pump house last night because she was getting rambunctious. I thought she might hurt one of them."

There was a tense silence as his words registered.

"You knew they weren't in the barn," Austin said.

Dane sighed heavily. "Better give me the rifle, son."

Blaze took two steps toward them and tripped. There was a loud crack. He jerked, then fell hard on his side and lay silent.

Chapter Twenty-Two

"Blaze?" Dane rushed forward.

"Hold it!" Austin grabbed him by the arm.

"What are you, crazy?" Dane jerked away. "He's been hurt!"

"You're about to get hurt, too." Austin grabbed him again. "Cheyenne, you stay right there. Everybody stay back! Don't you see that electric line? I caught sight of it in the beam of my flashlight. Blaze didn't get shot, he took a hit from that line."

He pulled his flashlight from his rear pocket and aimed it at the pole. A line had fallen across Blaze's path and now lay about a yard from his feet.

"You've got a live wire and wet ground," Austin said. "You can't help him if you're lying there beside him. Tell me where your switch box is and I'll cut the power."

"I'll get it," Dane said. "Cheyenne, get to Blaze as soon as I tell you. Austin, you help her." He ran up the steps and through the back door, yanked open the switch box door in the mudroom and pulled the switch that ran power to the barn. "Okay, it's clear!" he shouted through the open door.

He ran back out and found Cheyenne on her knees beside Blaze, with Austin standing over her holding his flashlight. Cheyenne had turned Blaze onto his back, and was bent forward with her ear close to his mouth, with two fingers on his throat, feeling for the carotid artery.

"He isn't breathing, no pulse!" She looked up at Dane. "He's in full arrest."

Austin pulled out his cell phone. "I'll call 911." He handed his flashlight to Dane. "Here, you hold this for her."

Dane took the light and held it on Blaze's lifeless face while Cheyenne worked over him.

"Somebody get my kit from the living room table, I need my stethoscope," she called over her shoulder as she placed her right elbow in the center of Blaze's abdomen. "Do we have a paramedic here?"

"No," Austin said, then spoke into his phone. "Yes, hello?"

Cheyenne raised her right forearm about a foot, and quickly struck Blaze's chest with her fist.

"What's that for?" Dane asked.

"Precordial thump." She felt again for a pulse at Blaze's throat. "It isn't used much anymore, but I've seen it work in cases like this." She nodded. "Got it."

"Thank God."

"Hold it." She leaned over Blaze's face again. "Dane, do you know how to do rescue breathing?"

"Yes, I've taken a CPR course."

"I may need you to take over." She positioned herself at Blaze's head, cradling his lower jaw with both hands. She lifted slightly, then bent forward and listened, with her cheek next to his mouth.

"Anything?" Dane asked.

She shook her head as she positioned herself closer to Blaze's face. She pinched his nose shut and sealed her mouth over his, gave two slow, deep breaths, then straightened.

Jason brought Cheyenne her stethoscope, and she used it to listen for breath sounds in Blaze's chest. "Still nothing." She breathed for him again.

"I've got the 911 operator holding," Austin said. "What all do I need to tell him?"

"You already told him we have an electric shock victim?"

"That's right. What's his status?"

"He still isn't breathing," she said. "We need the earliest available chopper they can get here." She breathed for Blaze again.

"Okay," Austin said quietly into the phone, "our patient is still not responding to..." He strolled away from them, keeping his voice low.

"Dane," she said, "I'd hoped once I restarted his heart and opened his airway by moving his tongue out of the way, he'd start breathing on his own."

"It hasn't happened?"

She shook her head and pressed her mouth against Blaze's again and breathed for him. "Austin," she called, "we've got to have that chopper as quickly as possible." Two more breaths. "Dane, see if the firemen have oxygen and a bag valve mask in their trucks."

Dane turned to find Cook standing behind him. "Would you do that for me, Cook?"

"I'm on it, boss." He took off through the crowd that had gathered in a group around them.

"Just a moment, please," Austin said over the phone, then stepped back over to Cheyenne. "The guy says the nearest air ambulance is on its way to another call. He can dispatch another one, but it'll be at least twenty-five to thirty minutes en route."

"We need the closest chopper here immediately," Cheyenne said.

Austin relayed the request, listened, then shook his head, grim-faced. "Cheyenne, he says he can't reassign an air ambulance that's on call unless a trained paramedic has assessed the patient."

"Then why did the guy even mention the other chopper?" Cheyenne muttered.

Dane knelt beside her. "I'll take over here. I can do what you're doing. You talk to the dispatcher."

"Okay, just be careful not to move his neck." She stood and took the phone from Austin. "Hello, this is Dr. Cheyenne Allison. I'm not a paramedic, but I'm a specialist in emergency medicine. Our patient was electrocuted approximately five minutes ago. He was in full arrest initially. I did a precordial thump and got a weak pulse, but the patient remains in respiratory arrest, still unresponsive. He is a sixteen-year-old with a history of hemophilia…that's right, he's a bleeder, which puts us in double jeopardy. We have no intubation equipment here at the accident site. I'm not sure about allergy history, but— Yes, thank you. I'll have a landing zone set up and relay that information to you. What's the ETA? Twelve minutes? Thank you, we'll keep you advised of any change in the patient's condition."

She handed Austin's telephone back to him. "The nearest chopper is on its way."

"Oxygen coming through!" Cook called, parting the crowd that had formed around them. A fireman came behind him, holding the equipment Cheyenne had requested.

Dane sat back, relieved when Cheyenne placed a bag valve mask over Blaze's frighteningly still features.

"You have excellent form," Cheyenne told Dane quietly as she worked. "You could teach a class on it."

"Thanks, but no thanks. What was the dispatcher hassling you about?"

"He wasn't hassling me, he was following proper procedure."

"What kind of procedure?"

"I don't know how many times I've heard of a panicked caller who tells the ambulance dispatcher the patient is unresponsive or isn't breathing, and then the ambulance arrives and finds out the person was only sleeping soundly. Would you expect a 911 dispatcher to divert an air ambulance that's en route to a heart attack victim or to a bad wreck until they knew for sure it was a patient in more serious distress?"

"I guess not."

Again, she listened to Blaze's heart with her stethoscope and felt the left side of Blaze's neck. "Hey, I think his pulse is stronger."

A few seconds later, Blaze's eyes opened. He coughed into the mask, then went nearly cross-eyed looking down at the apparatus on his face.

"Blaze!" Dane could have cried with relief.

"Well, hello there," Cheyenne said. "Blaze, can you hear me?" She reached for a pulse at his wrist. "It's strong, though a little irregular. Blaze?"

"Yeah." His voice was weak. "What happened? What's this thing?"

"You were electrocuted and went into cardiac arrest," Dane explained.

"Electrocuted?" Blaze reached up and tried to grab the mask.

Cheyenne gently restrained him. "Leave that alone, it's helping you breathe. Just lie still and stay out of trouble for a few minutes, if you can manage to do that. We don't know how badly you've been hurt yet. You may even have broken your neck."

"My neck isn't what hurts," he said.

"What does?" she asked.

"My chest is killing me." He raised a hand toward his head.

Dane stopped him. "Try to lie still, son. What else hurts?"

"My head." He grimaced. "My neck's the only thing that *doesn't* hurt."

"That doesn't surprise me," Cheyenne said, "considering what your body went through."

She punched in a number on Austin's cell phone and contacted the air ambulance dispatch again. She updated him on Blaze's condition, then told the dispatcher to hold and handed the set to Austin. "You need to give him all the information he needs to set up a landing zone for the helicopter. And make sure you keep everyone away from the chopper. Those rotor blades are deadly if you aren't careful."

"Consider it done." Austin took the phone and ran to the house. Dane could hear him speaking to both the dispatcher and to Cook, who continued to play bouncer to keep the crowd at bay.

"Please don't tell me you saved my life or something," Blaze said, watching Cheyenne with solemn dark eyes. "You'd never let me live it down."

"You're right. And you know what's even worse?" she teased, pointing at Dane. "He helped. You're beholden to both of us, and I expect to receive full credit for my services."

Blaze groaned.

"You're not out of the woods yet," Dane said. "You need to continue to lie still until the chopper gets here."

"But are you sure I have to go by helicopter? I hate heights."

"Sorry, you're flying," Cheyenne said.

★ ★ ★

Blaze was still arguing when Cheyenne heard the first thrust of rotating helicopter blades as they slapped the air. Moments later it hovered over the ranch, preparing to land in a hay field east of the house.

Blaze had fallen uncharacteristically silent by the time the huge bird landed and the crew emerged.

Cheyenne stayed in the periphery of the action as the flight crew strapped Blaze to the board, hooked monitor leads to his chest and established an IV. Cheyenne noticed with approval that the paramedic was drawing up an antiarrhythmic medication to treat Blaze's irregular heartbeats.

When they prepared to lift him, however, he called out, "Dane! I can't do this! Please don't—"

"It's okay, son. I'll meet you at the hospital."

"But can't you come with me?"

"Blaze," Cheyenne said, stepping to his side and putting a hand on his shoulder, "we've been through this. Every muscle in your body just endured grueling punishment, and that includes your heart."

"But I'm better now."

"Not better enough." She glanced at the monitor, taking care to stay out of the way of the paramedic and EMT. "Hear that beep? I know you can't see the monitor, but every time the beeps lose rhythm, that means your heart is feeling irritable. You need to get to a medical center with people who know how to handle this."

He closed his eyes and groaned. "I hate flying. I think this is overdoing—"

He suddenly stopped talking. His head went slack, eyes slid shut. The heart monitor shrieked the alarm for ventricular fibrillation. The crew stopped and put him down. The paramedic switched the Lifeback 12 monitor to the defibrillator mode, hitting the charge button.

"What's happening?" Dane asked, moving past Cheyenne toward Blaze.

She put a hand on his arm and felt the tension as he tried to pull away. "No, Dane, let them work. His heart lost rhythm. They're restarting it."

The unit surged with sound as the electrical charge built within it.

The paramedic said, "Everybody stand back!" He pressed the defibrillate button. Blaze's body jerked within the confines of the straps. The monitor once again beeped a strong rhythm.

Blaze's eyes opened. "—things a little, don't you?" he said, finishing the sentence he had begun before losing consciousness.

Cheyenne leaned close to the paramedic. "I think I would give him the high dose, four milligrams-per-minute lidocaine drip."

"Agreed." He looked at her and nodded as they pushed Blaze toward the chopper.

Dane stepped up beside her and took her hand, as if seeking reassurance from her. She squeezed it with both of hers.

The helicopter lifted off with Blaze in a storm of sound.

"Life is never boring around here, is it?" Cheyenne said as the noise once more grew bearable.

He glanced over his shoulder toward the people who continued to work around the burning barn. "Never."

"Do you need someone to ride with you to Springfield?" she asked.

"If you're offering, I'd appreciate it very much."

"I'm offering. They're going to Saint John's in Springfield. How long will it take to drive there?"

"A little over an hour. I need to call Clint and have him get in touch with Blaze's mother."

"Give me the number," Cheyenne said. "I'll call while you clean up and change."

Dane turned his ten-year-old Volkswagen coupe onto Highway 86 fifteen minutes after the helicopter lifted off, gripping the wheel so tightly his fingers felt numb.

"Are you sure you don't want me to drive?" Cheyenne asked. "I can do a manual shift, and I stuck my driver's license in my pocket before I left the house tonight."

"I'm fine. Really."

"Liar."

He tried to loosen his grip on the steering wheel. *Oh, God, please take care of Blaze. Please keep him safe, please keep watch over him. He isn't ready for You yet, Lord. Please.*

"Dane?"

"Yeah."

She put a hand on his shoulder and squeezed. "Try to relax, okay?"

"I want to relax, I just can't seem to do it right now." Highway 86 curved through the night with such abandon that he didn't dare try to look at Cheyenne through the dim glow of the dash lights.

Her hand remained where it was. "You know, if our roles were reversed right now, you would probably make some insane comment about trusting God's mercy."

He risked a glance at her then, and caught the imprint of her dark eyes and hair, the strongly chiseled features of her face.

He returned his attention to the road. She was right. He probably would have made that comment. Guilt added itself to the mix of his emotions. How could he talk about the peace and love of God, and then fail to exhibit that peace in his own attitude when the life of someone dear to him was in danger?

And yet, to paste a smile on his face and act as if nothing bothered him would be the ultimate in hypocrisy at this moment.

"Watch closely for deer, would you?" he said. "There've been several accidents along this section of the highway."

"Okay, I'm watching, but seriously, if you do believe God will take care of everything, then what are you worried about?"

He risked another quick glance at her. "I'm human, not a perfect, God's-in-His-box Christian. I love Blaze, and I want him to live. I can't be assured that he will. Can you?"

For a moment, she didn't answer. He didn't risk looking at her again.

"There's never any assurance," she said at last. Was there a slight catch in her voice? "None of life, and none of justice."

He heard the thread of darkness in her voice. "I'm sorry, I didn't mean to discourage you. I know you're going through a rough time with that lawsuit, and I also know you care about Blaze."

He hadn't been much encouragement to anyone lately. Just last week he'd been trying to teach the boys the concept of turning the other cheek, and tonight he'd nearly socked Austin in the nose—his knuckles had tingled with anticipation. What kind of an example was that?

"You know," he said as he negotiated another curve, "I've never quite grasped the impact of your job before tonight. You really do save lives for a living."

In his peripheral vision he saw her look at him. "ER docs don't have a corner on that market," she said. "Trauma surgeons would be more likely to claim the slogan."

"But you try. I could see that tonight."

"All I can do is try," she said. "It's never up to me. Sometimes it seems to me as if when I most wish for good results, the worst ones happen."

He thought about her sister.

"I'm sorry," she said. "That was a discouraging remark, and I didn't mean to sound that way."

"You have a right to say what you think. Tell me why you decided to get into medicine."

"I've wanted to be a doctor for as long as I can remember. My parents started taking me seriously when I discovered my sister's mitral-valve prolapse."

"Her what?"

"It's a heart condition."

"And when did you become interested in emergency medicine?"

"I became addicted to the adrenaline rush during my rotations. I think that's the case with a lot of us in that specialty. The schedule is crazy, and it can be overwhelming when five patients all present at once, all with true emergencies."

"All that adrenaline," he said, trying for a light tone and failing. "And here I had the audacity to suggest you might want to consider a solo practice in Hideaway. What could I have been thinking?" *What, indeed?*

Again, from the corner of his eye he saw her look toward him. She didn't say anything.

He slowed at the intersection of Highways 86 and 13 and turned south. He couldn't keep his thoughts from returning to Blaze, and with the thought came still more worry. Now, with Blaze's life hanging in the balance, didn't seem like a good time to suspect the teen's activities earlier tonight. But questions nagged at Dane. For instance, was it coincidence that had impelled him to remove his racing pigs from their mother? Intuition?

And had he really been sneaking out at night just to sit on the dock and think about his dad?

Dane had trusted in the system, and in a teenager, once before, and had been proven dangerously wrong. Were his instincts faulty with this one, as well? Was Austin right?

"Cheyenne, do you ever pray for your patients?"

She didn't reply.

Again, he glanced at her. She was staring out the window into the darkness. She shook her head.

"I've read some good articles about the positive results of prayer with medical cases. Have you seen anything like that in your medical journals?"

"Plenty," she said. "But trust me, you don't want me praying for Blaze. The only time I cried out to God, He took my sister."

Chapter Twenty-Three

By the time Dane and Cheyenne reached the Saint John's trauma center at two o'clock Thursday morning, the ER physician had done an initial exam on Blaze, called a cardiologist and was waiting for the radiologist to read the X rays before they could clear the cervical collar.

Cheyenne heard Blaze's laughter as she walked beside Dane down the hallway toward his exam room after speaking with the doctor who had treated him.

Dane released a breath of relief. "It doesn't sound as if this ordeal has dampened his spirits."

They entered the room and found Blaze teasing the nurse who was rechecking his vitals.

"I don't know what they brought me here for," he said as she stuck a tympanic thermometer in his ear. "I'm healthy as a Missouri mule. Shoot, I grab bare electrical wires every day for exercise. Can't you take this collar off and let me breathe for a couple of minutes?"

"You'll have to ask the doctor about that." The nurse jotted down her numbers. "But if you try to lower these rails again, I'll tie you to them." She gave Blaze a quick grin, then rolled her eyes at Cheyenne and Dane as she walked from the room.

Blaze's grin widened when Cheyenne and Dane stepped into his field of vision. "You came." He tried to turn his head and look toward the door. "Listen, you've got to get me out of here before my mother gets here. They warned me she was coming about five minutes ago, and here they've got me trussed up like a roped calf."

For emphasis he raised his right hand about six inches from the bed, then dropped it back down. He was connected to two IV lines, a blood pressure cuff, a pulse oximetry probe, and a myriad of wires hooked to the monitor.

"Don't they know you've already been electrocuted once tonight?" Dane asked.

"Seems like everybody in the hospital knows about that. I told the X-ray tech I was white before the accident."

"Please tell me you didn't show them that weird cross-eyed thing you do," Cheyenne said, "or they'll be hauling you off for more tests."

"Nope, I'm trying hard as I can to get them to let me go before my mother gets here."

"When will she arrive?" Dane asked.

"Said she was leaving when she called. How long's it take to get here from Siloam Springs?"

"Maybe a couple of hours," Dane said.

Blaze closed his eyes and moaned theatrically.

"At least she's coming," Dane said.

Blaze opened his eyes and scowled.

"Back to normal, I see," Dane said as he touched the youth's bare shoulder. "Driving everybody crazy."

"At least they took you off that long spine board," Cheyenne said. "I know that was uncomfortable."

"Uncomfortable!" Blaze said. "Can't you doctors come up with something better than that?"

"We're working on it."

"And when can I get rid of this stupid thing around my neck?" He raised his left arm and pointed at the Philadelphia cervical collar. "I keep expecting it to squeeze tight like the blood pressure cuff, and pop my head right off my body."

Cheyenne glanced at Dane and grinned. "You'll just have to curb your imagination until they clear you."

"But the ER doc's already seen my films. He doesn't think anything's broken."

"Then he's waiting for the radiologist to clear you."

"But—"

"Blaze," Dane said, "how soon are they going to get you to your room? I told the doctor you'd like one on the top floor, right by the window."

Blaze gave him a toothy, sarcastic grin. "If I could survive that crazy helicopter ride, I can survive anything."

"Actually," Cheyenne said, "I hate to spoil your fun, but they'll put you in ICU, and those are usually on a lower floor. I think they'll keep you here for a few days."

"Days? I'm going to be in here for days?"

"You had cardiac arrest secondary to electrocution, plus you have a bleeding disorder. They take those things seriously."

"Think of all that great hospital food," Dane said. "Yum."

"How many days?" Blaze asked.

"We'll have to ask your doctors about that," Cheyenne said.

Blaze lost his smile. "Doctors? More than one?"

"A cardiologist, a neurologist, an ICU intensivist, a heme-onc specialist—"

"Hold it, what's heme-onc?"

"A specialist who deals with blood disorders."

"They're going to turn me into a pincushion, aren't they?"

"It won't be that bad," she said.

Blaze moaned again. "When I get my hands on the person who did this—"

"The person who did what?" Dane asked.

"Set the fire." He blinked up at Dane. "Come on, you know bad wiring didn't cause that, not the way you always keep up the repairs. None of us smokes, because you'd kill us if we tried." He paused. "Besides, I saw somebody running away, along the edge of the woods down below the barn, when I first came out of the house. You were right behind me, didn't you see anything?"

Dane took a deep breath and let it out slowly. "No, I didn't, Blaze."

"Well, I did. Somebody set that fire, and it sure wasn't me."

Dane didn't say anything.

Blaze's thick brows met in the middle, eyes narrowing as he looked at Dane. "You can't be thinking my mother's right about that arson thing. Can you?"

"I thought she changed her mind about that," Cheyenne said.

Blaze continued to watch Dane. "Can you?"

"Blaze, I—"

"You know me. You know I wouldn't do that kind of thing anyway, but with animals in the barn? Come on, Dane."

"We have more important things to focus on now," Dane said. "The rest we can deal with—"

"Wait a minute," Blaze said, "That's why Austin Barlow was talking about those pigs not being in the barn with their mama. He thought...you thought—"

"I didn't think anything," Dane said.

"I saw something," Cheyenne said. "Down by the dock, when I was rowing across the lake. I didn't pay much attention because I was too occupied with the boat and trying to pull ashore, but someone was paddling a canoe, just a few yards out, along the shore."

"And I saw someone running down that way," Blaze said. "Dane, you've got to tell the sheriff, because somebody started that fire, and like I said—" he emphasized his words slowly "—it—was—not—me."

"I'll tell him as soon as we get back home, but right now, your health is most important."

There was a knock at the door, and the doctor entered. They discovered what they already knew—Blaze would be in the hospital for a while. The good news was they had a room ready for him, and he was getting the cervical collar off.

"Thanks, Doc," Blaze said as the man turned to leave the room. "Life just doesn't get any better than this."

The next morning, after sleeping late, Cheyenne drove to see if Red and Bertie would want to visit Blaze. No one answered the door at the house, so she went down to the milking shed.

The door stood open, with Bertie inside, wearing an apron over her clothes, milking a goat who stood up on a three-foot-tall wooden stand. The doe had her head half-buried in a grain trough.

"Bertie?" Cheyenne said softly, not wishing to disturb the animal. The doe continued eating.

Bertie looked around and smiled. "Oh, good, you're the person I most wanted to see this morning." She continued shooting milk into the bucket below the goat's udder with expert aim. "I've already gotten three phone calls from people who wanted to tell me all about the fire last night. You're a town hero. To hear some tell it, you pert-near saved the ranch."

"Wow. It didn't take long for that story to get distorted

beyond recognition." Cheyenne settled onto a plastic chair in the corner, a comfortable distance from the goat. "I called the hospital from my car phone this morning. Blaze is doing very well."

"That's what I hear. He's as tough as Princess, here." Bertie nodded toward the goat. "Now, tell me about last night. What really happened?"

"Okay, but first, where's Red?"

"I've got him tied to the bed again."

"He isn't feeling well?"

"Not the best, but you know Red, more stubborn than that buck that attacked you."

"I have my medical kit in the car. I'll check him if you want me to."

"I'll let you do that in a little bit, if you want. I reckon you're the only doctor he'll sit still for."

The goat Bertie was milking raised her head from the trough at last. She looked at Cheyenne as if she might have more grain for her.

"Bertie, that goat doesn't have any ears," Cheyenne said.

"Oh, she's got ears, alright, she just doesn't have the flaps. She can hear Red from practically across the lake, ain't that right, Princess?" She patted the animal on the back. "She took up with Red right after she was born, following him around the place like a puppy. Half the time she even sneaked into the house with him."

Chuckling softly, Bertie urged Princess off the stanchion. "Off you go, girl. Red won't be out to play today. I don't know what you're going to do when he's gone."

"Bertie—you think he's that bad?" Cheyenne asked.

"Who's to know? He won't leave the house except to fish or go to church or get groceries at Dane's store. You couldn't drag him to a clinic." Her voice faltered.

She covered the milk and carried it to a stainless-steel table at the other end of the long room. "Princess wouldn't never let me kiss Red when she was around. She'd throw a fit, stomping and shaking her head." Her voice faltered again. "Guess I'd do the same if somebody was trying to steal my man."

"Are you okay, Bertie?" Cheyenne asked.

"Oh, don't worry about me, I'm just shook up about the fire and worried about Red. Can't believe anybody'd do something like that, especially around here. It's just plain meanness. So what happened last night?"

Cheyenne told her about it, including the ride with Dane to Springfield.

"Lizzie Barlow can't believe I knew you was a doctor all this time and didn't tell her," Bertie said. "The gossipy old thing. You know what she told me? She said, 'I guess you know it was that black kid with the mop-head hairdo what started the whole thing.'"

"What did you tell her?"

"I told her, 'Lizzie Barlow, if you're talking about Gavin Farmer, you're shooting up the wrong tree with me. He ain't even got no mop-head hairdo anymore, and he didn't light no fire.' And then Lizzie said, 'That ain't the way Austin sees it.' I tell you, that Austin's got a chip on his shoulder all the way to his backbone."

"Maybe he does, but he was right there helping us last night. He was the one who called for the helicopter."

"Of course he was. You wouldn't expect to see a decent person just stand there and let Blaze die. The big blowhard does have a tender spot inside him. Somewhere."

Cheyenne suppressed a smile. "What else have people been saying?"

"Cook called me and wanted to know if you was open for

business," Bertie continued. "He said he'd've asked you last night, but you was a little busy."

"Speaking of which, I'll go check on Red now. I'm driving up to Springfield to see Blaze in a few minutes—do you want to ride with me?"

"Guess not, what with Red so poorly. Tell you what, though, I've got some of Blaze's favorite cookies in the freezer if you want to take them up when you go."

"He would love that."

Cheyenne gave Red another checkup with her trusty stethoscope and blood-pressure kit. His bp was still elevated, though it had been several weeks since his cellulitis. That concerned her.

When she listened to his chest, she heard an S-3 gallop rhythm. Had she heard that last time she checked him?

She straightened and placed the scope around her neck. "Red, I know you aren't feeling well, but I'd like to drive you into Kimberling City to the urgent care center. I'm afraid there's something going on with your heart."

He lay back on his pillows—three of them, which Bertie had given him in the night because he "just couldn't get comfortable" lying flat.

"What would they do for me there that you can't do for me here?"

"They could run tests on you to see how your heart's working, and if you've had a heart attack."

"Then what?" he asked.

"They can do all kinds of things these days."

His lids closed slowly over blue eyes that seemed to have lost the vitality that had been there when Cheyenne first arrived in Hideaway. "I'm eighty-five or eighty-seven years old. Nothing works like it used to."

"But we have drugs and procedures that can help your heart work better."

"I'm not going to no hospital, and nobody's cutting on me. If it's my time to go, I don't want no drugs or machines interfering with God's plan."

She nodded. "Okay, Red, I'll respect that." She repacked her kit. "Will you have Bertie contact me if you start to feel worse?"

He opened his eyes briefly and smiled. "We'll see."

As soon as Dane stepped into ICU at eleven Thursday morning, he could see Blaze wasn't alone. His mother, Dora Adcock, stood beside his bed. She was a voluptuous woman with skin as dark as Blaze's and thick black hair halfway to her waist. She wore a pair of figure-flattering jeans and a bright purple tank top.

Blaze did not look happy.

Her gaze swept over Dane as soon as he entered the room. "So here's the man who runs the ranch where my son nearly died last night." Her voice was deep and mellow.

"I didn't nearly die," Blaze snapped. "I'm fine."

Her gaze remained on Dane. "Did you find out how it happened?"

"I just spoke with the sheriff, and he didn't know what caused the fire," Dane said. "It's still being investigated."

Her gaze faltered. She glanced at her son, then looked away. "So Gavin tells me he flunked the written driver's test on Monday."

"You don't have to change the subject," Blaze said. "I didn't set the barn on fire, just like I didn't set your house on fire."

"Right, so it was just all a big coincidence." Her sarcasm carried a bite.

"He'll ace the test next time," Dane said, hoping desperately to derail the line of this conversation. "We have someone working with him, and she says he's getting along very well."

The woman's expressive eyebrows rose with disbelief, and Dane found himself wondering why she had bothered to come.

"Dane?" Blaze said. "One of my fifteen doctors wants to talk to you. He told me they were going to keep me in ICU until tomorrow morning, then they'll watch me for a day or so in the step-down unit, then onto the floor before they send me home. Oh, you'll be disappointed to hear the food's good."

Dane grinned at him. "Enjoy it while you can."

"By the way, Dane, my mother wants me to move back home with her."

Dane saw the flash of surprise on Dora's face, and the wicked gleam in her son's. He had a feeling Blaze wouldn't be leaving the ranch anytime soon.

He hoped.

Cheyenne took her time as she walked along the hallway toward ICU. The activity of the hospital no longer tightened her gut with tension as it had for so long after Susan's death. That was a good thing, since next month's schedule included her name for thirteen shifts.

As she turned a corner in the corridor, however, a depressing realization struck her. This place held no attraction for her. For the first time in her life, she had no desire to step behind those sacred boundaries where patients waited for someone to give them some miracle cure that would stop their suffering.

She knew, better than most, that there was no miracle cure. Red seemed to understand that, and even more important, he seemed to accept it.

She couldn't help thinking about her conversation with Red. He wanted to die at home, surrounded by his life, not by white-coated strangers who only wanted to delay the inevitable. Sure, they meant well, with all their rules and so-called standards, but she had learned that, in the end, it often became less about an issue of compassion, and more about an issue of following the rules and covering the bases to keep from getting sued.

There were always rules. For instance, if Red was brought into the ER unconscious, standard of care would require Cheyenne to do everything she could to keep him alive unless Bertie was there to relay his wishes, or unless there was a signed DNR sheet.

The rules were beginning to chafe....

"Cheyenne?" someone called from behind her.

She stopped and turned to find Dane coming toward her, accompanied by a beautiful woman who looked a lot like Blaze. His mother, obviously, since Blaze had never mentioned a sister. She hadn't arrived by the time Cheyenne and Dane had left in the wee morning hours.

"Are those some of Bertie's cookies?" Dane asked, indicating a small nearby waiting area. "Let's step in here for a minute and talk."

Cheyenne held out the package she was carrying as they entered the unoccupied room. "Blaze's favorite."

"Dr. Cheyenne Allison," Dane said, "meet Dora Adcock, Gavin Farmer's mother."

Dora held her hand out and took Cheyenne's in a firm grip. "Doctor? Which one are you?"

"She's the one who rescued your son last night," Dane said. "She's the person who's been tutoring Gavin."

Cheyenne gave him a quick glance. Was that an edge of irritation she detected in his voice?

"What kind of a doctor does that?" Dora asked.

"I'm an emergency physician."

"No kidding?" Dora laughed. "That's what it would take

for Gav to learn something. Emergency. Something like wanting to get his license."

"I think he'll do it next time," Cheyenne said.

"That's what Dane says too. I've yet to see this great new knowledge of Gavin's. Nice meeting you, Doctor. I'm going to go say goodbye to my son and hit the road. I've got to get back to work." She turned and left them.

Cheyenne stared after her.

Dane chuckled. "Close your mouth, you'll catch a fly."

"I can see where Blaze gets his attitude."

"I can see why he wants to stay at the ranch. Not that he has much choice. I think she suspects him again."

"Of setting the fire?"

He nodded.

"That makes two of you," she said quietly.

He closed his eyes and turned away. "Ouch."

"You really think he could have done it? And the other vandalism?"

"Obviously, you don't," Dane said.

Cheyenne was sorry the subject had come up. She realized she didn't like being at odds with Dane, and this topic definitely put them at odds. Still, Blaze didn't deserve all the suspicion being directed at him.

"You're right," she said. "I don't. If you can't trust yourself, trust me. I've come to know Blaze pretty well. In these past few weeks I've probably spent more one-on-one time with him than you have in all the time he's been at the ranch."

"I have other kids to keep up with." He sounded defensive.

"Would you relax?" she said. "I'm not criticizing you, I'm simply stating a fact. Blaze acts up in school to draw attention away from his dyslexia, and it becomes a habit. I know, because I've done it myself. But can you see him shooting the mother of those kittens he found in my closet?"

"I'm not talking about cats, I'm talking about the fact that I have to be certain about the safety of my kids. Did you know Blaze has been slipping out at night?"

"Slipping out?"

"I bet he wouldn't tell you that, no matter how much one-on-one time you spent with him."

"Watch it with the sarcasm."

"Sorry," Dane said. "I'm a little touchy about the subject. So you're saying he acts up now because of the dyslexia. Are you also saying when he becomes more comfortable with his abilities, he'll settle down in class?"

"Well, *I* did."

"Good, then you'll be happy to know he's going to settle soon. He's made more progress since you've started working with him than he's made in the past ten years."

"How do you know?"

"He's told me, of course. He said it was as if everything fell into place for him these past weeks. You were able to connect with him in a way nobody else has, because he could iden-tify with you."

"He said that?"

"No, I read between the lines on that one. And the other day, I casually asked him to make a list of the cows that had given birth so far this year."

"You asked him to write it?"

"I thought it would be simple enough, and he needed the practice if he was going to take that written test. We give our cows simple names like Bell and Rose and Gordy. Blaze gave me a complete list."

Cheyenne caught her breath. "He did? He didn't say any-thing to me about that."

"It's the first time he's done anything like it. I think every-thing is finally coming together for him."

"Except for his relationship with his mother?" she asked.

"Except for that."

"And for the fact that he's under suspicion for arson."

Dane stepped over to the window that overlooked the south parking lot. "Yes, that too."

"Lucky Blaze." It was her turn to be sarcastic. "He's got it made."

Chapter Twenty-Four

On Monday morning, Austin Barlow made his usual stop at the house before driving out to the barn to deliver a ten-pound bag of grain for Courage. When Cheyenne answered his knock, he was standing at the end of the porch, gazing across the lake toward the ranch, where several people from town had gone over to help Dane and the boys clean up the mess.

Cheyenne stepped out onto the porch. "Morning, Austin."

He turned around, hat in his hands. "Hi, Cheyenne." He pulled two yellow message slips from the front pocket of his blue Western-cut shirt. "Cecil gave me these to bring you when I picked up the grain this morning. Looks like the messages are increasing now that you're a short-timer."

She thanked him and glanced at the notes. One was from Larry Strong, requesting a call-back ASAP. Of course. Larry always needed his ASAP. The other one was from Jim, who wanted to make sure she knew her first shift was the first of July.

She knew. The nightmares, which had eased a lot in the past few weeks, now haunted her again.

"I guess you heard the latest about the fire," Austin said.

"The fire chief thinks it was arson."

He nodded. The morning sunlight struck his wavy auburn hair in a red-gold glow and emphasized the lines in his tanned face. He looked tired, and his usual come-to-visit smile was dull around the edges.

"That doesn't mean it was Blaze," she said.

"I know."

Oh, really? Sometimes he surprised her. "Austin, someone was paddling a canoe away from the ranch when I arrived there that night. Blaze says he saw someone running toward the lake when he first came out of the house. I know it's easy to blame—"

"Cheyenne, stop. Dane already told me."

"Okay. Well."

"Look, I didn't come to argue about the fire. I just came to bring you those messages and see if maybe you'd like to take a drive to Branson for a show before you left."

She couldn't imagine why her thoughts suddenly turned to Dane, wondering if he would feel betrayed. But why should he? It wasn't as if he had ever asked her to a show, and it wasn't as if riding to Branson and back with Austin constituted a deepening of their extremely tentative friendship.

And she also couldn't imagine why the idea suddenly appealed. Perhaps because she had grown more familiar with Austin during his short visits when he came to check on the horse. Besides, she simply wanted to see a show.

"That sounds like fun," she said. "Make it Wednesday night."

He blinked. "Oh. Really? Good." His smile brightened. "What show would you like to see?"

"*The Shepherd of the Hills,* and I'll pay for my own ticket."
No way did she want him to think this was anything romantic. "You can drive, but I'll buy dinner."

"Can I ask you something else?" He glanced toward the ranch again.

"You can always ask." That didn't mean she had to answer.

"What on earth does that Gavin Farmer do here all the time? Seems like half the time I come by, he's here."

"Could be he's wondering the same thing about you," she said.

"I come over to see about my horse."

"So does he." Austin didn't need to know that wasn't Blaze's only motivation. "Don't forget he's an animal lover, which is another reason he wouldn't have set fire to the barn last week. He also helps me out with yard maintenance while he's here. Speaking of Courage, what are you planning to do with him when I leave?"

"Do you think your friend would let us keep him here? I'd pay her, of course."

"I'll ask, but I feel sorry for Courage, alone here all the time except when you and Ramsay come to check on him."

"So you could just stay here," Austin said.

"Right. To keep a horse company? He'd be a great addition to the ranch when they get their new barn up. Where is Ramsay today?"

Austin indicated the ranch with a nod of his head. "He took the boat across the lake earlier this morning. He wanted to help with the cleanup. I'm heading over that way soon as I leave here."

"You are?"

He shook his head sadly. "Why do you have such a low opinion of me, Cheyenne? It isn't as if I'm a hard-hearted idiot.

Of course I'm going to do my Christian duty to help out a community member in need, and my son takes after me."

It was Cheyenne's turn to shake her head sadly. Poor Austin didn't even seem to realize how self-righteous he sounded. He was right that his son seemed to imitate his actions, though reluctantly at times.

"Is it possible you might want to retreat back down here on your days off?" Austin asked. "I know it's quite a drive down from Columbia, but—"

"I might just do that," she said. She'd been thinking about it lately, as the time to leave drew closer. Perversely, it disappointed her that Dane hadn't been the one to ask her about coming back. Not that she needed to be asked.

Austin cleared his throat. "Something else I've been meaning to talk to you about. Dane's mentioned it to me a couple of times, and Bertie Meyer's been twisting my mom's arm to talk to me about it. Of course, I told them you wouldn't be interested, and I feel a little foolish even asking you, but Bertie would never forgive me if—"

"Spit it out, Austin. The worst I can do is say no."

"I wondered if you'd ever consider opening a solo practice right here in Hideaway. Now, don't laugh until you've heard me out."

She wasn't laughing, though she couldn't imagine why not.

"That little episode at the ranch the other night opened a lot of eyes around here." He placed his hat on the porch wall and paced to the end of the porch again, combing his fingers through his hair. "Mine included."

"About what?"

"We're too far from medical care here. Shoot, we don't even have a paramedic. Since we're so isolated and more people are moving in here all the time, building nice new homes and all, I think we need to see about begging a doctor to open a practice. We've got a lot of retired people with health problems. Dane's already offered the use of his downtown property to put in an office, and to open a pharmacy."

"It would take awhile to build up a practice here," she said. "And it's a small town. A person could starve getting started." Why was she even thinking about it? This was impossible.

"I know. All that's true. It's a crazy idea, especially asking an ER doc to do it. But I see it like this—we need somebody here who's used to emergencies, because we're so isolated. As you've already seen, we get a lot of tourist traffic in town from the lake during the summer months, and I got word from the folks who run the bed-and-breakfast that they've got a tour bus line placing them on their travel agenda. I'm still not sure I like all the influx, but since it seems to be happening with or without my approval, we need to make sure the visitors can get to medical care while they're here—you know those busses are filled with retirees either on their way to invade Branson or on their way back. Somebody could keel over with a heart attack at any minute, and all we got's a couple of people who know CPR."

"I'll ask around when I get back to Columbia," she said. "That place is crawling with doctors fresh out of residency and looking for their first practice."

Austin's broad shoulders slumped a little. "Yeah. Well, sure, I'd appreciate that. Let me know if you hear anything, okay?"

As usual, Austin didn't stay long, and as soon as he drove away Cheyenne went to her car and plugged in the phone. People still teased her about not having a telephone in the house, or a cell phone, but this suited her well.

"Hi, Larry, this is Cheyenne," she said when he answered. "What did you need to talk to me about?"

There was a pause. "We received a complaint from Kirk Warden's attorneys last Thursday, and I'm checking it out."

"What complaint?"

"Did you attempt to contact Mr. Warden for any reason when you were in town last Wednesday?"

"Yes."

Another pause, this time a little longer. "May I ask why?"

"It had nothing to do with the lawsuit. I went by his house to request the return of a family album Susan and I had been working on before her death."

"That wasn't what we were told."

"Well, why am I not surprised? I've never known Kirk to be an honest person."

"Cheyenne, that wasn't the wisest move. This is obviously a hostile situation, judging by what you've told us about his actions at the funeral."

"I understand how Kirk will try to make it look to a jury, Larry. After I left there, I realized I shouldn't have done it, but I wanted that album."

"Did you get it?"

"No, Kirk denied having it, but Larry, he had a woman at the house with him."

"That won't have any bearing on this case."

"Why not? I heard her call him honey. Surely if the jury would take exception to my visit there, they would also take exception to—"

"We're hoping there won't be a jury," Larry said.

"Hoping?" She didn't like the sudden softness of his voice. "What do you mean?"

"We're expecting a settlement."

"No."

"It would be the least costly way for everyone concerned."

"Everyone but me," she said. "I would have that on my record for the rest of my career. It's a vicious attack, and it's totally unfair."

"We've already discussed this. I thought you understood."

"I understand that my professional liability premiums would go through the roof, my whole future—"

"A settlement doesn't mean a judgment. It would be confidential, with no admission of guilt in order to prevent a judgment against you."

"But the guilt is still assumed," she said.

"It happens all the time. Some of the best doctors in the city have been sued, Cheyenne, everybody knows that. It isn't as if you have to pay your own insurance premiums. An ER doc is almost always covered by the hospital where she works."

"You mean like the coverage that's paying for this case? And what if I don't always choose to work in a hospital setting? Or here's a shocking suggestion—what if hospitals choose not to hire me because of the liability? The applications always ask about lawsuit history. Forget it, Larry. I'm not settling. I want my name totally cleared."

He sighed. "But if you lose, it could be a lot worse. You may not have a choice. Warden's attorneys are already hinting that they might be willing to settle for five hundred thousand."

"Half a million dollars!" Were they insane?

"Ed is hoping they'll at least drop it to three hundred thousand, and maybe even two-fifty. If they do, I'm afraid it'll be a no-brainer."

"In other words, if that happens, I'm on my own." She felt as if her final support was threatening to buckle beneath her.

"Look at it from our perspective, Cheyenne. A modest settlement could cost less than the legal expenses to fight it for an extended period, even if we won the case. And keep in mind that the jury generally has the opinion that the big, nasty hospitals, doctors and insurance companies must be forced to pay something, and often that jumps over the million mark very quickly."

She felt sick. "But it isn't being decided today, right?"

"Not today, and probably not this month, but it looks to be headed in that direction."

"Thanks for the warning." She said goodbye and disconnected, slumping backward in the passenger seat of the car.

"I could've come over here myself, you know," Blaze complained as he tied their boat to Cheyenne's dock and stepped ashore late Monday afternoon.

"That doesn't make it the smartest thing to do," Dane said. "I just want to keep an eye on you a little longer."

"You don't think four days is long enough?" The teenager flexed his right bicep. "I'm in great shape."

He did look healthy, and Dane had managed to keep him away from the burned barn, where as many as thirty people at a time had been working to clean up the mess today. At this rate, with the other boys helping, they would have another barn up and operating in only a few weeks. Meanwhile, they had set up temporary headquarters in the milk room of a neighbor down the road.

Dane and Blaze climbed the bank toward Cheyenne's house and saw her out weeding the garden. She had brought sandwiches and cookies over to the ranch to feed the workers at noon, but she'd left again before Dane had a chance to talk to her.

"Don't pull out all the carrots again," Blaze called to her in greeting.

She looked up, stood and walked to meet them. She didn't smile or make a sarcastic reply.

"Uh-oh, looks like something's wrong," Blaze said loudly enough for her to hear. "What is it?"

When she reached them, she hugged Blaze. He hugged her back and gave Dane a "what's-up?" frown over her head.

The olive undertones of Cheyenne's face were tinged red from the heat and activity, and her black hair fell in moist tendrils across her forehead and neck. Her dark eyes were shadowed.

She released Blaze and turned to lead the way toward the shaded porch.

"Okay, out with it," Dane said. "What's wrong?"

"Why does anything have to be wrong? I'm happy to see Blaze."

"Then why don't you act happy?" Blaze asked.

"Because I'm hot and tired and it's been a long day, and I dread going back home to Columbia next week. You want some iced tea?"

"Yeah, but I'll get it," Blaze said. "I want mine sweetened." He pulled open the screen door, narrowed his eyes at Dane, and jerked his head toward Cheyenne.

Dane got the message clearly.

"What else is up?" Dane asked her as Blaze disappeared into the house with a quick greeting to Blue.

"The lawsuit." For the first time since he'd met her, she almost looked her age.

"You've heard from Columbia today?"

She nodded.

Cecil had told him about giving the messages to Austin to bring out to her this morning. She was getting more messages from Columbia lately—reconnecting her to her world.

But was Columbia still her world? Could that be, partially, what was bothering her?

"They want to agree to a settlement," she said. "That would place a permanent mark on my résumé, and it isn't fair."

No, it wasn't fair, but he'd learned long ago that life wasn't fair. Somehow, he didn't think she was in the mood for a sermon about real Life—the one after this.

"Won't they at least hold a deposition so you can share information?" he asked. "I don't know much about law, but you need to have an opportunity to see what kind of opposition you'll be up against. I've heard that if everyone can see a good defense, often the case will be dropped."

"Apparently, none of that is up to me unless I want to foot the bill for my own attorney—and I could still lose, with no financial backup." She slumped onto the top step of the porch. "I guess I shouldn't worry about it much. It isn't as if I have any huge accounts they can dip into."

He sat down beside her and took her hand. To him, it felt like a perfect fit. "I thought you said you lived in an apartment."

She nodded. "What does that have to do with anything?"

"And you drive a car that isn't exactly—"

"It's none of your business where I spend my money," she said. But a smile broke the surface.

"Let me guess. I doubt you have a gambling problem, and you obviously don't have a drug habit. You're apparently not much of a jet-setter. Something you said a few weeks ago gave me the impression you might frequent a soup kitchen or rescue mission somewhere near home."

She withdrew her hand from his. "What does Cecil do, tell everybody in town about my phone messages?"

The question stung. "He only mentioned it to me in passing, and I gave him a long lecture about confidentiality. I'm hoping it won't happen again, but I can't promise you anything."

She stood up and paced the yard, arms crossed over her chest. "I don't know if I could ever get accustomed to the lack of privacy in this place. A person might as well live in a glass house."

"So you wouldn't be interested in Austin's offer."

She pivoted, narrowing her eyes at him. "What did he do, drive over to the ranch and announce it to the whole crowd?"

"Why is that upsetting you so much all of a sudden? You know what a close community this is, especially since we're so isolated here."

She spread her hands in the air and continued pacing. "Maybe what's upsetting me is the fact that I'm tempted to take him up on the offer. I suppose he also blabbed that he's taking me to see *The Shepherd of the Hills* Wednesday night."

Dane felt as if he'd just been awarded a prize, then socked in the stomach. "No."

Blaze came charging out of the house with three glasses of iced tea clinking against each other. "Cheyenne, I can't believe you'd go out on a date with that blowhard mayor."

"It isn't a date, it's—"

"Hold up a minute, isn't that Bertie coming down the drive?" Blaze set the glasses on the ledge of the concrete wall.

Dane saw the small, stooped figure coming down the driveway toward them, waving at them frantically.

"Something's wrong." Blaze ran down the steps and raced toward her. Dane and Cheyenne followed.

Bertie stopped when Blaze reached her. She bent over, resting her hands on her knees as she panted to catch her breath. "I called the ranch, and they said you was here." She panted again. Her face was flushed, as if she'd run all the way.

"Bertie, what's happened?" Dane asked, reaching for her.

"We're getting too old for this," Bertie said, gasping for breath. "It just don't figure why all this has to happen at once."

"What, Bertie?" Cheyenne asked. *Red, it had to be. His heart?*

Bertie shook her head. "He's done it before, I know, but it still scares me every time. What could be wrong with him? Is his mind going on him?"

Dane took Bertie by the shoulders. "Has something happened to Red?"

Bertie nodded. "He's disappeared again, and I can't find him anywhere." She gazed up helplessly at Dane. "He got tired when he was over at the ranch today."

"That's right," Dane said, "but when I offered to take him home, he said he already had a ride."

"Did he say who with?" Bertie asked.

"No, it could have been anybody."

"It's nigh on sunset and he's not home yet. I think he's lost again, Dane, I do. Just like last time. Can you help me find him?"

Chapter Twenty-Five

"Don't know what I'd do without Red," Bertie said. She fidgeted in the passenger seat of Cheyenne's car as Cheyenne drove her back home, with Dane and Blaze in the back seat. "Don't know what could've happened to him."

"You said he's wandered off like this before?" Cheyenne asked. She'd never seen Bertie so upset, and she feared the worst.

"He did one night a couple of years ago." Bertie looked over the seat at Dane. "Remember that, Dane?"

"You mean when he and Cecil went fishing at Roaring River on the first day of trout season?"

"That's the time. We all thought it was funny then, 'cause Cecil was bringing him back home, had a flat tire and stopped to change it. It being dark, Red couldn't tell he wasn't home yet, and couldn't hear Cecil telling him to sit tight. While Cecil was changing the tire, Red just politely got out of the truck and started walking to what he thought was home, which was really across Lizzie Barlow's field. Her dogs got after him and nearly ate him before they realized who he was and stopped." Bertie shook her head sadly. "It's a shame when folks' eyes and ears go on them, and they don't keep up with the rest of the world."

Cheyenne pulled into the Meyers' driveway and parked. Dane got out of the back seat and rushed forward to open the door for Bertie. "I wish I'd made sure he was okay before he left the ranch today."

"Now, don't you go blaming yourself," Bertie said. "There was people all over that place helping with the cleanup, and Red was just one of them. Red can get himself into more mischief—" Her voice caught, and her chin quivered.

"The first thing we need to do is ask everyone who was there today if they saw Red," Dane said. "That's simple. I'll call Cook and Austin. They know everybody in the state, it seems."

Cheyenne picked up her car phone from beside her on the seat. "We can use this if you give me some numbers to call."

"I've got an extra phone book in the living room," Bertie said.

Blaze rushed ahead of Bertie and opened the front door for her. "Might not be that easy. You know Red, he could've rested an hour or so, then lit back out to go fishing."

"But I had the boat," Bertie said. "We went over together this morning, and then when he got tired, he said he'd catch a ride back home. You know how boats was coming and going all day today."

"Who does he usually fish with?" Cheyenne asked.

"Anybody who'll come by this way," Bertie said. "But first let's find out who brought him home. Could be they dropped him off down at the dock, then left, and Red got turned around again. It could've happened. He just forgets where he is sometimes."

"Shouldn't we start searching down by the boat dock in both directions?" Cheyenne asked.

"I done did that—that's why I'm so tired." Bertie led them into the house and reached beneath her telephone on an end table. "I went as far as the end of Lizzie Barlow's land, and as far as the beginning of yours. I didn't see no sign of him, not even a track in the mud. He's not been down your way, far as I can tell."

Dane picked up the receiver and punched his numbers. "If we don't find any leads soon, we'll get the boys to search up and down the shore on both sides of the lake. Hello, Jason? I need to talk to Cook. We've lost Red."

It was starting to get dark by the time Dane reached Austin on his cell phone. "Austin? Dane here. Thanks for coming out to help us today. Did you happen to see Red Meyer when he left to go home?"

"I saw him there," Austin said, "but I didn't see him leave. What's going on? Are you saying he didn't make it home?"

"He wasn't here when Bertie arrived home, and someone must have given him a lift with their boat."

"You might call Mom. She's probably got a list of everybody who was there and how long they stayed, what they ate for lunch. You know my mother. Red's probably just wandered off again."

"Thanks, I'll call Lizzie."

"I'm showing a place right now. Let me know when you find Red."

Dane disconnected, knowing this was not the time to brood about the apparently growing relationship between Austin and Cheyenne. Still, it rankled. She was going to a show with Austin Barlow.

He was dialing Lizzie Barlow's number when Cook and six ranch boys trooped into the house carrying flashlights.

"Would you look at that," Bertie said as she rushed forward to hug each one of them. "You boys've got to be tired after working on the cleanup all day long. You're just the best kids...." Her voice quavered. "I don't know what I'd do without my ranch boys."

After speaking with Lizzie and receiving no additional information, Dane gave up on the phone calls and sent the boys off in groups of two to scour the Meyers' sixty acres.

"It could be, if he was tired, he just lay down to sleep under a tree or a bush somewhere," Cook suggested as he headed out the front door with Jason.

Dane drew Cheyenne aside while Blaze held Bertie's attention in the kitchen. "Keep Bertie here. She's already worn herself out looking for Red."

"Keep us posted."

"We'll check back in every hour. Red and Bertie have an old cow bell hanging at the back door that they use to call the goats. If you hear any news, or if Red comes wandering in, you can use that bell to call us."

Cheyenne's gaze followed Bertie, and Dane could see the concern in her expression. "Dane, do you think something bad has happened?" she asked softly.

"I don't know. I'd sure like to find out who he was with. By now everyone in town knows about Red, so we'll hear if he turns up there." Dane felt suddenly weary. "Red's an impulsive old cuss. But I wouldn't have expected him to leave Bertie to do tonight's milking alone."

"Oh, that's right," Cheyenne said. "The milking."

"It'll need to be done. If that makes you nervous, I could have one of the boys stay and help, or I could stay."

"No, I'll help Bertie do it. She'll need to keep occupied. Watching me help milk her goats will definitely do that."

"Have you worked with them before?"

She grimaced. "You mean milked? I have a practical idea about where the milk comes from, but that's it. The only goat I trust is Mildred. The closest I ever came to the others was the day that buck chased me onto the roof."

Dane could have kicked himself. "I'm sorry, I didn't even think. Why don't I stay here, and you and Blaze—"

"No, I'm a big girl, I can handle milking a few little goats. Besides, they sold Roscoe." With a tentative smile, she reached up, as if on impulse, and touched the side of Dane's face, rubbing her fingers over his beard. "You look tired."

He placed his hand over hers, loving the gentle comfort. "I think we could all use a little less excitement for a while." Unfortunately, he couldn't see that happening any time soon, even if they found Red.

He prayed they would find Red.

"I'll be fine with the goats," she said, stepping back and withdrawing that soft, exquisite touch from his face. "I'll simply follow Bertie's instructions."

"Just your being here will help her. I'll be back soon, I hope."

"They'll find him, I'm sure," Cheyenne said, putting an arm around Bertie's slender, suddenly fragile shoulders, as they watched the shadowed figures scatter into the woods around the house. "Meanwhile, we might as well get started milking."

Bertie's shoulders stiffened. "Milking." She looked up at Cheyenne. "I can't believe I forgot all about my girls. They're probably wondering if I've lost my mind. You say you want to help?"

"Of course I do, Bertie." Cheyenne glanced through the

window toward the little milking barn at the far side of the yard. A comfortingly familiar animal stood at the door, nosing the handle. "Especially if they're all as tame as Mildred."

Bertie nodded and patted Cheyenne's arm. "Won't be no trouble, you'll see. You knew we got rid of that old mean thing right after he hurt you."

"Yes, I know."

Bertie reached for a red bandanna hanging on the hall tree beside the back door, then led the way outside. "Most goats won't be that way unless they're treated mean or teased a lot, and most goats won't have their horns. The owners usually cut those off."

Dane was right about the goats occupying Bertie. As she stepped into the barn ahead of Cheyenne, she kept up a steady stream of conversation. Cheyenne was grateful for something to do.

To her surprise, when she entered the milking area behind Bertie, the does entered behind them and stood in line, as if eager to be milked. They didn't look nearly as large or formidable as they had on Cheyenne's front yard and porch a few weeks ago, but part of that time she had been lying on the ground looking up at them.

Bertie laid a gentle hand on the head of one of the serene-looking does and reached up onto a shelf for a small stainless-steel bucket. The doe stood calmly as Bertie motioned Cheyenne forward.

"This one here's one of the gentlest, so I'll let you get started on her. Dane's boys built us these here milking stands quite a few years ago, and they're sure easier on the back than sitting on a stool and reaching down."

At her urging, the white-tan-and-brown doe stepped up an incline to a stand—or stanchion—that reached almost to Cheyenne's waist. The doe stuck her head through a partition, where a small trough had been built. "Now all we have to do is stand and milk, while the doe munches on her portion of grain. Don't worry, she'll wait for that grain all night if need be."

Cheyenne watched Bertie do the cleaning, then dry the udder and start milking.

"I'll let you watch me this first time, then I'll go to the other stand and start on my own." Bertie seemed to have forgotten about everything but the task in front of her.

She positioned the bucket. "See here what I'm doing?" She gave a demonstration, forcing a stream of milk downward into the bucket, then glanced up and smiled at Cheyenne's dubious expression.

"You know, I just thought about something," Cheyenne said. "What if someone tries to call us while we're out here?"

Bertie nodded toward the far wall, where a telephone hung. "Got us an extension a couple of years ago. Come on, you can do this. You'll have to practice a while before you get the hang of it. Give it a try."

The gentle-faced doe suddenly looked a little less gentle as Cheyenne approached the stand. "Uh, what do I do now?"

"Grab a teat."

Cheyenne reached forward tentatively and took one of the large, soft nipples. The doe jerked, and her head came around questioningly.

"It's okay, Dove," Bertie said calmly. "She won't hurt you. Talk to her, Cheyenne. Red and I do all the time. Make her think you know what you're doing."

"But I don't."

"Act like you do. Act like you mean what you're doing. Don't act afraid, or she'll take advantage."

Cheyenne did as Bertie instructed, and squeezed. Nothing happened.

"You're not holding firmly enough," Bertie said as she filled the small trough with grain for Dove. "And you have to pull gently. Try again."

When the doe's attention focused on the grain, Cheyenne squeezed again—this time more firmly—and was rewarded by a long stream of milk.

"Good," Bertie said. "Didn't hit the bucket, but it's a start. Try again."

Encouraged, Cheyenne squeezed with the other hand and received more milk, this time on her arm. "Ugh! What does it take to get this right?"

Bertie chuckled. "Practice, honey."

The next stream of milk caught Cheyenne in the chin, and Dove turned to look at her.

"Shut up," Cheyenne muttered. "I bet you never tried to do this."

At last, she got the hang of it. When she finished with Dove she looked around to see Bertie milking another animal on the second stanchion.

"What now?"

"Pull the trough back and let her go on out the other side. I've got… I've got Red's little sweetheart waiting in the wings." Bertie pulled off her glasses, and dabbed at her eyes with the sleeve of her denim shirt. "Can't think where he's gotten to, Cheyenne. I just can't stand to think about what might've happened."

"Neither can I, Bertie." She couldn't mention what she thought might have happened. What if Red had suffered a heart attack? She'd warned him about it last Thursday.

Even worse, what if he had been close to the water at the time? He might even have fallen into the lake. It could be days before they found him, and if the current of the lake carried his body elsewhere…

But she didn't want to think about the possibility that Red was dead. The nights were warm enough now that even if he was lost or hurt somewhere, an extended time of exposure shouldn't cause him too much harm, if he didn't have other, more serious problems. It wasn't as if he was missing any doses of medication, because he refused to take any medication on a regular basis.

In spite of Cheyenne's efforts to reassure Bertie, they eventually lapsed into uneasy silence. Between each milking, Bertie poured her bucket of milk into the stainless-steel drum and rushed to the door to look toward the house.

The tension continued to mount, and Bertie's movements faltered when the last goat stepped up onto the stand. Cheyenne grew more concerned when she actually finished with her last goat ahead of Bertie.

They put the milk into the cooler and cleaned up quickly, eager to go to the house in case someone returned with news.

Dane and Blaze arrived first, expressions grim as Bertie questioned them eagerly.

"No news," he said. "We took the boat along the shore in both directions, then went into town. I asked everyone who knows Red. No one seems to know what happened to him after he left the ranch today."

The boys returned soon after, two at a time, worn-out and dejected after the long hours of working all day and searching through the woods tonight.

"That does it," Bertie said firmly. "You're all going to bed. You're welcome to stay here if you want to keep searching in the morning, but you're all tuckered out, and you won't do no good getting sick."

"Bertie, we can't leave Red out there all night," Dane said. "I'll keep looking for a while. Several of the men from town volunteered to help search if we haven't found him by morning."

"A lot of good that'll do him tonight," Blaze muttered.

"And you, young man," Bertie said, taking Blaze's arm. "You need to rest up. You just got out of the hospital. And don't you worry, Red's a tough one. He'll wander up to somebody's house afore long, and they'll call us. You'll see." She sounded as if she were trying to convince herself as well as Blaze, and the boys all looked at each other.

"Dane, I'll go with you," Jason said, stepping forward. "I slept late this morning, and I'm not tired."

Dane finally decided to continue the search in shifts, making Bertie's house headquarters, and allowing some to sleep while the others searched. To Blaze's frustration, Dane decided he should stay and sleep before he went out again.

"It's not fair," Blaze fumed as Cheyenne rushed around to help Bertie unfold blankets to make pallets on the floor. "I should go with them. Red was my fishing buddy."

"Now, now," Bertie clucked. "Sounds to me like you need some sleep, grumpy. Wash off and hop in bed."

Feeling sorry for Blaze, Cheyenne said, "I'll go with you when Dane comes back. I haven't had a chance to search yet, and who knows better where to search on my land than you and me?"

Reluctantly, Blaze agreed. "We'll find him in the morning, though, Cheyenne," he said softly. "We've got to."

Chapter Twenty-Six

It seemed to Cheyenne that she had just placed her head on the pillow in the guest room when the front door squeaked open and Dane and Jason, Willy and Cook trooped in.

She climbed out of bed and pulled on her shoes.

She stumbled into Dane, tired and disheveled, in the dimly lit hallway.

"Hey," he said, placing his hands on her shoulders, "where do you think you're going?"

"With Blaze."

He shook his head slowly. "Half the town is out looking for him now. Why don't you stay here and sleep the rest of the night. Bertie might need you."

She heard the fatigue in his voice, and she reached up and touched his cheek again, tenderly, once more feeling the thick growth of beard beneath her fingertips.

"Get some sleep, Dane, I've had mine."

He held her gaze for a moment. Then, as if it were the most natural thing to do, he pulled her into his arms. She rested her forehead against his shoulder, allowing herself a moment to appreciate the comfort of his embrace. It felt right.

She wrapped her arms around him, hoping her closeness would offer him some comfort, as well. Red had been a good friend to him for many years, and the possibility of losing Red, along with the loss of the barn and Blaze's injury, must be weighing heavily on him.

"Would you two do that somewhere else?" came a familiar grumble from behind. Blaze. "You're blocking the bathroom door."

When Cheyenne and Blaze were ready to step outside, Dane followed them to the porch.

"Hold it, you two," he said softly. "I sent Cook home with Willy, James and Jason to get some sleep and then do the milking in a few hours. The only place we haven't covered thoroughly is the western perimeter of your acreage, Cheyenne. Keep a close eye on Blaze, and don't let him overdo it or injure himself."

"Would you stop it?" Blaze said. "I'm fine, okay? Besides, it'll be light soon. You don't have to mother—"

"The sheriff has called for search-and-rescue to come in at first light. The church in town has a prayer chain going." Dane put one hand on Blaze's shoulder and the other on Cheyenne's, and bowed his head. "Lord, please go with these two and protect them, give them sharp sight. And please, Lord, be with Red as You comfort Bertie. We need your continual touch."

It wasn't until he had ended the prayer and stepped back that Cheyenne had time to feel uncomfortable. It had seemed such an automatic gesture for him, not awkward or self-conscious.

"Are you sure you don't want to stay here until it gets light?" he asked her softly, his voice hoarse from overuse.

"I'm sure. Take the guest bed—it's still warm, and you need the sleep."

"You talked me into it." Once more, he put an arm around her. "Remember, as soon as you find Red, come and get me."

"We promise, Dane," Blaze answered for her. "Come on, Cheyenne. Can I drive the car to your place?"

"I thought we'd start searching from here."

"Dane said the west section of land. Besides, you need a jacket." He yawned. "It's colder than you think."

"I'll get one at the house. Fine, you drive."

Blaze reasoned logically that since Red was probably disoriented, he could be anywhere in the fields or woods, so after they reached her place and found her jacket, they walked down to the dock, then split up and went separate directions along the shore.

When they met back an hour later, Blaze slumped onto the dock. "Chey?"

"Yeah?"

"I think… I think Red is dead." His voice held a catch of grief.

She gently prodded a nearby bush. "Don't talk that way."

"It's too cold out here, especially for Red. You know how easily he got cold."

She shivered in spite of the warmth of her jacket. "I know."

"Then you think he's—"

"No." She sighed and reached for the rope that anchored the rowboat to the dock. "I'm a doctor, Blaze. I've learned not to think that way. Until the patient is pronounced, that patient is alive as far as we're concerned. I may not have Dane's faith. I don't have that confidence he seems to have that everything will turn out right in the end. But I'm not ready to give up on Red."

"I didn't mean that."

"I know," she said softly, trying to see Blaze's face through the darkness. "I just don't want to start grieving unless we know something for sure."

She moved her light in a circle around the dock. The movement had become automatic in the past hour. "Let's row along the shore."

"Fine, but I'm rowing. You'll take us right under the trees."

As they got into the boat, Blaze unlooped the rope from the post and pushed them off, then grabbed the paddles as if afraid she would try to take them.

"Hold both our lights," he said. "It'll give you a wider area. Yeah, like that. Cheyenne, I can't believe you're going out on a date with Austin Barlow."

"It isn't a date, and you had no right to be eavesdropping when I told Dane."

"The mayor's taking you to a show in Branson, and you don't call that a date? I bet it'll sound like a date to the rest of the town."

"I'm buying my own ticket."

"What? He's making you buy your own—"

"He isn't making me do anything, Blaze, I insisted. It isn't a date, I just wanted to see a Branson show before I went back to Columbia, and it isn't as if men are knocking the door down to invite me."

Blaze turned the bow of the boat toward the shore. "Is that just a clump of leaves?"

She shined the light on the form as he rowed them closer, and saw branches sticking out of the leaves. "Yes. Keep going."

"So if you wanted to go to a show, why didn't you ask Dane instead of Barlow?"

"I didn't *ask* Barlow, he asked me."

"So it's a date."

She gritted her teeth. "Is it my imagination, or are you a little more belligerent after your stay in the hospital?"

"I'm not belligerent, Barlow is, and you know it. He hates me—"

"It didn't look that way the night of the fire, when he called for a chopper and then prepared the field so they could land."

"He wouldn't've been a very popular mayor if he'd stood there and laughed while I died."

"You know better than—"

"You haven't taken a good look at the color of my skin lately, have you?"

"I know what color your skin is, Blaze. It's a rich, deep ebony, but that isn't the first thing I notice when I meet somebody."

"It is for some people, especially around here where they don't see a lot of black people. We stand out, and that isn't a good thing. There's still prejudice in the world, Cheyenne, and a lot of it. This isn't paradise."

"I know. It isn't fair of me to ask you to give people more time to adjust to you, just because of your skin color. It shouldn't be that way."

"But it is. And Austin suspected me when I first came here, just because I was black."

"I don't know Austin well enough to know that for sure, but I'd bet your nickname didn't help things. And you aren't the only one Austin picks on. You know how he is with Dane most of the time. And Dane sure isn't black."

Blaze was quiet for a moment. "Yeah. Austin was belligerent to Red yesterday, too. You should've heard them shouting at each other down at the dock."

Instinctively, Cheyenne shone one of her lights at Blaze, who squinted and glared at her in the circle of brightness. "Get that out of my face. I'm not lying."

She returned her attention to the shoreline. "What were they shouting about?"

"Austin was mad at Red about the goats in your yard, and warning Red how dangerous that buck was."

"How did he know about that?"

"Oh, come on, Cheyenne, you know this place. All it takes is one stray word, and folks around here can hang a whole story on it. Anyway, Red told Austin he got rid of the goat, and Austin said they should get rid of all the goats."

"And Austin was shouting at Red?"

"I heard Austin say later he wasn't shouting, he was just talking to Red loudly enough so the deaf old coot could hear him."

"That makes sense."

"There you go, taking his side again."

"I'm not taking—"

"So now what happens but I see you hanging on Dane tonight like a lovesick—"

"Just row the boat," she snapped.

She heard him chuckle behind her, and she ignored it.

They fell silent as they searched.

"You're right about Dane," Blaze said after a few moments. "He has a lot of faith in God."

She remained silent. This was an area she knew nothing about, and she didn't want her own doubts to affect Blaze adversely.

"I used to think this Christianity thing was just an act with him, like it is with so many other people," he said.

"I don't think so. Dane never seems to be putting on an act."

"What do you think about God, Chey?"

She glanced around at Blaze in surprise at his use—the second time that night—of the nickname Susan had given her and that was used by her closest friends. "I don't think I'm the person to talk to about Him."

"I thought you had all the answers. You're the doctor."

"I don't have a degree in theology. Why the sudden interest in God?"

Blaze paused thoughtfully. "Because of Red. He didn't go around talking God stuff all the time, but it didn't take too long to figure out what he believed just because of the way he lived his life."

Once again, Cheyenne noticed Blaze spoke as if Red were already dead. "What about his superstitions? He cut that little cedar tree out of my front yard because he believed it would curse me."

"Yeah, I know, but everybody's got their weirdness. Yours is going out on a date with Austin Barlow."

"Blaze—"

"Do you believe the soul lives forever?"

She believed she might dump this kid in the lake if he didn't drop the subject of her non-date with Austin. "I try not to think about it." But lately, she'd been thinking about it a lot.

"Dane believes in Eternal Life."

"I'm sure he does. Look, can we please change the subject?"

"What's making you nervous, talking about death or about God?"

"Both. Now, pick up the pace. At this rate, we'll never get anywhere."

They circled the cove twice with no success. When they returned to the dock, Blaze stopped and stretched wearily, then pointed toward the eastern sky. "Getting lighter all the time."

In a few moments the birds started singing.

"Where do we go from here?" Cheyenne asked. "Any ideas?"

Blaze stared across the misty lake. "I remember, lots of times, getting up before dawn to go fishing with Red. He always brought fresh fried pies and goat cheese he'd made himself, and we'd feast while we paddled to our favorite fishing spots."

She continued to scan the shoreline as the morning swept over them. "Where were some of Red's favorite fishing places?"

"Well, he especially likes the island, because of those cliffs that catch the afternoon sun. It's one of his favorites."

"I don't suppose there was any way he could have gotten over there, was there?"

"No, but we still haven't found out who brought him home from the ranch yesterday, either. Lots of people came and went, and everybody knows Red, even the people from our church in Blue Eye. Doug and Brenda Minton could've driven him, but it would've been pretty silly to drive all the way around to the bridge and back into Hideaway just to take Red home when there were boats coming and going all day."

"Okay, but we're sure he did get a lift across? If nobody remembers taking him, and he tends to get lost easily, couldn't he be wandering around on the other shore?"

"Dane and I looked over there, too."

"Fine, but just to satisfy my curiosity, why don't we check again, and then I can leave you at the ranch so you can get some more rest."

He hesitated. "You trying to get rid of me?"

"No. If you don't want to do the rowing, I'll do it."

"I'll do it."

She studied the island, with its thick growth of trees, steep, rocky cliffs and sandy beach on the east side. Though she had often gazed across at it, she'd never been there.

"Did you talk to him yesterday?" she asked.

"A couple of times. Guess he was worried about me. He told me shooting the sow was the right thing to do, and he even offered to help take care of the piglet orphans. He was always doing something like that."

Cheyenne sighed.

"I mean, he *is* always doing something like that."

The sun peeped over the eastern horizon, surrounded by soft, pink sky and gray clouds, and once it began its ascent, it rose swiftly. If not for the circumstances, Cheyenne would have reveled in the beauty of the morning, the songs of the birds, the fresh feel of the breeze lifting her hair.

Blaze directed the boat to a level section of the island, and they slid almost without noise to the edge of the grass.

As they stepped ashore, Blaze nudged her arm and pointed to the sky, where two vultures circled. "See them?"

"Yes, but—"

"It wouldn't be Red, don't worry. Probably a dead animal around somewhere close, but the vultures wouldn't start circling until something was dead for a while." He gestured along the shore, where the cliffs rose sharply from the surface of the lake. "You know those people who kept finding dead cattle out in the field, with their eyes and udders and…other parts of their anatomy cut out like a surgeon had been ahold of them with a scalpel?"

"Barely, but you're not even old enough to remember that."

"Dad did. He said vultures did that."

They climbed to the highest point of the tiny island, then descended down the other side. Blaze fell silent, and Cheyenne became increasingly aware of the birds circling above them, even though she knew they wouldn't be circling for Red.

A shadow passed over them, and Cheyenne looked up to see more birds. Above them, a cloud bank drifted across the sky from the west.

"Looks like we're in for a storm," she said.

Blaze looked up. "Come on, let's hurry."

Cheyenne stumbled over a rock, and Blaze reached out to steady her. She felt him trembling.

It was a long way down to the water from where they stood, and Cheyenne was surprised to realize how high they had climbed.

Blaze released her and went ahead, climbing over a boulder. Cheyenne was gazing down at the graying water when Blaze pivoted toward her abruptly.

"Cheyenne." There was a world of anguish in his voice.

She reached for him. "What is it?"

He squeezed his eyes shut, face contorting with pain as he gestured below them.

Cheyenne swept past him to see where he was pointing. She peered past a slab of stone.

Red's eyes were half-open, his face empty of expression. He lay sprawled awkwardly over a ledge, feet dangling into space. His right hand lay across his chest. His skin was white, waxy, and Cheyenne knew before climbing down to him that he had probably been dead since yesterday.

Chapter Twenty-Seven

Red's body was stiff, and he had dependent lividity, with blood pooling downward. A small trace of dried blood caked the side of his face.

Cheyenne touched the small wound at the site of the blood, which had probably been caused when he fell. She withdrew and closed her eyes as grief washed over her. No matter how often she came face to face with death, it still filled her with horror and anger. She fought it desperately, and though she had gained the upper hand from time to time, she never truly won.

Blaze knelt next to her. "I should've taken him home yesterday, Chey. How could this happen? There's no boat, nothing." He reached out and touched Red's hand, then recoiled. "Oh, Red."

Cheyenne took Blaze's hand. "Blaze?" She grasped his shoulders and squeezed gently. "Honey, we have to go get help."

She continued to hold him as he gritted his teeth. He took a deep breath and squared his shoulders, still staring down at Red.

With a hard sniff, Blaze dashed his right sleeve across his face. "I know. We've got to get Dane." He closed his eyes. "We've got to take him with us. We can't leave him here."

"We can't move his body."

Blaze waved a hand toward the sky. "Look at those clouds moving in. We can't leave him alone here to get drenched in the rain."

"I don't want to, but we can't handle him ourselves."

"I'm not leaving him here alone. We're taking him."

"Blaze, we don't know how Red died. We don't know how he got here to the island. If there was foul play, and we move Red's body, the police might suspect us."

"They'll suspect me anyway, and I don't care."

"Blaze, look at me." She caught his chin between her hands. It was slick with tears. "Red couldn't have gotten here on his own, you know that. It looks like someone brought him here, and then left him to die. Do you want them to get away with that?"

He looked down at his friend again, and shook his head.

"Come on," she said, taking his arm as she would a child's. "Let's go get help."

He pulled away. "No. I'm staying here with Red until he can leave the island with me. You get help, call whoever you have to call." He sat down beside Red, crossing his legs, settling in.

Cheyenne left them there.

It hurt to leave Red like that—dear old Red, whose tender heart had been so big, who had been such a good friend to her, to Blaze, to the ranch. It hurt to see him reduced to a lifeless shell.

Was this all there was?

The wind picked up velocity before she reached the house,

and the water grew choppy. She had to fight the waves to get the small boat to shore.

Dane stepped out the back door of the Meyer house and waved to her. He was waiting at the dock to grab the rope when she tossed it to him.

"Where's Blaze?"

"He's…at the island."

Dane tied the rope around the post and reached to help her from the boat. His movements slowed as her words seemed to register. "Cheyenne?"

"We found Red's body." Her voice wobbled. "Blaze refused to leave him."

Dane closed his eyes. "No."

Cheyenne touched his arm. "I'm so sorry."

He took a deep breath as tears filled his eyes. "On the island? Was anyone with him? What happened?"

"We found him on the cliffs where he and Blaze liked to fish. Dane, we need to call the coroner. I knew Red was having heart problems, but there was no way for me to know if that's what happened to him. He's been dead for at least several hours. I can't imagine how anyone would take him there and leave him."

The back screen door of the house closed quietly, and they glanced up the hill to see Bertie on the steps of the porch.

"I'll tell her," Cheyenne said softly.

"We can do it together. How is Blaze taking it?"

"Not well." She took Dane's hand and squeezed, hoping her touch could convey some comfort as she forced herself to slip into ER doc mode—compassionate, detached, searching for the gentlest way to tell a wife of sixty-six years that her husband was dead.

She pulled away from Dane and stepped off the dock. Bertie met them halfway across the yard.

"Cheyenne, what's going on? What's wrong? I thought Dane said you and Blaze..." Her words trailed off as she seemed to catch something in Cheyenne's expression.

"We found Red on the island," Cheyenne said softly. She wasn't prepared for this. None of this. She couldn't be detached about someone she cared about this way. "I'm sorry, Bertie, he's dead."

She knew it was necessary to say the words so there would be no doubt about the message, but the impact hit Bertie with an almost physical force. Her cry of comprehension and pain seemed to rip through the fabric of the day. She stumbled forward, and Cheyenne caught her. Dane put his arms around her and helped her back to the house.

"Come on, Bertie, let's get inside," Dane said. "You need to sit down."

They helped her to the sofa in the living room, and Cheyenne held her while she cried, answering her questions, then holding her some more, while Dane called the coroner.

"I want to see him," Bertie said. "And why is Dane calling Blakely? The funeral home can take care of Red. They've always—"

"Blakely is the county coroner?" Cheyenne asked.

"Yes, but Buchanan's Funeral Home can handle everything. I know them."

Cheyenne couldn't answer her. How was she supposed to explain that someone must have discarded Red on the island like an unwanted piece of clothing?

But she did explain at last, choosing her words with care.

Dane called the ranch while Bertie and Cheyenne sat in silence on the sofa. Bertie patted Cheyenne's hand idly, maintaining contact, as if Cheyenne were the one most in need of comfort.

"Red's fine now." Bertie's voice trembled. "He loved that island, and it could be there's one a lot like it where he is now."

Cheyenne grasped Bertie's hand and nodded, disagreeing with every word. How could she believe Red was fine?

Red was gone. The end. No more marriage to this wonderful, feisty, loving lady, no more gardening, no more fishing or milking his beloved goats or chopping down killer cedar trees. Cheyenne understood the need for these people to seek solace from some source of faith at a time like this, but that's all it was. Solace.

Thirty minutes after Dane called the ranch, Cook arrived with three of the boys. "Dropped Willy and James off at the island to sit with Blaze," he said as he enveloped Bertie in a long, hard hug. "When we pulled away, they were all sitting around Red. Don't worry, they took umbrellas and all. We called your pastor, Bertie, and he's on his way over with his wife."

While everyone surrounded Bertie, Cheyenne slipped out the back door and walked down to the lake, desperately needing solitude. She certainly hadn't helped Red, and that failure had cost Bertie everything.

The first drops of rain splashed softly against her face with a coolness that refreshed her. She thought of Red lying exposed on the cliff, and of Blaze and his buddies hovering beside that tired old body, grieving....

Those boys, who had already lost so much in their lives, would understand Bertie's loss more than the people who would come and prattle about Red's death being all for the best. Death was never for the best. When you were dead, it was over. All this talk about heaven was wishful thinking.

The main reason she had become a physician was to fight death until the last possible moment. In the end, though, death won.

The lake was still rough, but Cheyenne decided to row home anyway. Bertie would have a houseful of company soon, and didn't need someone else taking up space.

Later, if Bertie needed her, she would come back.

Dane looked out the kitchen window and saw the lone figure standing on the dock in the rain, hands stuffed into the pockets of her jacket, shoulders hunched forward.

How could he have been so insensitive? He'd been so focused on Bertie's pain—and his own—that he'd completely overlooked the obvious. Cheyenne was hurting, too. She, too, had suffered a loss, and this on top of another recent loss that had threatened to destroy her life.

He heard a knock at the front door, followed by the voices of Reverend Webb and his wife. Bertie would have someone with her the rest of the day.

He stepped out the back door to find Cheyenne reaching for the rope that moored her rowboat to the dock. "Cheyenne?"

She turned and gave him a casual wave. "I'll see you later, Dane. I need to slip home and take care of the animals and clean up."

She untied the boat, taking obvious care to keep from slipping on the wet wood as he crossed the yard.

"Cheyenne, please don't leave yet."

She looked up. "Why not? Is Bertie okay?"

"She'll be fine, it isn't a medical problem, but something tells me you might need to stay," he said. "For your sake." Or was it, completely, for her? Was he being selfish? He simply didn't want her to leave. He drew comfort from her presence.

"I appreciate the thought," she said, "but I need to be alone for a while."

He stepped onto the dock as the rain and wind picked up tempo slightly. "Please let me take you, then." The tiny rowboat looked like a toy between his own Mystique and the pontoon Cook had brought.

The rowboat bumped back against the wooden supports, knocking Cheyenne sideways. He rushed down to steady her and help her out of the boat, then took the rope and wrapped it back around the mooring post. "It isn't wise to be on the lake right now. Won't you just wait until this thing passes?"

She looked up at him, her dark brown eyes filled with sadness, her face wet with rain. Or did he detect some tears? "It isn't cold, and I'm not afraid to walk in the rain."

"Neither am I. Come on." He was relieved when she relented and walked beside him.

"I'm sorry it didn't occur to me sooner," he said, "but seeing Red must have brought back some horrible memories for you. I recall you mentioned to me a few weeks ago that one reason you came to Hideaway was because you couldn't stand going home to an empty apartment."

She caught her lower lip between her teeth as they stepped onto the muddy road that led downhill to her driveway.

"Have you considered coming back to Bertie's once the animals are fed?" he asked.

"She has a house filled with company already, Dane. I'm a temporary visitor whose stay is almost over. Bertie doesn't need—"

"You have the healing touch, Chey, and I think she does need you. I think we all do."

She gave him a skeptical glance. "Don't humor me, okay? Nobody needs a doctor right now. It isn't as if I'm a part of the community."

"I'm not talking about your knowledge as a physician, I'm talking about the way you comfort and care about others. In that act of comforting others, I believe you'll find healing yourself. And I disagree with you, because you are a part of the community."

"Look, I appreciate the thought, but I don't have anything to give right now." She held her hands out beside her. "Got that? I don't have any words of comfort, any answers about what happened to Red or where his essence went when he died. I can't talk the talk about heaven and God and all the rest."

"Then you can let me talk."

"I just need to be alone right now, okay? I can find my own way home." She quickened her steps.

"So you can hide again?" He hadn't meant to say that out loud.

For a few seconds she paused and glanced back at him. "I'm not one of your boys, I'm a grown woman, and you aren't responsible for me. I have my own way of dealing with grief, and if that's hiding—" She hesitated, her voice softening. "If that's hiding, then that's my business." She said it gently, but it stung.

He refused to take the hint. "I'm involving myself in your business because I care very much what happens to you. I can't just stand by and watch you struggle with this thing all by yourself."

"You're a little too pushy, Dane Gideon," she said, making an obvious attempt to revert to her typical dry humor. "It isn't an attractive feature in a man."

His footsteps faltered, then he caught up with her. "You don't call Austin Barlow pushy for unloading a poor old broken-down horse in your barn so he'd have an excuse to visit?"

"I certainly don't call that attractive. A little sad, maybe."

"So you feel sorry for Austin? That's why you're going out on a date with him?" He felt irreverent just asking the question. "I'm sorry, I know that's definitely none of my business."

And yet he caught the glimpse of a brief smile that quickly vanished to be replaced, once again, by grief. Her pace slowed as they approached the end of her driveway.

She turned to look up at him. "Thanks for trying, Dane." She stopped beside the rural mailbox that was big enough to contain a month's supply of mail. "I don't think it's possible for you to understand what's going through my mind right now. I told you I was the physician on duty when my sister was brought in by ambulance."

"Yes."

"They tell me I did everything right, went above the call of duty, was even too aggressive in my efforts to bring her back." She brushed sudden tears from her cheeks. "She died, and her husband lived, and now the greedy bottom feeder is suing me, while all the time proclaiming himself to be a Christian as my sister was. That's just one reason I can't deal with the belief you and Bertie and practically everyone else around here seem to have that Red's in heaven—the same heaven Kirk claims to believe in."

"That isn't—"

"I'm not buying. In fact, I take offense at it."

"I don't blame you."

She blinked against the rain hitting her face. "What do you mean?"

"Come on." He took her hand. "Let's get to your house before we're drenched."

She didn't pull away, and he had the sense to keep his mouth shut until they stepped onto her front porch. This time when Dane reached out for her, she went to him, pressing her forehead against his chest. He held her tightly, and he kept his prayers continuous but silent. He knew she could cry enough tears to overflow Table Rock Lake and still not wash the memories away. The wind died down and the rain diminished by the time her shoulders stopped shaking.

He didn't stir until her sobs receded.

"I'm sorry," she said at last.

"Cheyenne, remember when you were an adolescent, and baked those horrible cookies, and your girlfriends hurt your feelings?"

She nodded, wiping the moisture from her cheeks. "If you're a wise person, you won't even attempt to tell me death is like a bad batch of cookies, and I need some tissues. Can you come into the house for a minute?"

He held the door for her and followed her inside. "I'm not trying to say anything like that. But you were devastated when it happened, weren't you?"

She picked Blue up when he attacked her, and reached for two tissues. "I got over it," she said, wiping her nose.

"Meaning you can look back on that time and see things now that you couldn't have seen then, how your experience ultimately gave Blaze the courage, and you the heart, to help him break through that barrier that kept him from reading and writing."

"We're talking about death here."

"But I'm also talking about God."

"I knew it."

"Cheyenne, the death of Red's body doesn't end his life. In fact, it's only the beginning. It isn't some crutch that weak people have to lean on to help them deal with pain—it's reality to those of us who believe. It's a basic truth."

She shook her head. "I'm sorry, but I can't believe the way you do. I've seen too many people like my ex-brother-in-law—"

"I know. They brag about their special connection to God, and then they try to destroy wonderful people like you. They preach Christianity one moment, and then discourage anyone who might believe by living a lie."

"Yes."

"But that isn't God you're seeing. Please don't judge Him by the actions of humans. You'll never perceive Him clearly that way."

"Then how can I see Him at all?"

"Ask Him to show Himself to you, Cheyenne. Remember when I told you He's a pursuing God? The only reason you're asking questions about Him is because He's made Himself known to you."

"If you're saying God took Susan so He could get my attention—"

"No. You've told me your sister was a believer?"

"Yes, but—"

"God didn't take your sister just to make you sit up and take notice, but He knows how you're hurting and He wants to comfort you. Your sister would tell you the same thing, and so would Red. Just ask God for yourself, Cheyenne. He's waiting for you. He loves you."

"You mean just start talking to thin air?"

"Pray. Ask Him to reveal Himself to you. Read the Bible."

"The rule book."

"The guidebook. It'll point you to Christ. It's the Bible that will tell you that when you seek God, He will be found. To me, those words mean that He will make Himself known to you. It's something God alone can do."

She hugged Blue against her as if she craved the touch of something living and breathing.

"I'm sorry," Dane said. "You didn't want me to preach, and I did it anyway."

"Just don't make me recite a prayer and get born again."

"Okay."

She raised her hand as if to touch his face, then hesitated and sank her fingers into Blue's fur once more. "Will you be okay?"

"I'll be fine." He wanted to stay with her, but she didn't want him here. He had to respect her privacy and give her time to grieve in her own way. And he needed to get to the boys on the island. "You'll come to Bertie's later?"

"We'll see."

"If you don't, I'll be back to check on you."

She nodded. "Thank you."

He turned to leave.

"Dane?"

He turned back.

"I didn't mean what I said earlier."

He frowned.

"You're a very attractive man, pushy or not."

"Please don't give up on all Christians just because of the jerks."

"I'll see."

Cheyenne meant what she'd told Dane. There was definitely something about him that drew her, and she didn't think all of it was physical attraction. Not all of it.

Much of what he'd said made sense. If the words had come from anyone but Dane, she wouldn't have listened, and she was sure Dane didn't think she had. How could he know there was a large void inside her that craved a healing she hadn't found? Was it possible she could find that healing from the God Susan had believed in, and Dane and Bertie and Red? And Ardis and Jim.

As Dane disappeared over the top of the rise, she self-consciously glanced upward at the cloudy sky. There was no

God there. All she saw was cloud, which was water. But beyond that?

"Are You there?" she whispered. "I don't know why all these things are happening, and maybe I don't have to understand. But I need something more."

When you seek Me, I will be found. That was what Dane had said. But according to Dane, she wasn't seeking God as much as God sought her.

But why would He seek her, of all people? Her name and reputation were being dragged through a destructive legal process. She would never be the same, never be quite as trusting and open with her patients. She would depend less on her clinical skills, and would run more tests, which would increase the patient's final bill. And for what? To be able to defend herself in court the next time she was sued. In emergency medicine, it seemed as if there would always be a next time.

"So you see," she whispered, "I wouldn't be much good to You the way I am."

She lowered her gaze, then turned back to the house, feeling silly. God had more important things to do than listen to her whine about her career.

Chapter Twenty-Eight

On Thursday, the day of Red's funeral, the parking lot of the Hideaway Community Church was filling quickly when Dane pulled the van alongside the curb beneath the shade of a maple tree. He had all the ranch boys with him. Cook pulled up behind him in his own car with Brian, Wes and David, three young men who had spent a good portion of their teen years at the ranch. Jinx pulled in behind Cook in the rebuilt '55 Chevy, which Cook and the boys had been working on in the garage for the past two years in all their "spare" time.

"You sure Cheyenne's coming in the limo with Bertie?" Blaze asked as he opened the front passenger door and stepped out.

"That's what she told me when I called Bertie's."

Cheyenne had spent the past three nights at the Meyer house so Bertie wouldn't be alone. During the days, the other boys had taken Blaze's chores at the ranch so he could milk the goats for Bertie while she dealt with a steady flow of visitors who had come from a radius of twenty miles to pay their respects and bring food. Dane was ashamed of himself for being relieved that the date between Austin and Cheyenne didn't materialize.

Austin met Dane and his crowd of kids in the vestibule of the church. His son stood beside him, dressed in a suit almost identical to Austin's. To Dane's dismay, when Austin stepped forward to greet them, Ramsay pointedly turned away, ignoring Blaze, and stepped to the other side of the vestibule.

Blaze caught up with him and tapped him on the shoulder. When Ramsay turned, Blaze leaned close and said something. Ramsay shook his head and backed away. Blaze followed, raising his voice. Ramsay shoved him away.

"Stop it!" he said, loudly enough for the others to hear. "Leave me alone!"

Austin walked over to them. "What's going on here?"

Blaze and Ramsay stared at one another in tense silence, then Ramsay looked away. "Nothing, Dad. We were just having a little disagreement about schoolwork."

"School's out, and you two need to have some respect for the dead." Austin gave Dane a look of annoyance over his shoulder. "You'd think as much as this town—and especially this church—has done for you lately, you'd care enough to have a little more control over your boys when you're here."

Dane bit back an angry reply as silence descended in the foyer. In seven years, he had never been more aware of Austin's ugly personal connection to him—and to his wife. All the painful suspicion—the painful knowledge—that he had intentionally stored away in the back of his mind now threatened to spill from his mouth. He bit his tongue. Hard. Austin had changed since then. And he had suffered.

"Blaze," Dane said softly. "Let's go in and sit down with the others, son."

For a moment, he thought Blaze was going to argue, but

then Bertie stepped in the back door with Cheyenne. It became obvious that several vestibule loiterers had been waiting to greet Bertie, and she was immediately surrounded.

A soft voice attracted their attention from the entrance to the sanctuary. "Bert? Bertie Meyer?" A small, white-haired lady peeped around from behind Cook, and the boys made way for her.

Bertie's face crumpled with tears. "Edith Potts, where've you been?"

Edith crept past the boys and stepped forward to wrap her arms around Bertie tenderly. They held each other and wept.

"I know he's where he needs to be," Bertie said, "but if only I could've tagged along."

"I'm so sorry," Edith crooned as she patted and caressed Bertie's back. "I was gone to my niece's in Denver, and I just heard the news yesterday."

Cheyenne hovered beside them, looking so distracted and uncomfortable that Dane approached her. "You can sit with Cook and the boys and me if you want. We'd love to—"

"Thanks, but Bertie invited me to sit with her and her nieces and nephews." She took his hand and squeezed it. "Dane, I—"

"Ladies," Austin said in his deepest, most reverent voice as he placed a hand on Bertie's shoulder, "we've reserved a special section at the front of the church for you." He turned to lead the way.

Cheyenne squeezed Dane's hand one more time, then released him and followed Bertie.

Dane gestured to Blaze, and together they followed the rest of the group inside.

"You're not much of a mixer, are you?" Blaze murmured softly as he walked beside Dane.

"What do you mean?"

"You no more than get close to Cheyenne when Barlow works his way in between you. I can't believe she doesn't see through that guy."

"I think she does. Besides, she canceled her date with Austin to stay with Bertie. Now, are you going to tell me what's going on between you and Ramsay?"

There was no reply.

"Blaze?"

He looked up at Dane as they reached the two pews filled with ranch boys. "First you tell me something," he whispered. "Do you think I'm the vandal?"

Dane knew as soon as he hesitated that it was the worst possible thing he could have done. He saw the hurt in Blaze's expression. "My heart says you didn't."

Blaze slid in and sat down, leaving room at the end for Dane. He leaned close to Dane's ear. "When your heart finally convinces your head of the truth, let me know."

Cheyenne was helpless against the influx of memories that attacked her when a young redhead man by the name of Lyle "Jinx" Jenkins sang the identical song that had been sung at Susan's funeral—all about walking and talking in a beautiful garden with the voice of the Son of God in his ear.

This time she felt a difference, however. What if the words were true? What if there were a few special people who actually knew God the way they said they did? And what if these special people—such as Red and Bertie and Susan and Dane and Ardis and Jim—did exist spiritually in a different dimension, in a place where they could perceive God's voice, or even His touch? What a difference He would make in their lives.

Anyone could lie about knowing God, even to themselves. But Cheyenne couldn't allow them to lie to her.

As Jinx ended his song, Bertie leaned toward Cheyenne and

touched her arm. "That boy always loved Red." She sniffed and wiped her eyes. "He even looks like Red used to, with all that bright hair. Red was sure proud of him."

Cheyenne was glad Red's death had been determined to be from natural causes—his heart. The injury on the side of his face had apparently occurred when he fell. The sheriff was still trying to discover who had taken Red to the island and left him, but no one seemed to know.

Though the lack of a satisfactory conclusion frustrated most everyone else, Bertie didn't dwell on it. "After all," she'd told Cheyenne yesterday, "it won't bring Red back to us. For his sake, I wouldn't want it to."

When the pastor asked for people to approach the microphone and recall memories of Red, Dane rose and made his way forward.

"Red was one of my best friends," he began. "He befriended me when I first arrived here, ten years ago, and he and his wife, Bertie, helped us establish the ranch. They've been like grandparents to my boys ever since, and we will all miss him terribly."

He went on to tell about Red's history, about the many ways Red had helped friends and neighbors around Hideaway, about the goat cheeses and garden vegetables he had frequently given away as gestures of goodwill, and the many lawns he had mowed for the widows in the town.

Dane's attention focused often on Bertie, and then, as if against his will, went to Cheyenne. As he spoke of Red's deep faith, he continued to glance at her, as if to see if she was listening. She was.

When Dane stepped down and someone else took his place, Cheyenne glanced at Bertie to see how she was doing.

Last night, before bed, Bertie had said something that intrigued her.

"God's given Red and me a lot more years together than others get, nigh on sixty-six years," she'd said. "I reckon we'll recognize each other once I join him."

"You truly believe that, don't you, Bertie?" Cheyenne asked.

"Believe?" Bertie looked around at her.

"About Red being in heaven."

"Sure I do, but it don't make any difference whether I believe it or not, the truth's the truth. It says right there in my Bible that there's a heaven, and I know Red and I both belong there." Her eyes teared up, as they so often had in the past couple of days. "Someday soon I hope to join him."

"Oh, Bertie, please don't talk like that."

Bertie frowned up at her. "Like what?" She sniffed and wiped away her tears. "Honey, there ain't nothing wrong with crying over Red's death, and nothing wrong with looking forward to heaven. I know he looked forward to it. I just miss him, is all."

Cheyenne placed a hand on Bertie's arm as someone else took the microphone to eulogize Red. *I miss him, too, Bertie.*

Summer made itself impossible to ignore on the last Tuesday in June, with sunshine that threatened to melt the plastic clothespins on the line out beside the house, and humidity that made even Cheyenne's thick, straight hair curl into waves. She had promised herself when she first arrived that she wouldn't use the air conditioner, and she didn't want to break that promise this close to the end of her stay.

She was leaving Thursday. The closer the time came, the more her heart ached, and the more she wanted to impress the natural beauty of this place into her memory—even if she did suffer heat stroke in the process.

It felt good to be able to leave the windows open and feel

the fresh—hot, sultry—breeze blow through the house. She couldn't do that in her apartment in Columbia without the—

"Stop it," she muttered to herself. Making comparisons between this place and home only depressed her. This was not home.

She poured a glass of tea and stepped out onto the front porch. Domestic and wild sunflowers were thick this year, according to Bertie. The yard had obviously been tended in the past by someone who loved flower gardens. The blackberries in the woods were also ripening. She planned to fill a bucket with them before she left, and leave some for Bertie, and take some to Ardis in appreciation for allowing her to heal here for three months.

In spite of continued grief, Cheyenne knew she was, certainly, recovering from the worst of it. She had discovered that, in the richest sense, Susan's spirit, as well as Red's, lived on. If Cheyenne had come here for no other reason than to discover that for herself, this time of limbo was worth it. She avoided thinking about her own mortality. That, she would save for another time.

Blue scratched at the screen door, and she let him out to join her on the porch, in spite of his tendency to want to snuggle his hot, furry body against her sweaty, bare legs and stick his nose into her tea. She hoped he would adapt well to air-conditioning.

She had made special arrangements, and agreed to pay a monthly premium, in order to keep a pet at her petless apartment complex. She just couldn't face the loneliness of that place without the affectionate presence of at least one other living being.

Blaze had already transplanted her coop of Bantam chickens to the ranch, and Austin Barlow had agreed, reluctantly, to her request that he allow the ranch to have Courage. Dane had convinced Bertie to let him and the boys milk the goats in exchange for a steady supply of goat milk and vegetables from the garden. It was all working out.

Cheyenne dashed a stray tear from her cheek and looked up at the sound of a motor from across the lake. She glanced at the small Timex watch she had purchased at the general store last week. Blaze was on his way over for a final lesson.

She had a glass of tea waiting for him when he arrived, and he took it gratefully. He sat down on the steps of the porch and pressed the glass against the side of his neck. He seemed subdued.

"Is everything okay?" She sat down beside him.

"Nope," he said gruffly, not looking at her. "Nothing's okay."

"Has something happened at the ranch?"

He shook his head and took a long swallow of tea, then wiped his mouth with the back of his hand. "Grass is getting deep in the yard again. You want me to mow?"

"There's no reason to," she said. "There won't be anyone here to see it."

"Fine," he muttered, glaring at the yard as if it had personally offended him.

"Okay, out with it, what's on your mind?"

"You don't want to hear it."

"Of course I do."

He gave her a sideways glance, his thick brows drawn low. "It's all your fault."

"Please don't tell me the chickens are sick."

"No, that's not—"

"And Courage? Is he okay?"

"Courage is fine, I'm not talking about that, I'm talking about you leaving and never coming back. Dane's been moping around the house like the world's about to end, and—"

"He is?" She couldn't imagine why this would make her feel better.

"And," he said irritably, "I'm never going to pass my written test for my driver's license without more—"

"That's silly. Of course you'll pass it."

"And you're leaving and never coming back."

"You just said that."

He gave her an anxious look. "You mean you're really never coming back? Not even for the annual fishing tournament in August?"

"What tournament?"

"The one the ranch sponsors every year, the first Saturday in August. Dane calls it our goodwill tournament, to help promote goodwill between the ranch and the town. Come on, Chey, Cook says practically everybody in town shows up for it, and there's a great prize for the person who catches the biggest fish."

"What's the prize?"

"Slave labor. Whoever wins gets to boss the ranch boys around all day on any Saturday they choose until Christmas. We mow yards, trim hedges, do dishes, pretty much anything, Dane says. The locals love it."

"I'll think about it."

"Do you mean you'll really think about it, or are you just trying to shut me up?"

She couldn't believe she was actually going to miss this kid. "I mean I'll think about it."

"As in, 'Yes, Blaze, I'll check with my boss and see if I can get the time off—'"

"Blaze."

"Okay, I'll tell Dane to put your name down on the roster. Even if you're just blowing smoke, at least it'll cheer Dane up."

He finished his glass of tea and set it down on the concrete. "Chey, what do you think of Dane?"

"I think he'll make a go of the ranch. Why?"

He sat for a few seconds in silence. "Well, I'm not playing matchmaker or nothing—"

"Or anything. Watch your double negatives—"

"—but you sure would be a nice addition to the ranch, kind of a house mother, and maybe you could also open a clinic."

"Oh, Blaze, you too?"

He shrugged. "Well, but if you married Dane, it sure would put a strain on the relationship for you to be all the way up in Columbia, and him and me all the way—"

"He and I."

"And who's going to help me get my driver's license?"

"You can do that all by yourself."

"I flunked four weeks ago."

"You're not the only person who's ever flunked an exam. Just try it again. I thought I saw a computer over at the ranch the other day. Can't you e-mail me?"

"You mean you expect me to learn how to type?"

"Absolutely. A veterinarian needs to know those things."

"No way I'll get into college."

"Get on into the house and start your work. I have it laid out on the kitchen table for you, along with some of Bertie's gooseberry pie."

For once, he did as he was told. Cheyenne stayed on the porch steps, staring across the lake, savoring the intensity of colors, the rich smell of earth and blooming flowers, cherishing the peace that surrounded her here.

Even if she did come back in August for a visit, she knew there would never be another interlude like this one.

Dane knocked on Cheyenne's door less than twenty minutes after Blaze arrived home with the news that she was considering a trip back down to Hideaway in August. He might as well push the advantage for all it was worth. Funny, the closer her time came to leave, the more he realized how much he had come to enjoy her company, and her presence across the lake.

She came to the screen door, and he saw her gaze drop immediately to his bare legs. "Why, Dane Gideon, I didn't realize you even owned a pair of short pants."

He felt suddenly self-conscious—a sure sign of adolescent attraction. He'd seen it in his boys lots of times.

"You haven't gotten out much this year, have you?" she teased, gesturing to his pale legs.

"I guess not. Long pants are handier for ranch work. Blaze told me you were planning to come back down in August. I just wanted to know for sure, and since you don't have a telephone, I can't call you."

"You're kidding, right? You came all the way over just to put my name on a roster?"

"No, actually, I wanted to see how you were doing and ask if you needed any help packing." He paused and glanced down toward the dock, where his Mystique was moored. "If you want, I can take the rowboat back over to Bertie's for you."

"I don't mind the walk, really."

"Oh." *Say it, dummy. Just tell her you'd like to spend some time with her.*

"But now's fine," she said quickly. "We can do it now. Oh, and you've got great legs. You should let them out more."

"Thanks." Amazing what an inconsequential compliment could do for the ego.

She pulled on her shoes and walked down to the dock with him. "I know Blaze is afraid he's going to have trouble when I'm gone, but judging by the work I've seen him do lately, I don't think that'll be a problem."

Dane tied the rowboat's mooring rope to his boat and

helped Cheyenne on board. "It's as if something has clicked in his head. All he wants to do is study now. Or talk about the pig races. Or talk about you. He's going to miss you." *So am I.*

"Well, there's no reason he can't race his pig, is there?"

"Not unless Austin finds something else to get mad about and takes Blaze's name off the sign-up sheet. He's got a crush on you, you know."

"Austin?"

"Blaze. A lot of people are going to miss you."

"I'm going to miss this place, too, but a girl's got to make a living."

"Make it in Hideaway."

She sank into the passenger seat with a heavy sigh.

He silently berated himself for nagging her. "I'm sorry," he said. "I must sound like a broken CD player."

"No, actually, I was just thinking it's nice to feel wanted."

Dane Gideon was not a man to allow himself false hope. "You'll always have a place where you're wanted, Cheyenne. And you'll always be welcome here as long as I'm here. Or Bertie. Or Cook or the boys or—"

"Got it." She slanted a grin at him that made his breathing quicken just a little. "You'd make a great salesman."

"You mean it's working?"

"I didn't say that, I said—"

"Here's another angle—if you want to work in an ER, Branson has an emergency department."

"Too big."

"Dogwood Springs, then. It's even closer if you're driving there from our side of the lake." He was pushing, he knew, but he was hooked.

She turned to him and put a hand on the back of his seat. "Dane, I'm not exactly trying to change the subject, but I want to thank you for not giving up on me last week. And thank you for the things you said at Red's funeral." All of a sudden, the tone of the conversation had changed. There was no teasing thread of laughter in her voice or in her dark eyes.

"You mean you listened?" *Yes!*

"I did. My sister was one of those special people who belonged to God. So was Red."

"We all belong to Him."

"But they had that special dimension that tied them to God forever."

"Yes, Cheyenne, they did." He realized where his heart was going, and he couldn't stop it. This was the kind of woman he could love, who could be his best friend and whose heart he knew he could trust. Sure, he'd made wrong choices before, but it was almost as if God had brought her here to prove to him that not all women were like Etta, who had claimed a love she hadn't known...and who might have even shared more than friendship with Austin Barlow. Austin hadn't become a Christian until some time after his wife's death.

Stop it. Thinking that way solved nothing, and he was being selfish. This wasn't about him, it was about God's will in Cheyenne's life. He should be celebrating the fact that she was at least acknowledging His presence in her sister's life, and Red's.

"I can tell you from personal experience that God wants that special relationship with you, too," he said, before he could stop himself.

She withdrew her hand and sat back in her seat, facing forward. He knew he'd pushed too hard. "I don't think you have any idea what God wants for me," she said. "For your information, He isn't interested in me or my prayers."

"What gives you that—"

"I'm going back to Columbia on Thursday, Dane. End of story."

Chapter Twenty-Nine

Dane listened to the sounds of hammers, nails, saws behind him as he took a break down at the dock. After three weeks of hard work during some of the hottest days of the year, the barn was almost finished, and Dane was proud of his boys. He was proud of the whole town of Hideaway. They knew the meaning of community as men and women volunteered their days off and evening hours to help with the rebuilding.

For some reason, since the fire, and especially since Red's funeral, the community had seemed to embrace Dane's boys as their own. Finally. After all these years of struggle. It was as if they had chosen to honor Red's memory by recognizing the primary focus of the man's affection. To Red, Dane's boys were the grandchildren he'd never had because of the death of their only child. In effect, the premature death of the Meyers' son all those years ago had triggered a chain reaction that had led to this community outpouring.

Unfortunately, Austin Barlow's short demonstration of a thaw when he delivered Courage last month had dissipated as the weeks passed. He seldom came this way. He was busy with his mayoral campaign.

Dane hadn't even considered campaigning. He figured everyone already knew him, knew his work and experience, and if they wanted to vote for him, they could do it. He would have enough exposure to the crowd during the tournament and the festival, when he and Austin had their friendly debate. If he didn't win, he would be greatly relieved.

He gazed across the water at the empty house on the hill. He'd missed Cheyenne these past three and a half weeks more than he'd dreamed possible, and he found himself struggling with hurt feelings over her departure, over the things they had said, and over the things he had left unsaid.

He had no right to be hurt. It wasn't as if he'd appealed to her on a personal level to stay. Sure, he'd urged her to consider a solo practice. Big deal. Austin Barlow had done the same thing, but he'd also asked her to a show, and he hadn't bashed her over the head about her need for God in her life.

Dane knew that must have made her feel as if he were classifying her as a second-rate citizen.

After the divorce, Dane had been convinced he was meant to be alone, and until now he'd been at peace with it. If Cheyenne had never come, he still would be. Now, so many things had changed.

"Dane?"

He turned to see Blaze stepping onto the dock. "Sorry, Blaze, I need to be nailing on that south wall."

"Willy's taking care of it. That load of aluminum's in the drive. Where do you want it?"

Dane got up and gazed at the new barn. "Where they are is good. We'll start nailing it up in an hour or so. Has anybody mentioned anything about that new doctor Austin has coming for a visit?"

"Cecil says he's coming tomorrow. Says he's a young guy, just out of residency."

Dane couldn't explain his disappointment. "I'll be up in a minute."

"Okay, but staring at that house isn't going to bring her back, you know," Blaze said.

"Didn't she say she was coming for the tournament?"

"Last I heard, but it wouldn't hurt you to ask her yourself."

Before Dane could reply, Blaze went back up the hill, where seven men worked alongside the boys on the building. By the end of the day it would be nearly complete.

Dane had never felt less complete in his life.

"Cheyenne, have you missed me?" The exquisite lines of Susan's face glowed with life as she walked beside Cheyenne along a tunnel of green that was the Katy Trail.

The Missouri River whispered past them, about a hundred yards away. It was the same stretch of trail they had biked together so often. No one else was in sight.

"Where have you been?" Cheyenne asked.

"I told you where I was going. Why didn't you listen?" Susan laughed and ran ahead, the way she had done all their lives.

Cheyenne ran after her, cherishing the sight of her, the sound of her voice, but it was impossible to catch up. Susan remained a few steps ahead.

"Why won't you wait?" Cheyenne cried.

"Because then you won't follow."

"But I am! Please, Susan, come back."

"I can't. You've got to follow me. Please follow, Cheyenne."

Though Cheyenne ran as fast as she could, her sister disappeared into the haze.

Cheyenne was left in the darkness.

It was into that same darkness she awakened. Her eyes flew open, and tears trickled down the sides of her cheeks.

"Susan," she whispered.

She saw the clock on the desk beside the bed and realized she was in the darkened sleep room at work. It was six-fifteen in the evening, only forty-five minutes away from quitting time. She needed to get to work on her charts.

She turned on the desk lamp and checked the time again. Amazing that she'd been able to sleep for two solid hours at this part of her shift. She should have done her charts before she took a nap, but she'd just been too tired.

She shuffled into the bathroom and splashed cold water in her face, avoiding her reflection in the mirror. She didn't want another glimpse at the dark circles that had reinstated themselves beneath her eyes, like a constant reminder of the insomnia that had plagued her since returning here three and a half weeks ago.

The nightmares had grown less intrusive recently, segueing into dreams of Susan that were so vivid Cheyenne never wanted to wake up. But she always did.

The fatigue weighed her down. She knew it was depression, but what was she supposed to do about it? Even though she had brought Blue with her, the apartment still felt haunted. Her whole life felt haunted.

Maybe that was what Susan had been trying to tell her in the dream—or what Cheyenne was trying to tell herself. She'd tried to pray a few times recently but always felt foolish. She had no sense of anyone listening.

Columbia had lost its appeal with Susan gone, and though Cheyenne knew she could reach out to her friends here at work, spend more time with Ardis, or with Jim and Louise Brillhart, or with her old college friends she also knew that their kindness to her came from the goodness of their hearts, and not from any need they felt to have her in their lives.

She'd never before realized there was a difference. The only time she felt encouraged was when she was talking with Bertie on the telephone or e-mailing Blaze, or even when Austin had called her to invite her down to attend the festival in September. She looked forward to the fishing tournament in Hideaway the week after next. Maybe all she needed to do was return for a couple of days in the heat of the summer and realize it wasn't where she belonged, after all.

But what if she discovered it was?

Dane had been conspicuously silent, and that hurt. She knew he was busy with the boys and rebuilding the barn, but would it have been so difficult to pick up the telephone and call her? Why had she been so abrupt with him just before she left to come back? Had it been her imagination that he'd seemed to care about her? Not necessarily in a romantic way, but as a friend.

But friends would keep in touch with friends, wouldn't they? Even when she'd called the ranch to talk to Blaze, Dane was never the one to answer the phone. She'd asked Blaze about him, but had received unsatisfactory replies.

If even Austin Barlow could call her and invite her to a town function, why couldn't Dane?

She sat down at the desk and flipped through the stack of letters, lab reports and advertisements for medical education conferences all over the world—the kind she never attended because of the expense. She usually obtained her required yearly credits locally or via courses offered by mail or online.

She glanced at several lab reports for patients from recent shifts, then came to an envelope marked Personal and Confidential from the office of Larry Strong, Director, Department of Risk Management.

"Oh, brother," she muttered, rolling her eyes. Couldn't he have just called her on the phone if he wanted another meeting? Why did he have to summon her so formally? Unless...

She opened the envelope and unfolded the single sheet of embossed, typewritten paper, and skimmed the message. The hospital was agreeing to settle with Kirk Warden for a quarter of a million dollars. They needed her input.

With numb fingers, she refolded the letter and stuck it into the pocket of her lab coat, pulled on the coat and wrapped her stethoscope around her neck. Later. She could deal with it later. Right now she had charts to complete, and she wanted to think about anything but lawsuits.

Dane placed the final sheet of corrugated aluminum in a stack on the new concrete floor in the new barn and glanced up at the sky. It was clear, with no rain in the forecast for several days. For him, that was a good thing. Maybe they would get the barn completed and the animals moved back without being impeded by bad weather. However, the heat was oppressive.

He was closing the door, prepared to go check on the boys at the borrowed milking facilities, when Blaze came strolling out through the lot, hands in the pockets of his jeans, head bowed as if he was deep in thought.

"What's up, Blaze?"

"Nothing new," Blaze said without looking up. "Some guy called about renting that back counter down at the store and opening a pharmacy, and I've got to fix dinner tonight because—"

"What's wrong with Cook?"

"Hemorrhoids again."

Dane sighed. Cook had been told he needed surgery, but he refused to go "under the knife." Instead, he suffered a lot, complained a lot, and had earned himself the title of Hideaway's favorite hypochondriac. Dane had tried to convince Cook to take a vacation and get his mind off the daily stress of keeping up with all the boys. He refused. This was his life. To the crusty old bachelor, this was his family. It was Dane's, as well.

"Did you take a number so I can call the pharmacist back?" Dane asked.

"It's by the telephone, though you'd never notice since you never talk on the phone, and you're hardly ever even in the house lately, because you're out here working on the barn."

"I'm sorry, I know I've been preoccupied lately. The Marions have been more than generous to loan us the use of their barn, but this juggling act is a tough one. I want to get all our cattle back here and everything back into operation."

Blaze leaned against the doorjamb and looked up at Dane. "Cheyenne asked about you in her last e-mail."

"She did? What did she say?"

"Just asked how you were doing, and if you were still freaking over the barn not being done yet."

"Who said I was freaking?"

"I did."

"And you're learning to type that well after just a few weeks?"

"Pretty well. I don't type all the time. Sometimes she calls to talk to you, and I just happen to answer the phone."

"She asks for me?" Dane's spirits lifted with incredible swiftness.

"No, but I know she's hoping to hear your voice."

Those same spirits plummeted just as swiftly. "You should write fiction, Blaze. Come on, let's go to the house and get dinner."

"Cheyenne doesn't sound happy," Blaze said as they walked

toward the house in the heavy, hot evening air. "I don't know why you aren't keeping in touch. She's asked about you a couple of times—you know the way people do when they're trying hard not to show how interested they are. It wouldn't hurt to just call and ask her how she's doing, maybe let her know about that doctor Austin's trying to lure here to set up practice—which I think's a big mistake."

"You think getting a doctor here is a mistake?"

"I think getting someone who doesn't belong here is a mistake."

Dane glanced at Blaze from the corner of his eye. The kid was definitely smitten with Cheyenne, but Dane couldn't blame him. "I don't want to twist Cheyenne's arm. She knows what's here, and she's obviously not interested. Her life is in Columbia, and we have to get on with things."

"But you act like you don't even care about her."

"Would you back off? She left of her own free will." And she'd made it very obvious that she felt Dane was coming on too strong already. "Quit trying to play matchmaker and just concentrate on learning right now."

"I am. I'm not sure I like learning that much."

"Why not?"

Blaze stepped up onto the porch. "Because I've learned a lot more than I wanted to learn." He pulled open the storm door and barreled inside without waiting for Dane. "A whole lot more than I ever wanted to know. Like how a grown man responsible for a bunch of teenagers doesn't even have the nerve to call a woman and tell her how he feels about her."

"How do you know how I feel?"

Blaze snorted. "Right."

Dane followed him inside and closed the door, relishing the coolness of air-conditioning against his sweaty face and arms.

"Cook told me that you think just because one woman

couldn't stick it out, you can't ever be married again," Blaze said from the kitchen doorway. "I told Cook you weren't that stupid."

"Do you mind not broadcasting my personal business through the whole house?" Dane grumbled.

"Everybody's gone except Cook, and he's hiding out in his room. Willy and James went to Bertie's to milk the goats, and the rest are taking care of the cows. You know, if you got married again, you could fix up that cottage out back—"

"Not everybody gets married," Dane said in his drop-the-subject voice.

"No, but just because one woman couldn't hack it doesn't mean—"

"Blaze—"

"You know, it doesn't all have to be about romance. You could just be Cheyenne's friend. She needs good friends, and to her I bet it looks like you've said good riddance. What do you think that makes her feel about all that Christian kindness you keep preaching about?"

"I don't preach." Dane couldn't explain himself to Blaze. How was he supposed to admit to a sixteen-year-old kid that he was afraid a friendship with Cheyenne might turn into more than that for both of them? He'd felt a connection with her that he hadn't experienced with another woman since Etta.

He glanced at Blaze. "What did you mean a minute ago? You know, that thing you said about learning more than you wanted to?"

Blaze pulled out a big stockpot and put it on one burner of a six-burner stove top. "Never mind."

Dane would have dismissed the subject except for the way Blaze deliberately avoided looking at him. "Blaze, is something bothering you?"

Blaze didn't reply as he went out into the mudroom and

opened the freezer, shuffled through the bags of frozen meals, then shut the door and came back in carrying a two-gallon freezer bag of vegetable soup Cook had made a month ago. His thick brows were drawn together with apparently focused concentration.

Dane opened a cupboard and pulled out some bowls.

"Did you ever betray a friend?" Blaze asked suddenly.

Dane glanced at him. Was this some new approach to convince him to call Cheyenne? "Probably."

"Do you still think I might be the vandal?"

Wow, abrupt change of subject. Or was it? "I never felt you were the vandal, Blaze."

"I didn't ask what you felt, I asked what you thought. Remember the day of Red's funeral you told me that in your heart you didn't believe I'd burned the barn, but you left this honker of a question about what your brain told you?"

"I remember." Sadly, he did.

"We haven't had any vandalism since then," Blaze said. "Do you think it's possible the vandal was someone who wasn't from around here, and they just moved on?"

"It could be. I'm praying that's the case, and that they won't come back."

Blaze stuck the frozen bag into the microwave. "I didn't do it."

"I know."

That didn't seem to satisfy him. "I don't think anyone from the ranch did it."

"Neither do I." Dane watched him more closely. "Do you have some idea about who it might have been?"

Blaze set the timer on the microwave and punched it on. He turned and looked at Dane with eyes so filled with sadness it broke Dane's heart.

"Blaze?"

"I haven't slipped out of the house at night lately."

"Okay. Why not?"

"What do you mean? You told me not to."

"That didn't stop you before."

"I guess maybe I'm settling in a little. Anyway, I wasn't the vandal. I'm going to check on Cook."

Cheyenne perused the empty ER with satisfaction as Ardis glanced up at her from the nurses' workstation.

"There you are, Dr. Allison. Did you get some rest?"

"Not enough."

"There's a fresh pot of coffee in the break room."

"I'll get some."

"Nope, you stay right here." Ardis pulled out the chair at the doctor's workstation cubicle. "You'll want to get to work on those charts so you can get home on time for once. You still take a cream and a sugar, right?"

"That's right."

"I can't believe after all these years you haven't learned how to appreciate coffee in its natural state," she teased. "I'll be back with it."

Cheyenne grinned at her friend's retreating back and started on her charts. Her grin disappeared. On the top chart was a sticky note with a reminder that she had failed to do an HEENT exam on a patient with a triple A—abdominal aortic aneurysm.

She dropped her pen to the desk and hissed. "How stupid," she muttered.

Ardis returned with her coffee. "What's stupid?"

"The guy who was rushed to emergency surgery to prevent abdominal rupture? Med Records is complaining because I didn't document an exam of his eyes, ears, nose, throat while

I was at it. The guy's life was in danger, and all they can…of all the stupid—"

"Don't blame Med Records, blame the people who make up the reimbursement rules," Ardis said.

"Yes, but—"

Ardis leaned closer to her, frowning. "It's okay, Cheyenne," she said quietly. "The standards all clash, but that's just the way it is. Honey, are you all right? You just haven't seemed the same since you came back from Hideaway."

"Well, compared to the way I felt before I left, isn't that a good thing?"

Ardis hesitated, then shook her head. "It's almost shift change, and you're due back in the morning. Maybe a few of those charts can wait until then."

Cheyenne took a slow, deep breath and tried to calm herself. "That's okay, I'll get through them." She thought again of Hideaway, and realized how much she looked forward to her trip back down there in a week and a half.

Until then, she could endure.

"Aha! I've got it." Cheyenne raised her pen to the blank line of the offending chart. "Edentulous," she murmured. "There, now everybody's happy."

Ardis chuckled. "Nobody'll know what the word means."

"They won't care as long as their blank is no longer blank. You did tell me he'd been worried about his dentures."

As she completed the rest of her charts and paged through additional mail, she reflected on Ardis's comment. She'd been right. Nothing seemed the same. Cheyenne knew she'd complained about a lot since she'd returned. She felt constantly edgy…empty.

Again, she recalled the dream about Susan. *"Cheyenne, you won't follow…"*

But what was she supposed to follow?

At the bottom of her stack of charts she saw another envelope someone must have slipped in when she was sleeping. She slit it open to find a physician schedule for August. Her name was down for the first Friday and Saturday of the month, with a sticky note from Jim with an apology and an explanation that three other physicians had requested that week off before she made her own request.

The disappointment overwhelmed her.

Ardis looked up from her work. "Something wrong?"

"Just the schedule."

On the other side of the partition that shielded the ER proper from the waiting room and reception desk, the secretary greeted someone. Cheyenne glanced at her watch. Fifteen minutes to go before shift change.

"How can we help you today?" came Patty's voice.

"My little boy's sick. Can the doctor check him out?" came the voice of a young mother.

"Sure we can. Sign here, please," Patty said. There was a pause, then the sound of the chime that summoned the triage nurse. "Has any of your information changed since the last time we saw your son?"

"No, it's still all the same. Uh, could you tell me who the doctor is on duty?"

"That would be Dr. Allison for fifteen more minutes. She'll see him as soon as the nurse—"

"Allison? You've got to be kidding. She's still here?"

Cheyenne glanced at Ardis, who held her gaze.

The voice at the reception desk continued. "She's not touching my son. I heard she was being sued because she killed one of her patients."

"I don't know where you heard that," Patty said, her voice still soft and conciliatory. "Dr. Allison's an excellent physician, board certified in emergency medicine. She's—"

"She's a threat to my little boy. If she'll be gone in fifteen minutes, we'll wait."

Cheyenne suppressed a gasp of almost physical pain. She shoved away from the desk. "I'll be in the call room if you need me, Ardis."

Chapter Thirty

"Ardis, is Mrs. McKenzie's lab back yet?" Cheyenne asked. She was concerned about the risk of stroke for the seventy-three-year old patient, who'd presented by ambulance with chest pains and shortness of breath and dangerously high blood pressure Despite the clonidine pills, the pressure remained high.

"Yep, it all looks pretty good."

"Go ahead and call her family physician and I'll talk to him."

"She's new in town and doesn't have one." Ardis gestured Cheyenne aside. "She said a couple months ago she had to stop taking some of her medications because the total cost was eight hundred dollars a month and she couldn't afford it."

Cheyenne sighed and closed her eyes. She saw this kind of thing too much. "Okay, get me whoever is on call for family practice—Dr. Frazier, isn't it? I'll be in six." She washed her hands and entered exam room six, where a slightly impatient woman sat with her two-year-old daughter who had been in yesterday for an earache. Cheyenne was reminding the mother that it usually took two days on antibiotics before there was noticeable improvement. When the secretary slid the curtain back and leaned inside. "Dr. Allison, I have Dr. Frazier holding for you on line two."

Cheyenne apologized to the annoyed young mother and took the call at her workstation. As she had feared, she received the typical doctor-to-doctor brush-off. "She sounds too complicated, Dr. Allison. You need to have Internal Medicine take care of it."

Cheyenne brushed past Ardis on her way back to room six. "Okay, it's back in your court, Ardis. Dr. Frazier wants Mrs. MacKenzie to go to Internal Medicine."

Cheyenne returned to room six and repeated the exam she had given yesterday. As she'd expected, the involved ear looked the same. After some further discussion with the mother, Cheyenne wrote a script for a codeine elixir and requested that the patient be taken to her pediatrician in seven to ten days.

"Dr. Bagby is on line one, Dr. Allison," the secretary told her when she got back to her workstation.

Cheyenne picked up the receiver and explained Mrs. MacKenzie's situation to the specialist. "I'll be happy to consult, Dr. Allison, but Dr. Frazier should be able to take this patient," came the reply. "Mrs. MacKenzie's problems are obviously all secondary to noncompliance. Once she's back on her regimen, she should do fine."

She hung up the telephone to find Ardis standing beside her. "Hot potato."

"You want me to call Dr. Frazier again?"

"Let me check Mrs. MacKenzie first, and I'll let you know." Cheyenne returned to room four. A quick check of her elderly patient's lungs revealed mild expiratory wheezing that hadn't been apparent earlier.

"The IV medication we gave her must have aggravated her asthma," she told Ardis, and gave her the appropriate instructions. Cheyenne squeezed Mrs. MacKenzie's arm. "We're going to have to place you in ICU."

Back in the break room, she poured herself a cup of coffee and slumped at the table. She got one of the hot potato cases at least once or twice a week. The Family Practice guys didn't want to take on a complicated patient who could crash, because then they could get sued. The Internal Medicine guys didn't want any more complicated patients because their lives were full of complicated patients. Nobody wanted the patient, and those poor souls who were hurting and sick often fell through the cracks of the hospital politics game. And that was just in Columbia, which most of the rest of the country would consider medical care heaven, due to the high ratio of physicians to patients.

"Knock-knock, can I come in?" Ardis walked to the coffeepot and poured herself a cup of thick, black, ER-style coffee. No creamer, no sugar. What a woman.

"Didn't I see an envelope addressed to you from Larry Strong yesterday?" She joined Cheyenne at the table.

"Yes."

"So how's that going?"

"They've decided to settle for a quarter of a million dollars."

"You're kidding, right? You're just going to drop it?"

"It isn't as if I have a choice. Do you know how much it would cost to get my own attorney?"

"Okay, but who have you talked to about this?"

"I'm not supposed to talk to—"

"Baloney. How are you supposed to find witnesses if you don't talk to anybody? I can testify that you did everything right. We all did. And we weren't the only ones in the room. Didn't the police report absolve Susan of blame in the accident?"

"Kirk claims she could have avoided the accident if she'd been thinking clearly. I'm sorry, Ardis, but I give up. I can't fight it, and I don't have the strength."

"The old Cheyenne would have spoken to everyone who saw Susan that afternoon, beginning with the taxi driver and ending with the police report, or even eyewitnesses of the accident."

"Maybe I've just changed, Ardis," she said irritably. "Have you thought of that? I hate the ER abuse. I hate not having more control over the treatment of patients. It's frustrating."

Ardis sipped her coffee, studying Cheyenne in thoughtful silence. "The place in Hideaway is for rent."

"Good. You should be getting some income from it. That's a good, solid house. So what does that have to do with—"

"It's pretty, too, since you gave it a facelift. The rent would be reasonable." She put her cup back on the table. "Especially for you, since you've put all the time and work into the place."

"For me? Ardis, what would make you think—"

"You told me they need a doctor down there."

"Yes, but I didn't tell you I wanted the job."

Ardis winked at her. "You didn't have to. I wouldn't go making any quick decisions, but maybe you need to step back and take a look at what you really want in your life." She leaned back and stretched. "Who knows? I might be interested in a slower pace myself. Every good doctor needs a good nurse."

Cheyenne cruised down the street in front of Kirk and Susan's place—she refused to think of it as just Kirk's place. She desperately hoped he wouldn't glance out the window and see her car. Sooner or later, however, if this meeting went well, it wouldn't matter what he did.

She parked in front of the Harrison house, three doors down. This time, when she rang the doorbell, an attractive, plump lady in a red silk pant set answered the door. When Cheyenne explained who she was, the woman smiled.

"You're the sister! Please, come in. I can't tell you how many times I've thought about contacting you in the past few months."

Cheyenne entered the broad vestibule, caught by the blend of gemstone colors that were Susan's signature. "I came to speak with you once, but you weren't home. Your husband… seemed a little preoccupied."

"Oh, him." The lady dismissed him with a wave of her hand. "He never tells me anything, just treats me like a mushroom, keeping me in the dark and shoveling dirt at me every so often." She chuckled to take the sting from her words as she led Cheyenne into a bright room with a wall of windows offset with stone and at least thirty plants of various sizes and description. "I was at your sister's funeral, and I would have spoken with you then, but you were surrounded by so many family members, I didn't want to intrude. I just wanted to tell you what a treasure your sister was." She gestured around the room. "Susan was a true artist, and a kind person. I think of her a lot when I come in here, because this was the last room that ever felt the touch of her artistic hand."

Cheyenne sat down in an oversize leather wingback chair, and for a moment she felt caught by a tight band of unrelenting grief. "I was wondering, do you remember much about that last day? Did she say anything to you about why she might have been driving?"

"I sure do. Her husband told her to, that's why."

"How did he do that?"

Mrs. Harrison settled back on her sofa. "Well, right away when she arrived that day, I could tell something was wrong, because she wasn't her usual cheery self. But we knew she and Kirk hadn't been getting along that well—he and my husband golf together—and so I just figured that was it. But when she climbed up on her stepladder, she stumbled and nearly fell. When I asked what was wrong, she told me she was on medication and wasn't supposed to do heights or operate machinery."

"She told you that?"

"I wasn't the only one she told," Mrs. Harrison said. "When her husband called her to pick him up, she told him, too."

"She did?"

"Sure she did. Or at least, she tried to explain it to him, but he outshouted her. Typical hormone-stuffed jerk," she muttered.

Cheyenne refrained from saying what she would like to stuff him with. "So let me get this straight, Mrs. Harrison. My sister was completely aware that she wasn't supposed to be driving that day."

"That's right. Although she did say before she left that she thought the medication might be wearing off by the time she drove away. I think that was just an excuse, though. I think she was a little afraid of her husband, and he was shouting loudly enough that I heard his voice from the receiver all the way in the other room."

"Why didn't she have him take a taxi?"

"She suggested it, and he shouted again."

Cheyenne's fingernails stabbed her hands. "Mrs. Harrison, I know you and your husband are aware of the lawsuit Kirk has filed against me and the hospital. Has he ever given you any details about the case?"

"Never. That sounds like it must be top secret stuff, because

I've never heard a thing. I just figured Kirk wasn't supposed to talk about the case."

"He isn't." But that wouldn't have stopped him. "The lawsuit is actually being based on the allegation that I failed to warn my sister about the dangers of driving, operating other heavy machinery or climbing under the influence of the medication I gave her."

Mrs. Harrison frowned, leaning forward on the sofa. "But that's silly. That's crazy!"

"My attorneys are advising me to settle because we can't seem to prove we warned her. Apparently, my documentation was missing—"

"But they can't do that! You did warn her, and she told me."

"Would you be willing to testify about that?"

"Of course I'll testify. You just tell me who I need to talk to." She leaned forward and winked slyly. "Want to hear some good dirt on Kirk? The guys are all talking about it down at the golf club. Seems his secretary turned him in to the IRS, and he's in the hot seat for tax fraud."

But the news didn't please Cheyenne, as she would have expected. It saddened her.

Fifteen minutes later, she got into her car and plugged in her phone. She dialed Larry Strong's office. When he came on the line, she gave a brief explanation of her visit, and told him she would not be willing to settle.

When she arrived home she would type a letter with the same message.

Before going home, however, she drove to the cemetery and parked near Susan's grave marker. The evening was warm, and most likely filled with millions of hungry mosquitoes. She got out of the car and took her customary position by the marker with the picture of Susan's laughing face.

This time it felt different, however. This time the horrible grief, which had weighed on her so heavily every time she came here, had lifted.

"Sis," she whispered, feeling self-conscious even though she could see no other cars in the cemetery. "I miss you." She pressed her hand against the engraved words and closed her eyes. "And I'll always love you. I'm sorry I didn't bring flowers this time, but I think you have enough flowers where you are."

Did she truly believe that?

Yes. It wasn't wishful thinking; it was as if she had suddenly realized the enormity of the truth that had been dawning on her for a long time. "Thanks for never giving up on me, for telling me like it is, even though you knew how I felt about all that Christ talk."

A car horn blared in the distance, and an airplane droned overhead as she sat contemplating all the things she wished she could tell her sister personally right now. "You know how you complained so many times about my bossiness? From the day you were born, I felt so responsible for you. I felt that if I didn't take care of you, something horrible would happen."

She swallowed. Hard. "And then when it did, I believed for a long time that it was my fault."

But it hadn't been, she knew that now. "And it turns out that you were the one looking after me all this time, even in my dreams after you died, and I want you to know—I just wish I could tell you, somehow—that I'm listening."

Susan had been right all along.

Dane waited until all the boys were upstairs, and Cook was safely ensconced in front of the television in his room, before picking up the phone. He glanced at the number he had written on his bedside stand just before Cheyenne's departure, and he dialed.

When she answered, he was struck again by the mellow, sweet tone of her voice.

"Cheyenne? This is Dane."

Silence.

"Hello?" he said.

"Is everything okay?" she asked.

"It's fine, I just thought I'd call and see how you were doing."

There was a sound of soft laughter. "I can't believe you called just when I was thinking about you."

He smiled into the receiver. "You were?"

"I was just thinking about how surprised you would be by the things that have happened in the past few days. You won't believe it."

"Let's see…you came to your senses and decided to come back to Hideaway." There was a long pause, and Dane felt awkward. "I'm sorry, that was insensitive of me."

"No. Really. I was just wondering how you knew that."

For a moment, he forgot to breathe. "It isn't nice to tease me like that."

"I've never been considered a tease." She laughed again, and he loved the sound of it. "Dane, I think we've got some good evidence to help us with the malpractice case."

"You do? That's wonder—"

"And yes, I've been missing Hideaway a lot. I have to work the weekend of the fishing tournament."

"Oh." *And that was good news?*

"And I think it's a direct answer to my prayers."

"You do?" *She'd been praying?*

"Yes. This past month, all I've thought about has been the time I spent there. I've been daydreaming about what it would be like to live there instead of in my cramped, noisy apartment."

"I thought you loved what you did."

"I realized I love treating patients. I guess I'm not as addicted to adrenaline surges as I once thought. There would be one big problem, though."

Okay, here came the big kink in the works. "What's that?"

"Money."

"I know the setup expenses will be heavy, but I've been talking to a lot of people around here. You'll have a lot of community involvement. You'll probably have to take a big cut in pay at first—"

"There's the rub, Dane. You know I give a lot to the rescue mission three blocks away from where I live."

"I believe you could eventually earn enough here in Hideaway that you could start giving to them again. I can't guarantee that, however. Would it help you to know about how many people you would be helping right here? People like Red, who might be more willing to accept medical care after they've come to know you and trust you? People like Blaze, who might have died if not for you the night of the fire?"

"Red died." He heard the thread of self-recrimination. "If I'd tried harder to convince him to seek medical care, Bertie wouldn't be struggling with so much loneliness now."

"If you'd had access to a well-stocked and equipped clinic nearby, I believe you might have convinced him to see you, simply because he trusted you. He didn't want to be passed off to some impersonal doctor in some strange place."

"Yes, I know, but one doctor can't do everything."

"I'm not asking you to, but look how much potential you'd have right here to touch lives. And look at Blaze. Not only have you helped him break through that reading barrier, you saved his life."

"You could have—"

"I couldn't have started his heart again, Cheyenne. Just

listen to what I'm saying. How many more lives could you change right here in Hideaway?"

"It's all I've thought about lately," she said.

It took a great deal of effort not to let his hopes soar to dangerous heights. He couldn't jump to conclusions. She was just thinking about it, she wasn't doing anything about it yet.

"Cheyenne, are you coming to the festival in September? Blaze has been training race pigs for about half a dozen—"

"I'll be there. I've already asked for the time off, and I wouldn't miss those pig races for anything."

"And after that?"

A pause. "Under the terms of my contract, I have to give a ninety-day notice."

"Three months?"

"It could take awhile to find a physician to fill my position."

"Cheyenne, there's another physician checking out the town. He seems interested."

"Oh. How interested?"

"I don't know. You'd have to talk to Austin about that."

"I think I will."

Yes!

"Dane? Thanks for being so pushy."

"Pushy?"

"About God. I finally got the message. I'm going to see my sister again someday."

He closed his eyes. *Thank you, Lord. Thank you.* "Until then, you have a home waiting for you."

Chapter Thirty-One

Cheyenne awakened the day of the Hideaway celebration to the drone of the air conditioner in the living room. She glanced out the bedroom window toward the lake and saw the sky barely tinged with a golden-pink glow of early sunrise. She smiled and stretched, luxuriating in her surroundings—in spite of the heat that had forced her to use the window unit.

She'd turned into a wimp since leaving here.

Blue stirred beside her, and she shoved the blankets back. It felt strange to be back after two and a half months of long hours and longer weeks in the ER. It felt particularly strange to realize this was her new home. For good. She would be living here, rent free, with an option to buy. She'd turned in her resignation the day after telling Dane her decision, and Jim had arranged for her to get out of her contract early. One of the docs who had taken her place when she was on leave had jumped at the chance to have her position permanently. She, in turn, had jumped at the chance to escape the job she'd once loved.

Multicolored balloons floated from a vase of flowers in the living room—compliments of her going-away party yesterday at the hospital. A chocolate-cherry cheesecake waited for her in the refrigerator, a gift from Ardis.

As she stepped out the front door, holding a wedge of the cheesecake in her hand, she noted how the goldenrod grew in clumps around the perimeter of the field in front of the house. The lavender of chicory edged the drive from the road. Morning mist clung to the spiderwebs atop cedar trees south of the house, forming delicate lace in the topmost branches.

"Thank You," she whispered, turning her face to the sky. "How could I have missed Your masterpieces all these years?"

She glanced across the lake and saw the roof of the barn at the ranch. Today she would see Dane for the first time since she left here—and Bertie, and Blaze and the others.

But Dane...with him there was a best-friend kind of feel, yet a connection that went beyond even that. She knew he was going to be busy today, especially since he was leaving the store open in addition to helping with the celebration activities, but she couldn't wait to see him, touch him, and once again put a physical dimension to the sweet, supportive, intellectually challenging relationship that had formed between them over the telephone and e-mail these past weeks.

In two hours Bertie would be down at the dock waiting for her, and she would be ready.

She felt such a sense of rightness in this place. She would always miss Susan, but the darkness she'd felt when she first arrived here had disappeared.

The telephone rang as she was deciding which shoes to wear. It was Larry Strong. She sat down in the rocker beside the phone stand, and took a deep breath as the familiar tightness clenched her jaw.

"Cheyenne, you'll be receiving a letter in the mail next

week," he said by way of greeting, "but I wanted to tell you now. The judge has dismissed the case."

She nearly dropped her shoe. She leaned back in the chair, and the breath went out of her.

"Cheyenne?"

For a moment, she couldn't reply. "What happened?"

"Ed's office received notice yesterday evening. That new witness you turned up in July made the difference for us. It was obvious you warned Susan about the dangers of driving under the influence of her medication, and she not only told her neighbor about the warning but tried to tell her husband. I'm pretty sure that even if the case hadn't been dismissed, Mr. Warden's attorneys would have advised him to drop it. Testimony like that before a jury would damage them irreparably."

After he congratulated her and said goodbye, she replaced the phone on its base and sat staring out the window for a long moment. She was free. Her sister's name wouldn't be dragged through the dirt of a court battle.

The good news hadn't brought Susan back.

But Susan wouldn't want to come back.

Blue rubbed against Cheyenne's leg, purring like the motor on Dane's boat. She picked him up and carried him to the kitchen. Time for coffee, and then to get ready for the fair.

"I'm not going." Blaze stood staring out the barn window, ignoring the white-and-pink pig that nudged at his ankles, pleading for food.

"Of course you're going," Dane said. "You've been planning this thing for months, you've trained half the entrants."

"The other guys can race them. I'm staying here today."

"Please don't try to tell me you've suddenly developed stage fright."

Blaze lifted the lid from the grain bin and poured a scoop of dried corn kernels into the steel trough. The pig dived in eagerly, with her floppy-eared siblings surrounding her. "I don't want to go to the races. I don't need the pressure right now."

"For Pete's sake, Blaze, it's a homemade carnival in a tiny village. It's a pig race. All you have to do—"

"You know what I think?" Blaze scowled at him. "I think I'm some kind of experiment for you, to see if the great Dane Gideon can work his magic with a poor black boy with a learning disorder and a health problem and convince a town of rednecks to accept him."

The words stung. "You know better. Don't take your nervous tension out on me."

Blaze knelt to scratch the pig's head. "I don't want to go."

"Blaze, would you listen to yourself? It's a pig race. It's a fun little community competition with a bunch of cute little animals addicted to Oreo cookies. It isn't the Olympic games."

Blaze returned to the window and rested his forearms on the sill. "Everybody's going to be there today, right?"

"Everybody I know."

"And no one's going to be here to watch things."

"Why should they? We leave the place unattended a lot. We go to church and leave it—Blaze, why all this sudden concern? What's going on?"

"I don't have a good feeling about today, okay?" Blaze said. "This would be a perfect time for the vandal to hit again."

"Why? It's been three months."

"That's what I mean. It's like this person needs to let off steam every so often, and so he does something when no one's expecting it. The barn was a big thing, and so that eased a lot of this guy's pressure, but nothing's happened since then, and so that pressure's been building all summer."

"You told me you thought the vandal wasn't from around here, that he'd moved on."

"I don't *think* that, I *hope* that."

Dane felt the same way, but to hear it come from Blaze, as well—almost as if Blaze knew, somehow, who was responsible... "Okay, I'll ask you again, do you have some idea about who the vandal might be?"

"Not a fair question." Blaze closed his eyes and sighed. "No, I don't know."

Dane didn't buy it. "If you have a clue about who might have burned the boat this spring, and the barn, and—"

"Okay, I'll go to the stupid festival. I'll race pigs and play with the other kids and be nice, but we should come back home and check on things a couple of times."

Dane tried to hold Blaze's gaze, but couldn't. The kid had something more on his mind, but Dane had discovered early on that if Blaze didn't want to talk about something, he didn't talk.

"I had already planned to keep watch, Blaze. I'm taking my binoculars, and we can come back and do a physical check, but if you're protecting someone, or if you know something you should be telling me, and something happens today because you didn't warn me—"

"I know." Blaze rubbed his face wearily, staring out the window once more. "I'm responsible." He nodded. "I know."

Bertie showed up precisely on time, and Cheyenne was at the dock to meet her. The boat was so filled with Bertie's baked goods and crafts that Cheyenne had barely enough room to sit down.

"I wasn't going to go today, but Dane and Cook talked me into it," the older woman said as she turned the boat around and maneuvered it out of the cove. "They reminded me how I always loved setting up my little stall and mixing with the people."

Cheyenne had spoken to Bertie over the telephone at least twice a week since she'd returned to Columbia. She knew how deeply Bertie had mourned Red's death, how much she missed him. Though Cheyenne and Bertie had become good friends soon after Cheyenne came to Hideaway, it seemed as if they'd developed a special bond since Bertie lost Red—a sisterhood through grief.

"I can't wait to see what it's like." Cheyenne fingered one of Bertie's prized castles, made from the tiny clamshells that washed up along the shore of Table Rock Lake.

Bertie revved up the motor and picked up speed in the direction of town—barely a quarter of a mile from Cheyenne's cove.

They arrived at the public dock and parked in one of the few remaining available slips. A crowd had already congregated along the broad lawn that edged the lake, and cars lined the street on both sides. Dane and Willy came walking down from the general store.

Cheyenne watched Dane approach with mingled emotions of excitement and apprehension. After his first telephone call to her, he had begun to phone regularly, and she had anticipated those conversations, especially at the end of a busy day. It was Dane who had convinced her to apply for a part-time position in the emergency department at Dogwood Springs, where she could pull a few shifts a month to stay afloat financially until her practice in Hideaway picked up. He had even suggested she keep her car parked at the ranch, which would save her a great deal of driving time to and from work, since Dogwood Springs was south of the lake.

It was also Dane who had found a few generous souls to replace the donations the rescue mission in Columbia were losing with Cheyenne's pay cut.

Between her calls to Bertie, and her daily e-mail messages

to and from Blaze and the increasingly deep conversations she and Dane shared at the end of their days, Cheyenne had felt more than ever that she was coming home.

But now, as Dane approached the boat beside Willy—who had let his hair grow longer over the summer—Cheyenne felt suddenly shy. Had those intimate telephone conversations meant more to her than they had to Dane? Did he—as she had once accused him—see her as just another one of his responsibilities, taking the newcomer under his wing so she wouldn't feel ostracized?

She caught Dane watching her and smiled. He looked as apprehensive as she felt. She doubted, however, that his thoughts turned to her as often as her thoughts had begun to turn to him. She doubted he dreamed about her at night, or looked forward to their next conversation with as much anticipation.

She allowed him to help her from the boat while Willy stepped into the boat to unload Bertie's cache of goodies.

Cheyenne wrapped her arms around Dane's neck. "It's so good to see you!"

He caught her up against him and held her tightly. His arms were as strong as she remembered, the feel of his short beard against her cheek felt just right. "Did you see the groceries?"

"I saw them," she said. "Thank you." When she arrived last night, the refrigerator had been filled with produce, fresh milk from the ranch, eggs and her favorite bread from the general store. "How did you get into the house?"

"Bathroom window still needs fixing."

She looked up into his smiling forest-green eyes, and knew this was the thoughtful, compassionate man she would want to spend her life with.

"Okay, you two, make room for the working men," came another familiar voice, and Cheyenne turned around just in time to see Blaze moving in for his hug.

"Now," Blaze said, releasing her, "time for all that smoochy stuff later. We've got to get Bertie's things to her booth. People are already asking about her."

Dane, Blaze and Willy carried all of Bertie's freight to one of the small stalls that had been built at the perimeter of the church lawn for the locals to display their baked items and crafts, from crocheted doilies to walnut people to carved chunks of wood.

"You bring all the boys over already?" Bertie asked as they carried the last load into the little booth she had reserved in the shade.

Dane nodded. "Blaze has loaned his whole litter of racing pigs out to the boys, and they'll be out in back, putting the animals through their paces and talking with the other racers."

More visitors arrived via boat, and Dane was called to help set up more booths. Bertie led Cheyenne into the church basement, where the food had been laid out on long tables.

"Good, nobody else brought black-walnut pie," Bertie announced as she laid her offering on the table with the rest. "I see they've got a lot of breads this year—apple bread, zucchini bread, apricot bread, beer bread. Mmm, just smell that fresh-baked aroma."

Cheyenne breathed deeply of the warm, sweet, yeasty smelling air, and walked among the crowd, eyeing the pies—apple, cherry, raspberry, blackberry. In spite of her cheesecake breakfast this morning, she gave in to temptation once more and bought a wedge of raspberry pie.

"Why, I do believe you're eating some of my baked goods," came a friendly voice from behind, and Cheyenne turned to see Richard Cook smiling at her. "How is it?"

Cheyenne took her first bite of the tart, juicy wedge, and closed her eyes with pleasure. "Delicious."

Several women worked behind a makeshift counter, putting out hot rolls, coleslaw, baked beans and barbecued pork.

Cook took her arm. "You'd be surprised how many people will want their barbecue for breakfast."

"So you're saying that not only do you race pigs here, you barbecue them and eat them, too?" Cheyenne asked.

"Only the slow ones."

Cheyenne decided she wasn't much of a pork eater, anyway.

"I hope you won't miss the races," Cook said. "Blaze is excited about them, even though he tries not to show it. He asked me if I thought you'd be there to watch."

"I will be."

"I tell you what, Cheyenne," he said as he escorted her to a tent beneath two oak trees, "you're a popular lady around this place. If Blaze isn't talking about you, Dane is, or Bertie. Half the town's been calling to see when you're setting up your office. I don't think you'll have any problem keeping busy."

In this tent, a local artist painted clown faces on the children. Even white-haired ladies lined up to have tattoos painted on their age-wrinkled faces.

"They're setting up the music on the stage," Cook said. "Bluegrass, I hope, like they play every year."

The musical family of singers made themselves comfortable at the bandstand in the center of the broad lawn east of the square. The musicians plucked their banjos and guitars experimentally.

"I think I'll tickle the boys and get one of those tattoos," Cook said. "Want to come?"

"I'll wait a few minutes. I think I'll just mingle."

He nodded and headed toward the artist booth.

"Cheyenne Allison?"

She turned to see Austin Barlow threading through the crowd toward her, wearing a bright-red shirt and a white hat, with new jeans and high-heeled boots. His son walked beside him, but imitation of his father only went so far. The Western wear was not for him. His wavy auburn hair glinted gold in the sun.

Austin's political-campaign smile was in place, but he also seemed genuinely happy to see her. "Our new town doctor." He reached for her hand and pumped it up and down. "Good to see you, Cheyenne. We've missed you since you've been gone. Are you here for good?"

"That's right, I'm all moved in." She turned to Ramsay. "I heard you had an entry in the pig races today."

"Sure do. I plan on taking the grand prize, but I've got some good competition."

"You'll be there for the debate, I trust," Austin asked her. "Speaking of competition, Dane Gideon seems to have a lot more influence in this town than I do lately. I hear he's the one who talked you into coming back."

"Oh, really? You heard that?"

"Not that I'm complaining. I'm just glad you'll be back. What do you say we celebrate your decision and take in that show next week that we never got to take before you left?"

Cheyenne knew her sudden dismay was obvious in her expression.

"Or not." Austin covered the awkwardness with a quick laugh. "A guy can't be blamed for wanting to spend time with the prettiest lady in the county. Well, I see the musicians waving at me from the stage, so I'd better get." He tipped his hat to Cheyenne, and strode toward the center of the activity.

Ramsay turned and walked away without looking at Cheyenne again.

"Okay, I need to talk to you."

Dane turned from the cash register he'd been tending for

the past thirty minutes to see Blaze standing behind him, hands shoved into the pockets of his baggy khakis, face and bare arms glistening with perspiration.

"I hope I'm wrong, but I can't afford to take the chance," Blaze said.

"Don't you have a race in about ten minutes?" Dane asked, waving to catch Cecil's attention at the front door of the general store—which he had kept open today by special request. Business was booming.

"I can talk fast if you can listen fast. Then you can tell me I'm crazy, and I can get back to the racetrack in time to keep Austin from disqualifying me."

Dane turned the register over to Cecil and turned the Closed sign outward on the door, then moved the hands of the false clock face to show when they would reopen. He followed Blaze out the door and down the sidewalk, past the vacant, brick-front building that would soon be set up for patients.

"Tell me what's going on, Blaze."

"Okay, it's like this—I hope I'm wrong. I've even been praying I'm wrong, but what if Ramsay Barlow's the vandal?"

Dane stopped walking. Ramsay was one person Dane would have deemed to be beyond suspicion. Not only had he always reflected a sensitive spirit, but it seemed he barely left his father's side long enough to get into mischief. "You're not kidding?"

"No, I'm not."

"Why do you think that?"

"Well, first of all, he had to have opportunity to do those things, and he did. Remember when the barn burned? Austin came alone. Ramsay wasn't with him."

"Maybe Austin didn't want him in any danger," Dane said.

"Maybe, but if you're going to take the time to argue with me, I'm going to miss the races."

"Okay, I'll shut up."

"I've got to walk, I can't just stand here." And so they walked up the street, away from the crowd. "I've been thinking about it, and I realized every time something happened, it was to someone who had recently crossed Austin. Remember? He didn't want the public dock, and so a boat at that dock was destroyed."

"But if that's the case, then logically, he would have vandalized something of mine even before the barn," Dane said.

"You're arguing with me again, but now that you mention it, he did. Remember Cook told me about your tires being slashed last year? It just comes in spurts. Anyway, Austin had an argument with Mrs. Potts about something during a church business meeting—everybody was talking about it—and then her cat turned up shot. Then you decided to run for mayor against Austin, and the barn burned. It seems like anybody who crosses Austin suffers for it."

"Then why not blame Austin?"

"Because he couldn't have been the person I saw running from the barn that night. The shadow wasn't big enough, and besides, Austin arrived too soon afterward. He wouldn't have had time to paddle a canoe back to town and drive the long away around in his truck."

"I'm not so sure about that. He could if he'd had it planned just right."

"Okay, but that isn't Austin's style. He'd have his son write an editorial in the paper blasting whoever crossed him, but he wouldn't slash someone's tires. Can you see Austin doing that?"

"I can't see Ramsay doing it, either," Dane said.

"I've always thought there was something a little off about Ramsay's bond with his dad. It's almost like he doesn't have a mind of his own, and so when his father decided I was worthless, even though Ramsay and I had started to become pretty good friends, he stopped having much to do with me outside of school. And then there's the thing about Red."

"What about him?"

"We never found out who took him to that island. I know they said he died of natural causes, but he hit his head, too. About end of the school year, we had everything caught up in our English class, and so the teacher made us write a short story, then choose a partner and let them read our story. We got credit for it. Ramsay chose me to be his partner, and he let me just tell my story, then he gave me his to read. He didn't know I could read quite a bit by then."

"Please don't tell me it was a confession."

"Nope, it was about a little boy accidentally killing his mother."

Dane stopped walking.

"Come on, you're standing in the middle of the street," Blaze said.

"Ramsay wrote a story about his mother's death?"

"I didn't say that, but it sure did make me think. It talked all about how he knocked his mother down, and she hit her head and died. Then came all this weird stuff about how it was supposed to happen, and he'd been chosen, like one of those death angels."

Dane felt a chill grow within him.

"And then Red died, and no one seemed to know how he got where he was. Did you know Ramsay took off the day Red disappeared, and didn't come home until the next day?"

"How do you know that?" The police had not yet discovered who had taken Red to the island.

"I overheard Austin's mother tell somebody about it in the store the day before the funeral. Said Ramsay spent the night with friends in Kimberling City, and so he didn't know what was going on here. But we both saw him at the ranch. In fact, he must have left about the same time Red did, close as I could figure. Probably, he was the one who took Red home. When I tried to talk to Ramsay about it at the funeral, that's when he got all mad and everything. I figure Red might've talked Ramsay into stopping at the island, and you know how unsteady Red was on his feet. He probably fell and hit his head. Ramsay freaked and ran away. Ramsay does that when things get too tense. He can't seem to handle it."

Dane was beginning to feel sick.

The races intrigued and amused Cheyenne. She giggled unrepentantly when the pigs squealed and kicked against the little racing ribbons they were required to wear.

Austin, as mayor and official spokesman for the events, announced the race with as much flair as any professional sportscaster.

The piglets settled down to business the moment they saw their trainers scatter Oreo cookies at the end of the racetracks. When the rifle was shot and the gates opened, twenty little piglets lunged forward in a joyous flurry of flopping ears in their scramble to beat each other to the food.

Bystanders cheered their favorites, and Cheyenne shouted with the rest of them when Blaze's animal won the first heat, and another ranch pig came in second.

Austin seemed to lose some of his good humor when Blaze's pig qualified for the race for grand prize. Once or twice, his voice faltered over the announcements, and his eyes darted from Blaze to Ramsay, whose pig had also qualified. If Cheyenne hadn't known how seriously Blaze was taking this, and how much it affected him, she would have thought it ridiculous to be so serious about a pig race.

For the final race, the referee entered the racing ring as the squeal of pigs grew louder. The handlers—Danny Short, Blaze and Ramsay—tied the ribbons onto their pigs' backs and held them steady. Austin grew silent as the referee raised his arm, tensed, then shot the rifle into the air.

The handlers released their racers, shouting encouragement as the little pigs, silently intent, dashed around the ring toward their prize.

The crowd screamed and cheered and whistled as the pigs neared the finish line. Danny Short's animal rammed his stub nose into the fence and backed off. The other two pigs pulled ahead, nose to nose. With only seconds to go, Blaze's entry burst forward and surged over the finish line, claiming the grand prize for the day.

The crowd erupted with cheers. The other handlers rushed over to congratulate Blaze. All but Ramsay. Austin took his son aside, talking urgently. Ramsay finally went up to Blaze and shook his hand.

"Blast it all," Bertie muttered beside Cheyenne. "I forgot my cheeses at the house. I fixed them up special because so many'd been asking me about them. I can't believe I did that. And here I've got to get back to my booth. People are buying those castles like they was made of gold."

"I'll go get the cheese for you," Cheyenne said.

"No, I can't let you do that," Bertie said. "The boat's blocked in tight. You'd have to walk, and it's too hot."

"I'll take the shortcut along the shore, then get my car and bring the cheeses back."

"It's tough going along the shore, with those cliffs."

"Get back to your booth, Bertie. I'll bring your cheeses." Cheyenne needed a break from the press of the crowd, anyway.

As the pig race audience dispersed to other attractions on the grounds, Cheyenne strolled down to the shore toward home, eyeing the cliffs dubiously. She had never taken this route before, and she could see why. The cliffs and underbrush were not conducive to a leisurely exercise trail. She had reached her first thicket, and was almost ready to turn around and take the road, after all, when a boat pulled up beside her.

"Going home already?" It was Ramsay Barlow in his father's bass boat.

"Not this way, I'm not," she said.

"Want a lift?"

She smiled at him. She was going to love living here.

Chapter Thirty-Two

Dane stood beside the bandstand waiting to join Austin on the stage for the much advertised—and much dreaded—public debate. The musicians finished the final bars of their song, and Austin reached down at a control on his belt that regulated the tiny microphone clipped to the collar of his red Western shirt.

"Okay, folks, this is the hour we've all been waiting for," he said.

"Speak for yourself, Austin!" someone called from the audience. "We want more music!"

The crowd laughed, and Austin chuckled with them, though his face reddened with the effort. "Since it's an election year for our town, this seemed to be a good time for me to have a friendly discussion with my opponent, and include you all in the process. "Dane, why don't you come on—"

"Dane!" This time the interruption came from the other side of the audience, and Blaze wove his way through the crowd, waving his hand above his head. "Dane!" He broke through, breathless. "Dane, Cheyenne's out on the lake with Ramsay."

Austin chuckled again from the stage. "I don't think that's something worth interrupting the debate over."

"We've got to go out there," Blaze said as he reached Dane, panting to catch his breath.

"Dane," Austin said from the stage, "do we have a little discipline problem we need to take care of?"

Dane raised a hand for some time, and Austin's sigh echoed from the speakers.

"Cheyenne was going to Bertie's house to get some cheeses Bertie forgot this morning," Blaze said. "I was watching Ramsay after the races, and I saw him run out to his dad's boat. I was afraid he'd light out for the ranch, but he picked up Cheyenne. Dane, something's going to happen. We need to do something now. I mean *right* now."

"Any time, boys," Austin said. "We can't keep people waiting forever, or they'll start to leave."

Dane turned to the stage. "Sorry, Austin, but we have an emergency brewing. We need you to come with us."

Ramsay sped past Bertie's dock.

"Uh, Ramsay?" Cheyenne said. "I think you missed it."

He didn't respond.

She stood up and nudged his arm. "Ramsay?"

He jerked around and glared at her, his blue eyes fixing on her with sudden, surprising anger.

She took her seat as the boat curved in an arc toward an inlet. What was wrong with him all of a sudden?

"You're great pals with my buddy Blaze, aren't you?" he shouted over the whine of the motor. "And Dane Gideon."

What did that have to do with anything?

Ramsay glanced over his shoulder at her. "Dad doesn't like it."

She frowned up at him. "I'm sorry?"

He turned the boat so suddenly they nearly capsized. He steered it into Gulley's Creek—which fed into the lake east of Bertie's house.

Cheyenne felt the first flutter of tension. For the first time, she regretted not having a life jacket on. Ramsay hadn't offered her one, and as a strong swimmer she hadn't thought the precaution necessary for such a short ride, but if he was going to fool around with the boat... "I think you missed your turn, Ramsay."

He scowled. "You shouldn't have come here. Shouldn't've taken Courage, then tricked Dad into giving him to the ranch. You let us come out to your house and take care of that stupid horse, and you played up to Dad and acted all sweet and interested."

Cheyenne's breath caught. What was going on here? He sounded crazy. "Ramsay, what are you talking about? You act as if you think I was—"

"You were leading Dad on, but it's Dane Gideon you're really trying to—"

"I wasn't leading your father on." She glanced over her shoulder toward the lake.

"Now you won't even go out with Dad, after all he's done for you."

She tried to judge the distance between the boat and shore. She couldn't afford to panic. He was beginning to remind her of a psychotic patient she'd been forced to restrain in the ER last month.

"You don't know what that'll do to Dad," he said.

Cheyenne clenched her hands so tightly she felt the sharp implant of her fingernails into her palms. "I think he'll get through it." She forced her voice to portray a calm she didn't feel.

Ramsay cut the motor and steered the long bass boat around until it faced the lake. He folded his arms across his chest.

They were directly in the middle of the mouth of the creek, trees shielding them on either side. Isolated. Alone. With the motor turned off, all was quiet except for the gentle lapping of the water against the side of the boat.

"Suppose you try to tell me what it is I don't know." She trailed her hand in the water, focusing on deep, controlled breaths. "What has you so upset? Why shouldn't I have come here?"

Ramsay was silent for a moment. She could hear the uneven rhythm of his breathing. "My dad really liked you. He liked you a lot. Last week he asked me what I thought about you and him seeing a lot more of each other."

"But, Ramsay," she said gently, "that doesn't mean I have to see him."

Ramsay's unaccustomed scowl deepened. "Why did you have to go make friends with the ranch guys? Why couldn't you be friends with Dad? Maybe it would've worked out then."

He sounded like a six-year-old. "What would have worked out, Ramsay?"

He glared at the surface of the water, the wispy tendrils of a barely visible line of peach fuzz on his chin emphasizing his youth. "You had to get mixed up in this. Dad didn't want the boat dock, didn't want the town to turn into another big, cheap tourist trap like Branson. He never wanted that ranch across the lake, with new strangers coming in all the time. There wouldn't have been any more…vandalism. We were fine just like we were, and we didn't need a doctor or—"

"Ramsay, you can't be saying your father's been vandalizing everyone because he didn't want changes to take place."

Yet to Cheyenne's mind, that was exactly what Ramsay was implying.

"No, I'm not saying that." The words were slow and deliberate, the voice deep with animosity.

She watched the changing expressions on his face, as if metamorphosis between malevolent anger and the frightened-hurt feelings of a child struggled for control of his emotions.

"You're the vandal?" Her voice quavered.

Ramsay leaped to his feet, and the boat leaned precariously to the left.

She couldn't panic—could not afford to panic! The vandalism, the barn fire, Red. She would not panic. "What about Red?" she whispered.

Ramsay's face crumpled, and his shoulders slumped. "It had to happen that way. I know that now, but it was the worst… it was so hard…" Tears sprang from his eyes. "I was just taking him home because he was tired." He caught his breath on a sob. "That's all." He rubbed his eyes with his fingers, as a child would do. "When we passed the island, Red wanted to get out and just sit on the rocks for a few minutes. Blaze always talked about how much Red loved that place. So I thought that would be a good idea. I didn't realize what was supposed to happen."

"What do you mean by that, Ramsay? Why was it *supposed* to happen?"

He frowned at her. "Everything happens because it's supposed to. Grandma always said Mom died because it was meant to be. So it's like I was just doing what God meant me to do." His voice softened, as if he was reverting to a place in his mind when he'd been a child. "All I did was accidentally nudge Red when I was getting out of the boat. You know, we're not supposed to dock there because the motion of the water can damage the boats against the rocks, but I thought just this one time—"

"And so you accidentally nudged Red, who didn't really have good balance anyway," she said gently. "It was an accident." Which had possibly precipitated his heart attack. It wouldn't necessarily have taken much, considering the shape Red's heart had been in.

Ramsay nodded. "I didn't mean for it to happen. He fell and hit his head, just like Mom." He covered his face with his hands as the tears flowed more freely. His shoulders shook with his sobs. "I didn't mean to do it, but now I know it was meant to be."

Just like Mom? Cheyenne felt physically sick. "I'm sorry, Ramsay. I forgot about your mother."

"But I did it, don't you see? It was meant."

"No, you're saying it was an accident."

He shook his head. "I shoved Mom backward, and she fell and hit her head."

"Ramsay, you were a little boy."

"No!" He swung toward her, once more angry. "She shouldn't have been fighting with Dad. She shouldn't have accused him of doing those things with Dane's wife. She said awful things to Dad, and made him leave."

She felt gut-punched by that revelation. Austin with Dane's wife? Austin Barlow truly was a hypocrite—although Austin had told her, during one of his "visits" to see Courage, that he'd seen the true errors of his ways after his wife's death.

Ramsay's voice deepened. "She was screaming at him! And he left and I wanted to go after him and she wouldn't let me and I pushed her hard and she stepped on a spot on the floor and fell and it was meant—don't you see!" He ground out his words with increasingly angry precision.

"God wouldn't do that to a little child, Ramsay."

"What would you know about Him? You never go to church, you never—"

"I do go to church now, but not to one that would teach a little child things like you're saying. I know God wouldn't use a little child to kill his mother."

"It's what I am, like the death angel on that television show."

"Ramsay, no, that isn't—"

"You don't know! My dad's spent years of his life trying to keep the spirit of Hideaway as quiet and peaceful as it was before Mom died. He can't do it by himself, he needs my help."

"To preserve the whole town the way it was when your mother was alive?" And, possibly, to preserve to himself an image of peace in a world that had suddenly gone dark? Especially if he was showing signs of the emotional trauma he'd endured as a young boy.

"But Ramsay, your father has blamed one of the ranch boys all these years. He blames Dane, and it wasn't Dane's fault. God wouldn't want—"

"That ranch doesn't belong there, those boys don't belong. Blaze doesn't—" He stopped suddenly, and into the silence came the sound of a motor on the lake. A boat. It had a familiar cadence....

Cheyenne stood up and tripped over the spare paddle in the bottom of the boat. She caught herself as the craft wafted sideways, then she waved toward the approaching boat.

"No!" Ramsay grabbed her arm. "You can't tell anybody!"

She tried to reach the paddle at her feet.

He released her and grabbed it before she could get to it. "Stop it! You can't tell Dad! I can't let you!" He cast an anxious glance toward the lake, his eyes widening in alarm. "What have I done?" His breathing came in sharp, angry gasps. "You can't... I can't let you go home!"

"Ramsay, if you...if something happens to me now, everyone will know. You're not at the festival, and Bertie knew I was coming to her house to get something for her. Let me—"

"You've ruined everything!" he cried. Another sob escaped his throat, tears streaming from his eyes once more. "Don't you understand? If they know, Dad'll be ruined. I can't do that to him."

"Your father will forgive you. We can get you help. You're confused, and you've suffered more than any child should ever have to suffer. Please, Ramsay, listen to me."

The sound of the other boat grew louder, and Cheyenne braced herself to scream, jump from the boat, do whatever she had to do to get their attention.

She looked across the water. Dane's Mystique raced toward them. She raised her arms to wave them over.

"No!" Ramsay shoved her from behind.

She fell sideways, and the boat rocked. She lost her balance and fell into the sleepy green water. Her head cracked against something hard and pain blinded her. A hand caught her arm, and she fought against it. She opened her mouth to scream, and water invaded her throat.

A voice echoed through the darkness, as if it came through a long pipe from far away. Her head pounded, and with each jolt of pain the voices grew louder until they burst over her like the blast of a rifle shot.

She choked and gagged, spitting water.

"She's awake." Someone gently turned her onto her side, strong arms holding her. "Cheyenne?"

She opened her eyes, and looked up into the most beautiful pair of green eyes she had ever seen. Dane was dripping wet.

She coughed, and his arms tightened around her.

She tried to speak, but her mind felt as if it were struggling through quicksand. Her body felt numb. She drew another breath, and dry, welcome air entered her lungs to replace the lake water she had coughed out.

"It's okay, just lie here and breathe for a moment."

"My head is killing me."

"You hit it on a submerged tree stump."

"Ramsay?" she croaked.

"He and his father are in their boat," Blaze said from behind them. "We've got to call the police."

"He's okay?"

No reply.

She looked up at Dane.

"Physically, he's fine, Cheyenne," he said softly. "But he tried to kill you."

"Dane pulled you out," Blaze said.

"He thinks he killed his mother," she said.

"I know," Dane said. "Blaze figured some of it out."

"He thinks he killed Red," she said.

She heard someone crying in the distance. Ramsay? Austin?

"He needs help," she said.

"He's going to get it." Dane touched her face, a loving caress. "I was afraid we wouldn't reach you in time."

"But how did you know?"

"Blaze saw you in Ramsay's boat. He'd had his suspicions before, noticing Ramsay was gone every time something went wrong in town. I can't help thinking Austin suspected something, but wasn't willing to admit his own son might be the culprit."

Cheyenne couldn't think past the pounding in her head. Tears stung her eyes. "Poor Ramsay. All that guilt."

"He's psychotic," Blaze muttered. "And dangerous."

"He'll be institutionalized," she said. "At least for some time. He's sick, Blaze. But there are medications...." She wept for the child who had been wounded all those years ago, and for the father and son whose futures had now been destroyed. "And Austin…"

"He's got a town of people who will help him get through this," Dane said. "I'll be one of them."

She shook her head, looking up into that kind face. "You don't have any idea what he's done, do you?"

He nodded, closing his eyes. "I know," he whispered. "I think I've always known, deep down. But he's changed his ways, and he's sincerely tried to be a good father, a good Christian. He has a long way to go, and he can't do it alone."

Four months ago Cheyenne would have said Dane sounded naive and gullible. She didn't feel that way anymore. He sounded hopeful. He had a healing spirit, and it came from a source outside himself.

She wiped the tears from her face and looked up at Dane. "You have a more forgiving spirit than anyone I know. I need to do some forgiving of my own. Mind if I tag along and learn how you do it?"

He brushed a wet strand of hair from her face and touched her lips with his in a brief kiss. "I'll be right across the lake."

★ ★ ★ ★ ★

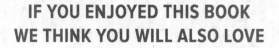

LOVE INSPIRED
INSPIRATIONAL ROMANCE

Save $1.00
on the purchase of ANY Love Inspired or Love Inspired Suspense book.

Available wherever books are sold, including most bookstores, supermarkets, drugstores and discount stores.

Save $1.00
on the purchase of any Love Inspired or Love Inspired Suspense book.

Coupon valid until August 31, 2021.
Redeemable at participating outlets in the U.S. and Canada only.
Limit one coupon per customer.

52616916

Canadian Retailers: Harlequin Enterprises ULC will pay the face value of this coupon plus 10.25¢ if submitted by customer for this product only. Any other use constitutes fraud. Coupon is nonassignable. Void if taxed, prohibited or restricted by law. Consumer must pay any government taxes. Void if copied. Inmar Promotional Services ("IPS") customers submit coupons and proof of sales to Harlequin Enterprises ULC, P.O. Box 31000, Scarborough, ON M1R 0E7, Canada. Non-IPS retailer—for reimbursement submit coupons and proof of sales directly to Harlequin Enterprises ULC, Retail Marketing Department, Bay Adelaide Centre, East Tower, 22 Adelaide Street West, 40th Floor, Toronto, Ontario M5H 4E3, Canada.

U.S. Retailers: Harlequin Enterprises ULC will pay the face value of this coupon plus 8¢ if submitted by customer for this product only. Any other use constitutes fraud. Coupon is nonassignable. Void if taxed, prohibited or restricted by law. Consumer must pay any government taxes. Void if copied. For reimbursement submit coupons and proof of sales directly to Harlequin Enterprises ULC 482, NCH Marketing Services, P.O. Box 880001, El Paso, TX 88588-0001, U.S.A. Cash value 1/100 cents.

5 65373 00076 2   (8100)0 12478

LICOUP0820TRADE